I0640038

The Healer

Aura Weavers, Book 1

LizAnn Carson

The Healer (Aura Weavers, Book 1)
© 2017 Elizabeth Carson
ISBN: 978-0-9949036-6-2

Cover photos used under license from:
Deposit Photos

Thank You

To the wonderful, supportive women of my critique group. You set me right and keep me going!

And always, to Michael, who puts up with my flights of fancy and obsessive streak, and has never been less than encouraging.

Prelude

"Get in here, girl. Herma's waiting for you."

Let her wait.

Ila ducked lower into the weedy field, trusting the plants to hide her. It didn't always work, but this time it *had to*. The plant the Healer had shown her was ready for harvest and processing into medicines. The energies lined up; she felt it inside, the same feeling she got when she knew the exact right herb to ease an ague or a toothache.

She would *not* spend the afternoon locked in the archivist's cramped biblio, learning *again* how to form the letters that recorded the events of the hamlet.

Bor-ing.

And not her destiny. She knew it right to her bones. Since she had been old enough to toddle around in the woods and fields, she had known.

But no one listened.

"*Ila!* Where the deuce are you?" Her mother's impatient voice portended a tongue-lashing in Ila's near future.

"She's down in the field, Jan." A man's voice. "Saw her going an hour or so ago."

And thanks a bunch. Wasn't Michel supposed to be off hunting? Instead of tale-tattling on her?

Ila thought frantically about the blooming heal-all plant, the scribing lessons waiting for her, and the possibility of bolting into the woods until her mother gave up. All useless. The whole hamlet expected her to be the next archivist, to sit in the dark little biblio and learn her letters and words and how to make the ink and which of the traveling vendors sold the best papers and the rest. Through most of her almost-thirteen years it had been pounded into her, like a ritual

1

chant. Ila, archivist. Ila, archivist. Blah blah blah. Sure, it was an honor; the mantle of archivist fell to only one person in a generation. But archivist was not who she *was*.

The heal-all plant would still be at its peak tomorrow, with any luck. Ila sighed and got to her feet. She treated her mother to a view of her slumped posture as she trudged back toward the hamlet.

Goodbye, sun. Goodbye, herbs. Goodbye, afternoon.

That night in the women's lodge, after the obligatory tongue-lashing and letter-learning and supper-making, while she listened to the other girls giggling about this boy or that game – which naturally she had missed – she caught a voice from the corner where the older women sat relaxing. Ila tuned out the other girls and listened.

"...be here in a few days. Just as well, with Cal's ankle not healing as it should."

Cal had twisted his ankle and perhaps broken it. The village healer had used every tool and herb available, but the swelling and pain persisted.

"Best see to tidying out the guest lodge. Sitting empty since that Bard came through."

The Bards brought music and stories, but not healing. If a Healer was coming, though...

Being the headmistress of the hamlet, her mother called forces into play. She appeared beside the cluster of girls. Ila sensed the ripple; when her mother descended, it meant work. Probably something distasteful.

"You, Ria, Jane. Tomorrow first thing, clean the Weavers' accommodation."

"Yes, ma'am." Even girls of fifteen jumped to obey.

Her mother's voice hardened. "Ila, when the Healer gets here, you are not to see her."

"Not—" The threat, for threat it was, sent shocks of horror through her.

"No. You are a woman now, old enough to put aside these dreams of plants and such. Time you settle into your responsibilities."

"But even Marie—"

"The hamlet does not need another hedge healer, girl. Best you concentrate on your real work." Her mother returned to the group of older women at the other end of the lodge.

Not see the Healer? When this new, inexplicable energy pulsed through every bit of her, calling her to the plants?

Ila slipped from the lodge and went out to the boundary of the hamlet. It was twilight, and only a fool ventured any farther. Animals lived out there, and dangerous people.

Since she became a woman, four months ago now, the pull had been stronger than ever. It peaked when she lay for hours in the field, her focus intent on a single plant, receiving its message. Ila studied the healings, simple ailments like scrapes and headaches, and more serious ones, broken bones and diseases, taken to the village healer. She sensed when the remedy failed to align correctly, and she knew – *knew* – that there was a better way, tied in with the messages in her mind when she spent time with the plants. But with insufficient knowledge, no training... and no one listened anyway. The Healers who visited the hamlet once or twice a season, they understood. She was sure of it. She *needed* to talk to this Healer.

She could not bear it if the Healer came to her hamlet and she, Ila, was barred from sitting by her, studying her ways, talking to her, learning from her.

Or him. Occasionally the Healer was a man. Not usually, though.

Ila's almost-thirteen-year-old body trembled, despite the early summer night's warmth.

She would *never* be the archivist. *Never.* No matter what they forced her to do.

But like it or not, the Healer came, and Ila found herself virtually imprisoned in the biblio. They piled lesson after lesson on her. The whole hamlet conspired to keep her from the learning she needed – *needed!* – and starve her soul.

"Goodness, Ila, a little dramatic?" her best friend Tula asked. "Calm down. You must be the only girl in the hamlet who gets an honor like being the next archivist and carries on as if they were torturing you."

"They are torturing me." The heal-all plant never harvested, the energy shifted, and it was too late for another year. Why could they not understand? Even Marie, their hedge healer, failed to grasp the importance of picking at the *exact right time*. To Marie, timing meant nights when the men's lodge, loud with drink and boasting, presaged babies to deliver in nine months. No more than that.

"Jonny was talking to you yesterday. I saw him."

Jonny had been talking to her since they were babies. So what?

"You gonna go with him, Ila?"

Her face flamed. Absolutely no. *Never.* They said that one day she would want to, but that day remained a mystery in the future.

"Gross."

Tula giggled. "You wait. You are a late bloomer."

No, she was not. She was a woman. She had bled. And now the dreams, the messages she heard in the plants, spoke more strongly than before. But lovemaking? No, thank you. Jonny had better understand that, and not try to put his hands on her the way some of the other kids did all the time these days.

And now the Healer was leaving. Tomorrow. Walking away from them on the east-west path, going to the next hamlet, then the next. Leaving her here with ink and quills.

Tears threatened. She muttered, "Later," and took off. To the biblio, of course. No one bothered her there. Because no one really cared about two hundred years of births and deaths and commitments. Her whole life, doomed to be meaningless.

The next day, watching from the edge of the gathering as the Healer completed her last-minute organizing and accepted a day's food from the hamlet, Ila decided. Stay here, to lead the barren existence they planned for her? If no one would listen, she would leave. The caravans of traders and the

Weavers – the Healers, Bards, and Scribes – walked the paths of the Midland with impunity. Could it be that hard or that dangerous?

"Tonight," she whispered.

"What's tonight?" Tula came out of nowhere, startling her out of plans she dared not share.

Ila blushed, which fit with the lie she formulated almost magically in her mind. "Tonight, maybe I will talk to Jonny. Maybe…"

She had said all she needed to. Tula's mind seldom wandered far from their new-found sexuality. "You will not be sorry," she whispered back.

Ila slipped away, her thoughts on what minimal supplies she would need for a day on the road. Because surely within a day she would locate a Weaver or merchant to help her.

A Weaver found her, not the other way around, and not within a day, but after four days, and numerous intersections in the tracks, relying on the sun to keep her moving east. Two days after she drank the last from her flask, refilling it from a clear stream that bubbled by the side of her path. Two days after she ate the last of her food, and that not nearly enough. Three days after a blister first blossomed on her heel. And three nights without sleep, because the forest, then the grassland, proved to be so much bigger and scarier than she had expected, and with the mountains still to cross.

Fatigue flattened her, and the blister, despite her best treatments, grew ever larger and looked red and angry. She sank down near a lone tree hugging the banks of a narrow stream and wondered if she would die out here. Around her the grasses rustled unceasingly. She leaned over to drink, then dropped her wooden clogs beside her and stuck her feet into the cold water.

As the throbbing in her foot faded and her thirst retreated, she studied her surroundings. A circle for fires, and grasses tamped down. So she was not completely alone. It only felt like it.

She had not minded the overcast day, because the sun of the days before had made her thirstier and burned her arms as she crossed the grassland. But now a rumble heralded something more ominous. She had no protection against rain.

When the first drops fell she scurried from the stream and settled against the tree's trunk. Its branches draped long and elegant across the land and the water, forming an umbrella that intercepted much of the rain. The tree's trailing branches meant safety. Its trunk felt sturdy to her, a sure thing in the vast uncertainty of the grassland.

The storm grew angry and loud, whipping rain to horizontal. No longer hot, now she shivered.

She was huddled in on herself, eyes pinched closed, miserable, all sense of time gone, when a woman's voice above her said, "My goodness."

A hand pulled her to her feet and out into the open, where the rain promptly drenched her. "Sorry, but you need to be next to me. It will get better, I promise."

Ila stood frozen, both literally and figuratively, watching the woman. She had been close for a while, because a pile of wood filled the fire circle. Between her misery and the chaos of the storm, Ila had not even noticed. A tiny piece of her brain wondered where the wood had come from, given the expanse of grassland. The woman placed Ila near a rolling pack, such as the Healers used to carry their supplies. She then stepped a short distance away, chanting under her breath and moving her arms. Gradually she inscribed a circle around them in the air, pausing at each quarter turn to chant and gesture. Then she raised her palms, and lowered them, and the rain stopped.

Ila looked around. The rain still lashed the ground, but within the circle it was quieter, and dry.

"Whew. I'd hoped for another half hour before the storm hit." The woman was as wet as Ila, her tunic and long skirt sticking to her rounded body and drips running from her gray hair onto her face. She knelt by the pile of sticks and hummed a few more words, and did something with her hands. When the soaked wood caught fire, the warmth drew Ila as if an unseen hand pulled her.

"Here, child. Sit." The woman dug into her pack and pulled out a ground cloth. "This should be fairly dry." Since her legs felt funny-wobbly, Ila willingly dropped onto the mat.

"Now," the woman said, "let's see what we have." Her hands moved around Ila, not touching her but sensing – what? Her face looked vacant, as if she were listening to hidden voices.

Her scan finished, she said, "You're hungry. This is a good place to get water, it's fresh and pure. Your foot – painful?"

Ila nodded, mute.

The woman dug in her pack. "Chew on this. I'll attend to your blister, but this will help." She handed Ila a short twig. She frowned at it, and the woman smiled. "It's safe. It's actually from a tree much like the one you found shelter under. We use it to take away pain and fever. You need both."

Ila chewed and grimaced at the intense bitterness. "I know," the woman said with a light laugh at the expression on her face. "Do it anyway. You'll be glad tomorrow." Then she set to work doctoring Ila's blister.

The fire burned for much longer than any fire had a right to. The woman shared hard bread and a piece of cheese, and the rain evaporated from their clothes. Relaxed and warming, as conscious thought returned she noted the woman's appearance. Elderly, not slender. A green sash crossed her plain tunic, the Healer's insignia.

"Now, as you're under the protection of my circle, tell me your story." A request, but Ila heard the command under it.

"Are you a Weaver?"

"I am."

"A Healer?"

"Yes, and a distance from my usual routes. And you are?"

Ila started talking as the woman removed the inflammation from her foot. She told of the need drawing her, the voices in the plants, the longing to learn what it meant, to control it and use it. The woman nodded occasionally.

Her energy departed with the last of her words. As if she read her mind, the woman said, "Yes, you must rest." She put a hand on Ila's head, and a curtain fell over her mind. Ila settled on the sheet and lost herself in sleep.

When she woke the rain had stopped, and around her the earth steamed in the morning sunshine. The woman bustled about, tidying up the camp. She handed Ila a piece of bread. "Supplies are low, but we'll reach a town soon. You wish to come with me?"

"Ye... yes, I do. Where are you going?"

"A wise question." The woman laughed. "Nowhere to benefit you. But soon we'll meet with others. One of them will assist you on your way."

"But..." She bit into the bread. Stale, but she was too hungry to care. "What is my way?"

"Oh, dear. You've run away from your own hamlet with no idea where to go?"

"I hoped someone would help me."

"And we will. You need training. It's irregular, but we'll get you to the Motherhouse one way or another. Now, it's time to leave. That rain cost me an hour's walking, so we're late."

"I want to be a Healer. I *must* be a Healer."

"Perhaps, if it's meant to be. It won't be easy."

"I understand." Though she had believed it might be.

"Seven or eight years of study and practice, followed by a journey year, traveling with another Healer. Get your pack."

As they left the camp, the woman said, "Tell me your name."

Ila thought, quick and hard. If she gave up her name, her hamlet would find her and drag her back. "What do you call that tree back there?"

The woman smiled. "A willow. Not the strongest of the willows for healing, but useful in its way."

And good for shelter, when shelter was needed. Graceful, and it removed the pain and fever. Ila nodded. Her old life fell from her shoulders as if it had never been. "I am Willow," she said.

Chapter 1

Day lay on the land, bright and already hot. By Willow's calculations, Summer Solstice was no more than a nine-day away. The ripest time of year, burgeoning with growth.

But not this morning. A strange, acrid tinge hung in the air, tainting the sweetness of midsummer. No birdsong, no rustling in the undergrowth.

She raised her hands, palms open to the sky. "Sustainer and defender of life, I call you. Your daughter calls to you."

Nothing.

Anxiety, alive and insidious, threatened her focus. Around her, the cold blue flame of her circle of protection faded in and out, far weaker than it should be. Never, in her twenty-four years as student, journeyer, and Healer, had she experienced anything like this.

"Please," she whispered.

A ripple, then only the soft touch of the morning air. It was as if the planetary Aura of elemental energies had shattered, leaving fragments and empty space. She lowered her hands, curling her fingers around her vulnerable palms.

She'd camped in this spot innumerable times over the years. The trail by the waysite took her through these leafy woods, a pleasant walk on a warm day when sunlight dappled the ground and the path lay soft under her sandal-clad feet. This forest had always been a magical, fertile place, nothing like the hollow sterility she felt now.

None of her training, the fine-tuning of her senses, told her the cause of this wrongness. The Aura was an inviolable constant. Not even in legends had it ever broken apart this way.

The night before, when she was unable to cast a strong protection circle, mounting dread had made swallowing her supper difficult and sleep impossible. Through the dark hours she'd sat hunched by her small fire, wrapped in her cloak and waiting, listening.

Now she rose and turned to the north to begin her releasing ritual, raising her hands and her voice. "May the energies of earth align truly with the land. May the power of earth flow from me and to me, in healing. I release the powers of earth, my protection through the night, with thanks." Casting and releasing the protection circle had been part of her earliest training, when she'd first learned to gather, merge, and work with the elements' energies. Healing was possible without this ability, but happened more slowly and with less certainty. The familiar touch of the Aura danced over Willow's palms.

Then the warm tingle that signaled her Entrée, her ability to access the Aura, vanished.

It returned, faintly. Growing, pulsing... then gone again, leaving only emptiness.

Trusting the land to recognize her efforts, she completed her ritual, moving around her protection circle, making similar invocations to water, fire, and air. The words she used didn't matter, for the power lay in speaking them aloud, acknowledging how little she could do on her own.

The faint line of blue flame dissipated. Relieved that she'd mustered at least enough connection to release the circle, she changed into a fresh tunic over her ankle-length skirt and added the sash that identified her as a Healer. She bound her long, cornsilk hair with a thong, then ate a minimal breakfast of a grain cake and an apple. By walking briskly, she'd be in Stanstead in time for a late lunch.

Her meal finished, she again opened her senses. A void, with only a faint trickle of power. The very land she relied on felt untrustworthy, and she suspected that any medicine she created from its bounty would fail.

"I'm scared." She spoke to no one, seeking the reassurance of her own voice. Then she stood and prepared her pack for travel.

She was bent over to spread out the last of the cinders from her fire when she heard a twig snap and a rustling behind her. Before she could straighten, a smelly giant in filthy, torn clothing crashed into her. She lost her balance and cried out.

Bruising hands caught her before she fell. "Got you." A man's voice, coarse and grating.

No. No! This didn't happen!

No one, not even the worst of the worst, interfered with the Weavers, the Healers, Bards, and Scribes who followed the tracks from hamlet to hamlet. They treated illness, carried news and entertainment, and recorded stories wherever they went, with no concern as to rights and wrongs. Everyone needed access to Healers. The covenant held, and Weavers moved freely, to everyone's advantage.

But now the grip of this unclean *brute* with wild, greasy hair held her captive. He stared at her as if she were a new, exotic species, then said, "You're coming with me." His massive hand binding both of her wrists, he dragged her toward the woods.

It never occurred to her to fight. She'd never had to, in all her years of walking the roads and trails of the Midland. She resisted, though, a thread of panic tightening around her. "Stop, don't—"

The man didn't answer. His hard hand twisted her arms at a painful angle as he crashed like an enraged bull through the forest, and with her skirt catching on every twig and shrub, Willow struggled just to keep her feet under her. Her mind rejected everything that had happened. The elemental energies, unresponsive. The tradition of safety, gone.

After walking nearly an hour at their stumbling pace, they broke out of the forest into a small clearing. The coarse man released her with a shove that drove her to the ground. Shocked, she barely registered the pain of new grazes on her palms and knees. Her body froze as she vacillated between anger and fear, between astonishment and tears. She sought alignment, but despite the gentle landscape around her, the land gave off no radiance, as if life had fled from it, leaving only the illusion of plenty. Unable to attune her personal energy to the Aura, she had never felt more alone.

Pull yourself together. Use your training. After a minute, she rose to her feet and studied her surroundings. A fire struggled in a makeshift stone circle. A battered cookpot sat by the embers. On the far side of the clearing, in the earth quadrant, lay another man. His face bore the drawn, pinched look of pain.

"It's a damn woman, Kiril," the brute said.

The man on the ground made a feeble gesture to wave her closer. "Come here. Joss, back off."

Willow approached him. Neither man had shaved in five days or more. This one's short hair might be blond or brown or gray under the layer of soot and dirt that blanketed him top to toe. He was not an elder, and although thin, he looked to be strong when he was healthy. His shockingly blue eyes stood out in the frame of his grimy face.

Blue eyes were rare. The legends claimed they foretold a special destiny.

Only dead leaves cushioned him. She nodded approval. Positioned so, he'd be close to the healing energies of earth.

Which didn't do either of them much good. "I can't help you," she said.

The man named Joss came at her, but the one on the ground stopped him with a gesture. "Why not? You don't know how? Can you find someone who does?"

Indignation gave her courage. Not know how? Was he blind? Everyone, everywhere, recognized the sash of a Healer. "You doubt my skill? However, this *creature* forced me here against my wishes, and without my tools and medicines."

Indignant or not, she obeyed her training and knelt beside him. Her hand on his brow confirmed her suspicion. *Hot. Much too hot.* Those portentous blue eyes glittered with fever. To remain conscious and converse with her, he must have enormous strength of will.

"Is there any water?"

"In the pot. It's almost gone."

She sighed. Water was crucial. She pulled his tattered shirt loose from his trousers and sensed a desire in him to recoil, although he lacked the energy to do so. Curious, and to distract him, she said, "How did you find me?"

"I'll show you." He held up a small box in an unnatural dull black color. He tapped it, and the front of it lit up. "When it detects life, a dot moves on the screen. It was odd, though. Your dot kept fading in and out."

Her pathetic protection circle. It hadn't hidden her from these men.

His voice was thin and uneven, and his hand shook as he made the lit-up place on the box disappear and set it beside him.

Willow opened his torn and seared shirt, of a shiny, unnatural fabric, exposing pale skin over a muscular chest bearing numerous scrapes and a flaming burn on his right arm, shoulder, and pectoral. As she hovered her hands over his crown, his torso, his limbs, she kept her face neutral. "Nothing."

"What are you doing?"

"Sensing your energy, or trying to. You know you're feverish. I suspect your body is toxic. Are you injured beyond this?" She let her hand hover over the burn.

"My leg's broken. Rough landing."

"Landing?" She frowned as her gaze swept their camp. "What do you mean?"

"Over there."

Willow straightened and turned to her right, to the east. With a quelling glance at Joss, she walked across the clearing and into the forest, where a trace of a path led into the underbrush.

Thirty paces in, she stopped dead. A blackened, twisted thing the size of a four-room cottage filled her vision. Its overwhelming, alien energy forced her backwards. She stumbled as she turned and fled back to the camp. "It must be destroyed." She struggled to speak, fighting off terror. "It is evil."

"How?" Kiril's voice had weakened in the short time she'd been away from his side.

But she couldn't explain; she could hardly talk. "I can't heal you," she blurted. "No one can." Now that she'd experienced it up close, she felt the dead weight of desolation, the denial of life surrounding them. Nothing would thrive near it, no Healing be possible.

The men didn't understand. The deadness failed to touch them. Saving Kiril, and possibly saving Joss and herself, rested on her shoulders alone. She swallowed back her panic. "If you cannot destroy that thing, we must go as far away from it as we can."

"Don't be stupid." Joss made a dismissive gesture, as if her opinion was not worth considering.

Kiril shook his head, a small movement. "...safe when they come..." His voice was a bare whisper.

She spoke to Joss. "Injured, fever, and no water. I cannot access the Aura, and without it he will die."

"*We're not moving anywhere!*" Joss roared. "Just set the leg, and we'll let you go. Maybe." He took a step toward her.

Desperate, she stood her ground and adopted the voice that had commanded countless sick rooms over the years. "After we deal with his leg, we move him, or, I repeat, he will die. Only deep Healing can save him, and that requires the energies of the Aura. Now, we need sticks for a splint, and to make a litter." She drew herself up to her full height, barely past Joss's shoulder, and looked him square in the face.

Pure antipathy filled his answering look to her, but after a moment he crashed off into the trees.

Kiril's eyes closed. She sat and took her knife from its sheath under her tunic. With it she cut the bottom of her skirt into strips for makeshift bandages and ropes, hoping that the break was a simple one. Without the Aura, without her medicines, without water, she could do little else.

Willow looked up as Joss entered the clearing with an armful of branches. He dumped them at her feet and turned away.

"Stay. I require your assistance." By then she had cut off Kiril's right pant leg. The fracture itself appeared to be straightforward but had pierced his skin, and putting the bones into alignment would go more smoothly with Joss's strength.

"Don't you give me orders, woman —"

Willow rose and walked toward the gap in the underbrush created by their trek from her waysite to theirs.

"*Bitch!* Where do you think you're going?"

She rounded on him. "You are unwilling to assist in your friend's healing. I conclude that I am no longer needed here. I am leaving."

"Like hell." He crossed the clearing in two bounds and planted himself between her and the trail.

"Then help me. Because there is no other way."

Again they stared each other down. Again, he looked away first. She worried she had made an enemy, but that was a problem for another time.

"What do you want me to do?" His voice was grudging.

Between them they aligned the broken bone and bound it. She had hesitated to lend Joss her knife to smooth branches for splints, but Kiril's fever raged and she was desperate to get away from their camp. At least he wasn't conscious while they tended the break.

She handed Joss a pile of the fabric strips to tie more branches together for a litter. While he worked, Kiril surfaced into consciousness, so she held his head up and encouraged him to take the water remaining in their battered pot. He barely managed a sip. She soaked a linen strip and put it over his forehead. Little of her skirt remained, but her tunic covered her to mid-thigh.

When he'd finished, Joss lifted Kiril onto the improvised litter. The men had no possessions other than what they wore or carried, and the pitiful pot. Thinking it might be useful, Willow tied it to the litter, then picked up Kiril's box with the moving dots and dropped it in a pocket of what remained of her skirt.

It did not escape her notice that Joss retained her knife.

She hoped never to repeat the trek away from their camp. Her muscles screamed in protest and branches scratched her legs as they fought their way through the trees and undergrowth, she carrying the foot end of the litter. They stopped frequently while she rested her arms, and each stop meant finding a smooth place to lay Kiril. He remained unconscious, but his occasional groans filled her ears. It was midafternoon when they lowered him to the brushed ground of the waysite.

She sensed, barely, the lessening of the poison in the Aura. Not enough, though, for her to Heal.

"We'll stay here tonight," Joss informed her. "Where do we find water?"

"There is none here, which is one reason we must leave. But we can try this, to make the journey easier. My pack is on wheels."

While he studied her rolling cart, Willow dug her flask from her reclaimed pack and poured water into their pot, then handed it to him. "This is all I can spare. I too am thirsty, and he needs more, if he wakes long enough to drink it." Joss downed the liquid in one go, but at least he didn't quibble about quantities.

They worked in silence, she tending Kiril and Joss reconfiguring the litter and the pack, until he straightened from his construction. He had attached the wheels, but... "This isn't stable," he grunted. "We need more binding."

She looked at the contraption and agreed. Reclaiming the knife, she sliced the last of her skirt, other than the waistband and pockets, to secure the reinforcements.

She applied a salve to Kiril's wounds, but was unable to rouse him to drink. That worried her. She hated to continue on the trail so late in the afternoon, but he was worse. He might not survive the stress of further travel, but without greater distance from that *thing*, his fate truly would be sealed. She chose another small bottle from the pack and moistened his lips with a drop of its contents.

She'd charged these bottles with Healing energy before sealing them. Right now she doubted their efficacy. How much of Healing depended on the continuing presence of the Aura? Had the medicine retained its potency? She still felt nothing, or only the barest flicker, when she tried to touch her powers.

"You got any food?" Joss growled at her.

Willow dug her single remaining apple from her pack. She'd hoped to share it, but it made sense to appease his hunger before hers. She suspected he hadn't eaten since the day before. "Here. Take this." She handed the apple to him.

He looked at it and frowned – not that he had done anything else since she'd met him. "This is it?"

She shrugged.

"What about you?"

"What about me?"

"Food," he snapped. "You've got no fat on you. What are you gonna eat?"

"You need it more than I. If we arrive at the next waysite in time, I may be able to catch a small animal. If so, I'll make a stew when we camp tonight."

"You sure?"

"Please eat, so we can go. His condition – I'm worried."

"Yeah. Me, too." Joss studied the apple for a moment, then bit into it, finishing it in under a minute, eating right into the core.

She hoisted the heavy pack onto her back. Joss picked up the front of the litter and started forward. The wheels wobbled, which she'd expected, given the unusual weight and the use of her skirt as a construction material, but held, and rolled tolerably well. She hoped the cart would last until they reached the next waysite on the road to Stanstead, which provided both safe respite and fresh water, but it lay at two hours' walk under normal circumstances – and probably twice that today.

She prayed that the distance would be adequate to restore her Entrée. His leg and burns demanded her attention, and soon.

Willow plodded after Joss, feeling the abrasions on her hands and knees, her hunger, the weight of the pack.

One foot after another. One step at a time. She had made this walk in equally desperate situations, when she herself ailed, or when rain chilled her to the bone.

Sustainer of the land, align my energies, strengthen my footsteps.

And grant freedom from the trembling that clenched her stomach into a knot so hard she could not have eaten the apple if she'd tried.

These men and their wreckage had brought calamity with them. Kiril had spoken of a rough landing. Landing from where? Had the thing flown? And if their wreck wrought such damage to the Aura that the templates, her Healing techniques, were gone, what harm might they themselves bring?

"Where are you from?" she asked Joss. "Not from the Midland. Your clothing and accent are not familiar."

He gave a hoarse laugh. "I bet they're not. We're not even from this planet, never mind this country of yours."

Planet. She knew the word, that their world could be called a planet – but from a different one? His reply made no sense to her. Instead of pursuing it, she dropped back to walk beside the litter, studying the drawn face of the man lying there.

What is your fate? Do you come to bless us or destroy us? With your magnetic eyes, are you doom or savior? Doom how? And savior from what?

They paced themselves, moving patiently so that the litter remained on the wheels and Joss could pull it without overtaxing himself. Willow walked beside Kiril most of the time, channeling any random bits of Healing energy she picked up into his abused body.

It was early evening when Joss next spoke. "How much longer?" His voice was ragged. Like her, he had exhausted his reserves.

"Not far. It's hard to tell, without the Aura—"

"Let me guess. That Aura thing tells you how to get there."

"I chart my progress by it. Usually."

"Stop blaming me, woman."

"Nor was I."

Silence as they trudged on.

"You say 'woman' with disgust."

"Are you surprised?" he snapped.

"Half of all people are women."

After a time he spoke again. "Suppose we don't make it?"

"We must. Without water, your companion is not the only one in trouble. There is no spring before the waysite."

The trail joined the trunk road a short time later. Her least favorite part of this route, the road was wider than the tracks she preferred, and more heavily traveled. But today it meant smoother, faster progress.

And not a minute too soon. Willow's feet dragged as she walked, and what she saw ahead added to her burden of worry.

He glanced back. "So we're almost there?"

"We are close, and it's imperative we finish this quickly. Look above you."

Clouds piled up to the east. She and Joss risked illness, Kiril risked worse, unless they reached the waysite.

"Rain?"

"A thunderstorm. Within an hour. We must get to shelter."

"You didn't say there's a building."

"A hut."

"Which way do we turn off?"

Conversation, however unpleasant, kept them both moving. "To the right."

Willow fell silent. Not long after she resumed her walk, when she spotted a stump, a gnarled tree, she almost cried with relief.

"There."

He stopped and squinted. "That deer track?"

"That is our trail. Not made by deer, however."

He scowled, and with reason. Navigating this path, given its narrowness, bade fair to be as difficult as bushwhacking from his camp to hers. She waited for the litter to pass her, then stayed close in case the wheels chose this moment to detach.

When at long last they came in sight of the shelter, she realized with a sinking heart that others had arrived before them. A donkey with its nose in a bag of oats was tied to the post.

"Wait here." She directed Joss to rest his end of the litter on the porch step, knocked twice, and opened the door.

"Sister," a woman's voice said.

She'd walked in on a group of three, clearly a trading caravan. Various well-wrapped bundles lined the walls, kept indoors to prevent thievery. The woman who greeted her sat at a table tucked into a corner, bearing a lone lantern, while a man worked the cookfire, and another, older, lounged on the solitary cot. They looked travel-worn and weary, so the greeting she received was less than hearty.

"I am very sorry to trouble you," Willow said. "We are three, and two are patients, one grievously injured and the other traumatized. I need a bed and water, and a meal if there is food to spare. We haven't eaten today."

"Always room for a Healer," the woman said. "Name's Zelda."

"Willow. The man accompanying me is Joss."

The older man rose and went to the door, just as Joss appeared at the threshold.

"By all the powers of creation," Zelda sputtered.

The man reeled back. "A demon." Raw fear crossed his face. "Yesterday the fireball, now this."

One glance at Joss and the reality of their appearance sank in. He towered over them. Coated in dirt and soot, with a wild look in his eyes, and herself with her clothes in tatters…

"Sister, you can't seriously—"

"I can. For his companion's sake." Dealing with the trading party pushed her to the end of her strength. She couldn't keep the irritation from her voice. "Joss is bordering on collapse himself. We require shelter, water, and rest." Her word was law, and the others knew it, but that didn't guarantee smooth times from here on.

"Get that monster away from us, then we'll let you see to the other one." The man backed from the door. "I don't intend to be murdered in my sleep."

"He's like something out of a nightmare," Zelda said.

True.

"Joss, wait outside while we shift Kiril to the bed."

Instead, he shoved into the room, his glare taking in the inhabitants and the limited furnishings. Willow held her breath. He'd been acquiescent so far, but she couldn't guarantee it would last. Once again it fell to her to control a situation she didn't understand.

Sustainer of all that lives, how much more?

As she had done that morning, she planted herself in front of him before he could advance any farther. "Outside, now. Before there is trouble."

Their battle of wills ended when he spoke. "You take care of him. I'm holding you personally responsible, got it?"

"I am a Healer." As should be obvious. "But I will do nothing until you leave and the energy in this room stabilizes. Do *you* understand?" she shot at him.

He grumbled something unintelligible, but stepped back. Willow released a breath she hadn't been aware she was holding.

As he moved out onto the porch, the first round of thunder shook the cabin.

She addressed the traders. "May I ask you to bring the litter inside? I cannot manage it myself."

Zelda and the older man maneuvered the litter into the cabin, uneasily passing Joss, who hovered just to the side of the door, his narrowed eyes watching every move. Under her direction, they shifted Kiril onto the cot, then propped the makeshift conveyance in a corner.

A pot of water simmered on the cookfire. "Figured you'd need it," the younger man said. He seemed the calmest of the group, assessing but not making assumptions.

"You keep that *thing* outdoors and we'll be fine." The older man was prepared to be courageous as long as Joss kept his distance.

At that, Willow's strength gave out. She wasn't equal to arguing with the traders, channeling random shards of energy to Kiril, and seeing to her own need for food, water, and rest. She stumbled, lightheaded.

Zelda caught her. "Sister, sit here. She's ailing herself," she told her companions. "Bring water." To Willow she added, "We've barely enough to share. We'd expected to be in

Stanstead by now, but it's been a troubling day." The younger man pressed a mug into Willow's hands.

"Please, will you take some out to Joss? There's a cooking pot tied to the litter."

The older trader freed the pot, filled it, and passed it through the door before darting away. Joss lingered near the entry, wary as a cornered wild animal but silent.

Willow drank, then staggered as she attempted to stand.

Zelda supported her to Kiril's bedside. As she settled on the floor, Zelda said, "Good looking fella. What ails him?"

"Burns, cuts, general body trauma, and a break to his right leg. The skin was split, so I fear infection. Hot water is a blessing."

The storm picked that moment to unleash its fury over their heads. The cabin shook with the next blast of thunder as rain pelted the roof.

Willow managed to stand and grasp the doorframe. Joss stood out in the downpour, his arms spread, allowing the water to sluice layers of filth from him. The older trader watched from the sheltered porch, while the donkey ignored everything but the oats in its bag.

Confident that the state of affairs was as stable as it was likely to be among the members of their blended party, she knelt by Kiril and pulled every scrap of occasional, disconnected Healing energy she could find into herself. Then, settling into a familiar trance, she began her work.

Sometime later she woke up with a start. Her head rested on the edge of the cot. Disoriented, she slowly straightened and looked around. Night was near, and rain continued to pound the cabin, drowning out other sounds.

"Come, Sister. Let me serve you a bowl of stew." Zelda put a hand under her elbow and eased her up. The cabin was dark, the lantern providing a weak, flickering light.

"Stew? I thought you said..." Her feet had gone to sleep, and her hand gripped Zelda's arm as her legs threatened to collapse under her.

Zelda settled her in the lone chair. "Not much, I said. Happens we had some dried rabbit in reserve."

Unseasoned stew had never tasted so good. The men from the caravan lay curled up in a pile of blankets in the far corner, but did not appear to be asleep. She wasn't sure, given the dim light, but she thought Kiril breathed more regularly. Joss was nowhere to be seen.

"Earlier, you mentioned a fireball."

Zelda shuddered. "Lit up the sky, it did, and that in the late afternoon. We were to the west, in the grass hills, but it landed in the forest. Expected the place to go up in flames, we did. But no fire. I call that odd."

So did she, but then nothing about the last two days had been normal. Her stomach no longer clenched with hunger, Willow returned to Kiril's side. His breath did flow more evenly. She touched his forehead. Hot. With several layers of the grime removed, she confirmed Zelda's observation. He was good looking. Thin face, firm mouth, strong jaw under the untrimmed beard.

And the blue eyes. She hoped to avoid the traders getting a glimpse of his eyes.

Seeking air, she pushed open the door and stepped outside. Joss sat on the porch step, sheltered from the downpour. He ignored her. The donkey stood close by; the man raised no trepidation in the animal.

"Have you eaten?"

"Yeah."

"You must be cold by now. The cookfire will warm you."

"I'm fine out here."

"You are not, and I cannot afford for you to catch pneumonia. Come in."

His hesitation might denote reluctance or fatigue, but he stood and stepped across the porch to the doorway. From within the cabin she heard Zelda begin to protest.

"No." Willow cut her off. "He will not harm us, and sleep is essential if we are to make Stanstead tomorrow."

"You won't object if we stand guard, turnabout."

"If it sets your mind at ease. Joss, rest by the fire. I must work with Kiril, or at least attempt to." She gave a conspicuous yawn. Let the traders believe her fatigue presented the only challenge. The last thing she needed was for word to spread that the Aura had become unstable.

Willow settled beside the cot and sought her Healing trance.

Chapter 2

Sustainer of life, align your energy to ours today. Give me the tools to help these men. Sustainer of the earth, return to us, strengthen us and feed us.

The day had dawned clear. Willow expressed her gratitude in her morning ritual as Joss watched from the porch and Zelda heated the remaining stew for breakfast.

According to the unofficial code of the roads, when groups met, they merged, allowing safer passage for everyone. As well, it made more sense for the donkey to pull the litter than to subject Joss to it. The daylight revealed the hollows around his eyes. Despite his quiescence during the night, with a resultant reduction of stress levels among the others, the traders maintained a healthy distance between themselves and him as they went about their business of loading goods into packs and onto the donkey, tidying the cabin.

She chose not to confirm that Joss and Kiril had indeed arrived in their fireball, although they'd obviously drawn that conclusion. Her best hope was to get them to Stanstead with a minimum of fuss.

The heat had broken with the storm, and the day held the freshness of wet earth and new-washed foliage. As they trundled along the trunk road, she studied her patient. She'd been able to capture shreds of Healing energy in the night and channel it to him, but never enough to construct a proper template. He had awakened briefly, long enough to take a few sips of the broth, but she wished for more alertness in him, and a lessening of the fever and flashes of pain that crossed his face. She leaned over to drape yet another cool rag across his forehead.

Nobody had slept well, but it wasn't so far to Stanstead, two hours at a normal pace. As they walked, they split into distinct groups, one exhausted and wounded, the other deeply suspicious.

Joss said nothing but kept near the litter. The sun beat down on them, and he pushed up his sleeves, revealing raw, blistered skin on his arms. Neither his nor Kiril's clothing had burned, yet underneath they both bore the marks of fire.

"You're injured."

He didn't reply.

"I can apply a salve. It will soothe — "

He stopped and glowered at her. "You keep your hands off me." At the menace in his voice she froze, then took a step backwards.

He lumbered forward. The litter moved well ahead before her heart rate settled. Joss had *threatened* her. Only in the direst pain, the most fraught of sickbed situations, had anyone dared turn a threat on her.

She corrected herself; he'd threatened her *again*. The scene at the men's camp might have been a dream, were she not constantly reminded by the Aura's erratic behavior.

She swallowed. At least he was moving. If he chose to deny himself succor, why should she be bothered?

They were nearing the ford, perhaps another half hour's walk, when she heard a voice she knew as well as her own heartbeat, calling her name.

"*Bryar!*" she shouted back.

They had gone through training together, she as Healer, he as Bard and Minstrel. They had been first lovers for each other, and much later had created a child, a daughter now herself in training at the Motherhouse. Along with their friend Quinn, no one was closer to her, and no one more trusted.

So the sight of Bryar sprinting toward her eased her fears and made her believe, however temporarily, that things would be all right. She drank in his short golden hair, his muscular, stocky build, the birthmark covering most of the left side of his face, marring his beauty.

"Willow. Thank the Sustainer." He threw his arms around her as they met; she felt his chest heaving as he embraced her, smelled his so-familiar scent.

She pushed him away to look at him. "Were you aware of it? Are you? Is anyone else in Stanstead?"

"One from your guild, Agatha, but she's moved on to the south. What happened?" Bryar grasped her hand as they walked back to the others.

"I will tell you as we go." She spoke for his ears only. "We must move far away from the last waysite on the northern track. There is a poison there, a danger. How strong is your connection?"

"Variable, not as it should be. When I performed in Stanstead last night, I resorted to old material, the things I do by rote. The energy was unreliable."

She nodded, for a moment unable to speak. Bad enough the terror of it when she let her mind pretend it was only her own problem. But she could no longer deny that other Weavers felt the disruption.

The story emerged, laced with her fear and his incredulity. No one treated Weavers that way, and the Aura… neither of them knew what to believe.

They reached the ford before midday, just as two men waded across from the Stanstead side. Young and well-muscled, they approached their caravan cheerfully – until they caught sight of Joss. The wary look she was growing accustomed to marked their faces as they hesitated.

Willow selected a level site where the road paralleled the river before turning into the ford. "Rest him here," she said to the traders. "And thank you. We can manage now. I regret taking so much of your time, and I wish you well."

"And to you." Clearly more than happy to escape, the members of the caravan freed the donkey from the litter, handing the front end over to Joss. They nodded a brusque farewell and set out across the ford toward Stanstead, a quarter of an hour away.

Willow wasted no time watching them go. "Joss, support the litter while Bryar and I remove the wheels. Then bathe in the river. It will soothe your burns." To the new men she said,

"I will need your assistance to carry my patient. I believe you came to swim? Please do so. I will signal when I am ready."

She thought Joss looked uneasy, but her attention focused on his companion. She longed to linger herself, to pull off her tattered clothing and let the river's waters wash her, but treating Kiril was critical.

"Bryar, will you allow me to link? I expect this to be difficult. He's been too long without help, and there's this..." She trailed off, allowing a gesture of her hand to indicate the erratic energy.

He gave her a half smile. "Take as much as you need, Wils."

Removing the wheels allowed the litter to lie flat, connecting with the earth. Bryar sank to the ground next to her, asking no questions. They had linked energies in the past; he understood what she required of him.

The two of them settled in, both seeking attunement to the Aura, the unseen, life-giving force that dominated their lives. She sought and found Bryar's connection and claimed it, joining it with her own. They sat unmoving while Willow did her work.

Joss watched the weird behavior of the healer woman and the man still as stones beside Kiril. Their actions did nothing to ease his mind. If this was what passed for medicine in this benighted land, they were both in trouble – and if the commander died, he'd be alone here, with no trace remaining of the life he'd lived before.

Did that matter?

The men at the ford kept their distance, but didn't show the fear that marked the traders' behavior. He followed them to a small beach, praying for shallow water. Obsessive cleanliness had been drummed into him from childhood as necessary to prevent epidemics, and he longed to wash properly. But first he had to survive the river, because he had never learned to swim.

"Might as well take advantage," the taller of the men said. They both wore tunics like to the healer woman

Willow's, with trousers. Before his disbelieving eyes they peeled out of their clothes. All their clothes. Without a stitch on they waded in.

Joss had not been naked before another human being in his life. Personal modesty was a corporate regulation back home. He could no more casually remove his clothing than he could return to Terra.

First a *woman*, then the gibberish about this Aura thing and healing powers. Followed by the realization that he was fated to spend the rest of his days on this planet, and then water and nudity.

He'd fought it off as long as he could. Overwhelmed, his remaining strength seeped out of him. He allowed himself to drop onto the little beach.

The men noticed and returned.

"Name's Rick. Need help?" the taller one asked.

"You look pretty bad. Remember that barn fire?" the other man said, glancing at Rick. "Thought I'd never walk again, I was that exhausted. Wife wouldn't let me in the door till I'd scrubbed up, and me staggering like I'd been in the beer instead of a damn fire. I'm Ab. We'll get you straightened around." He continued to chat as they hauled him to his feet, both of them stark naked. With no drive to resist, he let them do it. They settled him, fully clothed except for his boots, in shallows near the beach, no more than knee high and flowing over sand.

Relief. He leaned back on his elbows as the water cooled his battered body, and rinsed his singed skin and filthy clothing.

After the better part of an hour by his reckoning, Joss returned to land, letting the sun dry him. Unfiltered sun was nonexistent on the settled parts of Terra, and he worried, briefly, about burns or cancers. But at this moment he was too drained to care.

Willow and the blond man, whose name he had already forgotten, sat like statues over Kiril. The men dressed and joined him on the beach, chatting about their lives and work. They lived in Stanstead and worked as agriculturists, which Joss concluded meant they were farmers.

He listened and said little. The last thing he'd expected to find on this planet was other people. People the same as them. And people who – *hell*. He must have been more shocked than he'd known not to realize it before. They spoke a language he understood. Not Northam Standard, but similar.

How in the blazes was that possible?

He hoped Kiril pulled through. And soon. To stand any chance of coping with the challenges of this place, he needed the commander.

Word of their arrival preceded them. A few minutes later Joss watched as a party of perhaps twenty people, led by a short, elderly, and angry woman, crossed the ford.

The healer and her friend were just shaking themselves free of whatever kind of trance they'd been in. She rose and approached the new arrivals. Rick and Ab scrambled up and joined friends in the crowd. The blond man remained seated by Kiril, his face buried in his hands.

"Marla."

"Willow." Marla's greeting was terse and unfriendly. "I hear you bring trouble with you, and I've come to stop it in its tracks. These newcomers, they aren't welcome in Stanstead unless you can prove their origins. Caravan says they dress strange, speak strange. And something about arriving in a ball of fire."

"Partially true. Both are ailing, one severely. I require use of the healing room, and lodging for the other."

Joss got to his feet, keeping an eye on the crowd and attempting without much success to brush away the sand sticking to his wet clothing. The woman named Marla watched him and swore under her breath.

"He's not dangerous," Willow said.

"Are you sure about that? You found them on the road?"

"No, in the woods, north of the main waysite on the northern track."

"Fireballs?"

"True, I expect. There's wreckage. The big one, Joss, gave no trouble last night at the shelter. The other, Kiril, is not out of peril. Bryar and I linked, and that helped. But we must get to the healing room and gain greater distance from the wreck." She dropped her voice. "The fireball they spoke of affected the Aura. Near where it crashed, it's as if it isn't there. Or inaccessible."

Marla paled. "Crap. That explains the Weavers' agitation yesterday. And you want to bring these men to Stanstead? You understand my position, Willow. As mayor, my responsibility is to protect my town."

"He seems like an okay guy." Rick must have overheard the conversation; he gestured to Joss. "We've been chatting."

The rumblings from the group accompanying Marla had grown louder, drowning out the man's testimonial. Before Joss could process what was happening, four men broke free and darted at him. He twisted to run, but too late. Egged on by the small crowd, they jumped him. Someone landed a punch in his ribs he wasn't braced for, knocking him sideways.

"*Don't!*" Willow's voice, shouting. "*Stop, leave him alone!*"

The struggle on the beach was over in a moment. Outnumbered, he went limp. They seized his hands and yanked them behind his back. The coarse bindings of a rope circled his wrists, pulling tighter than necessary.

He risked a glance at Willow as she took a step toward the crowd. Marla gripped her shoulder, stopping her. "Let them go," she said, her voice hard. "There'll be less trouble that way. We'll deal with it when we get back. Until then, at least we know where he is."

The men shoved him along the road, the mob pushing and elbowing. He glimpsed Rick and Ab as he was driven into the ford. Both had stepped aside. Hopefully, that meant they intended to stay behind to help Willow with Kiril.

Logic staved off panic. Joss figured he shouldn't be surprised by the hostile treatment. He'd already scared the traders with his blackened skin, his size. No one he'd encountered so far came anywhere close to matching his heft or height. The tallest man here stood closer to Kiril's height, about average on Terra but well short of his own. As well, water had been insufficient to remove the greasy soot, and rumors and fears spread fast.

He tested the ropes, but they held. He'd been too worn out, his instincts too numb, to resist them in time. Now he found himself a prisoner, at the mercy of a mob.

He had no idea how far to expect to walk, and cursed himself for not putting his boots on when he left the water, despite the blisters.

The crowd grew the farther they went. Hysteria grew along with it. Two or three voices rose above the general clamor, inciting them all to riot. They poked and shoved him, threw clods of dirt and rock. He tripped and fell flat, knocking out his breath and muddying his clothes and face. They yanked him upright amid jeers and drove him forward.

Don't fight.

So much for logic. After the fall he was scared shitless. He kept his head down and plodded on, mentally cursing Northam Corporation, the Amalgamated Expeditionary Force, the exploration pod that had landed him here, his injuries, Kiril's injuries, the mob, the day... in fact, everything. Except the donkey. He'd never seen a donkey, and the animal's placid companionship had relaxed him, however temporarily.

And Willow. He didn't understand why she wielded so much power, but she made things happen. She'd get him out of this mess.

They paraded him through town to a small building on a side street. There, he was cut from the crowd and harried through the door into a room he recognized as a cell. It contained a cot, a bucket, and nothing more. They gave him a shove, sending him flying, shut him in, and left him.

He lay still on the floor for long minutes. Then, using a wall for leverage, he clambered upright and sat on the cot, arms pinioned, helpless, wondering what else could happen. On Terra, the rabble-rousers leading the charge against him would be executed. Here... hell, for all he knew they were cannibals.

The pain in his bound arms had gone from uncomfortable to excruciating by the time the door opened. Three cudgel-armed guards grudgingly stepped aside to let Willow and Marla in.

"Did they hurt you?" Willow kept her distance, as did the older woman.

"Yeah. Some." Scrapes, bruises, a sore rib, swelling on his face where he'd smacked his head on the floor when they shoved him into the room.

"I apologize. I am Marla, and I am the mayor of Stanstead. You represent a threat to the stability of my community. Do you understand that?"

Joss seldom said much, but now he needed to find words, in a hurry. "Yeah, I get it. You don't know who I am or what I want."

"Perhaps you'd care to enlighten me?"

He sighed and looked up at the women, one of whom had allowed his brutal treatment at the hands of her mob.

Kiril would say, name and rank only. But what was the point? It wasn't as if he'd be released to go home again.

"We're from another planet. I'm no —"

"Hold it. What was that again?"

How was he supposed to explain intergalactic travel to a woman whose civilization transported goods by donkey? "Look, it's complicated. For now, can you just accept I'm no threat? Believe me, I don't want to be here, but I don't see there's a choice."

Mercifully, she let it go. "And the reason you're here?" Implacable, Marla showed no sign of the hysterical fear that had infected the mob.

"To learn what's here."

"Wherever they came from, their arrival was not gentle," Willow said.

"Ah, yes, the traders' fireball."

Joss looked at Willow. "Kiril, he's..."

"Stable. He's in the healing room."

Marla studied him for a long minute. He forced himself to meet her eyes steadily. Throughout his life he'd acknowledged rank by lowering his gaze. But their survival training taught otherwise. Show dominance, never weakness. Fighting his instincts, he sat still, waiting.

She spun from him and addressed the men with cudgels. "Untie him, escort him to the men's lodge for a bath, and arrange for a room. Guard on the door. Let him move around the village and be sure he makes it to the dining hall, but not alone. Report regularly."

"Fresh clothes and sandals," Willow put in. "And bring him to me. I will attend to his wounds."

"If you say so," one of the guards said. "But I don't like it."

"And watch your tongue," Marla snapped. "Obviously, this man's no demon. He's big, that's all. We show him respect, and we keep an eye on things. Clear?"

Willow sat next to him and dug at the knots holding his wrists behind his back. "I'm sorry," she said after a brief struggle. "It's too tight. I can't undo this."

The guard took her place. Much less gently he tugged at the bindings until the ropes fell away. Joss clenched his teeth at the cramp in his arms as he moved them forward.

"You're going to need healing yourself if you don't get food and rest," Marla told Willow. Then she turned and stalked off.

Willow looked around at the guards. "Can you see to him?" Her voice was gentle after Marla's. "He gave no trouble on the road. I do not believe he is dangerous."

"We'll keep a watch out, just the same."

She left. Joss stood, uncertain what to expect next. At a curt gesture, he joined the men and walked in the middle of them as they departed the jail.

A few minutes later they had crossed an open square and arrived at what he was told was the men's lodge. This he understood; he'd lived in some form of barracks his whole life. Alone at last in a bathing room, he stripped off his ragged clothes and wallowed in the bliss of warm water and soap, ignoring the wounds on his body as best he could. A tunic, loose trousers, and sandals of leather and rope waited for him in the anteroom. He abandoned the remains of his Terran uniform in a grimy pile.

Next they led him to a clean, simple room. There, disregarding the guard outside the closed door, he sank onto the hard bed and fell asleep before he had time even to wonder how Kiril fared, and whether the purported healing had been successful.

Only to wake up with a lurch. Based on the angle of the sun coming through the small window, he guessed no more than an hour had passed. Recognizing the improbability of returning to sleep, he spent a minute gazing out, studying the scene on the square below him, then shoved his feet into the sandals and set off to find food.

Chapter 3

Stanstead was a clean, prosperous crossroads town. A veneer of ground white rock that came from much further north coated its one- and two-story buildings. Tradition claimed the mixture kept illness at bay, so most settlements in this part of the Midland glowed white.

A plaza surrounding a well, paved with flat stones instead of the more typical hard-packed dirt, held pride of place in the center of town. The well's strong-flavored water rose from deep in the earth and caused grimaces at first taste, but Willow had come to trust its healing properties.

In the shade of early evening, she sank onto the bench outside the healing room, itself attached to the Healers' lodge south of the plaza, enjoying the relative quiet of the courtyard garden and breathing deeply of the fresh air. Fatigue clawed at her nerve endings, as much mental as physical. The night on the road, Joss's chaotic energies, the near riot at the ford, the strange behavior of the Aura – still a noticeable disruption at this remove – had left her in a mental fog. She longed to be alone to work with the plants, to create medicines. To ground herself in her everyday life, in the earth.

Soon the bell would ring for supper. Much as she liked Stanstead, the thought of the noise and chatter in the dining hall was almost enough to make her skip eating. Her hollow stomach prompted her otherwise.

Most routes she walked started with the track from the Motherhouse to Stanstead. A town, not a hamlet, it offered variety as well as a chance to meet with her fellow Weavers. Besides the workroom in the Healers' lodge, Stanstead provided a fully stocked textile center, varied food, and things like bottles and corks, which had to be imported since the Midland produced neither.

Tomorrow she would visit the textile center to replace her destroyed skirt. While she was perfectly content to wear a tunic only, the extra layer provided protection against typical hazards, from scrapes to sunburn.

Some scrapes, anyway. She studied her grazed hands, the crusted scab on her knee. With distance between herself and *it*, she might begin to heal.

Kiril was improving, but not with the speed or smoothness she expected. Without the infusion of Bryar's energy, she doubted she could have triggered even this much healing.

Bryar's baritone voice floated from the plaza, where he spoke and sang a legend, a standard he'd performed hundreds of times before. He'd be nearing the end of his performance, and probably the end of his strength; shadows had haunted his eyes as they made their way to Stanstead that afternoon, the two agriculturists carrying Kiril's litter.

Speaking of whom…

One of the men who had accompanied them earlier came through the gate to the courtyard. She managed a weary smile.

"Thought you should know, Sister. That man —"

"Which man, please?"

"Joss, he called himself, the one so reluctant to enter the river. He's wounded."

"As I noticed. That is why I asked that you bring him to me."

"Tried. He won't come."

She could have gone a season without dealing with this kind of irritant. "Where is he now?"

"Don't know. Moving around."

A young woman joined them, attaching herself to the man. These girls. One thing only on their minds. Had she ever been so carefree?

Although to be fair, at that moment the release of lovemaking sounded blissful, if only she and Bryar weren't both so worn out.

"That new fella, he's down in the fields," the girl said. "Staring, like. At the cows."

"I'll find him." Willow shifted the conversation to another concern. "When last I came through here, a girl named Missy was apprentice to your healer. Is this still the case?" *Sustainer, let it not be so.* Olyve, the local hedge healer, had grown too old to handle her responsibilities, but Missy had proved to be lazy and intractable when she didn't get her way.

"She's on the plaza. We're just heading over there."

So be it. Swallowing a sigh, she said, "Please send her to me, here and now." She was a Healer. However exhausted, she lived her commitment, even if it meant dealing with Missy. And Joss.

As the young people went away, she delved into her pack to check her supplies. If the Aura held stable, healing Joss would not be difficult, other than his own strange resistance.

In no rush, Missy wandered over.

"I've a person who needs me," Willow said bluntly. "What took so long? There is work to be done and a patient to be attended. I expect you to be here."

Unimpressed, the girl said, "I can watch him from the plaza."

"You cannot even see the door of the healing room from the plaza. Stay here, and I will return as soon as possible. If Kiril wakens, apply cold compresses to his forehead, but nothing else."

Missy whined. "There hasn't been a Bard here in forever. I don't wanna miss the fun."

"I am sure you attended Bryar's performance yesterday, so you will remain here. While you wait, please consider your position as apprentice to the town healer and the responsibility that entails."

Missy recoiled at the sharp words. Willow turned her back on the girl and walked away. Nominally, the Healers who passed through Stanstead held authority over her, but in practice it was not so simple, since Healers seldom were present for more than a couple of days. The health of the town, as well as maintenance of the lodge and the preparation of medicines, became a challenge without a responsible and competent local healer.

A problem for tomorrow.

Joss had propped himself against a fence, his attention fixed on the brown cows as a man rounded them up for milking. A guard from the jail stood at a little distance, cudgel in hand, watching. Unaware of her coming up behind him, Joss jumped when she spoke his name.

"What?" he snapped.

"You are drawn to the cows?"

The purposeful innocuousness of her voice took the edge off of his. "They're different." Fidgeting, his attention once again on the beasts milling about near the gate, he turned away from her.

"How so? These are common enough."

"Not where I come from. First those trees, now this." He gazed into the distance, along the lane, sweeping his hand in an arc to encompass the valley. "So those are cows. I never imagined they'd be so big. Or so tight together."

"Really? In what way?"

"They just are. Like they support each other." He frowned, as if his own words made no sense to him.

Willow broached the reason she had ventured into the fields. "I say again, you are injured. A festering wound will leech your strength, and may cause death. I will Heal you, if you allow me to."

An instant, negative reaction. "I don't need your hocus-pocus. I'm doing fine as I am."

Her instincts, however muddled they might be by fatigue and the fluctuations in the Aura, told her he was afraid of her, which made no sense. His size alone should be enough to establish his safety in her hands.

She stepped forward and quickly touched the back of her hand to his forehead, ignoring his instinctive flinch. "You are mistaken. You should not be so warm. A fever must be treated, and soon."

"Sister!" The cowherd approaching them. "Can I assist you?"

"Only to convince this bull-headed man to accept my help."

"She's right," he told Joss. "She saw to my ankle when I sprained it a few years ago. If she says you need Healing, you need Healing. No point in fighting it."

"Thank you." Willow placed a gentle hand on the man's arm. "I appreciate your words."

They exchanged smiles. "I have to go," he said. "The cows won't wait. See you around."

She nodded. Possibly two thousand people lived in Stanstead, but yes, they would meet again. No avoiding anyone in a settlement, even one this large.

When the herd started on the road to the barns, she said, "Please let me treat your burns. I can provide a salve to ease pain and fight infection." She reached toward his arm.

He backed away. "I'm fine." Shifting sideways, he removed himself from her proximity. "Just fine," he muttered, and took off at a near run, outflanking the cows, only to stop without turning when she called his name.

"Visit your friend. When he wakes he will be confused and disoriented, and will need your support."

"He's not my friend." Joss spoke to the valley rather than to her. "He's my commander."

Then he left in a hurry, leaving her with a new puzzle. *Commander?* What did that mean? She understood the word, but not the context. People did not hold positions of such dominance, except sometimes with children.

Like your mother. Commanding you to be an archivist.

Whatever Joss meant, it wasn't good. She was sure of that.

Yes, he'd run. Run like a baby.

With a safe distance between himself and the woman, Joss slowed his pace but kept moving with no particular destination in mind. He wasn't in a hurry to return to Stanstead, so he allowed himself to wander, still amazed by the clear sky, the rutted track that emitted a rich aroma as he trod on it, the grasses and weeds growing waist high outside the fence corralling the cows' pasture.

A path forked off to the left, following the fence – north, he'd worked out. He took it and before long found himself in a stretch of woodland similar to where they'd crashed. With no one else in sight, he dropped to the ground and leaned against a tree without thinking, then jerked upright again as the burns on his back flared. With his arms wrapped around his knees, he allowed his body to relax – for what felt like the first time in a month.

She was right, he knew it, but *damn*. The horror of their crash landing after the nightmare of the weeks preceding it, losing the rest of the crew, men he'd known and lived with for over two years, then the controls failing in a cascade he and Kiril fought to contain, most of their food destroyed, their lifeline to Terra severed, only to find himself in an unexpectedly populated land, Kiril injured...

What the hell was he supposed to do now?

Joss had never been in the situation of having no one to tell him what to do. Never, from his infancy through the years of training, culminating in his unexpected promotion to the Expeditionary Force. He should be on a factory floor, working the line, kicking back over sports on the video in the evenings. Following orders. Not sitting in a forest on a new planet, under unfiltered sun, catching scents he'd never smelled, touching leaves and dirt...

Overhead the breeze set up an unnerving rustle in the treetops. Trees, and for that matter wind, were rarities on Terra. Joss struggled to his feet, worried by the effort it took, and followed the track farther into the wood, curious about what he'd find next and hoping for solitude.

It appeared that they'd provide food and shelter, and that nobody much cared what he did otherwise. No cameras watching him, only the one lackadaisical guard. He'd seen few people, compared to Terra. But so many of them were *women*. Women everywhere.

Alone. The thought made his mind twitch. He, a competent man, taller and stronger than most – at least when in health – found himself marooned in a strange land. It would make a damn fine video game. *Expeditionary Force 3: Fighting the Aliens.*

Except that so far, discounting the hysterical mob, there was nothing to fight.

Members of the Expeditionary Force didn't admit to fear. But as the forest ended and the trail led him to what he recognized as the back of the cows' field, he admitted, if only to himself, that yes, the suddenness and quantity of the changes scared him. He accepted that as a normal reaction and assumed he'd get over it once he found his footing. But bottom line, for the first time in his life he was completely on his own. The corporation that had fed and housed him, provided him with work and entertainment, was a thing of the past.

His guard kept a good distance between them but stayed in sight. Well, he understood that, too.

Joss set out to circumambulate the field, his thoughts spinning through his mind.

The Commander would expect assessment, recognizance, that he learn everything possible about these unexpected people and how they lived. He only had to wait for Kiril to recover, to take charge.

The breeze, which had been tangled up in the leaves, played across the open field, cooling his face. It never got this hot in Northam Corporation, not in his province anyway. The moving air brushed against his skin, but not enough to cool. He worried that his body heat might be not from their sun but from fever.

And that brought him back to the woman, and, coincidentally, to the place along the fence where she'd found him. Willow. Sooner or later he suspected his burns would demand attention. But allowing a woman that close to him was too much to deal with.

He'd eat, sleep, keep the wounds clean, get himself healthy again. And for his own sake he had to start learning the ways of things. Because he was dead certain he'd never see Terra again.

Standing leaning on the fence, missing the cows no longer in the pasture, he wondered if he cared.

Willow sank with relief into a chair at one of the smaller tables in the dining hall. She had arrived right at the peak, at the end of the workday when everyone was ready for sustenance and socializing.

Stanstead, being bigger, meant more commotion. Wearily but with good grace she had fielded questions from the townsfolk, denying any real knowledge about the strange visitors, urging them to visit her during clinic hours. When they finally left her alone, she consumed her mushroom cutlet and vegetables, barely tasting them. As she ate she scanned the room for Olyve, the resident healer, but failed to locate her.

No other Weavers were present at the meal. She assumed she and Bryar were the only two in town.

One of the servers brought her a small piece of cake, an unusual courtesy since protocol dictated she queue for dessert. Willow didn't want the sweet, but smiled her thanks and ate it anyway. Part way through, she felt her head lift off her shoulders and recognized the signs of overwhelming fatigue. When she stood to leave, she gripped the edge of the table for a moment to steady herself.

"Let me help you." Marla appeared at her elbow. Willow nodded, failed to produce a smile, and allowed the mayor to escort her from the hall.

Once outside, her head cleared. They paused on the plaza, taking in the early evening scene. Marla ran Stanstead with an iron hand, but the result was peace and prosperity. Willow had known her for years, and trusted her, so during their walk from the ford she had told her about the disappearance of the Aura and its subsequent instability, and the sequence of events that had landed her in town with the two strangers.

The plaza presented a scene of tranquil content. The sun wanted another couple of hours before setting, and the surrounding buildings cast long shadows. Children ran and shrieked, enjoying their freedom. A group of gray-haired men waved. Families leaving the dining hall walked together, returning to their homes.

All as usual... but not.

"Are you personally aware of the trouble?" Willow asked. "Do you sense it?"

"I'm not sure if I pick up the unease from you or from the earth."

"I would prefer this be kept in confidence. Truth to tell, never have I been so frightened."

Marla placed an arm around her waist. "How can Stanstead support you? We stand ready to assist, however possible."

She managed a faint smile. "Thank you. The disruption is less here, more a fluctuation. With Bryar's aid I was able to do a Healing, but alone—" She broke off, the reality of the situation flooding into her. "Alone I'm not sure I could have done it."

The women walked across the plaza toward the Healers' lodge. "Anything we can do to help," Marla reiterated. "Stanstead supports our Weavers, whatever is required."

"I know it." She gave Marla's arm a grateful squeeze. "I must notify the Motherhouse. Then we will see."

They parted at the gate to the Healers' lodge. Willow went inside to her room, comforted by the older woman's reassurance.

Chapter 4

Willow woke to find early morning sunlight brushing her bed. She had slept soundly, free of the dreams she had feared might disturb the night. After a quick wash, she went downstairs to the herb garden to enact her morning ritual, feeling, if not quite herself, at least renewed from the shock and exhaustion of the previous two days.

Just as well, because today shaped up to be busy, and not with enjoyable activities. The matter of Missy, for instance.

The girl's insolence troubled her, as did the state of the Healers' lodge, which barely met minimum standards. She had actually noted a film of dust on the water in the ewer beside her washbasin.

More important, though, was explaining the events of the last two days to the Motherhouse. Between her plummeting energy levels and the vacillations in the Aura, she had been unable to maintain a connection the day before. But communication was vital, even if it meant linking once again with Bryar. Linking placed a serious drain on his energies, so was not to be taken lightly.

And her patient, who had slept through the night. Neither Missy nor the other girl she'd employed to keep watch had reported any change.

To sustain her spirits, she bent to rub a sprig of lavande and inhaled the scent. The heat of the sun later would bring out the medicinal properties of the plants, a perfect time to replenish her supplies.

She peeked into the healing room. Kiril slept on, and Missy was nowhere in sight. Sensing nothing to give her concern in his condition, she let the curtain drop and made her way to the dining hall, where she downed a soft-boiled egg and a cup of life-sustaining caff.

With the Aura stable, if weak, and her energy levels propped up, her attention turned to her patient. Kiril. A strange name – but everything about these men was strange. She returned to the healing room and hooked the heavy curtain aside.

She studied him. Fast asleep, but sleep only, not unconsciousness. A handsome man, once the layers of dirt had been washed off. His face thin, chiseled. Light brown hair fell over a cowlick onto his forehead. She was glad she couldn't see his disturbing blue eyes.

Willow crossed to him and rested the back of her hand against his temple. Only a little warm, nothing to alarm her, and sleep could be as therapeutic as any of her medicines. She realigned his energies, then left, letting the curtain swing closed behind her.

Now, Missy.

With three private rooms, a workroom for formulating remedies, and a common room, the Healers' lodge ranked among the larger accommodations Willow stayed in. Most hamlets offered only a one-room edifice for whatever Weaver came through, be it Healer, Bard, or Scribe. If two of them turned up at the same time, they shared. It was just another aspect of life as a Weaver.

The healing room adjoined the lodge, the buildings forming an el around the courtyard and herb garden, separated from the lane by a low stone fence with an arched gateway. She found Missy in the lodge, sullenly swabbing the floor of the common room. The girl ignored her.

"Missy."

"Yeah." She remained on her knees, pushing the brush back and forth in the pooling water.

"You can see to this later. Get up and come with me. We must talk."

Willow did not wait for her to comply, but turned and walked toward the main door. She settled on a bench in the herb garden, allowing her muscles to relax in the warmth of the morning sun and relying on completion of an unpleasant task to make the world seem right again.

After a time, Missy sank down beside her, a shapeless bundle of sullen misery in her scullery clothes.

"Tell me this. Have you any true wish to be a healer?"

The girl reared back. "Course I do. Only an idiot would do the cleaning and stuff, otherwise."

"Why?"

That perplexed her. She fidgeted. "I guess... thing is, I like messing around with the plants and all. Only I don't know how."

"But that's Olyve's job, to instruct you. Do you not ask her?"

"She don't help."

"Why not?" Ancient now, Olyve should have passed on her responsibilities years before. All beginning healers needed a mentor.

Missy shrugged and kicked at the paving stone under her foot with a heel. "She just tells me to pick this or that. But maybe I don't know what it looks like, and she don't go into the fields anymore."

"But how are medicines made?"

The girl reddened. "Healers that come by, they 'splain things or give me stuff."

"And are you practicing healing?"

The blush deepened. "Don't dare, do I? What if I got it wrong?"

So Stanstead effectively had no healer. Fortunately, because every woman and many men grew up with some knowledge of healing and herbs, the town was not completely without support.

"And what if a Bard came, and listening to him was more interesting than keeping watch on an ailing man?"

Missy's slump became more profound, so she resembled a pile of rags on the bench. "All's I ever do is clean," she whined.

"What is your age, Missy?"

"Seventeen years, Sister."

"Tell me truly. Do you want to heal, or would you be happier working with plants and remedies only – an apothecary, they are called."

"Never heard of that." But the bundle of rags unfolded as the girl sat straighter.

Willow noted the change in posture. She said gently, "I think it might be best to find another candidate for healer, don't you? We will arrange instruction for both of you. The current situation meets no one's needs."

"Can you do that?" The members of the Healers' guild offered advice and assisted with training, but the town itself chose the local healer, or hedge healer as they were called.

"I will speak with Olyve. Finish what you are doing, quickly, then go to the healing room. I need you to listen for Kiril's waking. Not glamorous work, but necessary. And perhaps we can improve things for you. The idea is not that you be unhappy."

"Yes, Sister. Thank you, Sister." Missy practically tripped over her dragging skirt in her haste to get away.

"And Missy?"

The girl stopped but did not turn around.

"Today, please refresh the linens and water in my room, which are several days overdue, I believe."

Missy's body tensed, but when Willow said no more she plunged for the door, leaving the uneasy conversation behind.

Olyve lived in a small apartment next to the Healers' lodge. Willow called out to announce herself, but receiving no answer she let herself in. The sight of the old woman shocked her. More than a year ago, when she last passed through Stanstead, Olyve had been mobile and opinionated, if not vigorous. The woman she found in a chair by the single window, looking out over the street and unaware of Willow's hail, was shrunken and tremulous.

She tried again. "Olyve?" She placed a hand on the woman's shoulder.

Olyve turned toward her, a vague smile on her face. "Thank you, Missy. Yes," she said. "A small bowl, please, made thin the way I like it."

She crouched beside the chair. "It's Willow. My dear, how can I help you?"

Olyve frowned. "There's trouble, you know. No one tells me, but I can tell. That girl Missy, go get her. She'll tell you."

"She has told me." The eyes failed to focus, the elderly brain no longer grasped changes in her environment. Willow resolved to see that Olyve's remaining years offered more than a thin gruel and a room with no visitors. "I will bring your porridge." She gave the bony shoulder another gentle squeeze and left for the dining hall.

As she crossed the plaza to fetch Olyve's breakfast, a man who worked in the cobbler shop waylaid her. "The new fellow. His sleep was that troubled, he woke up the whole lodge."

"From pain, do you think, or from toxic dreams?" She bit back the sigh fighting to emerge and updated her mental list. Porridge, then Kiril, then Joss, that obdurate, idiotic man. Why suffer, when healing was offered? And then the Motherhouse.

"At a guess, I'd say both. They thought to call you in the night, but you were exhausted."

"True, but my duty is to be there. I can recover later. Where is he?"

"Saw him walking out of town, toward the ford."

The sigh escaped. "I will find him. How is your daughter? Has there been any recurrence of the breathing difficulty?" The girl was a patient from her last visit; she remembered the concern etched on the father's face.

"No, and I thank you. She's flourishing now. That stuff you gave her, it does the trick."

The man went off in the other direction. Willow continued to the dining hall, then a little later re-crossed the plaza, a bowl of gruel in hand. She passed the porridge over to Missy, with orders to return as soon as Olyve finished her breakfast, and ignored Missy's put-upon sigh. Like it or not, for the moment this was her work.

Willow checked on her patient. Still asleep. She took the time to once again align his energies, noting the relaxation in his body as he responded. Then she gathered supplies from the locked closet adjacent to the healing room, which the

Healers and local healers jointly maintained, and took a mental inventory while she awaited Missy's return.

Finally, with the discontented girl in place on the bench outside the curtained door, she set off after Joss, wondering why he had returned to the ford. Even she, with the fatigue and worry she'd carried with her, had seen that he and the river were not friends.

She greeted the ever-present guard lounging against a tree beside the swimming beach and found Joss alone in the shallows. He had removed his tunic but left on his trousers, and was scooping water with his hands, pouring it over himself. Either for pain relief or for cooling, she guessed, and made a mental note to request a second change of clothing for him.

She assessed him as she approached. Washed and shaved, he appeared much less the dangerous brute of yesterday. Tall and heavy boned, curling brown hair shaggy over his neck, and a toned torso, although he and Kiril both showed signs of insufficient food and exercise. Angry burns covered his back and shoulders, bruises and abrasions peppered his upper body. A bruise on his face had swollen to force his right eye nearly closed, likely from the mob's rough treatment.

He caught sight of her and shot a panicked look toward the beach, where his tunic lay. Her own tunic covered her to her knees, so she pulled off her skirt – he turned his head – and fished a cup from her pack, then waded into the river. Before he had a chance to recoil, she touched her hand to his forehead.

"You should have let me help you. Now, you are blazing hot, and you *must* submit to my Healing, or expect your friend to be walking while you fade away on a sick bed."

Markers of pain and fatigue showed on his face as he glared at her. "It's wrong. You and your magical thinking. I can't—"

"Can't?" Willow knelt beside him, soaking her tunic almost to her waist. Using the cup, she joined him in pouring cooling water over his head and back. Once again he flinched.

"You do not want me to touch you."

"It's wrong," he repeated.

"In what way? That I should wish to ease your discomfort?"

He responded by shifting slightly from her.

"Very well." She stood, waded to the beach, and rummaged again in her pack. Finding what she sought, she smeared salve into the cup. "I offer you this. When you are clean and dry, smooth it onto your burns. Not as efficacious as a proper Healing, but better than nothing. Today, drink water and eat when food is offered." She extracted a small bottle. "Two drops of this, no more, in your water, now and at mid-afternoon. Come to me this evening and I will replenish the salve. As you refuse to allow me to help you, you must help yourself."

He stood and followed her to the shore, snatching up and donning the tunic before accepting the cup and bottle. He stared at the remedies, frowning.

"You cannot reach some of the burns. Ask one of the men for assistance if I am such anathema to you." Willow folded her skirt over her arm. The wet tunic, the sun on her bare legs, felt delicious. She left him standing there, radiating distrust. Joss would have to tend to himself. Her more pressing client waited in the healing room.

Kiril became aware, first, of darkness. The shifting lights no longer tormented him like knives piercing his head.

He'd been hurt in the landing. He remembered heat, consuming him. A fever? The heat was gone, in fact he shivered.

Eyes closed, he lay still, waiting for his senses to catch up with consciousness.

He experimented with moving, starting at his feet. The heaviness and pain in his right leg restored part of the memory.

Broken leg. Joss pulling him from the wreck of their ship. Lying on the ground, shivering, burning.

An angel touching him. He'd died, then. He tried to swallow his bitterness. The mission a failure, most of his crew dead.

Surely goodness and mercy will come to me...

Or not. The words of the ancient chant hadn't done the job so far. Goodness and mercy might exist in an alternate universe, but not in his own.

Kiril continued his survey, working up his body. Burns, the worst on his arm and chest. He remembered that one, when a piece of the ship's wreckage fell on him, pinning him in hell until Joss hauled him out.

His arms lay beside him. Slowly, because of the burn, he turned his palms down, then up. Smooth. Not the rough, uneven surface that had imprisoned him for that agonizing trip to wherever. A lightweight covering draped him, soft, silky.

Not warm enough. He shivered.

While Kiril explored, his mind became more aware, his senses more alert.

Indoors? The smell's different.

Where was he? How could there be an indoors on an uninhabited planet? A cave?

And where was Joss? Kiril swallowed his panic, talked himself down. Of course he hadn't been abandoned. Unless Joss was dead.

Not uninhabited. People around him, talk. When? Had they taken Joss prisoner?

The leg throbbed. How long before he'd be able to fend for himself?

Helpless. Justified or not, bitterness welled up in him again.

He slitted one eyelid open, then the other, and froze, waiting to see what would happen next.

Nothing. Unless there was a camera somewhere, nobody watched him. He opened his eyes, carefully, and equally carefully turned his head to survey his surroundings.

A small, dim room. It looked like a structure of sticks, the gaps filled with mud. Hangings on the walls, too dark to be sure of the colors. No windows, but a curtained doorway divided him from whatever lay on the other side. Light filtered in around the curtain's edges, and it shifted gently, so he suspected it opened to the outside. He saw no furnishings other than a straight-backed chair.

Kiril risked shifting on the bed and gasped. The burn must be more extensive than he thought.

He touched his body. No clothes. They'd taken his clothes.

The heat, suddenly unbearable.

With great care, he raised his head, ignoring the pain.

To be sitting, instead of lying flat... Again fighting panic, he struggled to get his elbows under him, relying on the sheet for modesty. He had to show them he was capable.

Except he was shaking, no strength in his arms. He would never make it to the chair if he couldn't even pull himself up to sit.

So hot. Burning.

The curtain twitched. An animal entered the room.

A giant, muscled cat, as big as himself.

He'd seen them in picture books from the old days. Cougars, they'd been called, or maybe lions. The cat paused near the door and stared at him, its eyes glowing.

The beast crouched, readying itself to pounce. Horror-struck, he sought frantically for something to defend himself with, and succeeded only in falling back onto the mattress.

His voice. Frighten it off, call for help.

He screamed as the animal pushed off with its muscular hind legs and flew through the air toward him, giant paws reaching...

"He's awake!" Missy called across the plaza.

Willow had initiated an impromptu clinic while she waited for one or both of her irritating patients to need her. She hastily completed her consultation with a woman whose energetic imprint pointed to menopause, not pregnancy as she hoped, and hurried to the healing room, looking around for Joss as she went. Predictably, he was nowhere to be seen.

"I heard 'im whimpering," Missy told her.

She paused at the door and sought the Aura. This morning the energies were weakened and erratic, but at least accessible on a minimal level. Satisfied, she steadied herself and pushed aside the curtain, draping it over a hook to allow fresh air and light to enter.

He'd wakened, or thrashed in his sleep. His covers were askew, and he had thrown the healthy arm over his face. She tested his crown energy. Not pain, more like panic. After such a crash, it made sense that he might suffer from nightmares.

She touched his forehead. Dry and too hot; the fever was back.

A quick assessment of his energetic pathways pointed to another loss of alignment, and his heart beat more rapidly than it should. She began passing her hand slowly up and down his body, not quite touching, again and again until she sensed the free movement of his core energy. Blue eyes or not, the man's pathways became unstable quickly. The effect of the crash? Or a deeper disturbance?

As the flow of his essential energies aligned, Kiril's body relaxed, his face grew peaceful. She continued until she was sure the alignment was stable, because whatever torment bedeviled this man, he needed a respite.

His eyes opened. Willow stilled her hands and smiled at him. "You're awake."

"The angel," he whispered. "I didn't believe it."

She'd heard Healers called angels of mercy; was that what he meant? "Hardly an angel, but your leg is healing. You're in the town of Stanstead. Joss is here, too, probably out with the men. I'll bring him to you when he returns." A shadow crossed his face, so she added, "You're safe here."

"Did you catch the cat?"

Willow glanced around. "There is no cat. Did one come in?"

She registered the agitation in his energy field and almost absentmindedly began smoothing it again.

"Giant. Big as me. Attacked me. Claws..." He tapered off.

The fever. "When?"

"Here. Right here." He struggled to pull himself upright.

Willow put a hand on his chest; he cringed. *The same as Joss.* "I will help you to rise in a moment. I must tell you, though, there are no cats that size in the Midland. Only small animals to hunt rodents. Can you take water?"

He nodded.

She shouldn't be surprised that the flagon of drinking water was empty. She went to the door. "Missy?"

"Yeah?" Missy had wandered into the herb garden, where she sat idly on a bench.

"Renew the flagon from the well, please. And if Joss is anywhere to be found, would you ask him to come to the healing room?"

"Yes'm." Missy took off, and Willow returned to her patient.

Kiril struggled to rise. Willow brought a stack of pillows from the supply closet and supported him as he settled into a partially upright position. He kept the light blanket wrapped firmly around himself. Emotions danced across his face when she touched him – fear, despair, an overarching weariness that set up a less than optimal healing environment. This man had not lived an easy life.

Missy tapped on the doorframe and handed over the water. "I can't find the other man."

"He will come eventually." Willow retrieved a cup from the cabinet and poured a little water into it. She added a few drops of feverfight, then held it for Kiril. "Put your hand over mine. You lack the strength to hold this yourself." He was reluctant to touch her, but eager to drink, a sip at first, then as if he craved the very taste of the water.

"More," he croaked when he finished. She shook her head. "Too much would make you ill. In a little while."

He steadied himself against the pillows. "Clothes."

"The town will provide new ones soon. Your old clothes were destroyed."

"But I can't stay like this." His voice was growing stronger.

Willow frowned. "It bothers you to wear nothing? Why?"

"Please."

He didn't need to add despair over his lack of clothing to his other challenges. "I will find you a nightshirt."

Relief washed through his pathways.

At a brushing against her legs, she glanced down to see a familiar ginger cat twining around her ankles. Absentmindedly she bent and scratched behind his ears, then scooped him up. "Is this what you saw? You're a big guy," she said, nuzzling into the orange fur. The cat purred ferociously and struggled to leave her arms in favor of Kiril's bed.

Kiril stared as if he'd seen an apparition.

"Shall I allow him on the bed with you?" She watched his face, puzzled.

He didn't hear her. "He clawed me," he whispered. "But he was huge. He attacked, and his mouth, the teeth—"

"Quiet." She put a hand on his shoulder, bringing him to a stop. "This cat, attack you? It's not likely. He's a familiar character around here. He's never hurt anyone."

"Look." Hesitantly, Kiril lowered the blanket, revealing four raw, shallow scratches on his torso, such as a cat might make. But a cat many sizes bigger than this one. A cat with a paw the size of his hand.

This makes no sense.

As the reality of the purring creature in her arms sank in for him, she put it on the bed. He tensed, then relaxed as the animal settled at his side, kneading the bedclothes to soften them. The purrs hadn't diminished. In fact, she'd never heard this particular cat so determinedly content.

He stammered an excuse. "I've heard of cats. They're wild things. Vicious."

"Not here. They control the mice and rats, and they make excellent companions."

The size of his hand. She hovered her own hand over the new wounds, sensing their energy while being careful not to touch her patient. They had not come from a cat. In his panic, he had clawed himself.

She poured water, cleansed and disinfected the scratches.

Exhaustion was catching up with him. She pulled the wrap up, covered his eyes with her hand for a moment to encourage sleep, then settled into the chair, a silent observer of the man and the cat, now curled tightly against his hip.

Not a quarter of an hour later Joss arrived. She could tell when he was close by the chaotic energy he brought with him, an urgent, edgy drive. The limited rapprochement they had attained during their walk had been used up by her attempts to offer him healing.

He shouldered his way into the room without concern for who might be sleeping, who might need peace.

"Out." She was on her feet in an instant, extending her hand to stop him. He drew away and backed through the doorway. She followed him outside and released the curtain over the door.

His eyes narrowed. "Is he okay?"

They stood there in the herb garden like combatants. "The healing is progressing, but slowly. I could use your help. Information."

He turned his back on her and strode through the courtyard gate, then headed around the healing room toward the plaza. Willow stuck at his heels.

He stopped at the well. "What?"

"Your burns – they are better?"

"Yeah." He must hate admitting they weren't as painful; his brown eyes shifted here and there, anywhere but to her.

Willow perched on the stone rim of the well and waited.

"Why?" he demanded.

"Why what?"

"Why isn't he getting better? Kiril – Colonel McKettrick's the best commander I ever served under. You'd damn well better take care of him."

Kernel? Another puzzle. First commander, then kernel, like the corn you feasted on in late summer. And McKettrick. Were these second and third names?

"As I said, he is improving, but more slowly than I like."

That got through. "So, what do you want to know?"

"Will you sit?"

"No." He stood in front of her, arms folded across his chest, radiating exasperation.

She considered. "His energies slip out of alignment much too easily. It would help to understand why. Do you know of some event in his past that might disturb him still?"

"No idea. I was on his crew, that's all."

"So you never saw...?"

"Nah. He keeps to himself. And the mission went fine, right up to when the..." He paused. "Okay, yeah, he took that hard."

"Took what hard?"

"When the refrigeration system failed. We were in the cargo hold. The others... died. That got to him. Not that he showed it, except for not sleeping much."

"How many others?"

"Four."

His voice became huskier as he remembered the day Kiril lost most of his crew, and Joss lost... comrades? Friends?

"Is he subject to visions?"

"Don't be absurd."

"Why is asking about visions absurd? It is a part of the healing process."

He shot her an exasperated look. "Look, you strike me as a reasonably intelligent woman, okay? But visions? Give me a break. You're delusional."

"And you are wrong."

"We're scientists and engineers. We deal in facts, not crazy fantasies."

Purely for the shock value, and because she had had enough of his attitude, she said, "One of the visions you fail to believe in clawed scratches across Kiril's chest this morning."

He stared at her, dumbfounded. Then he raised his voice. "I told you, I hold you responsible."

"Nothing disturbed him. Stay away for a while, Joss. Your energy will not help him heal."

His lips pinched in a tight, angry line. "I'm the only familiar thing he knows. I'm not deserting him."

"Nor do I want you to. But not today." She wished he would meet her eyes, or let her touch him, let her calm him. "I will provide you with a tisane this evening to give you a calm sleep. Last night you disturbed the men's lodge, or so I'm told."

He gave her a contemptuous look and stormed off across the plaza. He wasn't going to accept calming. He wasn't going to accept anything from her, but at least she had gained a partial picture of her patient's mental state.

This could be a long healing.

Chapter 5

Willow watched Joss leave, taking the road that led to the barns. Why did the animals hold such allure for him? Based on his limited and reluctant communication, he was some kind of specialist, a person who fixes things and studies how they work, not a man to be fascinated by cows.

At least his wounds were healing. Olyve had received her porridge, and a little company to go with it, and Kiril – commander, kernel, McKettrick, whatever name belonged to him – rested comfortably, likely exhausted by his fright earlier.

Next on her list was the Motherhouse. She slid from her seat and walked back to the Healers' lodge.

The Aura remained stable, but weakened.

Alone in the herb garden, she paced in a slow circle, beginning in the north, the direction of her earth clan, greeting the energies of each direction in turn. Then she stepped into the middle of her circle, raised her arms, and spoke, aloud but quietly. "Sustainer of the land, I call you, your daughter asks for true alignment and clear communication, to nurture the health of the Midland. Grant me the grace of Healing, others and myself. Ease my fear."

As she lowered her arms she became aware of another person close by. It was Bryar, waiting in the west near the gate. An unspoken message flowed between them, and he stepped in to join her. Her circle had been one of benediction, not of protection, so it was open to him.

When he added his own invocation to hers, he eschewed the drama and theatrics of his performances, speaking somberly, weaving his own words into hers, and into the fabric of existence. "Sustainer of water, giver of life and rest, align with us now. Flow through us and inspire us. Sustainer of the land, grant us courage as we do what must be done."

Their ritual complete, he took her hands. "Motherhouse?"

"It's past time, but I had no energy to spare yesterday. And with the fluctuations... But today my connection is stronger."

"Do you need to link? Or shall I stand sentinel?"

She smiled. "Sentinel. I think I can do this. Thank you."

He went to the arch at the entrance to the garden and shut the gate, a rare move. "When you're ready."

Willow settled on the stone bench and allowed herself to sink more deeply into her working template than she usually found necessary. Bryar faded, as did the intoxicating scents the herbs released in the sun. Her eyes closed, and she was still.

A quarter of an hour later she gave a violent shiver. "Gently," Bryar said. His arms wrapped around her.

"It's done." She sagged against him while she waited to return fully to normal consciousness. Long distance contact always drained her. Being of air, Quinn used this form of communication regularly; thoughts and logic were her natural milieu. But, Willow reminded herself, Quinn could never focus her mind on a plant and discern its medicinal value. They each manipulated the templates of the Aura in ways suited to their guilds and their own clan proclivities.

She wished she could avoid the trembling and hint of nausea, though.

"I didn't bring food. Are you able to walk to the dining hall?" Bryar had seen it before, but he still sounded concerned.

"The kitchen baked seed pastries this morning. I'll tell you what I learned as we go."

Amusement danced in his eyes. She loved seed pastries, as he well knew.

They made a short reverence to the four directions and to the overarching Auric energy that governed their lives, then walked together across the plaza.

"The Scribes pinpointed the location, but not the cause of the disruption," Willow said. "They didn't know about the wreck or the two men."

Bryar nodded. "We're not helpless, not with the Motherhouse involved. We can neutralize it, whatever it is."

He did not say, *before it destroys us.* But she was sure it filled both their minds.

She tried to prevent it, but cynicism trickled into her voice. "All we have to do is figure out how."

"Don't, Willow." His strong arm came around her, hugging her before letting her go.

"I'm frightened, Bry."

"We all are, I expect. I wish there was another Healer here. You need support."

"A seed pastry will help."

At the dining hall they found both the pastries and the mayor, Marla, with her council.

"I have a performance," Bryar told her. "I'll talk to you later." He kissed her temple, saluted the council, and left.

Willow brought her pastry and a mug of caff with her to their table.

"It's time to tell the others what's going on, Sister," Marla said. "All of it, now that you are rested." For all her polite delivery, a command lay behind the request.

Grateful that Marla had kept her confidence, Willow allowed herself a bite of the pastry before presenting as complete an explanation as she could for the obvious agitation she and Bryar exhibited. Most people had no energetic connection to the Aura, but everyone trusted the role it played in maintaining their land.

"I contacted the Motherhouse this morning," she concluded. "The effect fades with distance."

"We need to look over this wreck," one of the men on council said. "See what's left and what it looks like. From the picture you paint, I don't have any concept of it."

She swallowed another bite. "There's no point of reference, so it's impossible to describe clearly. I'm reluctant to send anyone to the site, but if someone has to go, then please, be sure it is a person without Entrée. Anyone who touches the Aura could be at risk, but whatever is causing the disruption, it did not appear to bother either Joss or Kiril."

"So it might be safe enough, and a way to provide more information to the Motherhouse." Marla nodded. "Yes, I think we must do this. If for no other reason, the northern track is heavily traveled this time of year. We'll post a warning for others if there is danger."

"It's most of an hour's walk through brush from the main waysite, so I doubt anyone will stumble on the wreck." Willow sat with one hand gripping the mug of caff as if it connected her to life itself. Recounting that day brought back memories she would rather forget.

But she had to review them, or be haunted by them, until she contacted another Healer and received a Healing.

With efficiency that Willow admired, the mayor assigned members of her council to select participants, gather supplies, and prepare to leave within a couple of days. Five or six hours at a healthy person's pace would bring them to the waysite, another hour to the site of the crash.

"I want to include the foreigner Joss in the party," Marla said. "I've heard no negative reports, only that he spends his time in the fields and barns. Can we insist he participate? And could he find it? He might identify things in the ruins that are unfamiliar to us."

"Ask him. He is a mystery to me."

Marla nodded to one of the council members. Task assigned. Willow was happy enough to be relieved of Joss's disruptive energy for a few days.

"I'm concerned about how this will be received among the population."

"We don't want to cause a panic," Marla said. "We've already had to discount the traders' talk of demons and such. For the moment, we'll restrict the information to the council and those selected for the trip to the site. A softly worded explanation will do for everyone else. Don't worry."

"Impossible."

The impromptu meeting adjourned. Out on the plaza, Willow checked the position of the sun and calculated that she had time before the call to lunch. Kiril was still asleep, so she returned to her room in the lodge, kicked off her sandals, collapsed fully clothed on the bed, and fell into an uneasy slumber.

The healer woman, Willow, allowed him to go outside, escaping the tedium and darkness of the room they'd confined him in. He had insisted on wearing trousers, as well as one of their loose-fitting tunics. Then been embarrassed as hell when he needed help to put them on.

Pain shot through the broken leg as Kiril walked to the door, but it was bearable. And he was walking, only three days after she began her so-called treatments. He didn't like to admit it, but there might be something to her rigmarole. He shuffled forward on his own, refusing help despite his weakness.

Behind him, she sighed.

She was an attractive woman, all that long, pale hair. Not as young as he'd first thought, not a child. Too slender for his liking, but with an air of command about her he found appealing. On the whole, her presence pleased him, if only she'd keep her hands to herself. Medics on Terra were men.

His only experience of women had come because of his caste – in upper management, they had been provided as an occasional reward, interludes that had been compelling in the moment if mildly distasteful in memory. Joss must be in a state of shock; in the working caste, relations with women could lead to castration or worse.

"Commander." Joss's familiar rumble, waiting for him.

Once past the curtain, he slammed his eyes shut against the blinding daylight. By his reckoning, it was near the time they brought him his lunch, so call it high noon.

"Here. Sit. Feel the bench against the back of your legs," Willow said.

He got himself settled, the injured leg straight out in front of him. Gradually he opened his eyes, adjusting to the light. He and Joss were alone.

"This planet is closer to their sun," Joss said, reminding him. "Class seven, smaller sun, weaker. Shorter orbiting time, fewer days in a year."

"Much brighter."

"You've been in that dark room, remember. And no filters."

On Terra they lived under filters to prevent the sun from baking them to a crisp. Kiril allowed his body to relax, soaking in the warmth.

Joss settled next to him, legs out, propped against the wall of the healing room. The ginger cat wandered over and twined itself around Kiril's ankles, then jumped to the bench beside him, and from there onto his lap.

He placed a steadying hand on the cat's back before speaking. "Nice shiner."

Joss shrugged. "My arrival – some people objected. A couple of rabble rousers mainly."

"You injured otherwise?"

"The salves and hocus-pocus took care of most of it."

"How's the political situation? How much danger are we in?" No one was around, as far as he could see, but Kiril kept his voice low.

"None, I'd say. I hear the mayor laid down the law. The kids on the plaza made up a new game about being chased by black demons."

Kiril gave a short bark of a laugh. "Nice to be a legend in our own time."

"Maybe. I don't like that they scatter when I turn up."

"Get over it." He knew he sounded irritable, but Joss would be no different if his leg felt as if it might snap off and he'd been flat on his back in enforced seclusion for days.

Joss ignored the snipe and grinned. "Looks like you've got a fan."

"Stupid animal." But Kiril's hand of its own accord moved over the cat's fur, absorbing the rumbling. No need to mention that the warm, vibrating weight had soothed him to sleep the last two nights, when the threat of nightmares led to wakefulness.

Squinting, Kiril studied his surroundings. A courtyard full of plants, which he assumed were herbs. A two-story building to the left, abutting his one-room hovel. Around them were whitewashed stone buildings, mostly single story and small. A few larger buildings lined the lane bordering the courtyard, none taller than two stories, all surrounded by flowers and shrubs.

Noise came from behind them. He looked at Joss, questioning.

"Your room backs onto the plaza. A guy performs there at lunchtime. They're narratives, like legends. I haven't paid much attention."

"I've heard him. He's impossible to shut out."

Joss said nothing more, just sat there waiting. Typical. Throughout the voyage he'd done his job, but volunteered little.

"Tell me what you've learned."

"There's not that much to tell." Joss didn't move, didn't turn to address him or look at him. "The farmers – they call them agriculturists, I don't know why – they seem friendly enough. The food's the best I've ever tasted. No one's trying to restrict what I do. They put a tail on me for a couple of days, but no more. I spend a lot of time in the fields, walking around. There are animals here, cows, donkeys, sheep and goats, so I've been helping in the barns, learning what they eat, stuff like that."

"Not helpful, Sergeant."

"I guess not. What do you need from me?"

"First, has it occurred to you that we understand them?"

"Weird, isn't it?"

"Well, what do you think?"

"Obviously our people are connected, but when and where... I didn't want to question anyone too closely, in case they started asking questions themselves. Anyway, I can't figure out who to ask. Willow seems to be the best educated person around, but it's not her field."

"Do you remember when you were a kid, learning about the lost ships?"

"History? No, sir. In my caste, we didn't bother much."

In the lowest caste, a decent education wasn't a priority. Given his background, that Joss had been selected for the Expeditionary Force was a miracle of sorts. His voice stayed carefully neutral when he mentioned the worker caste, but Kiril wondered what he really thought about the system, and the way he had bucked it.

"Four hundred years ago or thereabouts, they sent out ships packed with settlers. A dozen of them. Only one landed on a habitable planet, as far as we know. The others vanished."

"Could be we just found one of them."

"Could be."

"So this happened around the time things started to go bad."

Kiril nodded. "Language evolved quickly when the corporations took over. The people here probably speak an archaic form of Northam Standard, what they used to call English."

Joss folded and unfolded his hands on his thighs, taking in the theory. "But if their ancestors arrived on a ship, shouldn't they know it? Four hundred years isn't that long ago."

"Provided they kept records."

"I haven't seen any sign of records. Or of paper, for that matter."

"Find out. Report back tomorrow."

"It may not be that simple, sir."

"Make it simple, Sergeant." The heat was getting to him. He could see Willow crossing the courtyard.

"I'll do what I can. But as I told you, I haven't found the right person to ask yet. And I don't want to raise any alarm bells."

Willow stood before them. "This is enough. You're flushed from the heat."

Joss rose and held out a hand, helping him to his feet and sparing him the indignity of relying on a woman. The sun had leached him of energy, though, and he required Joss's support to walk back to his bed in the dark room.

The cat followed and jumped up beside him, settling next to his leg and making that soothing rumble. The woman stayed with him for a few minutes, working her mumbo-jumbo over him, then left, promising to see to his lunch.

Getting up had sapped his strength, but he refused to doze while he waited for the food to appear. He slumped against the pillows, staring at nothing, turning over the events of the past few days and hoping that his mental focus returned soon. He'd expected to settle an unoccupied land; now he was faced with conquering a settled one.

Chapter 6

Joss saw the ford ahead and something came over him, which he didn't immediately identify as happiness. He was glad to be back.

His game plan involved adaptation, since going home wasn't an option. The three days away from Stanstead, leading the others to the wreck, only reinforced his resolve.

Remembering, he picked up a stone and threw it into the trees. Before they left Terra, the Northam CEO had promised they'd return heroes as he pinned on their insignia. Instead, four dead, and he and Kiril marooned in an alien civilization.

After his promotion, he'd been subtly isolated because of his working caste status. Only in the exploration pod, their little spaceship that carried them across light years to prove the suitability of this planet for settlement, had he found men he could call friends.

By contrast, the three men accompanying him were... well, ordinary guys. Doing a job together, on task, kicking back in the evening with gossip and beer. Relaxed and easy. A joke or two about his size, but not mean-spirited.

He hadn't been comfortable enough to ask the questions piling up in his mind, though. About their history and language, for instance, their technology. The cows and the weird way their perceptions trickled into his head, more and more clearly with every day that passed. Now that could freak him out, if he let it. It was as if they invaded his mind with theirs. Maybe it was usual, but he didn't think so. No one talked about what the cows were thinking.

And then there was the big question, the one that he couldn't avoid much longer, the nature of male-female relations.

Women. That they were everywhere, even running things, made Joss more than uneasy. Yet the men around him talked about women, and sex, constantly.

Sex. Another cause for unease. The private bathing rooms at the men's lodge met his occasional need for relief, but obviously there was more to it. His mind flashed to the cow and bull in the field a few days before, the way his gut had clenched, believing the cow was being attacked, before he sorted out the reality. And she'd been fine, pretty damn full of herself in fact, as the bull ambled off. He'd concluded that men and women...

He turned hot.

"Want to stop for a swim on the way in?"

"Weather's gonna break sometime this evening." Sure enough, clouds piled up on the horizon.

"By which time we'll be snug in the lodge. Ready to get beaten at checkers again, Joss?" The first man nudged him with an elbow.

"Whatever." He understood this kind of casual camaraderie among men. "I think I'll just head back." Though he was drawn by the thought of cool water flowing over him; the trek through the scorching afternoon had left him sticky and dusty.

The third man, Rick from that day at the ford, said, "You can't swim, can you?"

Joss turned his gaze to the river, but didn't deny the fact. "Never learned."

"No time like the present."

Laughing and jostling, his companions surrounded him.

Accept the inevitable. He was going in the water if they had to throw him in.

Just one day. Just one day without a new challenge to deal with...

At the beach near the ford the others stripped off and ran into the river. He could see no choice but to join them, so he shed his clothing and hastily immersed himself.

Nobody stared. He'd get used to the nudity. Eventually.

Later, having pleaded fatigue and avoided the drubbing at checkers, Joss stretched out on his narrow bed. The water hadn't been so bad, splashing and roughhousing. And he'd gone underwater. Damn, but he was proud of that. Not only dunking his head, but staying there for seconds at a time. Tomorrow, they promised to show him how to float, sometime in between visiting the barber's room in the men's lodge for a shave, hanging out with the cows, and checking in with Kiril. What passed for a full day.

At least the rough-and-tumble in the water helped him avoid the memories brought on by the wreckage. Nights, though, it all came back.

A sharp flash of lightning, then thunder, disturbed his reverie. He winced and commanded himself to relax. The northwestern province of Northam Corporation's territory never experienced anything like these thunderstorms.

The uneasiness and mild headache that had stayed with him while they were close to the crash site troubled him. He needed to debrief, talk to someone about... well, everything he'd learned, or sensed, since landing here. Not Kiril, because he knew Kiril wouldn't get it. Willow? Or that musical guy? Joss had never associated with men in pansy occupations like music, but he worked with that energy thing, so he might understand.

Rain lashed at his shutters. At home on Terra, every available surface caught rain and funneled it into holding tanks. Nature tamed, for the good of mankind. The wild, tumultuous storms here, water sluicing off the roofs, the room obscured by the closed shutters – just another thing to adjust to.

The next day, after communing with the cows and sensing their concern for an aging member of their herd, and after sitting with Kiril and listening to him rant about superstition, dirt, food, even the cat, who remained loyal and draped itself across Kiril's lap, he went in search of the musician, whose name, he learned from a man in the barn, was Bryar. He found him by following the sound of a flute into the courtyard of a small house to the east, just off the plaza.

"Mind if I join you?"

Bryar sat cross-legged on a patch of grass in the shade. He moved the flute from his mouth and stretched. "You're welcome. Is here okay? I've been cooped up indoors all morning."

"Yeah, fine." He settled next to Bryar on the lawn, already dry after last night's thunderstorm, and concentrated on not staring at the purple mark marring Bryar's face. No one on Terra bore such a defect.

"What can I do for you?"

Joss rubbed his hands on his pant legs and took a deep breath. "About this Aura thing. And Entrée, I've heard that word, too."

"Oh, that," Bryar said, and grinned. "Here's an overview. Entrée is the ability to access the Aura. Those whose Entrée is strong become Weavers – if they want to. It's not a life for everyone. We train for eight years or more, followed by a journey year."

"So you weave something?" Joss felt his forehead crinkle in concentration.

"Yeah, currents of energy in the Aura. The pattern of the weave forms a template for whatever work we're doing. Willow created a template to heal Kiril's leg, for instance. I maintain a number of templates that I use to store my music and build performances on. What else do you want to know?"

Everything? "The Aura... What is it?"

Bryar shrugged. "There's no definition. It just is, like the sky or breathing. It emanates from the planet and surrounds it, like a blanket. It's an energy, or an energy source... we don't really know."

"But you sense it. You're aware when it disappears."

"As we found out a nine-day ago. Until then no one had experienced life without it."

Joss detected no accusation in Bryar's words, so he went on. "What's it like? Is it physical? Or a voice in your head?"

Bryar scrunched his face and lay back on the grass. "Let me think how to explain." He closed his eyes.

Joss waited; he was a patient man.

After a minute, Bryar sat up in one lithe move – clearly, he was no weakling – and said, "Neither, but the second's closer. The Aura isn't a voice, more an awareness in your mind. A sense that you're in touch with a power, or an energy, mightier than you are, but beneficent, not hostile. There to support you. It's intrinsic, a part of you."

"I see," Joss said, dragging the word out. Whatever was going on in his mind with the cows felt pretty damn intrinsic.

"Now, the templates are practical, like patterns for making use of the Aura, based on the individual and his work. You're familiar with the clans and guilds?"

Joss shook his head. "Healers, because of Willow. But not the others."

"The Weavers belong to one of three guilds, Healers, Bards, and Scribes. Our guild affiliation determines how we work with the templates, although there is some overlap. For instance, I draw on it for inspiration, and as a way to record what I compose. For Willow, it enhances her healing abilities. Those are guild qualities, but it's individual, too. I see the Aura sometimes, as colors corresponding to music, but I don't know anyone else who does."

"Then the Aura isn't one thing." This was nothing like an engineering problem. Just trying to grasp the concepts and retain them without a concrete, physical application to attach the information to stretched his logical mind to breaking.

"We assume it is, but filtered through our individual affinities. Now, the clans are different. Everyone belongs to a clan. They're concerned with which of the elemental powers resonates with you."

"Elemental powers?" As he'd half feared, Bryar was descending into the realm of make-believe science.

"Earth, air, fire and water, beginning in the north and working around the circle. North, east, south, and west. Willow is almost pure earth, I'm primarily water. You're earth."

"Why do you say that?"

"Instinct, and years of practice. It's usually obvious. Take your interest in the animals, for instance. Your size, the way you move. I'm an anomaly for water clan, most of us are slender, not stocky like me, but I carry a hint of earth, too. That's what makes it subjective. You'll figure out where you fit."

Fair enough. Joss relaxed, leaning back and propping himself on his hands. "If all this is true, what does it feel like when an earth person experiences the Aura?"

"Why do you ask?"

The crux of the matter. Did he dare say? But what difference did it make? "The thing is, when we got to the wreck, I had to force myself to go near it. I felt sort of dead inside. It wasn't like that when we first crashed, but yesterday and the day before... it was spooky."

Bryar didn't laugh, as Joss had half feared he might. Instead he fixed grave brown eyes on him. "Did it weaken you?"

"Shaky. As if... I can't explain."

"Try."

Joss gave his head a minute shake.

"This could be important. Please, try."

How to explain the unexplainable? He hated this. But he needed facts. Objective facts. "As if I was missing something, like a part of my brain had been sealed off. As if I wouldn't be able to hear the cows. Once we left the wreck, I got a sort of tingling sensation for a while, like my whole body had pins and needles, and today I could hear them fine."

Bryar studied Joss through narrowed eyes. "Tell me what you mean about hearing the cows."

"Not voices, not even thoughts, but... kind of my interpretation of what's happening in their minds. For instance, right now they're worried. One of them is older, and she isn't well."

Bryar stood and offered him a hand up. "Have you told anybody about the ailing cow?"

"No. Should I? You're saying that not everyone —"

"No one that I've ever heard of."

Shit.

"I'd speak to the head agriculturist, if I were you. He needs to know she's sick."

Bryar started for the gate that separated the courtyard from the lane. Joss reached out to stop him. "Wait. You're saying..."

Bryar stopped, facing Joss and fiddling with the flute. "History tells of such people, but I've never known anyone who reads animals that way. I need to find Willow."

Thoroughly puzzled now, Joss said, "Why?"

With the resigned look of a man accepting the inevitable, Bryar said, "Because you may have a gift, and if so, we need to figure out what to do with you. It sounds like you're touching the Aura. And at your age, that's a problem. Not insolvable, but a problem nonetheless."

"For me or for you?"

The slight tension snapped; Bryar laughed. "Good question. I guess we'll find out."

The two men walked together as far as the plaza. Bryar clapped him on the shoulder and headed toward the healing room, leaving Joss to return to the animals.

That hadn't gone too badly. He rolled his shoulder under the tunic, where the skin was still a little sensitive from the burns. Which Willow's salve, miraculously, had healed.

He walked along the lane leading to the field, considering his new problem. He'd assumed everyone understood the cows. If not, if he were the only one, what kind of freak did that make him?

Chapter 7

The day of Summer Solstice, Willow and Bryar claimed the afternoon for themselves. Barefoot, they followed a path along the river to a glade familiar to them both, far enough upstream to be private.

Her patient had been as irascible as expected that morning, despite standing, walking, and spending time in the sun. What did he expect? Normally, a leg required a minimum of five nine-days to heal. Instead he was up and moving around, although not with perfect ease, in little more than one nine-day. Yet he chose to be dictatorial, complaining about everything from the food, to the itching of his burns as they healed, to the ginger cat who, contrary to previous behavior, appeared to have adopted Kiril as his own.

The cat visited the healing room regularly, but its reaction to Kiril was a mystery, his rejection of it more so. Many considered the purring attention comforting. One day she had hovered outside once she'd settled Kiril, and sure enough, the man reached over to stroke the cat, triggering another burst of rumbling affection, as he fell asleep.

Still he complained. Why?

But today she had better things to occupy her mind.

The Solstice festival was in full swing on the plaza, showcasing delicacies from the dining hall and fancy clothing – dyed, embroidered tunics that were more difficult to launder, and town tunics, with an opening down the front held closed by colorful ties.

And courting... plenty of courting going on. She smiled.

Apart from her work, she had spent the morning singing the old songs and dancing, along with most of Stanstead. She loved Solstice festival, marking as it did the true beginning of summer.

Like her, Bryar had participated in the celebrations, and had taken his turn performing for the crowds, but she sensed the undercurrent of trouble in his mind. She saw it in the absence of his usual smile, the set of his shoulders. As a performer, he maintained consummate control of his body, but now, alone with her, he released his public persona and allowed her a glimpse of the man underneath.

A worried man.

"I hope there's a devil in you today," she said calmly. "You're much too contained."

A grin that was decidedly devilish rewarded her. "Perhaps you should show me what you mean."

"Idiot."

He grabbed her and swung her around. She'd made him laugh, and the tension they shared dissipated.

Willow inhaled and shoved the mystery that surrounded the Aura from her mind. Better to luxuriate in the spicy green scents of summer, the lushness of the fields and meadows, the dense shade of the trees bordering the river, which flowed less sluggishly than usual for this time of year, swollen from the rain two days before. It gurgled along beside them, heading for its destination far to the south. The breeze blew her tunic against her bare legs, a respite from the heat of the summer sun.

Bryar reached out, and Willow took his hand. Languid anticipation of what was to come between them seeped into her, her body as well attuned to his as it was to the earth.

Neither wore a Weaver's sash. Off duty, for the first time in days, she sighed with relief.

At the glade he spread the ground cover he'd brought with him, and without speaking they knelt. Their hands worked together as they removed clothing and sank into the luxury of lovemaking. Weavers seldom formed lasting relationships, for very good reason, but she and Bryar had managed it. The closest of friends... they both had other lovers, but still turned to each other. And of course, they shared their daughter.

Later, sweaty and considerably more relaxed, they sat side by side on the mat and watched the river tumble by. "I love the rolling lands," she said, while the languor of the afternoon filled her. "More than the plains."

"Anywhere with lakes and rivers."

"Because you're half fish," she teased.

"Want to swim back?"

"I wouldn't mind, provided you stay close. I'm not as adept in the water as you."

"It's hot enough, a swim will feel good." He dropped down on his back.

Bryar was a strong man, incorporating acrobatics into his performances as well as playing flute and chitarre, writing and performing songs and poetry. He was stocky and sturdy, and bore the marks of his share of boyhood brawls.

Inspired, she ran an idle finger over one scar, then another.

"Trying to heal them?" he asked her.

"Not likely. You've borne them too long." She trailed her hand down his torso.

He caught her intention, but shook his head. "Soon. Maybe I'm getting old, but I'm not well recovered yet."

She kissed his chest, but moved her hand away and lay beside him.

Plenty of time, the whole afternoon of Solstice. Time to laze on the bank and watch the unfolding of summer.

"We don't do this often enough," she said.

"No. And we should. I miss our days traveling together."

After Romarin's birth, they'd stayed together for almost three years, raising their infant daughter and squabbling over whether she would grow up to be Healer or Bard as they walked from hamlet to hamlet. Then Bryar had struck off on his own once again.

"We are together now," she said, "and for a while to come. I assume the Bards' guild received the notice not to travel?"

"Yes. Stuck in Stanstead. I'm ready to move west."

"And I to rest a few days at the Motherhouse. Spend time with Mari, if possible."

Instead of replying, he sat up and gazed into the far distance, for all that his eyes watched the water tumbling by.

"Bryar?" Her muscles weak from heat and their earlier lovemaking, she remained lying on the mat.

"It's still difficult for me to comprehend. That she is born of me."

"Romantic." Willow rested a hand on his muscular thigh. "Every child has a sire."

"But that I should be among them, and acknowledged as such."

"Now that she's at the Motherhouse, she's no longer our responsibility."

"Sad?"

"Not today." But his reflective mood had caught her up. "Bryar, what are we going to do?"

As usual he made her mental leap with no trouble. "There isn't enough information about why their wreck disrupted the Aura. It makes me close to nauseous at times, the way it surges, then retreats until I'm afraid I've lost it forever."

"The men seem normal," she said. "Joss spends his days in the fields. If it's true that he understands the beasts, he may find a role for himself here. The other one, Kiril, is an impossible patient, demanding and irritable. I'll be happy to see him gone from the healing room. And his eyes – did you notice?"

"They were closed. I haven't seen him since."

"Blue," she said. "The deepest imaginable."

"A portent?"

"I don't know. Perhaps that's merely a tale, because blue eyes are so rare. Perhaps he's fulfilled whatever destiny he bears and it's no longer a concern."

"By bringing destruction down on us."

Bitterness laced the words; she reached up to brush a finger over his chin, his cheek. "Not today."

"The turning of the season into summer. Don't worry, I won't ruin it for you."

"Thank you." Rising onto an elbow, she continued to caress his face, damp with humidity and perspiration, tracing the edge of the birthmark that had cost him half a year of training as he fought to overcome his aversion to it.

He leaned back on his arms, looking up into the dense leaves. "All I ever wanted was to walk this land with music. I'm afraid what we're facing will end that, change our whole way of life."

"I fear the same. But what it might be and how we repair it..."

He smiled. "You're wise. Not thoughts for today."

She grabbed his hand and lowered it to touch her. "No," she agreed. "I want to make love with you. And then we swim home."

Laughing, he collapsed onto the mat. She adjusted herself against him and once again allowed the comfort and familiarity of Bryar's fine body to soothe the raw edges of her worry.

Later, she swam next to him with her tunic flowing out around her – although to be honest, the river did most of the work – enjoying the chilly current and gentle exercise. When they got to the ford he said, "Not a peaceful swim after all. I've received a message from guild. We're to make our way to the Motherhouse."

"Yes, the same message. But more, I'm to bring the two men with me."

"That should make for an exciting journey." But he saw her dismay and pulled her up out of the water. "We'll be together, you, me, and Quinn, just like always. We'll figure it out."

"Or try to, at any rate." She freed herself but tangled her fingers into his. "I expect I need food. But Bry..."

"Hush." His lips sealed her mouth. "Dry clothes, then food. It *will* be all right, Willow."

It has to be, she thought a little desperately as they made their way along the road to Stanstead, their tunics dripping a trail behind them.

"Get me away from here."

By the time Joss turned up that afternoon, a couple of meat pies in hand, Kiril thought he'd go mad with the boisterous festival and the heat radiating off the plaza in waves.

The healer woman had told him to venture no farther than the courtyard outside his door. He'd ignored her and settled on a bench on the edge of the plaza – although damned if he knew why. Now that he was there, he'd do anything to escape. Except return to the dark room.

At least he was in the shade.

His brusqueness didn't faze Joss, but breaking Willow's commandments apparently did. "That may not be a good idea, sir. It might set things back—"

"My leg's doing fine," Kiril grumbled. "I'm not sure how far I can walk, but I've got to get away from this bedlam before it drives me out of my mind." Summer Solstice, they told him. But after two years in the relative silence of the pod, the chaos on the plaza shredded his nerves.

Typically, Joss made no comment. They walked through the village, eating the pies, Joss pointing out landmarks. The leg hurt, but Kiril refused to let that stop him. To be using his body again... a walk like this would do more good than any amount of the healer's incantations.

Moving slowly, they had cleared the town and were working their way along a track between pastures when a man going the same direction caught up with them, exchanging pleasantries, driving a flock of animals that swarmed around them.

"Sheep," Joss said without further explanation.

As a member of the upper management caste, he'd once owned a wool sweater, and had even eaten mutton on occasion. But he'd never laid eyes on a sheep. He watched, and smelled, the creatures as they waddled past them and down the lane.

The flock rounded a corner up ahead about the same time his leg sent a bolt of pain up into his hip, warning him not to walk any farther. Heading off disaster, he leaned against a tree, which brought the added benefit of shade. On Terra, trees existed only in the vacation parks. There were artifacts in museums, relics of the days when they grew so abundantly they were a construction material. Like the fencing here, he realized with a mental jolt. He failed to understand the allure of anything so inherently imprecise.

Sheep. Wood. Festivals. Voodoo.

He was sweating; he wiped his face with the sleeve of his tunic.

Joss noticed. "You shouldn't even be on your feet yet," he said mildly.

Building his strength was crucial, because the more he tired the more a feeling of uselessness invaded him. A weak, lame man, fit for nothing. His heart had lurched when the sheep milled around them. *Don't topple the cripple.* He admitted resentment, if only to himself. But he'd never show weakness. Never.

He was the commander here. Time to take command.

With the weight off his leg, he said, "I have to get out of that healing place."

"I'd stay where you are as long as Willow says to. From what I hear, she's a respected healer. What they do here isn't the same as our medicine, but it works. When we stopped at the ford on the way into town, she and Bryar, the one who's been singing, they just sat there like statues next to you, as if they were in a trance."

Kiril made a short, rude noise.

"Yeah, I know what you mean. But your leg's some kind of miracle, not to mention the burns, and it's been less than two weeks. There's more going on than we understand."

The state of his health took second billing to his main concern. "Yeah, but we have work to do. First, establish communication with Terra. We need a comm link, if we can build one."

"We can't." Joss's comment was flat and final. "None of our gear survived. And the technology here – it's weird. I don't have a clue how to use it or even access it. One night, late, I watched the musician cross the plaza. He made a fist, and when he opened his hand there was a light on his palm. He used it like a flashlight."

"Magic trick."

"Or maybe not. This isn't home."

"I intend to find a way to send a message back to Terra. Let them know this place, from what you've told me and what I've seen so far, is perfect."

Joss fixed him with a look. "I hope you're not serious, sir. There's already a civilization here."

Kiril shrugged. "If we can't contact Terra, we have no way to prevent it. Our mission – our *mission*, Sergeant – is to locate a habitable planet. This is. Lots of vacant land, and a culture so primitive they'll value what we bring to the table. With solid groundwork, the takeover will go smoothly. No rebellions."

"What worries me is that we've already affected them," Joss said. "Disturbing their Aura. Willow's healing power got messed up, whatever that means. She was adamant we had to move you away from the wreck, or you'd die. I expect she was right. I'm still kind of surprised you're alive."

"Irrelevant."

"No, sir, it's not. What's irrelevant is our own medical procedures. We have to adapt, or we put ourselves at risk." Joss rubbed a hand over the faded bruise on his face. "I like it here, Commander."

"You're letting their hocus-pocus get to you. I want you to go to the ship and assess what's there. There might be something that's usable."

"You okay to walk?" At his brief nod, Joss offered his arm to begin their slow return to the village. "Stanstead isn't a superstition-ridden bunch of hovels in a circle. There's a well developed culture, a stable way of life. Letting our people come here —"

"Is going to happen. You can't stop it. Neither can I, even if I wanted to. Which I don't. This planet is ideal."

And he intended to get the credit for a successful settlement. But that was classified.

As they moved along the track, Kiril noted the fields, which appeared to prosper. The inhabitants seemed healthy and content. There were crops and meadows, and vast swaths of undeveloped land.

The open spaces made him uneasy, probably the result of the tight quarters in the pod, although nothing like this existed on Terra, either. The China Pacific Corporation had even started blasting mountains, leveling them to accommodate the overwhelming population demands. More than enough room here for Terran settlers, especially with their much more advanced technology.

"They don't restrict your movements?"

"No. Not at all."

"Good. Leave as soon as possible. Traveling light, you should get there in a day, shouldn't you?"

"I've been," Joss said. "We got back yesterday."

Kiril stopped and stared, his gaze cold. "You went to the wreck without notifying me?"

"Sorry, sir. The town wanted to send an expedition. We didn't stay long. I poked in the wreckage, but to be honest, the place creeped me out."

"So it wasn't a thorough recon."

"Not really."

"Go back. Spend several days there, dig around."

Joss looked uneasy. "I'd prefer not to."

The insubordination rankled. "An order, Sergeant. Prepare to leave tomorrow."

Joss stopped walking and removed his arm, which Kiril hated to admit he'd clung to as his strength waned. "Commander," Joss began, slowly but with complete assurance, "the rules have changed. We're here alone, and our best option is to integrate into what we've found. It doesn't make sense for me to report to you anymore."

Speechless, Kiril stared. A big, phlegmatic man, Joss had always been tractable, willing to undertake any task for their mission. "You're aware you're defying a direct order?"

Joss shook his head. "I've thought this through, sir. The thing is, there's no military structure anymore. It's just the two of us. But to make it formal, I'm tendering my resignation, here and now. I'll put it in writing, if I ever find pen and paper."

Kiril tamped down the blaze of anger that tore through his gut. "You will pay for this," he said, his mouth tight.

"Not in the sense you mean. Let's go." Joss turned them toward the town. "There's a lot to learn here, and I'm happy to work with you. But I can't take orders anymore. I need to make my own decisions. We both do, because we may end up going different directions. The Expeditionary Force is history. There's no escape, we're in a foreign culture, and it's up to us to accommodate, not up to them."

Kiril said nothing, but fumed. Unarmed and without effective authority, he had no tools to bring Joss into line. He'd always listened to his team and respected their opinions, but he expected to have the ultimate say. Being in the military wasn't about collaboration.

They walked back to the healing room, exchanging few words. If Joss sensed his ire, he ignored it.

When the next ship arrived, the game would change. In the meantime, with or without Joss, he'd get a feel for the sociopolitical situation and be as ready as possible for the influx of settlers, bringing a life he understood with them.

He couldn't admit, even to himself, that they might not come.

Joss delivered Kiril to the healing room, although he refused to go inside, instead collapsing on a bench that received shade from the building across the lane, scowling all the way.

That went well.

Freed of his irritable former commander, he crossed the plaza, heading straight for the table where cheerful men poured oversized mugs of beer. His first mugful went down in about fifteen seconds, the second in a couple of minutes. The third, he took away with him, to the ford and beyond, into the forest.

It had taken every ounce of his self-possession to stand up to Kiril, and at the moment he questioned his decision. Cutting the ties, becoming his own man, had seemed like a good idea earlier. Now, with the unknown pounding through the mild fug from their potent beer, he wasn't so sure. What difference did it make if he obeyed Kiril's orders rather than his own? It would be so much easier. Kiril had always listened to him, and occasionally even followed his advice. Leave the thinking to someone else.

No. Not gonna work. Because of the cows.

Joss spotted a narrow trail, let it lead him to solitude, then sat on a rock, staring out at the trees.

Kiril saw a land ripe for conquest, which was true enough as far as it went. He didn't see the depth, the way the earth responded to a rainfall, or that the cows took turns babysitting the calves, or the miracle of Willow's healing. By rights they both should be laid up in bed still. Or dead.

He pulled off his tunic to let the air touch his torso, much thinner these days than it should be, and studied his taut, unscarred skin.

The third mug of beer, as he ruminated, lasted a good fifteen minutes.

Joss stayed alone in the forest until sunset, when the thought of the tantalizing aromas drifting across the plaza from the food stalls lured him… home? No, not home, not yet. But the land… yes. Something about it drew him, making him wonder if he had stumbled on what had been missing most of his life.

Back in Stanstead, the fourth and fifth mugs lasted the rest of the evening, until the festivities wound down, by his estimation around midnight. He skirted the rambunctious crowd on the plaza, usually holding a meat or vegetable pie – pasties, they called them – or some sweet concoction in the hand that didn't grip the mug, and got thoroughly lightheaded, maybe even a little drunk, before he stumbled to his room in the men's lodge and sank into an uneasy sleep.

He'd pay for it the next morning. But however briefly, he relished the freedom from all the new, intimidating things assaulting him.

Chapter 8

"Willow. Here you are."

Three days after the Solstice festivities, Willow was deep in preparations for the journey to the Motherhouse, including remedies to be left behind for Missy. She'd sensed a new presence in the workroom at the Healers' lodge an instant before he spoke. Without looking up from her work, she grinned and said, "I know that voice."

"You ought to." He came over to the workbench and perched on a stool.

Willow finished her task and, still grinning, shifted her focus to the man across from her. "Working on supplies for the medicine cabinet. How are you, Dal?"

In his early fifties, with hair already gray, a finely drawn face, and serious brown eyes, Dal was fit, but bore the marks of having recently come off the road, dusty and travel worn. On a hot afternoon such as this, the cool stone room must be a relief for him, as it was for her.

Perhaps a third of the Healers were men, and Dal had been part mentor, part lover to her during her journey year, when she first began traveling.

"Troubled. Same as you, I'd guess. Having any luck?"

She shrugged. "The energy's unstable today, but these are simple herbs. I'm just packaging them, nothing extra needed."

"And you. I miss your usual radiance."

"I find myself at the crux of a situation I don't know how to handle."

"Tell me what's going on. When you're in the middle of a Healing and your energy dissipates like that, it's frightening. I feel a need to be at the Motherhouse."

"It is scary." Willow settled on her stool and told the story, all the while keeping her hands busy processing the herbs on the workbench.

Dal followed her narrative intently. "At first I believed it was happening only to me," he said when she finished, his eyes narrowed with concern. "This is beyond my understanding."

"I'm to bring the two men with me. I daresay the council is curious," she added with deliberate understatement. Council must be climbing out of their skins with curiosity. As she hoped, she got a smile from Dal.

Willow finished the last bag of herbs and shook out her arms. "There. Now to tidy up here, then clean out whatever's in the closet and store these."

Dal let the topic shift to more immediate matters. "Missy hasn't improved, I take it?"

"I've spoken with her. She's young and immature, and I don't believe she wants to be a healer. It's the plants she loves, not the healing. Might we set her to work as an apothecary? But that supposes the town can find another candidate to replace Olyve."

"Has Olyve suggested anyone?"

Willow lost her smile. "We let her stay too long. Now she thinks only of her next bowl of thin porridge and the view across the valley, and reminiscences from forty years ago. She cannot help, not even as a mentor."

A hint of color rose into Dal's face. "But I might be able to. As it happens, I'm courting here in Stanstead."

Happy news to counteract the sad. Willow's smile returned. "Really? Who is it?"

"A weaver. Her name is Charlotte. I had hoped for a reason to spend more time here. The need to train both an apothecary and a village healer makes a solid argument."

"Stanstead is too large to be without a resident healer. Wonderful news, Dal, for both reasons."

"Thanks. Wish us good fortune." As they tidied the room he asked, "The trek – how do you plan to transport your patient? How much remains to be done?"

"We depart in two days. I've been organizing clothing for the men, provisions, camping gear. And I arranged a donkey and cart for Kiril," she added with a chuckle. "Which he will find humiliating, and I expect him to insist on walking more than is advisable."

"From the way you described his wounds, it's a miracle you've accomplished anything. Between us we should get him there in one piece."

"We need all we can learn from these men. So far they've been acquiescent, if not communicative."

With the workroom considerably tidier than Missy had left it, she said, "Next, to stow these in the cabinet."

"I'll join you." They left the lodge for the small courtyard, lingering as they entered the herb garden.

"He's a strange man – they both are," Willow said. "But Kiril more than the other. I have heard him addressed by many names, Kiril and Kernel and McKettrick, and sometimes Joss calls him commander. What do you know about commanders?"

"Nothing, but I can guess."

"Yes, I as well. And he does attempt to command." She sighed. "They did not recognize, or at least did not honor, the Healer's sash. And there is something about me personally... he cringes when I touch him. Both of them, in fact." Out of earshot of the healing room, she related her encounter with Joss at the ford, when he'd shied away from her. "It's as if my hands are poison to them. I don't understand it. I've never experienced such a reaction before."

"Nor have I, but I doubt it's you. If these men truly are from a different planet, they won't be acquainted with Healers, or with Auric energy and all it implies. He doesn't say?"

"Since the fever broke, he's strong and silent."

"Foolish man."

The throwaway comment made her giggle. Kiril would die rather than allow himself to be thought foolish. "In more ways than one. He went walking, Solstice afternoon. Now the leg is painful, the healing set back a few days. He can hardly put weight on it. But still I'm sure he'll expect to walk. Perhaps before we leave you and I could link?"

"I'd be happy to. You're agitated, Willow."

She kicked at a stone on the path with the toe of her sandal. "I am. I find it hard to stay in balance these days."

"So do I, and I haven't been carrying around your extra burden of concern. Would it help if I look in on your refractory patient?"

She brightened instantly. Assistance with caring for Kiril, since he so obviously longed to be free of her, took a load off her shoulders.

The supply cabinet held medicines and other sundries needed in their work. Its two doors opened to the outside and to the healing room itself; the outer door allowed access without disturbing a patient. Dal freed the lock, and together they discarded old, no longer potent herbs and replaced them with the freshly dried ones. When they finished, he said, "Shall we see what your patient's up to?"

"Let's."

They found Kiril propped up in bed, the orange cat snug against his leg, looking as if he might crawl up the walls if he weren't free of the room, or of her, or of the whole planet, soon. "Kiril," she said smoothly, one of her professional voices, "I wish to introduce you to Dal. As you can see, he also is a Healer. He has offered to assist in your care."

Dal reached out a hand. The brief shake they exchanged was... manly, Willow decided. An accord had been negotiated in their unspoken communication. Kiril relaxed against the pillows.

She returned to the door and pinned back the curtain, allowing in light. Dal settled on the stool beside Kiril's bed. "I want to scan your energies, although today isn't a good day. Do you agree, Willow?"

He had subtly established that she still directed Kiril's Healing. "Completely. I'll leave you now. I have other errands to attend to."

She lingered at the door briefly, watching Dal as he first talked Kiril into greater relaxation, then began a systematic scan. With the Aura uncertain today, she doubted he would learn much, but the process seemed to put Kiril more at ease. The session was going well. Then she left them and directed her footsteps across the plaza, where Bryar was setting up for a performance. She planned to conduct a clinic later, but a period of rest, listening to Bryar's rich voice, could only be to her benefit.

She fixed her hopes on Dal's help with Kiril. Linking their energies might set his healing on a proper track. His rejection of her made no sense, but it seemed to rise from a deep-seated suspicion of women. She'd seen it happen before, but never extending to a Healer.

And Joss had said that her touching him was wrong.

"Willow." She heard Dal's voice behind her and turned.

He caught up with her and spoke quietly. "Please leave time free this evening. I want a Healing session with you."

"Oh, are you ill?" She had been so absorbed in her own concerns that she had failed to scan him when he arrived.

But he smiled. "No, not for me. For you. Let me help you. You're at the end of your energies. Let me help," he repeated.

Healers were notoriously poor at caring for themselves, so Dal's offer was welcome. "With gratitude."

"Good. See you later." He squeezed her arm and returned to the healing room.

Later, she thought, and continued her walk, waving to and chatting with the people she met. A comforting word, implying as it did a next time, a future meeting. As she crossed the plaza, Bryar barely acknowledged her. He was deep into his own process as he attuned himself to his performance. Probably, like her, he sought some hint of Aura connection to do his job. Time enough later to tell him about Dal's arrival. For now, she wanted to lose herself in his wondrous stories for a short time before her clinic.

The next day Willow crossed the plaza, keeping pace with the man beside her. Kiril took in everything, especially the buildings.

"Your room is on the ground floor," she told him. "I checked, it's bright and airy. A good thing in the summer."

"Is it clean?"

She shot him an exasperated look. "Of course it is. Why would you think otherwise?"

Her tone had no effect on her companion. He eyed the men's lodge with only a little less distaste than he showed for the healing room. "Explain why I need a room in this place."

"Because most uncommitted people live in lodges. For companionship, and to avoid the upkeep of a private residence."

"I'm not staying here."

"I wonder if you expect to find better elsewhere." In her experience, Stanstead was among the cleanest and most interesting settlements, being on the intersection of two major tracks, one of them a trade route between the Northlands and Southlands. "In any event," she continued, "you require a base, however temporary. To store your belongings, if nothing else. Joss's room is upstairs, so you will be close."

An expression combining anger and pain, quickly suppressed, flashed across his face. Something had happened between the two newcomers, and Willow was no longer confident that Joss's presence reassured him.

"Belongings," he muttered. He glanced at his light linen outfit, the same as worn by almost everyone. "Bloody pajamas."

"With the heat, you may elect to skip either the tunic or the trousers. Most find it expedient to wear one or the other, for cleanliness. But I meant your other possessions."

He stopped walking. "What other possessions?"

They stood at the entrance to the men's lodge. "The things salvaged from your wreck. The strange box you showed me, with the moving dot. As well, there is a metal pot, which Joss retained. And an object attached to the clothing you wore – the crash destroyed your clothes, but the object is here. It looks like a bird."

"My insignia survived?" A flicker of excitement displaced his habitual irritation.

"In your room."

"Where?" He shoved past her into the building, only to stop at the cross corridor.

"To the right. The third door on your right."

Kiril was staring at the two pitiful artifacts of the wreck when she reached his room. The mysterious objects lay on his bed. He sank down beside them with the aspect of a man whose brain had not lined up with his emotions. Lost, and remembering a life beyond reclaiming.

He picked up the box and fiddled with it. "Nothing," he murmured. He let it fall and reached for the bird. She had washed it, but he rubbed at it with a finger anyway. Then he looked up at her. "Thanks for hanging onto this."

"We do not disrespect others' belongings."

The bird joined the box on the bed. He studied them. "Not much point, is there?" he said, speaking more to himself than to her. "All those years, and this is what I'm left with." The bleakness of his expression, his hollowed-out voice, told of isolation, regret, longing... a dozen things.

Instead of commiserating, she gave him facts. "You will find two changes of clothing in the cupboard. Nightshirts also. Soiled clothing is placed in the bin outside your room. The dining hall is on the north side of the plaza. Services such as bathing and shaving are available. I suggest you talk to Joss about them. If you want to share your bed, make arrangements at the guest lodge."

He didn't reply. Fatigue had caught up with him, although he fought not to show it.

"You are welcome to stay here for a while," she continued. "but I require you in the healing room this afternoon. Dal and I plan to do another linked healing for you, to strengthen you for the journey tomorrow."

He nodded.

She left him sitting on the bed, looking from the items in front of him to the view through the small window and back again.

More than once she'd tried to cast herself into their mindsets, Kiril's and Joss's, how it must be to lose everything familiar. Understanding came all too easily, and with it the echo of her mother's words, once the Motherhouse tracked down her identity. *She is not welcome here. Tell her not to bother coming back. We do not want her.* As a result, she had never walked a route that took her across the mountains to the far southwest, near her childhood hamlet.

The familiar heaviness invaded her heart. She shook it off.

As she crossed the plaza she picked up snippets of a conversation between two men, agriculturists from the look of them, walking in the same direction. "...knows what they're thinking. I swear he does."

"Nah. Making it up."

"He pegged the ailing cow in number three herd. How'd he know that, then?"

"Training at that place he comes from?"

"Better'n ours?"

The first man conceded the point. "Thing is, he's spooked. He'd assumed we all heard 'em. But when he told us about the heifer, and we didn't know, he went quiet like."

"Strange one, he is."

"Fits in well. Shy, I'd say."

"I wonder what the full story is."

The men drifted off toward the barns on the western outskirts of town. Willow reflected on what she'd overheard as she made her way to the textile center.

Talks to the animals. Understands what they communicate.

They must be speaking of Joss. She and Bryar had discussed it, but surely it wasn't possible. Surely Joss, from his faraway planet, could not create or utilize a template. There had been only a handful of animal whisperers in the known history of the Midland, men and women who held a weak connection to the Aura, and used it to communicate with animals. If Joss fit this profile, she had a new concern to add to the list she'd present to the council when they got to the Motherhouse.

Picking up waterproofed cloaks topped her agenda. A soaking would do Kiril no good. Even though he seemed determined to thwart her at every turn, she guarded against setbacks to his healing. The capes reeked of lanolin, and she preferred not to use one herself, but he would need it if they encountered inclement weather.

Chapter 9

To no one's surprise, her recalcitrant patient kicked up a fuss about the donkey cart. Kiril had been a strong man before his injuries drained his vitality, but did he really think he could manage a four day journey, seven hours or more each day, on foot? Dal, Bryar and she regularly walked such distances, and she didn't doubt Joss's strength. Even at their slower pace, dictated by the carts, she reckoned Kiril would not last a quarter hour.

Willow was in no mood to dally.

Kiril stood arguing with Dal, who exhibited more patience than she did. With a sigh she approached the two men in time to hear Kiril at his most adamant. "Understand this. I will not be carried by that thing like a damn baby."

The flat-bedded cart had been equipped with cushions and blankets for the journey; it also carried their packs and assorted provisions. The donkey's owner waited on the box, reins in hand. The donkey, she'd swear, rolled its eyes at her.

"You don't have a choice," Dal said.

Her patience was at an end. "You are injured and weak, however much you deny it. This petulance is inconveniencing everyone."

"Not my problem," Kiril said. He wheeled and started toward the men's lodge.

Dal seized him by an arm.

"I can compel you to stop resisting," Willow said to his tense back. "I do not want to, but I can and I will, if you do not give up this childish stalling."

He shook off the grip, but turned back to the cart, lips pinched in a grim line. As he climbed onto the bed of pillows and blankets, he shot her a look that was as poison as his crash site.

Bryar chatted with Joss at the head of the procession. She watched their exchange, glad Joss had found someone he felt comfortable talking to. Bryar would handle the man with sensitivity.

Unlike Quinn. Quinn tended to be acerbic. And she, Willow, had borne all the irritation she intended to from these men. Joss was better off with Bryar, the gentlest of the three of them. He must have hundreds of questions about their way of life in the Midland, some best answered by a man. Not to mention the possibility that he communicated with animals, which, if true, would rattle anybody. But Joss said little to her, leaving her to guess.

Quinn played in her mind these days, and she hoped to see her friend at the Motherhouse. It had been several years since their schedules last intersected.

Besides the three Weavers, two foreigners, and the donkey cart driver, their caravan included a husband and wife planning to visit their son. The couple had arrived with their cart and belongings an hour ago and were impatient to leave.

Kiril glared at her, but said nothing.

The ginger cat jumped onto the cart, butted his head against Kiril's hand, and jumped down again, disappearing in the direction of the stables.

Never in history has it been so difficult to begin a simple journey.

"We're leaving. Now," Dal called from near the front of the procession, in a tone that brooked no objection. The caravan lurched into movement, heading east across the plaza toward the track that led them to the Motherhouse.

She stayed beside the cart. "You can't keep me imprisoned forever," her patient said, a threat underlying his voice.

"Until you are healed, I can. After that, believe me, nothing could force me to. You make this far more difficult than necessary."

Kiril shrugged. As the caravan made its way through the eastern fringes of the town, he sat up and surveyed the rolling, agricultural terrain. "I need paper and a pen."

She raised her eyebrows. "Paper is an unusual commodity, and not in great supply. I carry none with me, nor pen or ink. You may find them at the Motherhouse. I assume you can read and write?"

He looked to the heavens as if to say, *how many kinds of fool are you?*

She ignored the implied sneer. "Few here learn. Weavers are required to, as part of our training, and most hamlets appoint an archivist."

"This benighted place doesn't have books?"

"Village archivists use books to record such things as births and deaths and crop yields. It does not make for captivating reading."

Or a way to spend a lifetime, recording the mundane events of a hamlet.

"Figures." He settled himself, plumping a pile of pillows to form a backrest and turning his attention to the buildings, then fields, on the other side of the cart from her.

Snubbed. Well, his problem. In a while, when they were some distance from Stanstead, she would permit him to walk, thus providing exercise for him and a respite for the donkey. His leg was sufficiently healed for a short walk to strengthen it, not hinder its mending, so she would require that much, unless he collapsed.

Foolish man.

Joss noted the changes in the landscape. Three days out from Stanstead, he found himself in a hillier land, with fewer fields, more forest, the trees intimidating in their size. Northam Corporation boasted of once owning trees bigger than these, but they had long since disappeared.

The walking was easy, partly because of the lumbering speed of the cart. This road carried less traffic than the trunk road going west, as evidenced by the weeds populating the center strip. Bryar had told him to expect few settlements in this direction, and sure enough, so far they had passed through only two hamlets. None of the three Weavers wore the sashes they crossed over their tunics, marking their professions. They traveled incognito, not stopping to tend a wound or sing one of those songs that went on forever.

He and Kiril had established an uneasy détente, discussing what they passed, both of them hoping to cement the memory by talking it over. Like his erstwhile commander, Joss missed paper and pen, missed even more his comm, the little computer that let him record his observations and communicate with the others. But the comm had disappeared in the crash.

The linen clothing was cool; the sandals, while not military-issue boots, protected his feet and felt comfortable enough. The weather remained clear and hot. He'd been able to wash at the campsites – waysites, they called them, at least the established ones. All in all, this walk provided the respite Joss needed to sort through his tangled thoughts.

Willow dropped back to match her pace with his, behind the other walkers but ahead of the carts. "I am curious. Bryar tells me you understand animals. Is this so?"

"Seems to be, yeah." The cow thing was bad enough; a one-on-one with a woman threatened his tenuous sense of security. Not tolerated on Terra.

This isn't Terra. Calm down.

"Are you willing to talk about it? People who work with animals develop instincts, but nobody knows their minds with certainty."

"It's just impressions," he mumbled. "They don't think. Not like we do."

"All animals?"

"Don't know. Cows, yeah. Maybe not sheep."

"They say sheep aren't very bright. I guess it's possible there's nothing going on in their brains."

"Sure."

She changed tack on him. "When we walk, we talk. It passes the time and gives us a chance to share information. I'm not trying to make you uncomfortable."

Well, you're succeeding.

He didn't answer. No point signaling that her walking beside him, the two of them a little apart from the others, made him uneasy.

Her long hair? Her unfamiliar shape? He'd noticed that about the women of Stanstead, how unfamiliar their bodies were, how... uncomfortable... he felt around them. How aware.

Serious, she stopped, forcing him to stop, too. "If this with the animals is true, Joss, it is a gift, but it needs training. It's good you're going to the Motherhouse. You will find support there."

The carts rumbled by them, leaving them at the end of the procession. Kiril shot a questioning look his way.

"I can figure it out myself," he said when the last donkey cart was out of earshot.

But she shook her head. "You don't know yet what you are capable of. The training at the Motherhouse will help."

He flushed, embarrassed. "Yeah, well, we'll see."

"Yes. We will see." A last quick brush of her hand on his arm – he'd swear it burned his skin – and she ran forward to fall in with the woman going to visit her son.

Joss lingered behind the caravan, in no rush to be with people for a while. Because it seemed as if every time he learned something, he grew more confused.

Chapter 10

Kiril had slept well, the two nights they'd been at the Motherhouse, and his leg gained strength from regular exercise. The guest lodge was clean and Spartan, the way he preferred it. Food was simple and plentiful. A massive stone outcrop dominated the landscape north of the complex, out of place in the broad valley. Conifers competed with deciduous trees for dominance on the steeper, more rugged terrain. The wild river just east of them added a thrilling edge of danger, unlike the lazy ford where Joss had taken him the day before they left. The healer woman had thrown a fit when they returned. She'd wanted him under lock and key, to cosset him as if he needed babying. And then sadistically force him to walk halfway here from Stanstead.

The leg had hurt like blazes that first day on the road; when Willow let him off the cart, he'd been forced to fake enjoyment. The ride had proved to be a blessing, not that he'd ever admit it.

Kiril sat on the slope overlooking the gray stone buildings that made up the Motherhouse complex, only one of them taller than two stories. Lodges, the dining hall, and a handful of smaller structures strung out on either side of the main building, which they called the Centra. The land formed a natural amphitheater with a level, grassy space in front of the buildings. The slope faced north and didn't get too hot, making it a good vantage point to watch the comings and goings on the green.

He started to reach beside him, then snatched his hand away. He'd never admit to missing the cat, or that the beast's rumbling weight had been a comfort during his interminable convalescence.

As he leaned back, soaking in the sun, Joss came up the slope and dropped next to him.

"Sergeant."

The appropriate response was, 'sir'. Joss didn't say it. He just nodded. The man was a fool to give up his place on the Expeditionary Force. Kiril needed Joss's expertise, and preferred to keep him close, preferably in a subordinate role. He questioned Joss's allegiance these days.

"When you can make time in your busy life," he said, leaning on the sarcasm, "we need to start planning. Work out effective strategies for when the next ship turns up."

"Whenever you want. Nothing much happening around here. The couple from Stanstead and the donkey man left this morning. Did you notice?"

"Not pertinent." No, he hadn't noticed. His room faced back, toward the woods, and he'd spent far too much time gazing out at the forest, resting his mind from the haze of worry and to-do lists that usually clogged it.

When Joss didn't reply he added, "They brought us here for a reason."

"We knew that. They told Willow to bring us."

"Any idea why?"

"To learn who we are, probably, and what our intentions are. To them, we're a threat. They need to figure out how to neutralize it."

Kiril regretted the loosening of rank distinctions during the final stages of their flight to this place, after the catastrophe. Joss spoke as if they were equals. Unfortunately, he lacked the power to counteract Joss's determination to put Terra, and the military, behind him. To pave the way for the settlers, he needed Joss, his eyes and ears and his expertise.

"They aren't coming," Joss said, reading his mind. "Until they find out what happened to us, they might send another exploration pod, but they won't risk a whole settlement party."

"They're coming."

He had to believe it. His reputation hung on this expedition, which already had two massive black marks against it. His entire career, everything he'd built for himself, hinged on establishing successful settlements here.

Joss leaned back on an elbow. "They blame us for the disruption in their Aura, but I don't sense any threat. It's not the way they are."

Kiril snorted. "They'll try. Just wait and see. In case things turn nasty, do you have a plan for getting out of here? An escape route? I figure we'd better be prepared to take down one or two of them, if they—"

In the next instant a nerve pain shot from his ankle to his hip, so acute and so agonizing that he groaned, twisting as if to separate himself from the fire blazing along the outside of his injured leg.

"Are you all right, sir?"

"No, dammit. Help me up."

Standing, he put experimental weight on the leg and quickly retracted it. Vicious spikes of pain crippled his hip, but he released Joss's arm, steadying himself by force of will more than anything else.

"I figure we should cooperate," Joss said. "No point getting anyone's back up."

As long as it was an equal exchange. There was a lot he wanted to know, anything to help him paint an accurate picture of their culture.

One of the younger teenagers who swarmed all over the place, a girl, approached them. "Lunch will be served soon, if you'd care to go to the dining hall." Like everyone here, she spoke with perfect politeness.

"Thanks," Joss said, and smiled. The child smiled back, then turned and skipped away.

Willow appeared around the corner of the Centra, talking to another girl about the same age as their messenger. Almost as tall as the healer woman, the girl's hair was shorter and darker, her build stockier.

Willow made an elaborate gesture with her hands. The girl tried to follow the movements. Willow guided her hands, adjusting the positioning of her fingers. Kiril couldn't see what happened, but they both broke into giggles.

Surely goodness and mercy...

That damn chant, the one the nursemaid in his dormitory used to sing when he was a boy. Illicit, because of the religious overtones, but they hadn't been as rigorous about destroying the old superstitions back then. Willow brought those words to his mind; they'd haunted him during his time in the dark room, at least until the cat started haunting him instead.

Fanciful nonsense; he'd long ago given up on ideas of goodness and mercy.

Willow glanced up at them and frowned.

Kiril focused on the present. "If they do intend to question us, what strategy do you propose?" Give Joss a say, make him useful. Draw him back in.

"The truth, I guess. Anything else would be impossible to sustain."

"If they hear about the settlers, they might try to raise a defense."

"They know."

Horrified, Kiril glared into his sergeant's eyes. "I didn't expect you to shoot off your mouth."

"I told Willow why we're here. She saved our lives."

"We'd be fools to trust her," he spat.

"I doubt it. These are good people, sir. I'd hate for them to be harmed any more. I'm going to lunch. Do you want help?"

"I'll manage," Kiril snapped, and removed his hand. He was sick of being helped.

"See you there." Joss ambled down the hill.

He'd seen his mistake as soon as the words left his mouth, but something – pride? – didn't let him retract them. Helpless, he stood on the slope, his weight on his strong leg, watching his onetime sergeant leave.

Willow parted from the girl she'd been talking to and came up to him. "The midday meal smells good."

"I'm not hungry."

"Yes, you are. Let's go."

Damn rescuer. But with no better option, he accepted her support. "What the hell happened to my leg?"

She smiled. "You underestimate us," she said.

Shit.

❖

Kiril and Willow joined Joss and Bryar for a lunch consisting of bean cakes with a sauce. The others chatted together, complained about the heat, although Kiril thought it cooler here than in Stanstead. He rubbed his leg. The pain had vanished as quickly as it had come, but a residue of weakness lingered.

As they were finishing, a statuesque, gray-haired older woman approached their table. Their companions rose to their feet. Joss followed suit, and after a moment Kiril joined them.

"Still together," the woman said.

Bryar grinned and gave Willow a shoulder hug. "Can't be separated."

"Quinn should arrive today. We require an hour or so of your time." Her gaze moved from the healer to the singer.

Willow started gathering up their dishes. "Your office?"

"Yes." The gray-hair turned to speak to Joss and him. "I am Arwen. I hope to make your further acquaintance this afternoon. Someone will come for you."

Her words carried the heft of a command. The woman nodded and left.

"See you later," Bryar said. He and Willow stopped by the slot in the wall where they dumped the dirty dishes

On their way from the hall, Willow came back to their table. "I was teasing you," she said, a twinkle in her eyes. Then the two of them followed Arwen.

Great. Now he had to decide which version of events to believe. Idly he rubbed at the residual ache in his leg.

Joss scanned the room, confirming they were out of earshot. "I think we're going to find out what they plan for us. What happened to your leg back there?"

Kiril forced himself to shrug. "Just a pinched nerve."

"Running isn't an option, sir. There's nowhere to go. We need them as much as they need us. I'm getting caff. Want some?"

He had hoped and prayed for caff to be coffee. In his dreams. But it was bitter and caffeinated, or whatever they used instead to keep themselves awake, so he let Joss bring him a mug.

They lingered over their drinks, watching as the residents, most of them teenagers, filtered in and out. Kiril estimated they'd been there an hour when two of the kids approached. "If you'd come with us, please?" the taller of them, a boy, said.

Their escort led them to the Centra, then through labyrinthine stone corridors to a heavy wooden door. Kiril had learned to recognize wood, but still considered it an odd choice for construction. "Good luck," the boy whispered. "We get called here when we're in trouble." He knocked twice, pushed the door open, and left them.

They stepped into the room.

Willow and Bryar sat at either end of a long wooden table. On the far side, two women and two men conferred quietly together behind five chairs. There were two more chairs on their side.

An inquisition, then. He wondered if the pain really had been a pinched nerve, or if they were capable of long-distance torture.

Kiril sat without waiting to be invited, establishing his authority early. Joss took the other chair.

Since Arwen and the other three remained engrossed by their conversation, he looked at Willow. "Why are we here?" he demanded, his voice low.

She smiled, as if to reassure him. "You must expect questions. You keep a lot to yourselves. Which is your right, but you are new and we don't know what sort of men you are."

The stone walls held neither adornment nor windows. The door was dark, heavy, and solid. He frowned. There was no obvious source of illumination, yet a soft white light filled the space. The day was hot, but the room wasn't. Kiril felt sweat congeal on his skin and shivered.

The Weavers wore their sashes. Two of them green, like Willow's. One in red, another entertainer. Arwen's was brown, making her a Scribe. The function of Scribes remained murky, but there didn't seem to be many of them. They settled at last, leaving the chair closest to Bryar unoccupied, and Arwen took control, addressing her words to Joss and himself. "I'll begin with introductions. I am Arwen. As the head of the Weavers' council, it is my responsibility, shared by the council and the full community of Weavers, to assure the integrity of the Midland. That is the reason for this inquiry."

Inquiry. So that's what they're calling it.

His mind turned over the possibilities, not that he'd thought about much else since he recovered from the crash. How to cast their presence in the best possible light, how to convince these backward people that the Terran settlers would enhance their lives with benefits they couldn't even imagine. From comms to pesticides, settlement implied an improved standard of living.

Arwen continued talking. He forced himself to follow. "On my right are Daren, the head of the Healers' guild, and Cynth." Daren, he noted, was late forties, with a receding hairline, a sharp nose, and sharper eyes. Cynth was nondescript, a mouse of a middle-aged woman, although he got a feeling that she missed nothing.

"On my left is Fergus, head of the Bard's guild."

Fergus was a middle-aged man with a face like rubber as it moved from expression to expression. A born clown, Kiril decided, hardly worth considering.

He came to with a jolt when Arwen spoke his name.

"Stand," Willow whispered.

Show respect or defiance? He reluctantly decided that for the moment, deference was the best strategy, but took his time as he got to his feet, facing the council.

"You are Kernel Kiril McKettrick of the Amalgamated Expeditionary Force, from a planet called Terra. Is this correct?"

He shot a glance at Joss, who shrugged.

"Can you explain these words, please? McKettrick and Kernel. Then tell us about this expedition."

"McKettrick's my last name —"

"Meaning you have two names. Kiril and McKettrick."

"Yes."

"And you prefer to be called?"

He preferred to be called Colonel McKettrick. *Sales job*, he reminded himself. "Kiril's fine."

"We rarely use surnames, and not all hamlets assign them." Arwen switched into teaching mode. "For instance, Willow's childhood home is isolated, and she came to us without a second name. In Bryar's homeland far to the north, they use town designations, so he is officially Bryar of Newcastle. You have yet to meet Quinn, although I don't doubt you will. Quinn Featherstone, the only one of the three to have a full two-part name. As a result, they are rarely used here, unless needed for clear identification.

The Three. What made them the Three?

"And Kernel," she continued without missing a beat, "a word whose meaning appears to be inappropriate in this context."

His mouth was developing a rictus from all the smiling. "It's not the same word." He spelled it. "It's a rank – a fairly high one."

"So people report to you. And you report – to whom?"

"On our ship, I was the senior officer, the commander. The others reported to me."

"Those you report to are on Terra planet?"

He nodded, amused by her unusual syntax.

"And they are your superiors?"

"Yes."

"And you consider them such?"

He frowned. "Higher rank, but not necessarily smarter or more capable."

Joss shifted in his chair. He'd be curious to hear his sergeant's opinions. But then, most in the Force held a less than positive opinion of their superiors.

"You didn't respect them?"

This was harder. "Respect is earned. I respected those who deserved it. I followed orders."

Short, to the point, unrelenting, her questions fired at him. "Without due consideration?"

"No military can function unless everyone accepts the chain of command. You do the job." He heard the exasperation in his voice and did his best to suppress it.

"Explain military, please."

"The organization that defends the corporation. Keeps invaders out."

"Fighters."

"When necessary, yes."

Arwen never took her eyes from his face, compelling him to speak unvarnished truth. Which was impossible. He'd cloud the issue, even lie, if needed.

"And as a member of this military, you fight and kill, without question."

His leg began to throb. Willow must have sensed it, because she spoke up. "Arwen, Kiril is in pain."

"My apologies. With your air of vitality, I neglected to consider your injuries. Please sit."

He did, hiding his relief.

"To rephrase, are you a man of integrity?"

"Yes." He held himself straighter, offended.

"Yet you blindly follow orders."

His exasperation crested, and he bit down on his emotions to stay calm. "In the military, there's no choice. Ignoring orders leads to disgrace, imprisonment, even death."

"Hmm."

The council members huddled for a moment, then Arwen said, "Yes or no, please. Do you consider yourself a good man?"

Yes or no? "Yes." Keep it short, to the point.

"Have you ever purposely lied about a matter important to you, or to anyone else?"

Everybody told lies. Not lying when you needed to could get you dead in a hurry. What the hell did she want from him?

"Sometimes it's expedient—"

"Or kind. I'm aware of that. Please answer the question."

Heat washed across his face. He opened his mouth to deny it and heard his voice say, "Yes."

"Have you taken a life?"

He didn't need bullshit questions like this. No way was he going to allow them to invade his privacy. "What I've done or haven't done is none of your goddamned business."

"Did you just answer my question, Kiril?"

Did he? Willow touched his arm, and the anger drained from him. More of her voodoo, probably. Trapped, he played for time. "A human life, you mean?"

Arwen nodded, her lips thinning.

The four men lost on the pod? Not his fault. The bar brawl, during his days as a cadet, had been covered up. It was self-defense; his conscience was clean.

But he felt compelled to say it. Was it her eyes? Had they doctored his lunch? "Yes," he mumbled.

"I thought as much. Have you been in love?"

"You mean, with another person?"

"Man or woman."

"No. Love is a weakness."

"Love is the greatest of strengths. Tell me about your childhood."

He closed his eyes briefly and wished he were back in his room at the guest lodge, staring at the trees. He felt sweat dampening his underarms and shivered. "Same as everyone's. I'm from the upper management caste. Nursery until age three, then dormitory, school. I entered the cadet corps at eleven, after the aptitude tests. Military academy until I was twenty-one."

"Your parents?"

"We don't have parents."

All six Weavers sat up straighter at that.

"You are taken from your mother at birth?"

"No, nothing like that." He glanced at Joss, then back to Arwen. "We're created in a Petri dish." He saw her frown and added, "In a laboratory. They combine the right compounds and grow the children."

"Sustainer of life," Willow murmured, shocked.

"You are aware that this is unnatural," Arwen stated.

"But necessary." Time they stopped badgering him about things that didn't matter to them. "Terra is overpopulated. It's vital to control births, so that everyone born is healthy and engineered for a purpose. Otherwise, we'd starve."

"And your purpose is to serve in this military, in which orders must be obeyed without question. What is the purpose of your colleague's birth?"

He glanced at Joss. "I suggest you ask him that."

"I'm asking you. As the commander on that ship of yours."

Speaking for Joss felt wrong, as if he were throwing his rank in the other man's face. But he sensed they were both better off not crossing Arwen. "Sergeant Worthing was born in the worker caste, which generally consists of factory workers and manual laborers. However, he tested much higher than expected and entered military training. Joss is a genius at fixing things and keeping them running."

"Then you blame him for the problems on your ship?"

"No." His reply was unequivocal. "The sealed refrigeration system failed, and gas escaped into the main compartment. Nothing Sergeant Worthing did or didn't do could have made a difference."

He didn't let himself think of the instantaneous deaths of his crew, or how the loss of refrigeration meant they'd survived on painfully limited rations for the month before the crash.

"The purpose of the voyage?"

An easy, factual question. "The Northam and Amsur Corporations instituted a program to create settlements on other planets. The Amalgamated Expeditionary Force exists to confirm that planets are habitable. We believed this one to be unpopulated."

Arwen nodded and started to walk him through the accident, asking about the other men on the ship, his relationship to them, how he and Joss had survived.

A tall woman with skin the color of a strong mug of caff came into the room and circled the table, interrupting the interrogation – for that's what it had become, an interrogation, and he'd been sucked into it and didn't see a way to extricate himself without getting their backs up. At a nod from Arwen she moved to the empty chair and coolly surveyed the men and women around the table.

Kiril noted a slender, upright body under the ubiquitous tunic, hair worn close to her scalp in tight, black curls, dark, assessing eyes that made him long to seize her and shake up her remote confidence. Take control. She bore herself with an imperiousness that added to her stature. When her gaze landed on him, his heart jerked in his chest. Her mouth twitched, then she looked away and sat.

He had never felt such a desire to dominate another person.

Willow and Bryar both shot delighted grins at the new woman, who winked at Willow and leaned forward to squeeze Bryar's hand.

Joss, unaffected by the newcomer, rose to his feet. "May I speak?" he asked. That unfailing politeness used to get on his nerves, especially after the catastrophe when they were both frayed to breaking.

"Please," Arwen said.

Joss stood silent for a long moment. "I believe you're trying to determine whether the commander's a good man. He is. I've served under five different men since I went into the military. Kiril's the best. He's fair, and he has integrity. He means what he says. You don't need to continue this."

Arwen looked to the end of the table. "Willow?"

She stood and spoke without emotion. "Kiril keeps to himself. I sense he has an intention here he does not want to reveal. He can be petulant and is quick to anger. I believe him to be both highly intelligent and highly strung. I have not been able to observe his integrity in action." She sat.

A damning summary.

Still on his feet, Joss said, "We're here to lay the groundwork for settlement. Our planet is not merely overcrowded, it's dying." He glanced at Kiril and added, "The official word claimed otherwise, but it was obvious to anyone with a brain." He turned to the council. "A single ship might hold ten thousand. They targeted a million or more for one settlement."

The council members looked at each other. No one spoke.

"We estimate the population of the Midland at twenty-five thousand," Arwen said. "Are these people coming?"

Kiril reclaimed the conversation. "According to protocol, no, not without a positive report from us. But the way things were going on Terra, there's no guarantee they won't send the ships."

"And we have no means to tell them not to come," Joss concluded. "Our communication system was destroyed in the wreck. I regret bringing this on you." He sat.

"Thank you," Arwen said, then paused. "We have a situation." She looked at each person around the table, then nodded. "As I see it, we face two threats. First, the mystery of the fluctuations in the Aura, and second, the potential for our way of life to collapse with the arrival of so many people, who will bring with them foreign ideas and habits, not to mention diseases and conflict. Put your minds to these things, please – I mean all of you," she added, looking at Kiril and Joss. "We reconvene after lunch tomorrow. We need to discuss the damage you have caused to the Aura. Bryar, Willow, take a break, then return here. We aren't done." She rose.

Willow raced to the new woman and Bryar grabbed her in a hug. While they chattered in what was obviously a reunion, Kiril faced his sergeant. "You told me they knew about the settlers."

"We did," Arwen said. She'd appeared silently at his elbow. "But not the scale. The situation is more serious than I understood, and we rely on you to consider how to stop the migration from your planet. And what it is about your arrival that destabilized our world."

Joss shook his head. "I wish I knew."

Arwen left. The chattering group broke up; the new woman fixed him with another level stare before leaving on Arwen's heels.

"Now what?" Kiril asked.

"First, food," Bryar said. "I'm starving, and I need to get grounded. The council wants answers, but this isn't meant to be torture."

"Although it can feel like it," Willow murmured. At Joss's questioning look she added, "We got into our share of trouble when we were students. Everyone did."

Only the four of them remained. The leg twinged, but Kiril refused to show it. As they left, the light dimmed, then went out.

Joss, he noted, hung back, walking at his slower pace. Taking care of him. He cursed his leg.

"Walk us through it one more time."

Willow fought to maintain both an upright posture and a positive attitude. Beside her she recognized growing tension in Bryar, his intrinsic light-heartedness overwhelmed by the onslaught of questions they and Dal had endured for the last two hours. With no windows in the conference room, and concentrating on the reasoning behind the questions, she had lost all sense of time.

Arwen shared her mind; they had agreed to allow this. Scribes used mind linking to extract information, and they needed that information. But Arwen's demanding presence in her head further exhausted her, costing her much of her autonomy. She'd begun to feel like a machine, not a human. Daren and Fergus were present from the council, but not Quinn; Willow suspected their closeness precluded her participation in this examination.

Wearily she recounted, once again, Joss grabbing her, the scene at the wreck, piecing together every half-forgotten strand of dialogue, every observation. Among them they reconstructed the history of Kiril's and Joss's stay in the Midland, all the conversations, observed actions, worries or questions about the two men. Drained, she reached over and took Bryar's hand, needing his warmth.

At long last, Arwen nodded and released her grip on Willow's mind. "Thank you. I'm sorry to inflict this afternoon on you."

Dal wordlessly left them, a gray pallor to his skin. Shortly thereafter, she and Bryar emerged into a fiery sunset.

"Quinn's sky, not ours," he commented. Quinn carried a portion of fire in her makeup, as well as her clan energy of air.

"We missed the evening meal."

"I bet they set something aside for us." With shared intent they turned toward the dining hall.

As they focused on their meals, she could see Bryar begin to unwind; the interrogation had shaken him, challenging his positive nature. He shifted their empty plates and replaced them with bowls of spiced custard.

Feeling like a shadow of herself and more troubled than before, she asked, "Do you trust them, Bry?"

"Kiril tried to deflect questions about his past, remember? He's ambitious. And Joss reports to Kiril."

A new voice entered their conversation. "Does he?" Quinn pulled out a chair with her foot and sat between them. "I'm not sure that's true. Joss seems like his own man to me. I met Kiril only briefly, but he masters his thoughts with an efficiency I find a little scary. Do you know how long they were in space?" Quinn hesitated before the unfamiliar concept. Space, travel through the heavens, from one sun to another.

"Two years?" Willow said. "I'm on overload. Could you read his mind, Quinn?"

"I've done crazier things, but that would be a mistake, even to try. He'd sense it, and he'd freak." She cupped a hand over her mouth, resting her first finger along her upper lip, a typical Quinn gesture when she was working through a puzzle. "That might be a strategy to break him down a bit. But not until we get him where we can control him."

"I hate this," Bryar said. "Control him? Enter his mind? This isn't who we are."

"No," Quinn said, "but it may be where this is going, if we want to save ourselves." Her hand covered Bryar's. "And the three of us... we're senior Weavers. We can't avoid whatever is coming."

Bryar looked from Quinn to Willow. "Let's get a room in the guest lodge tonight. Stay together."

She thought Quinn might shrug off the suggestion, but she nodded. "Good idea, I'll arrange it. Enjoy the custard. They used muscade."

A rare spice from the Southland. No wonder it tasted so good. Even the kitchen staff conspired to ease the tension permeating the Motherhouse.

They watched Quinn go, then finished their treat in silence. Bryar squeezed her hand as they separated to pack a few necessities for a night with friends.

Chapter 11

Sustainer of us all, let me be calm and find strength in the face of my challenges.

The Motherhouse was in a stew, everyone agitated. She and Bryar had hoped to spend time with Quinn last night, catch up and hear about her promotion to the council. But Quinn hadn't reappeared since their evening meal.

This morning, though, word traveled through the Motherhouse as if by osmosis.

The Old Man had arrived.

Willow had seen the Old Man from afar, and he'd occasionally sat on one of her assessment panels during her training more than twenty years ago. He was still alive and able to travel? Even then he'd been, well, *old*.

But he'd come in from the north yesterday afternoon, and he'd huddled with the council ever since. His elderly wife had appeared at breakfast, but she greeted them with a vague smile and few words, not sharing in the trouble swirling around the Motherhouse.

The Old Man worked with the Aura in ways that no other Weavers did, according to rumor. His power was legendary. He had been a Scribe, but as far as she knew, he no longer belonged to a guild; he transcended them.

Willow supposed he'd come because of a summons from the council. She hoped he held the key to the mystery of the Aura, so weak today that once again she'd found herself nearly pleading when she made her morning invocation.

And how much did Joss and Kiril know, really? The disruptions troubled Joss, but Kiril had the air of a man who took advantage of situations, not remedied them.

When Quinn tracked her down, she was on a bench in the extensive Healers' garden. "The board room, as soon as we can gather everyone," she said after they'd hugged. Her fingers tangled with Willow's. "It's a freaking mess."

Quinn had an edge to her that neither she nor Bryar shared. Today that edge was prominent.

"The Old Man?"

"Not as scary as you think. We're starting as soon as everyone's gathered. I need to find Bryar and Dal, since you're the ones best acquainted with the newcomers." A final squeeze of her fingers and Quinn pulled away.

"I couldn't attune this morning," Willow murmured.

Quinn stopped. "Honest, Wils, I've never experienced anything like this. Not just the Aura, but this surge of hatred, as if I'd murder in cold blood to put things right. If this is what those men have done to us, if everyone's having these feelings…"

"I'm not, so don't worry needlessly. Hold on." She extracted a tiny vial from the pocket of her skirt. "For stress. Open up."

"Not now. I don't have time to —"

"Quinn. Just do it."

Her friend smiled and shook her head. "Only you." She obediently opened her mouth. Willow delivered two drops under her tongue.

"Go on. Try to relax."

"Dreamer. See you later."

"And you." Quinn strode away.

"Dal left the lodge early," she called to Quinn's back. "He might be in the fields."

"Damn inconvenient time for him to disappear," Quinn muttered as she went through the garden gate.

Willow headed upstairs to sit alone in meditation until it was time to cross the green to the Centra and whatever awaited her there.

Willow sat next to Bryar and reached for his hand under the table, grateful for his familiarity, the texture of his skin, his smell, his thoughts and actions so predictable. Today he shared her agitation.

The Old Man hadn't changed in twenty years. His presence escalated the situation to crisis point.

From the moment Joss had seized her back at the waysite on the North Trail, crises never abated. No wonder she battled fatigue all day, then lost sleep at night.

The council members gathered. Quinn arrived last, with Dal. From his unusually disheveled appearance, she suspected he had indeed been in the fields, working with the plants. Probably Quinn had given him scant time to clean up. Her friend's mouth was set in a line that suggested…

"Best not to mess with Quinn," Bryar whispered to her.

She giggled, and the tension let up.

"Did you find the two men?" Arwen asked.

Quinn nodded. "They're prepared for a meeting this afternoon. The thin one, Kiril, you can almost see the strategies and plots whirling around in his head."

"Do we expect trouble from them?" the Old Man's voice was gravelly and quiet, but side discussion ceased the moment he spoke.

"Joss, no," Quinn said. "Kiril, I'm not sure. You agree?" she asked Willow.

"I do."

Arwen made brief introductions. "Let's begin."

The Old Man, whose proper name was Ezra, commanded the room. "I came to help, if I can. Like you, I have struggled against the disruptions. With limited success."

Any success would be an improvement.

"I do not recommend that any of you attempt to explore deeply through the templates. The danger is much too great. But here is what I've seen."

Listen, Quinn. Believe him. Don't be foolish. Quinn took chances with the Aura that Willow and Bryar deemed foolhardy, delving deeper and longer than either of them dared. Risking herself in the name of knowledge.

The Old Man sipped water. "We have known for some time that our Aura originates from a general area on the other side of the hills. I have been unable to pinpoint it accurately, or to determine what creates it or how it works." Watching the others, Willow saw the incredulity that greeted these words. "But now there is an antagonist to that energy. In all probability, the strangers brought it with them. Not intentionally, however. Or so I believe."

Bryar spoke. "A team from Stanstead went to the wreck. Joss went with them. They found nothing."

"I understand that the newcomer Joss connects to Auric energy," Ezra replied.

The council knew this, from the exploration of their memories the day before, but nonetheless reacted with raised eyebrows or looks around the table.

"It is not certain," Willow said, "but he shows signs of being an animal whisperer."

More shuffling as the council members processed this information.

"Then he would have been eager to leave their wreck. And influenced the others, consciously or not, to rush their search."

"So, if there is some object at the site that conflicts with Auric energy, we must find it and neutralize it," Arwen said. "That is the purpose of this meeting. How to deal with the threat. Willow, please tell Ezra of your experience."

She briefly recounted the first meeting with Joss and Kiril, her despair and fear at losing touch with the energies. Explained how things gradually improved, until once they reached Stanstead she could heal again by linking with Bryar. Her words formed a springboard for questions, most of them speculative. If she might have accomplished more powerful Healing had there been another Healer present – for Bards used the Aura in very different ways from Healers. If the transition had been smooth or erratic. If she experienced any lasting effects.

She responded, draining her energy in the recounting, until Arwen called a halt. "Willow is pale, and we all will benefit from a break. I'll call for caff and cakes, and we'll plan on a late midday meal." Brooking no nonsense, she stood up, and the meeting temporarily adjourned.

Willow leaned against Bryar for a moment. Quinn disappeared with Daren. The Old Man sank into a reverie; no one dared approach him.

"Bryar?"

"Hmm?" He wrapped an arm around her shoulders, lending her his strength.

"Did I understand this properly? The Aura – there's a cause? It isn't just there like the land, the planet?"

"The idea isn't comforting."

"Maybe it's like a rock formation? Or a really deep pond? Or —"

"Hush," Bryar whispered. "Whatever it is, it's stable. It's been there forever." His hand tightened on her shoulder.

Bryar's energy wrapped around her. He could be a part of her, their connection was so profound. It was the same with Quinn, and also between Bryar and Quinn, although the energy manifested differently with each pairing. But they made up a unit, the three of them, going back years, to the days when they frustrated Arwen every time they got hauled up before the council for some illicit exploit or other. Times had changed; they were all experienced Weavers and respected guild members now. Quinn's promotion to council delighted her; it meant she played a role in this – this whatever to call it.

Disaster?

The meeting reconvened, plates of abricoe cakes and hot cups of caff set out in front of them. The Old Man came out of his reverie and said, "Until we speak with the foreigners and discover what causes the disruptions, we can't know how to contain or destroy it. But we can explore its effects, which may be crucial when it comes time to deal with the thing. Tell me your experiences."

What followed was more a presentation of horror stories than anything that should occur in real life. The Healers and Bards present gave on-the-road accounts of interrupted healings, faltering performances. When Bryar's turn came, he flushed a little. "I forgot the words to 'The Lay of Tommy Thompson'," he said. "A song we learn as children. The newer works, even my own..." He trailed off, perplexed. "I couldn't find them, as if they'd been erased from my mind. I've been faking my performances since this thing happened, relying on old material and hoping I'll remember, cutting songs or stories short."

Fergus, the Bard on the council, nodded. He told much the same story, with equal embarrassment. The Bards were renowned for their prodigious memories.

Dal spoke next, echoing Willow's experience, although he brought other nuances into the tale. The plants, for instance. "They were just plants," he said. "With stems and leaves and flowers and roots, but it was as if they were without healing properties. Perhaps that is so, and this *thing* removes their energies, or warps them."

Willow hadn't contemplated anything so terrible. She had assumed that the intrinsic energies of the plants were there, even if the extra power she, as a Healer, imbued them with, was not. She shuddered, and Bryar's hand gripped hers under the table. The room fell silent for a minute, giving them time to absorb the information.

Most Scribes traveled less and spent more time closeted at the Motherhouse. Looking from Quinn to Arwen and back, Willow noted the tight mouths, the tense postures. Then Arwen said, "Quinn, Ezra, and I did a deep template exploration last night. Do *not* try it," she added, shooting a look around the table. "In fact, I forbid it. Am I understood?"

She waited until each of the Healers and Bards in the room assented before she continued. "In sum, we learned this. Whatever this alien force is, it affects the templates in the most shallow levels. It masks the Aura and renders it inaccessible. It is not native to the Midland, or to any of our neighboring lands, and its energy clashes with ours. The deep templates seem to be immune to it, so far. But we believe its energy is insidious, and will ultimately destroy the Aura, and possibly life as we know it."

No one moved. Having the threat spelled out so baldly terrified Willow. As did the idea of Quinn plunging helter-skelter through a template, even with a powerful lifeline to get her out should she fall into difficulty.

Arwen continued. "For this reason, we also believe that destroying the originator of the alien energy is ill advised. It is possible that attempting its destruction would spread its poison further, and faster. So containment is our best option."

The Old Man, Ezra, stood and looked them in the eye, each in turn. "Arwen speaks true. Once we locate the thing causing the disruption, we must find a way to bind it. This may be physical or energetic, and there may well be risk involved. Keep that in mind."

His eyes surveyed the room again, taking his time, leaving no doubt he was serious.

Then he sat again. "Next," he said grimly, "we find out what it is."

A different atmosphere, Joss thought as he and Kiril entered the conference room that afternoon. Less collaborative, more threatening.

An elderly man, introduced as Ezra, sat dead center at the table. Rather than the ubiquitous tunic with trousers or skirt, he wore some kind of robe, though woven of the same neutral linen. His eyes were dark with concern and necessity.

The room deferred to the old man. Joss wondered what his presence meant.

Beside him, Kiril was closed off. Other than banalities over lunch, they hadn't spoken that day, so he had no idea how Kiril spent his morning. Most days he either drove himself, exercising to exhaustion, or stared out at the forest. Joss himself had wandered a little way from the Motherhouse, to a field with a herd of goats. He'd tried to get a reading on them, but failed.

He felt edgy, as if he were unprepared for an expected disaster. From overheard conversations, he gathered that the Aura was unstable. That likely affected his ability to connect to the animals.

Arwen's grim face reflected the mood of the rest of council. Willow looked as if she might jump out of her skin any moment. Bryar sat next to her, holding her hand. Why? Among men, a clap on the back established a bond. Arwen sat beside Ezra; the others ranged around the table. They settled quickly, deferring to Ezra.

"The problem is clear. You hold the solution. What is causing this disruption?" Ezra's cold voice belied his frail-seeming body.

Kiril held himself straight, every inch a commander. "We don't know, although naturally we'll assist you in your research. Our intent was never to harm your culture. I'm not convinced our arrival had anything to do with your problem, though."

"You cannot mean that," Willow said, then fell silent.

"I don't believe you," Ezra said flatly. "For your own reasons, you choose to hide your knowledge. We will speak until the answer reveals itself. Do not play games with us. You both understand the workings of this vessel that crashed. Tell us what you suspect."

Joss spoke, at least in part to deflect attention from Kiril. "I didn't spot anything obvious at the crash site."

"But you didn't dig deep, did you?" Ezra said flatly. "You fled."

His mouth twitched. *Fled* implied cowardice. "Maybe we left too soon. I admit the place made me uneasy."

Ezra's face softened. "So they tell me," he murmured, as if to himself.

"It didn't bother the others."

The old man spoke more forcibly. "To me this seems a simple problem. If your ship traveled from another planet, you had a means to power it. What?"

"A propulsion system. That's gone. It was almost as big as the vessel. I identified a few burned-out remnants."

"What else? For light, heat, whatever you needed?"

"Those ran off of a power cell."

Next to him, Kiril tensed.

"Describe it, please."

"It's a box, the size of..." He tried and failed to come up with a cultural reference. "It's approximately the size of my hand, as thick as two hands together. Heavy. I don't think I can explain how it works in terms you'll understand."

"This thing survived the crash?"

Joss paused. "It could be there. Its workings are well shielded, because of the —" He broke off, suddenly aware of the realities behind what he had been about to say.

The cell radiated a dozen types of energy.

"Please continue."

But Joss wasn't ready to speak yet, except to swear under his breath. The implications slammed into him. If the cell was leaking, they might have their explanation.

When he hesitated, the Old Man changed his focus. "Kiril. What is the threat that this thing poses, that it must be 'well shielded'?"

All business, Kiril moved his gaze around the table. "It emits several types of radiation. Gamma, proton fusion, nuclear, and lower level emissions from its chip board. Electronics, chemical reactions. It could kill you if the casing broke."

Kiril was management. He had only the faintest idea of the cell's functioning, but he could pitch the shit with the best of them. This was a power move, establishing rank.

Ezra didn't rise to the bait. "Or destroy slowly, if it cracked? Or perhaps it wouldn't even require a crack. Perhaps the thing, intact, is powerful enough to conflict with other energies."

"It never bothered us on the ship," Kiril replied. "And our scientists put it through rigorous testing. It doesn't leak radiation. I'm simply not convinced this is the problem."

Ezra pounced. "But you suspect. And you have suspected for a while, have you not? Joss, what is your opinion?"

He took a breath. He had a sudden hunch about the nature of Kiril's plans, and he didn't like it. Not at all. "I think it's buried in the wreckage. I doubt it's cracked, because we'd see the effects much sooner, and in everyone, not just the Weavers. Like a poison."

"It's intact then, and destroying the Aura."

A bleak assessment, and Joss bet an accurate one. He looked around the room. Their eyes focused on him, not Kiril. "It puzzles me that it would bother me now, when it never did before. Or anyone else. But there was no other energy consolidator on board."

"You're exposed to the Aura," Ezra said, "which, in your terms, is probably another type of radiation. That may have affected your reactions. How do we defend against it?"

"I don't know. So help me, I don't." He covered his eyes with a hand for a moment, then met Ezra's level gaze.

Kiril radiated frustration. That worried him.

Ezra's tone changed. "You believe your technology to be far beyond ours. Is this true?"

"Yes, sir. Except that here, the more I learn, the more I question my assumptions."

"But you have no equivalent to the Auric energies on your planet?"

He shook his head.

"And you consider us primitive, backward, and uneducated."

Honesty. Be honest, because the old man will know for sure if you're not. "At first, but not anymore. Not since I started to understand more about your culture."

Ezra nodded. "You will lend us your expertise to design the best way to contain this *thing*."

"Yes."

"And you?" Ezra turned his attention to Kiril. "You believe you have landed in a backward, primitive culture?"

"No, of course not. I appreciate what you have here."

"And you also will assist us to defend against your cell?"

"We'll both help in any way we can. But I have to emphasize, I'm worried that this is the wrong direction. Something else is disrupting your Aura. We may be wasting time pursuing this avenue." Kiril's voice was smooth; you didn't become a commander in the Force without being able to play the political game.

Ezra made the decision for all of them. "First, we eliminate this possibility. If it's not the power cell, we will move on. All of you, please be prepared to reconvene at a moment's notice."

"And consider what we face," Arwen added. "How do we contain a box we can't even approach safely? We need ideas."

Joss anticipated a tense conversation ahead. Not only was Kiril lying through his teeth, he wanted to get his hands on the cell.

Willow had watched the confrontation between Ezra and the two alien men with mixed feelings. She was sure Kiril was lying, but not sure why. Joss… perhaps he was what he seemed to be, a good man, ready to defend their way of life.

Or perhaps not. She wasn't prepared to trust either of them.

Arwen adjourned the meeting soon afterwards on a positive note. "Tension is much too high here, and that affects our work. Tonight, we dance. Quinn, Daren, Fergus, inform your guilds, please. Bryar, kindly notify the village, and ask them to bring music."

Bryar nodded and grinned at Willow, echoing the cautious cheer on the faces around the table at the prospect of an evening of movement to shake free the pressure growing throughout the Motherhouse.

Willow smiled back, pleased. A dance would clear her nagging headache, release her worry, drive a hundred unanswerable questions from her mind.

Bryar kissed her cheek and left. Quinn shot a smile at her but filed out with the council. The two foreigners followed, leaving Willow with the impression that Joss had herded Kiril from the room. In their previous lives, Kiril had outranked Joss – another foreign word, implying the ability to dictate actions – but Joss showed no signs of blind obedience these days.

Arwen and Ezra sat at the table, talking in an undertone. Dal stepped behind her chair and placed his hands on her shoulders.

"Rough day."

She leaned into him, feeling his fingers dig into her knotted muscles.

"The bone-knit is coming into bloom," he told her. "I can't decide if it's worth risking a harvest."

"I've wondered, too. You sense nothing from the herbs?"

Dal, always fastidious, released her and brushed at his soiled tunic before settling in the chair Bryar had vacated. "No, I couldn't judge. Is that the plant, or the Aura, or us? The plants' healing compounds are intrinsic, but..." He shook his head.

Willow closed her eyes. "And we risk losing a year's worth of medicines. Or we wait until tomorrow and hope for a more powerful day."

"Come to the fields later? You're earth clan, you might pick up something I don't."

Dal was air clan, although his work with plants kept him in contact with earth. He lived in his head, his love of healing academic, not organic like hers.

"Were any of the others out?" Herb harvest was a favorite activity.

"Yes, most of us. Same results. I'll talk to Daren about calling a guild meeting over dinner. Calm things down a little." As head and deputy head of their guild, Daren and Dal would present the situation factually and put rumors to rest. Willow's conversations with her fellow Healers ranged from worried to panicky.

"Dal, Willow." The Old Man's voice interrupted them. They both looked up. "You may harvest, but only to dry and prepare salves. The extra power needed to create elixirs and tinctures isn't present."

Dal tipped his head in acknowledgment. "Thank you. In terms of energetic alignment and blooming date, there's a two- or three-day window. I'll arrange a party for picking and processing."

"Excellent." Ezra stood. "Now, I'm an old man with a craving for a seed pastry. Willow, my dear, may I ask you to escort me to the dining hall?"

"I'd be happy to." She exchanged a hand squeeze with Dal, then went to the Old Man's side. They departed with Arwen and Dal, separating outside the Centra.

Ezra took her arm as they crossed the grass. A slender woman herself, she realized that he was no taller than her average height, and probably weighed no more. "This has been hardest on you," he said. "You've burdened yourself with responsibility. That's a false perception."

"I try not to. That they found me first was an accident. After that, I did what my training and my pledge dictated. Otherwise, Kiril would be dead, and Joss wandering wild. I hope they can help us."

"Kiril will not. Joss will if he can. That may, of course, change."

The bald words chilled her, but she recognized the inherent accuracy of them. "Kiril is angry."

"He sees himself as a failure."

"I regret I saw only the anger. That explains…"

"He keeps it well hidden. Secretive, that one. He is desperate for his fellow Terrans to arrive, as a vindication."

His straight talking relaxed her. She found herself enjoying their short stroll in the sunlight. "The accident, when so many died… neither of them was to blame."

"True, but two thirds of his crew dead and his ship beyond salvage? And the remaining one turning away from him. There is no love lost between them, Willow."

"I encouraged Joss to visit him, when he was immobilized. Was that a mistake?"

"No. We all need the familiar around us. But my old legs grow tired. Would you mind running into the hall for our pastries? I'd like to eat in the sunshine."

"You are sure you're able to negotiate the slope?"

He gave her a smile such as she hadn't seen before from him, warm and open. "My talents are many and varied. Go."

When Willow returned with the treats, she found him on her favorite spot, where the grade briefly leveled out, making a flat place from which to watch the comings and goings below. "You knew," she said as she handed him his pastry and settled beside him.

"They say I know everything. They are wrong, but yes, I knew about this little patch. You three made quite a mark during your training."

"I love them both." She bit into the pastry, savoring the spicy, nutty warmth.

"And they, you. But I wanted a moment to speak with you only. Because you are destined to play a significant role in the upcoming days. Your friends, also, but it is most certain for you."

All smiles vanished. She swallowed her bite. "How?"

Ezra sat with his forearms resting on his knees, the pastry dangling from his hand, staring out between buildings, across the valley. "I don't know yet, but difficult times lie ahead, more difficult than you can imagine. You will be called on to make sacrifices. However, if you choose not to, no blame will attach to you."

The hard question. "Will I survive this?"

"I wish I could say yes. But the truth is, the future is never so clear." He turned to her. "You have my support, and the Motherhouse stands behind you, as always. Follow your training and your instincts, and trust in a positive outcome."

She wrapped her arms around her knees and looked down at the green, where a class of apprentices had started a game of dodge-the-light-globe. "This is my world. My calling. What would be the point of going on, if it ended?"

He followed her gaze and spoke quietly. "That is my great fear, that it may come to an end. Not merely the ultimate collapse of the Aura, but the poisoning of the land. It might take generations, but I believe it is possible, if we can't rid ourselves of this thing."

"Thank you for warning me."

"I regret adding to your burden."

"It's better to know." She returned her attention to the pastry, scarcely tasted, in her hand. "I will do what I must."

"And that is why you are among the best Healers currently traveling. Among the most powerful also, not because of your Entrée, but because of your dedication."

She shrugged and looked around. Weavers, apprentices, and support staff from the village came and went, everything peaceful and normal, on the surface.

The conversation had become stiff, because what more was there to say? Even in the heat of a midsummer day, she felt chilled by the nameless challenges facing her. If only...

If only it would all just go away.

Angry at her negative thoughts, she rose. "Shall I escort you anywhere else?"

"Assistance is always available. Thank you for spending some of this beautiful afternoon with me. Take care of yourself, my dear." He touched her hand. "You, the three of you, are the epitome of what we hope for. You have lived your life well, Willow. May the Sustainer of the land bless you."

"And you, too."

She started down the slope, only to be called back. "Willow? One more thing."

She looked up at him, her brows drawn together.

"I have seen something about the east. I don't know what it means, but I thought you should know in case events make it clear. Something about the east," he repeated, as if musing over a puzzle.

With his mysterious words adding to the whirlwind of thoughts and feelings tearing at her mind, she hurried down the slope, pausing to look back only once. Ezra sat, the remains of the seed pastry forgotten as he stared off into the distance. He looked smaller, tired and very old.

She ran, aware that she didn't have much time to reach her room in the Healers' lodge before tears started.

Chapter 12

Joss settled on the slope, waiting for Kiril's opening salvo. His former commander sprawled next to him, clearly pleased. Weavers and students crisscrossed the green. Across the amphitheater, Willow and Ezra talked together. She looked troubled, more so than before. He wondered why.

Kiril wasted no time. "We agree it's the power cell."

"I'm sure you suspected that."

"But now we know it survived the crash."

"Your point?" He'd bet Kiril had his own plans for the cell – if he got his hands on it.

"Don't be dense, Sergeant. We'll jury-rig it. We need power if we're ever going to contact Terra."

"The only ethical future for that cell is to render it inoperable, if we can figure out how. The thing's damn near indestructible."

Kiril scowled, annoyed. "No one's destroying anything. There must be crystals, or metal, or *something* on this backward planet to build a transmitter."

"Not gonna happen. Forget it. I'd rather help them save their Aura than chase a crazy dream about getting word to Terra."

Kiril sat up and gripped his forearm, hard. "It's not crazy. And you're helping me."

"No," Joss said calmly. "I'm not."

Fingers dug into his flesh. "Let's be clear. There will be another ship. A pod or a full fleet of settlers, I don't know, but they are coming." Kiril's voice grew taut, matching the tension on his face. "And if you refuse this assignment, I'll see you court martialed and hanged." He gave Joss's arm a shake and let go.

"Won't work." Joss faked indifference, ignoring the clenching in his gut at the dreaded words *court martial*. After the lifetime he'd devoted, pulling himself up the ranks, proving his worth despite his caste, to end it in ignominy...

He shook the thought off. Even if a ship did arrive, they'd find a different ball game from what they'd expected.

As his gaze swept the slope, Willow stood and hurried away. The old man stayed behind, watching her go. Whatever had passed between them, neither looked happy.

Kiril backed off. "We'll make it work. Hell, Joss, with a decent transmitter you could tell them *not* to come. Soothe your conscience."

Kiril had used his name, not his rank. A slip, or a gesture of friendship, or a new strategy to win him over?

"Thing is, to build the simplest ham outfit we'd need materials I'm not sure exist here. And where do we start looking?"

Kiril's face went cold. "You're so enraptured by this place it's blinded you. Obviously, once we've secured the device, they'll give us anything we want."

Joss stared into the hungry eyes of the other man. "You would do that, wouldn't you? You'd hold these people for ransom. Force your ideas on them."

"And you wouldn't? Don't be a fool. And don't limit your options."

Joss bit back a sigh, wondering how to persuade Kiril away from his plan. "They deserve better. There's a good way of life here. Air to breathe, the trees and the fields — "

"And the cows," Kiril muttered contemptuously.

"Those cows provide milk and butter, and meat. Maybe it's different in the management castes or in the officer ranks, but where I come from, those things didn't exist on Terra except artificially. And the artificial can't hold a candle to what I'm finding here. I'd never tasted real beef."

"All of which is why this planet's perfect for settlement. But go on, Sergeant. Get it all out." Kiril sounded bored. He flopped back, his fingers playing in the grass.

"Okay." Joss leaned forward, resting his arms on his knees, and watched the bustle down below. "It's civilized, the people are happy. There's meaningful work. They share what they have. That didn't happen at home. We'd hoard if we could get away with it, and no one helped anyone."

"Out of curiosity," Kiril said, "are you going to mention the women?"

He hadn't been, but what the hell. "Tell me this. Were women on Terra really so inferior?"

"Enjoying them, are you?"

"What do you mean?"

"You had a woman yet, Joss?"

It took only a second to puzzle out Kiril's words. His face flamed.

"Didn't think so. Use them, but don't trust them." he made a disparaging gesture with his hand. "They're dangerous."

"Willow saved your life."

Kiril let out a sigh, as if Joss were missing the point. "Someone else would have found us."

"Not another Healer. And not in time."

"Men are Healers, too. And women are less trustworthy."

That sounded wrong. More Terran propaganda? Funny how when you're in the middle of it you can't separate the truth from the lies. No woman he'd met here was inferior to a man.

"The settlers – I assume they planned some kind of reproductive technology?"

"Most likely doing it the old fashioned way. Hell, I don't know. Whatever's expedient, I suppose."

Anger flared. "Women aboard to breed?"

"What else is there? Cooking, cleaning?"

"This culture's light years ahead of concepts like that." Joss stood, aware he'd better leave before he said things he'd regret later.

Kiril watched him from his place on the slope. "The settlers will adapt. They train for it, how to survive on an unfamiliar planet." He shrugged.

"Too little, too late."

"I need your help."

"You won't get it. Sorry, *Commander.* Perhaps you should consider going native."

Joss stalked away, annoyed with himself that he'd let his temper get the better of him. He'd always been so controlled, kept his own counsel. But Kiril was pushing the limits.

The green fronting the Motherhouse was alive with movement. The Weavers in residence, perhaps twenty-five in total, another three dozen apprentices, and everyone from the village nearby, men, women, and children, had shown up. A couple of babies slept under a table tucked against the wall. Older kids ran around the buildings and joined in the dances. Men from the village had hauled over a large drum made from a hollow tree trunk with a skin stretched tightly over it; the penetrating bass rhythm dominated the music.

Joss stood on the sidelines and took it in. Fires at either end of the green fought off the dark, augmented by lanterns on posts along the Centra's frontage. People avoided the fires, given the heat of the night. Shadows heightened the air of revelry, of something wild and pagan transpiring in front of him.

Men didn't dance on Terra, but threw their excess energy into sports. He was fine with that; his big body lacked an innate sense of rhythm, and he liked the framework of rules, practice, competition. The raw, pulsing rhythms unnerved him.

Couples and groups moved with those rhythms, almost touching each other at times, triggering a body awareness he did his best to ignore. He'd yet to see anyone on the planet who matched him in height. He was healthy again, a big, virile man since regaining some of the weight and muscle mass he'd lost during the last month of their voyage, and he felt conspicuous among these lithe people. Self-conscious, he ignored his bodily response to the music and looked away. Better to hang out at the tables bearing fruits, cakes and pastries, meat pasties, cheeses, and the ubiquitous flat, crunchy bread.

He sensed rather than heard someone approach and turned to his left to find Quinn standing beside him, her dark face glowing in the heat and lantern light. Her body shifted underneath the shapeless tunic, unconsciously keeping time with the drum. "Have you considered that we speak the same language?" she asked him without preliminary.

"Yeah. Kiril figures one of the lost ships settled this planet. We sent them out to colonize other worlds, but most of them vanished."

"When?"

"In Terran years, about four hundred years ago. How long is the year here?" They'd had this information, down to the second, before they left Terra, but that was in a different lifetime.

"Three hundred sixty days. Ninety days to a season. That isn't precise, but we don't have a way to measure it more accurately. We speak of months, but as a length of time between a woman's courses, not a celestial measurement."

A woman's courses? Joss seized what he understood and chose not to ask about the rest. "Almost the same as ours."

"Most believe that we've always been here. I'm skeptical, myself. You know I'm a Scribe."

"I don't understand what that means."

"It's my job to discover things and build them into the pattern of our knowledge. Whereas Willow uses the templates to deepen her connection to the plants, and occasionally minerals, and to Heal, I use them to track history. But we're stuck at about a hundred and fifty years ago, because it's too dangerous to go back any further. We have legends, but no idea how old or accurate they really are. We've searched the records in hamlets all over the Midland. None of them covers more than a couple hundred years, so our origins are shrouded in mystery."

"Are those records written? I haven't seen any paper."

"Each hamlet has a book and an archivist. Paper's rare, because of the expense. It's imported from the Southland. They make it from a kind of reed that grows there."

"There's a lot to learn." And learn he would. Not for the benefit of Kiril's purported future settlers, but to recreate himself as a part of their world.

"I'm open to an exchange of information," she said. "You already know far more about us than we do about you. The absence of women, for instance. How can you exist without women? How can babies be born in a laboratory?"

"Technically, I can't explain it." The driving bass rhythm worked its way through his nerve endings, pulling at his muscles to move. He tamped down the impulse. "And there are women on Terra. In Northam Corp they live in different cities, so there's no mixing. They do their jobs, we do ours."

"Makes no sense to me."

"Terra's far too crowded. Everything's controlled, including births."

"Do you have alcohol?" She gestured at the mug of beer in his hand. He'd finished his first mugful quickly, but having no desire for either light-headedness or a headache tomorrow, was nursing his second.

Joss didn't mind Quinn's pumping him for information. What difference did it make if he revealed facts about life on Terra? "Yes, but limited to Friday or Saturday night, depending on your registration number, and two pints. There used to be other alcohols, but not anymore."

"Here, beer's most common, but we brew fruit-based wines and meads, and there are a few distilleries around. Weavers rarely drink alcohol. The others do, but usually at celebrations. Conservation of resources."

He understood that. "This is a prosperous place."

"We work at it. That's why the disruption in the Aura upsets us so. It supports us in so many ways, and in a more general sense supports the land. That sounds like nonsense, but all my research tells me it's the truth."

"How about manufacturing? The Motherhouse has glass windows. In Stanstead I only saw shutters."

"The windows there are covered with treated skins and shutters, come winter. It's a dark time, but the only way to keep out the cold and snow. The glass was a donation, years ago. We're careful with it."

"Where's it made?"

The music stopped, and the dancers swarmed the food and beverage tables. He and Quinn stepped away.

"The Northlands. Also metal and earthenware." She nodded at the plates covering the table. "We manufacture some pottery here, but The Midland's primarily agricultural. We trade butter and meat, grain. Fruit's everywhere, but in the winter there's a demand for our vegetables."

"I never knew real food tasted so good. Not much is grown on Terra anymore. Mostly it's synthesized in the lab."

"All those labs. Making babies, making food."

"You do what's needed, to keep civilization going."

"I guess." Quinn sounded doubtful. "It sounds so artificial. And regimented."

"It is. You live in a dormitory, go to your work and your scheduled times at the gym or the pub or a social function. You watch videos in the common room." When she frowned, he added, "like a picture, only moving."

The music began again, a dark, pounding rhythm overlaying the melody from the small band. He couldn't put a name to any of the instruments, although they resembled ones at home. Guitar, violin, flute, broadly speaking. This must be a popular song, because literally everyone surged out onto the green except Quinn and himself, and Arwen, standing on her own on the far side.

"There they are," Quinn said. "I worried a little that Willow wouldn't turn up. This whole thing's hit her hard."

He grimaced. "I feel bad about my part in that. I was a lot rougher than I needed to be, that day I found her."

"You were injured, and with no idea what you were up against. Here, we'd call it panic. Where's your friend?"

He'd given up telling them that Kiril wasn't his friend. "I don't know."

Quinn's attention wasn't on Kiril, in spite of her question. "This is good... I suspected she'd end up with Dal tonight, but this is better."

When he looked in the direction she nodded, his gaze snagged on Willow and Bryar.

Even with the loose-fitting tunic – no skirt or trousers under it – he could see her movements. And his. Bryar wore only trousers; perspiration gleamed on his muscular chest. Their bodies followed each other, twisting and twining, growing closer. His hands rested on her hips, hers on his biceps. Her bare legs intertwined with his. Willow's face was flushed. It suited her, Joss thought, and once again turned away.

"It's no secret what they'll be doing tonight," Quinn said. Then, glancing at his face, which he was sure conveyed a strong desire not to know any more, she grinned and added, "Think of it academically, as a form of mating ritual. I'm glad. Bryar's a skilled lover. Just what she needs to get her head straightened out. You're aware that sexual release is an excellent antidote for tension?"

Sometimes gathering information resulted in information he wasn't ready for. "Yeah, sure," he mumbled.

"I expect you'll find out," Quinn said unhelpfully. He noticed the way the skin around her eyes crinkled. Did they all recognize he was a neophyte where women were concerned?

"Could we continue this another day?" she asked. A polite enough request, but he thought, not for the first time, that he'd as soon not cross Quinn.

He nodded and sipped the beer.

"There's so much I want to know about your society. And about that possible missing link, where we came from. I'm intrigued."

"Sure. And the more I can learn, and the faster..."

"You're not drowning. You're doing well, in fact. I need to talk to Arwen. Enjoy the dance."

Quinn disappeared around the edge of the bobbing crowd of dancers. Joss returned his scrutiny to the surging mob on the green. Willow and Bryar were gone.

Chapter 13

The sun shone through the little window in their room at the guest lodge, and Willow stretched, feeling lazy happy. In no small thanks to Bryar, she had slept well. He knew where she hurt, how to pleasure her. More than twenty years, she thought idly.

And Romarin. The child they shared, deepening the connection still more.

Things were falling into place. The Old Man was here, and they had good reason to suspect the cause of the disruption. As Ezra had promised, today would be perfect for harvest with the sun's heat encouraging healing properties in the plants. In the wake of days of meetings and tension, Willow looked forward to getting her hands dirty.

Bryar had left an hour ago, after warming her early morning. She'd claimed this hour for herself, to let go of responsibility and luxuriate in the sunshine.

But not forever. With regret, she threw back the light cover.

Back at the Healers' lodge she made her invocation in the herb garden, honoring a stable Aura. Healing energy flowed through her; her hands tingled.

Thank you, Sustainer of all, for the gift of today.

She joined several other Healers in the dining hall for a loud and cheerful breakfast, all of them more relaxed than at any time since they'd received the summons to the Motherhouse, thanks to Daren's pep talk and the dance. As they walked back to the lodge together, they planned their preparations for harvest.

In the workroom they organized supplies and cleaned out herbal remedies too old to be useful. Together they checked the stores of dried herbs, scrubbed containers, boiled water to purify it, checked supplies of tallow and beeswax to melt into salves. Willow tried to remember the last time she felt so positive. She knew it dated to well before the strangers arrived. Happiness, for her, meant traveling, but also being with Bryar, Quinn, or her daughter, and that happened so rarely. She'd relished that shared laughter with Mari two days ago as she demonstrated the hand gestures to manipulate the softer energy of soothing.

No time for introspection today, however. She hauled several more containers to the workbench and began assessing their contents for potency.

That afternoon the sun drenched the land with heat. Willow wore a floppy hat to shield her head and neck. She and Dal left the tiny distillery tucked into a hollow behind the main Motherhouse complex, pulling a cart bearing a small cask of alcohol, and were turning onto the track to the fields when Bryar and Joss appeared ahead of them. Both men looked troubled.

They pulled alongside and stopped. "Have either of you seen Kiril today?" Bryar asked.

"Not at breakfast, I don't think," Dal said.

Willow shook her head. "I ate late, but I didn't see him." She frowned at Joss. "He hasn't been with you?"

Joss ran a big hand over his face. "Not since yesterday afternoon, after the meeting broke up. He wasn't at the dance, and his room has that empty look about it. I don't believe he's here."

The words landed among them like a death knell. If Kiril had disappeared... she and Bryar exchanged a glance. Dal's brows drew together as the implications sank in.

"The power cell?" Willow asked.

"That's my guess." Joss frowned. "But with his leg? Walking's still a struggle, even though he tries to hide it."

"With a walking stick, he could manage," Dal said. "But where to? And why?"

"And how do we find him?" Bryar's question brought it home; Kiril's disappearance meant trouble. "We've asked around the complex, but no one remembers seeing him."

"We can put out a call," Bryar said. "Most Weavers are on the road. If everyone's alerted to watch out for him..."

Joss spoke up. "We learned a lot of skills in training for this mission, including surviving in the wild, living off the land. He's capable of avoiding people and foraging, or stealing."

Willow looked up at the clear sky, watching her dream of a happy day with the plants vanish. "We have work to do. The harvest takes precedence over Kiril." She glanced at Dal, who nodded his agreement. "Later we'll go to Ezra together. He'll expect to see us all."

Willow dutifully went to the field and set about her harvest, but without her earlier optimism. Sometimes she wondered what could go wrong next.

The next morning, restive in the mugginess, Joss crossed from the dining hall to the guest lodge, hunched against the weather. Unlike the thunderstorms, the warm rain had fallen for hours, not strong but steady. Scraps of conversation floated his way over breakfast; the Weavers were happy about the rain. Life here was lived close to the land's cycles of growth and rest, even for the ultra-cerebral Scribes.

After alerting Willow and Dal to Kiril's disappearance, he'd spent yesterday afternoon wandering the valley, drifting ever farther from the Motherhouse, expecting that any moment they'd come for him, demand he produce Kiril. But they never came.

Questions bombarded him, questions about the crops, the seasons, raising the animals. Who ground the flour, who decided who did what work, what they used for money – if it existed. How did they survive winters? What kinds of industries did they have up north? Why was so much communal, right down to the clothes he wore? Women...

The dance two nights ago had been its own form of misery, driving home his size, his loneliness, the thousand things he didn't understand. Yet the dance had gripped him like a moth to a light, dredging up the longing to claim what they took for granted.

Willow, the expression on her face...

His other question superseded those. The weirdness in his brain was growing stronger, and he had no control over it. As usual, yesterday he'd found himself in the agricultural lands, watching the cows and goats and listening to them. What he heard was trivial. That he heard anything at all scared the bejeezus out of him.

He missed Stanstead, eating and talking with the agriculturists, hanging out in the men's lodge, and learning. Not to mention getting a shave; like so much else, razors were held communally, and his beard sported ten days' growth. Not unlike many other men, but he wasn't used to it and would rather get rid of it.

Hell, he even missed Kiril.

He needed answers.

The Old Man and his wife shared a suite in the guest lodge. She answered Joss's knock and smiled in that vague, kindly way he'd noticed before. With a hand resting on his arm for a moment, as if to assuage his disappointment, she said, "You'll find him in the common room at the end of the hall. He asked me to tell you he's expecting you."

"What do you mean, he's expecting—"

She closed the door gently in his face, leaving him to contemplate a new mystery as he made his way along the corridor.

Joss hesitated at the entrance to the common room, composing himself and plucking his damp tunic away from his skin. The Old Man, robe tucked at his feet, was settled in one of two upholstered chairs near a small fire. Why a fire? The land, heated from the summer sun, steamed in the rain.

The Old Man laughed, as if aware of his internal monologue, and twisted around to greet him. "Welcome. And please forgive the extra warmth. My joints protest on damp days. Take a seat, join me."

Joss shoved the second padded chair away and replaced it with a slat-backed one from the table to the right of the doorway, placing it so his wet back faced the fire. A pottery vessel they used to serve caff waited on a small stool at the Old Man's elbow. Without asking, Ezra poured into the miniscule mugs. "Do you take milk?"

"However it comes."

"The least of your worries, I suppose. When the brew's strong, I enjoy a little. Try it. Milk is a soporific." When Joss frowned, he explained, "Medicine for the nerves. Helps you sleep."

Joss accepted the caff. "You knew I was coming," he said.

The Old Man nodded. "It's too difficult to explain at your level of education. One day you'll understand. Until then, take it on faith – or believe as some do that I have mystical powers that transcend even the Aura." He chuckled and leaned back, holding the tiny cup.

"Then you know why I'm here."

"Probably. Don't expect everything to be resolved today."

Joss surveyed the room. Plain, like all the other interiors, stone walls broken by two small windows looking out over the green. The table and chairs, the pair of upholstered chairs, and the stool holding the caff were the only furnishings. A cookfire occupied a corner, and a built-in cabinet ran along the wall under the windows.

"Let's dispense with a few basics first. I'm aware I'm known as the Old Man almost everywhere, but I prefer that my friends use my name. I would be honored for you to do so."

"Thanks," Joss mumbled. Ezra's friend? How was that supposed to work?

"And you are Josiah Worthing. Do you use Joss by preference, or for another reason?"

He thought back, cradling the tiny mug. "It started when I joined the military," he said. "Nobody in the higher castes gets a biblical name. When you're an anomaly, you do what you can to fit in. And to get ahead."

"And biblical means?"

"It's an old religious term. The corporation suppressed all that, but they still assign the names. They brand you as belonging to the worker caste. They're not acceptable once you move up the ranks."

"Changing castes is unusual?"

"Change?" He snorted. "You don't change. I'd never be anything but a worker, no matter what job they gave me."

"And that has left you bitter. Need I remind you that you're living a different life now? With that comes the freedom to discard what no longer works, including your name."

The Old Man – Ezra – raised his mug briefly, as if toasting him, then drank.

Suddenly Joss got the humor of it. "I'm evolving into some kind of freak, and I obsess about my name? Joss works for me."

Ezra smiled, and Joss relaxed, in the back of his mind wondering how Ezra had made it happen.

"It's time to set aside whatever you were. Because you are becoming something else entirely."

"I wish I knew what," Joss muttered. He ran his thumb over the tiny mug in his hands, took a sip – yes, the milk did improve the flavor – and put it on the table.

"You do know, or at least you suspect. But to continue, you are not a prisoner here. We prefer that you stay at the Motherhouse until Kiril returns, but we will not compel you to do so. As you may imagine, we seek your assistance in solving the puzzle of this cell of yours."

Joss let silence build for a minute. Then he said, "Once he's got the cell, he'll track me down. He lacks the knowledge to make use of it himself."

"What does he want it for?"

"A radio." *And power.* But he didn't say that. At Ezra's puzzled look he added, "It lets you send your voice over long distances, and receive others' voices."

"And whose voice does he hope to receive?"

"He wants to contact Terra, our planet."

"I understand. To tell them to come… or not?"

Joss gave a humorless chuckle. "Kiril says they will, unless I find a way to stop them. Maybe another small party, or maybe — "

"Millions," Ezra said gently. "Numbers we can hardly fathom here. More than enough to disrupt or destroy our civilization."

"They might not settle in the Midland."

"But we are interconnected. The Northlands and Southlands are a part of us, serving different functions. This is the agricultural heartland of our world, but our continuing existence with any level of comfort requires them. As for the land on the other side of the hills…" Ezra drifted off, as if debating what to say. "We cannot go there. But it is essential nonetheless."

Why not? Why?

"Is there anywhere else? Another continent, perhaps?"

"I don't know. I suspect so, but I have no proof."

On Terra, the scientists had acquired only the sketchiest picture of the land masses. Joss cursed himself for not paying more attention as they approached. But by then they'd been close to freefall, with not a second to spare away from the failing controls. It was a miracle he and Kiril had both survived the landing.

Ezra sipped his caff, then said, "So, Kiril returns with the cell. And by now you can imagine the effect."

"Yeah."

"We've ruled out destroying it, because releasing whatever is inside it could make things infinitely worse. So how do we neutralize it, Joss?"

The fire had dried his tunic; he swung his chair around to sit next to Ezra, the caff table between them. "No one's ever tried, far as I know. We never had to."

"We could attempt to surround it, contain it. What materials might block its energy?"

"We'd have to experiment, I guess."

"While every Weaver in the Motherhouse is crippled by its effects. Not an optimal solution."

"No."

"Give it thought, please. Bring your ideas to me, or to Arwen."

Joss mulled it over. "I wonder if I should go to Stanstead. That would keep the cell farther away and buy you time to decide what to do next."

Ezra pondered the suggestion. "That might be best, if we can guarantee no adverse effect on the residents."

"Kiril and I lived with it for a couple of years. For most people it's innocuous."

"I'll bring it up with the council. Are you ready to move on to your bigger concern?"

Joss looked at Ezra and away again. The Old Man had given him time to grow comfortable by opening their conversation with more ordinary matters – if anything about the power cell could be considered ordinary. He took a breath. "It's the animals."

The way their brain processes got into his head. The way he understood them.

Ezra's hands formed a temple. Joss would swear the man's gaze pierced right though him. "Animals' brains don't work like ours do, but you have the ability to translate the workings of their minds into words."

"It seems so, yeah." Ezra's reflecting his thoughts back at him no longer surprised him.

"And it's getting stronger. Clearer."

He nodded.

"You can't make sense of it, and it frightens you."

"Makes me feel like I'm going crazy. I mean, what the hell am I?"

"You're not a freak, Joss. Don't you think that every one of the Weavers experienced being an outsider, growing up in an isolated village and aware of things the others were not? What you are is unusual, but normal. And fundamental to how we live."

"But I didn't grow up here. And I'm not a child." He rubbed his scratchy chin, then passed a hand over his head.

Ezra noticed – or read his mind. "Go to the men's lodge in the village. They'll cut your hair and give you a shave. That's what the Weavers do." He stood, placing his empty caff mug on the table. Joss followed suit. He towered over the older man, feeling every bit as awkward as he had at the dance.

"Life here isn't easy," Ezra said. "It can be harsh. Right now, the middle of the summer, everything's lush, but there are bleak times, too. We pull together because of the calamitous effect of not doing so. Make no mistake, you must find your niche. Your mind is a gift, Joss. Your connection to the Aura is weak, but viable. You're drawn to agricultural work. As a member of a team, you'd be invaluable, especially as you learn control, but it's your choice whether to go in that direction. To run from this or nurture it."

"I want to be useful. I'm strong, I can do manual labor. And I'm good with my hands."

"You've been discussed, of course. To partially answer your question, we believe the best for you would be to spend a year here at the Motherhouse. We'll devise a training program to help you come to terms with what you are and refine your skills. After this other mess is concluded."

"If it ever is."

"Oh, we will find a solution." Joss heard the determination in the other man's voice. "I worry about the sacrifices, though."

"I guess I do, too."

Ezra twitched his robe, straightening the hem. "I wish we could make this easier for you. You've already been a positive force. We'd be pleased if that continued."

"I'll do my best." Aware that he'd been dismissed, Joss asked, "Should I take those to the dining hall?"

Ezra smiled. "If you don't mind. Thank you."

Joss picked up the tray with the tiny mugs and container of caff and crossed to the door, strangely reluctant to leave, and with no fewer questions. Different ones, but at least sharing his concerns lessened their impact.

At the threshold, he turned back. "I've heard the phrase 'animal whisperer'."

"An old term, for which I feel a certain nostalgia, however inaccurate it may be. It's been fifty years or more since an animal whisperer walked these roads. That's the name we give people like you. One who hears the whispering of the beasts. A blessing, if you choose to see it that way."

A blessing. Sure. Joss managed a crooked smile, then turned away and left the room.

Chapter 14

It took Joss several hot, sweaty days in the hills outside of Stanstead to find the spot he wanted, a pile of stones, boulders, and dirt deposited by a rockfall. Another day to reshape the landscape into what he needed. It was a long hike from town along a seldom used track, and he'd left civilization behind him an hour from the site.

He expected Kiril to turn up any time now.

Of Kiril's eventual return to Stanstead, he had no doubt. A home base of sorts, it was also the gateway to the Motherhouse. As well, Kiril's knowledge encompassed management – personnel issues, scheduling, and so forth – but he lacked the technical skills to manipulate the cell himself.

Joss leaned on the pick he'd borrowed from a barn and studied first his scraped and bruised hands, then his handiwork. Humid heat such as he'd never experienced danced over his face. His gut twisted at the idea of leaving the power cell undefended, here or anywhere, but after a long day of meetings, he, Ezra, and the council had concluded that non-crystalline rock offered their best hope to shield the world from its rays while they figured out what to do with it. Once he'd buried it, he'd make the stones look so natural, no one stood a chance of locating it.

Safely in the sanctuary of the nearby forest shade, he stripped out of his tunic. Pale from a lifetime under the filters, his skin hadn't yet hardened to their sun. He gulped from his hide water flask, then squirted the tepid liquid over his head. As he started for town, looking forward to sinking into the river, he dug a couple of pasties from his pack.

Everything he possessed had been given or lent to him. Pack, flask, food. Tools. Tunic and trousers, sandals. Soap, the razor they shaved him with at the men's lodge, the rough comb he dragged through his thick curls in the morning. Everything. In return, he'd told them about one sick cow and brought destruction to their Aura with his arrival.

Not a subject to dwell on, but he wouldn't forget, either.

While he walked and ate a chicken pasty, he considered the potential for confrontation, based on his and Kiril's conflicting ideas about adapting to life here. If the settlers came, Kiril intended to play a role in making a place for them. Joss couldn't prevent their arrival, but he could assure the cell didn't become a bargaining chip. This new world opened so many possibilities, compared to what he'd known. And he suspected the technological skills they'd bring would be of little use here.

With a twinge of nostalgia, he remembered a larger wardrobe, faster transportation, ready hot water, videos and filters, the regimentation that gave order to life.

The segregation from women.

Through gaps in the trees, he studied the sky and predicted a storm by evening. Thunder and lightning still triggered his nerve endings. He'd watched Willow; the storms energized her. He understood the physics of them, but it was different when you'd grown up never seeing one.

He felt for his comm to check the time, a reflex that dogged him even though the comm was long since destroyed. Midafternoon, anyway. That day length corresponded so closely to earth days made adapting easier.

Nobody told him what to do here. He was free, freer than he'd ever been in his life. Nothing was restricted, there was no requirement for an ID card or a pass. Half the town must have seen him leave every morning, but they let him go. Nobody tried to stop him or question him, other than the mayor, Marla. On his return the first day, when he longed to cool off and wash in the river, she'd cornered him and herded him into a cubbyhole of a room in one of the buildings surrounding the plaza. "What's going on?" she demanded. Politely, but without doubt a command.

"I'm looking for a place to bury the thing that's disrupting the Aura." No point embellishing. She understood the importance.

"You're earth clan."

According to everyone. He supposed they were right. It made sense.

"And not from here." The implication: why should we trust you?

"Do you have a better idea?"

They had locked eyes for a long minute. She would have been a first-rate warrior, Joss thought. Like in those video games he'd played back on Terra. Indomitable.

She met his gaze steadily. "The Motherhouse?"

"We planned it together. Arwen and the Old Man and me."

"If something happens to you before we dispose of it?"

"If it's not shielded, any Weaver brave enough to try could locate it, just by tracking its effects." Maybe. He suspected that only his lesser Aura connection had allowed him to approach the wreckage. Based on its effect on Willow, the thing had the potential to blow a full-fledged Weaver out of the water before they got anywhere near it. "If this works, what difference does it make? No one's going to stumble over it."

Marla considered, then gave him a curt nod. "See to it. Let us know what you need."

After that short conversation, he went his own way unmolested.

Now, back in Stanstead, he stowed his tools in the barn and trudged across the plaza, which bustled with activity. Children chased each other shrieking, agriculturists made for their homes or lodges, several women gathered near the well, chatting. A Healer he didn't recognize talked with the old men who sat in a corner of the plaza all day, her hand resting idly on a child's head. A girl carried a board holding unbaked loaves to the communal oven in the kitchens. He weaved his way through the bustle and walked the extra twenty minutes to the ford.

Something niggled at him, a tightness in his gut and a mild headache, making him uneasy. He'd first registered it as he approached Stanstead, and it grew stronger the closer he got to the river. He wanted to attribute it to the approaching storm, but by now he recognized the effect of thunderstorms on his body. This was different, but familiar.

The beach was deserted. He stripped off and sank into the gentle current downstream of the ford. He let the water flow over him, relieving his taxed muscles, then he soaped himself and pitched the yellow bar onto the sand. Although readily available, soap's value was such that no one wasted it.

Relaxing in the late afternoon sun, he finally identified the uneasy feeling. He'd last experienced it at the crash site.

Kiril was close, with the cell. Less than a day away.

A group of men arrived. Joss recognized most of them, and everyone exchanged greetings as they stripped and plunged into the river. In no mood for company, he dressed and walked back to town, thinking he should find the Healer he'd noticed on the plaza earlier, to warn her. It was one thing to sense the energies were out of whack, another to experience it the way Willow had, the bleakness on her face, her fear and bewilderment.

Willow. She'd become a marker for how much he had learned, how far he still had to go.

In the dining hall that evening Joss introduced himself to the Healer, a woman named Beatris.

"You must be one of the newcomers," she said.

He nodded as he pulled out a bench and sat. "You need to know what's happening. We can talk now or later."

"I'm conducting a clinic after dinner. You'd best tell me now."

"You're on the way to the Motherhouse?"

"I am." She took a bite of her cutlet.

"You feel the disruptions?"

Abruptly Beatris looked years older. "The fluctuations… they're driving me crazy."

"It's going to get worse." He filled her in on the power cell's imminent arrival, without mentioning Kiril. "Soon, before it's shielded you may lose all contact with the Aura. I can't do anything about that. If everything goes according to plan, by tomorrow evening it should be all over."

She gave him a tired smile. "But no guarantees, right? I'd best see as many patients as I can today."

"I'm sorry."

"So am I. How's Willow?"

"Fine. Stressed, like everyone." Joss chewed and swallowed, watching the mild-mannered woman across the table from him. "You could leave," he said. "Put distance between you and Stanstead."

She shook her head. "The clinic. Tomorrow…" She shrugged, as if to say she had no choice but didn't regret it. "I've come from the south. I noticed that the disruptions lead to more accidents. It's never lasted long enough to be sure if more people got sick. But I'm needed here. Aura or no, I can tend cuts and set bones."

Joss didn't believe she grasped how bad it could be, but said nothing. He'd developed a solid admiration for the Healers. They followed their vocation, even at the cost of personal discomfort or threat to themselves. He'd seen it in Willow and Dal, and now in Beatris.

"I've filled Marla in," he told her, and got an answering nod. "I'll keep things as controlled as possible."

"What will you do? Destroy it?"

"Whatever we do, it'll be risky. Contamination, for instance."

"I don't understand. But then I don't understand any of this."

"None of us does, really. I'm grasping at straws."

She tipped her head, puzzled. "What does that mean?"

Funny how the basic language had translated, but so many idioms had not. "Something like, I don't have a clue what to do so I'll try almost anything. There's a plan. It should work."

But might not.

"I'll do my best to minimize the impact," he concluded. "Are any other Weavers here?"

"No. I wish there were."

Not half as much as she'd wish it soon, when the cell hit full power on their doorstep.

After parting with Beatris, he went to his room in the men's lodge, where he napped, then spent a long time in the same mindset he used when he communicated with the cows. It was the only way he'd figured out to access his limited Auric connection. After darkness fell, he quietly slipped out.

Morning, and no sign of Kiril. Following a restless night, not helped by a fierce storm in the early hours, Joss arrived for breakfast fighting off a sour mood.

Beatris sat hunched, looking as gray as her bowl of porridge. She waved him over. "You're right," she whispered. "It's terrifying."

"Gone?" he asked.

She shook her head. "But it's so faint it might as well not be there at all."

He put his big hand on her shoulder for an instant, as he might do with a male colleague – and marking the first time he'd voluntarily touched a woman. "It'll get better."

I hope.

He did his best to down a plateful of eggs and a mug of caff. Like Beatris, he could barely sense the Aura, and his body was reacting to the nearness of the cell. Kiril had hidden it but not well, attenuating but not completely shielding its power, a fact that had allowed him to do his nighttime sleuthing.

Time to start. Joss went to the barn and retrieved the pick and shovel, and added a pack loaded with dirt to provide a temporary shield, stowing them outside of town in a fold of the hills. Then he returned to the men's lodge to wait for Kiril.

By mid-morning, Joss concluded that Kiril must be camped near Stanstead. It didn't take long to track him down. No one in his right mind would have stayed outdoors in last night's storm. Joss systematically checked the numerous outbuildings west of Stanstead, many of them huts for the shepherds or shelters for the men and women who worked in the more far-flung fields.

He found Kiril resting against the north wall of a wooden shed. Even with a beard and wearing the ubiquitous tunic, even sitting on the ground, Kiril looked every bit the leader he was. His eyes tracked Joss, alert, missing nothing.

Joss noted his blue eyes. Funny; eye color had never mattered before. But he'd seen only a handful of people with blue eyes since they arrived. Kiril stood out.

"Commander."

"About time you got here."

"Took me a while. I expected you at the men's lodge."

Kiril shook his head. "Join me," he said, an order.

Joss settled on the ground against the wall, legs outstretched. "You ate okay?"

"What you can't forage, you take. I raided the kitchen in Stanstead."

"Impressive that you kept going this long. Nine days?"

"The hardest was locating that hut with the water supply."

"Funny, I thought you were unconscious when we stopped there."

"Not entirely. And I overheard talk afterwards. When something's important, I don't forget it."

"You did good, avoiding traffic on the road."

"I am good. Aced the survival training."

"Yeah, I remember."

They sat in silence for a while, staring out at the rolling pastureland in front of them.

"What's next?" Joss asked.

Kiril sat up, pulling rank. His straighter stance placed him above Joss, who had slouched, relaxed, against the wall. "Next, Sergeant, is you decide whose side you're on. Are you helping me contact our people, or are you going rogue?" He twisted to face Joss head-on.

No problem with the leg, Joss noted. He'd bet it still ached, but with their strange healing techniques, maybe not. Nine days of walking must have strengthened it.

He hesitated, feigning a man reluctant to admit a mistake. "I've had time to think this through. You're right, we need to try to re-establish contact, whether it's to tell them to come or tell them to stay away. I'm in."

"That's what I expected. I'm glad you've come around."

"Thank you, sir. What's the plan?"

Kiril stretched and gazed out over the fields, his hands fiddling with a flower he'd plucked from a weed next to him. "Building a comm might be an impossible dream. I'm not underestimating the challenge, but it's our duty to try. So, we assemble materials."

"Anything useful at the crash site?"

"Not a lot. The cell, of course. Scraps of metal and polymer."

"Yeah, that's my memory, too."

"I expect a receiver's easiest to tackle first."

"Agreed, transmission opens a whole other can of worms," Joss said. "Some of what we need, the rare metals and such, don't exist here. And I wouldn't know where to start to create a signal strong enough to clear the planet. I didn't qualify in communication technology." Addison, a lost crew colleague, had held that role. Joss tallied what he'd located so far. "Metal's around. I've pilfered a couple of spoons from the dining hall at the Motherhouse, but no idea what their composition is. Glass comes from the south, so that means silica. I haven't seen any sign of crystals, but they'd be useful if you hear of any. It'll take experimentation, and whatever we build will be crude."

"Any major dramas in Stanstead?"

He forced himself to shrug. "A Healer's there. She's in a state, I gather."

Kiril glanced toward the heavens, a useful alternative to rolling his eyes. "How much of their mumbo-jumbo do you believe?"

Joss retained his casual, loose-limbed posture. "Some of it. Too many people are involved for it to be a total sham. But how much is placebo... hell, I don't know. They did fix your leg."

"I've always healed fast." Kiril dismissed Willow and Dal's healing with a sentence.

In the silence stretching between them, Joss picked up the song of some bird or other, the rustle of the hot breeze in a nearby hedgerow. Finally, he spoke. "It's a good land."

"Perfect for our purposes."

"How many do you reckon they'd send at once?"

"A different branch of the Force dealt with settlement, so I only heard rumors. It depends on the size of the fleet."

"There might be better places for them than the Midland. Up north's more industrial, whatever that means in the context of this planet. The south's a mixed bag, everything from glass to silk. We're in the agricultural heartland, obviously. They're hoping for a good harvest this year."

"Still talking to cows, Sergeant?"

"Nah. No time for playing around." True, but he missed the animals.

"Good."

"Sir, it's a half hour walk into town, so they'll be serving lunch by the time we get there. Are you ready? I checked, your room's waiting for you."

"You didn't have any trouble getting away to meet me?"

"I've been told more than once that we're free to come and go as we please. Life's more interesting in the men's lodge here than the guest lodge at the Motherhouse."

Kiril rose to his feet. Joss caught a moment's hesitation as the muscles in the injured leg kicked in.

"You haven't asked where the cell is."

Joss stood and gave himself a shake. "I assume it's safe. We can't afford for anyone else to get hold of it."

"Let's go." Kiril struck out, Joss in his wake.

As they walked, saying little, Joss studied the land. A pasture close to Kiril's shed usually held sheep, but today was empty. His eyes tracked the narrow paths the sheep cut in the gentle slope. Further ahead they'd pick up a trail that led through cultivated fields. He hadn't learned the crops, but guessed the tall plants were corn. The first corn of the year marked a holiday – corn festival – so great was the anticipation.

He looked forward to it, too. He'd play the game with Kiril as long as necessary. But he wasn't about to let their power cell, or their civilization, destroy the Midland.

Besides, he knew where the cell was, more or less. He'd tracked it down from his bodily reaction last night, and only uncertainty about Kiril's proximity kept him from taking it then.

Chapter 15

Joss's former commander had more drive and energy than he'd ever met in one person before. Restless when not fully occupied, Kiril seldom had enjoyed a decent night's sleep on the pod. But Joss expected a busy night, and since he didn't want interference, he plied his boss with a beer, noticeably stronger than Terran beers, followed by a heavy meal, then dragged him out on a brisk hike into the neighboring hills, using an ongoing narrative about their new planet as a lure.

As he'd hoped, by twilight Kiril was ready to retire to his room, exhausted for once.

Joss waited until full dark before he quietly departed. He collected the pack, then made his way across the ford to a shed half filled with hay, northwest of Stanstead.

Even with what he'd learned from last night's surreptitious exploration, he wasn't absolutely sure of his facts, but he knew, because of the cramp in his gut, that he had to be almost on top of the cell. He dropped the pack and got to work. After half an hour rummaging in the scratchy stalks in the dark, he closed his hand on it, buried in the hay.

The sultry night left him drenched in sweat by the time he brushed off as much hay and chaff as possible and stepped outside. The cell had triggered a cascade of cramps in his gut to go with a peculiar, empty sensation in his head, as if he'd left part of his brain behind. He couldn't even imagine how much worse it must be for the Weavers.

So perhaps it was because he wasn't thinking clearly that he walked right into Kiril's fist, aimed at his face.

Kiril was half a head shorter and lithe rather than heavyset, but his unexpected punch sent Joss reeling against the doorframe. Watching the shadowy, bearded figure every moment, he tossed the cell back into the haystack and straightened, rubbing his jaw.

"I don't fool easily, Sergeant."

"I'm moving the cell. To a secure place, and the fewer know about it the better, including you. It's done enough damage."

"And you claim not to believe in their Aura?" Kiril scoffed.

"I told you I'm not one hundred percent convinced. But I've seen the results."

"You aren't walking away from here with it."

"And you're not walking away alone."

Joss made a rapid recalculation. If he went into the hut, he'd lose track of Kiril, and his instinct warned against that. The best bet was to get both of them, and the cell, to Stanstead. "It's not worth fighting over who carries it, but don't expect to leave with it, except with me."

He stepped aside to allow Kiril to enter the shed. His eyes never leaving Joss, he felt around until he located the cell.

Joss blocked him at the door. "I'm serious, sir. Once we're at the lodge, we'll figure out how to deal with it."

"You're willing to sit up all night and guard it?"

"I am."

"Let's move." Kiril's capitulation was a little too swift, a little too smooth. He elbowed past Joss and set out on a narrow trail cutting through the forest.

"At least put the damn thing in the pack," Joss shouted. Kiril ignored him. With barely enough starlight filtering through for Joss to see, he hurried in Kiril's wake. The man moved like a cat through the trees.

"Where does this go? I don't know this track."

"Stanstead. That's what you wanted, isn't it?"

After ten minutes or so, they reached the bank of the river, a deep, dark stretch flowing swiftly toward the ford.

Joss realized with a start what Kiril planned. He grabbed for his arm, but an instant too late. Kiril leapt into the river and disappeared.

Overland, unsure of his way, Joss knew he'd never reach the ford in time. His swimming was still rudimentary at best, but he muttered a curse, dropped the pack, and followed Kiril into the river.

The rough current pummeled him, sucking at his feet. Beyond his limited skill, he thought as he surfaced, sputtering.

He'd watched other men swimming, studied their arm and leg movements. While he lacked technique, the river itself would move him forward. All he had to do was stay afloat. Not much of a plan, but the best he could do, given the critical urgency of keeping up with Kiril.

And when he caught him, he thought with a savagery foreign to him, he'd beat the crap out of him.

A passing notion; the ache in his jaw reminded Joss why he avoided fights. Then the current snatched him, and the challenge of staying afloat and in the center of the turbulent river absorbed his mind and his muscles.

At the ford the river was three times as wide and shallow enough to wade through. Relieved to get out of the water, he scouted both banks in the dark before finding a wet track heading toward Stanstead. Joss followed, wringing out his tunic as he half walked, half jogged, his sandals squelching, relying on his familiarity with the path to move rapidly.

At least the river had flushed the last of the hay.

Half way to Stanstead he rounded a bend and caught a glimpse of a shadow ahead. It disappeared to the right. With his eyes adapted to the dark, it didn't take him long to spot the break in a hedge where Kiril had left the trail. Joss shimmied through the narrow gap and paused. The corn stood eye height, but by standing on tiptoe he tracked a rustling in the stalks.

He wove between the corn plants, watching their tops for movement that shouldn't be there and making no effort to disguise his advance.

As Kiril approached the far southern edge of the field, Joss heard voices.

"Hey, what's that?"

"Wait just a minute there."

"Grab him, Steve."

A thump.

"Damn. It's one of them strangers."

Joss recognized the voice and called out, "Don't let him get away!" Then he plunged through the corn.

The two men had taken him at his word, and his arrival interrupted a three-way scuffle. But holding onto Kiril proved to be a challenge. If Joss were a betting man, he'd wager Kiril, revealing himself as a born street fighter, would win it.

That couldn't happen. He grabbed Kiril by the back of his tunic and hauled – and noted the woof of relief from the man underneath him. "Sorry, sir," he said. He spun Kiril around, landed a punch to his midsection, then another to his jaw. Kiril doubled over and collapsed to the ground. The local man stood, somewhat shakily. Panting, Joss and the locals eyed each other until Joss broke from their uneasy group and searched the ground for the cell, locating it a row into the field. He retrieved it, then turned to the men. "I apologize, but it was necessary."

"We ought to haul you both up," the man who'd been on the bottom grumbled. "Whadaya suppose the town's gonna eat all winter, you go trashing the crops?"

"I'll make it up, if I can, but right now I have to get my colleague to Stanstead. Will you help me?"

"And why should we think you're any better 'n that one?"

He reminded himself that these guys were as frustrated as he was. "Ask Marla. She knows what's going on."

"You're good with the cows," the man named Steve conceded. "I reckon that counts in your favor. I'll carry that for you, if you want." He nodded at the gold box.

"I'd be grateful." Shifting Kiril promised to be challenge enough.

Recovered from the dustup, the other man said, "I'm staying here. No telling what other varmints are out wandering."

Joss stood over his former commander, who still lay on the ground, retching. "We have a walk ahead. Get up."

"You'll pay for this." Kiril's voice sounded strangled, but even so Joss detected impotent fury in the words.

"That could be, sir. But for now, we're going to Stanstead. And I'm dealing with the cell." Joss hauled him to his feet. Kiril was unsteady, but stayed upright.

He followed Steve, supporting Kiril, his wet sandals chafing as their little procession made its way toward town.

They stopped in the plaza, where Joss settled Kiril on the low stone wall surrounding the well. "Would you track down the mayor?" he asked Steve. "Tell her I need backup. And give her that." He gestured at the box in Steve's hand.

"She's not the most amenable to being woken up in the middle of the night."

"She's expecting this."

A tray holding small mugs sat on the wall. While he waited he worked the pump and passed a cup to Kiril, then drank himself. The water had a strong flavor such as he'd never experienced on Terra, where water came from the condensers and tasted of nothing at all. He was developing a taste for the stuff.

Kiril was silent, but Joss felt the waves of rage pouring off him.

"I'm sorry, sir. You didn't leave me any options."

"Getting over your fear of water, I take it?" Kiril's voice dripped with frustration and bitterness.

"Not so much a fear as unfamiliarity. That wasn't fun, though. A good strategy on your part."

"You've been busy."

"Yes, sir."

When Marla appeared, Joss laid it out. "The cell disappears tonight. He stays here."

She asked no unnecessary questions. "Steve's gone back to the fields. I need to get hold of one or two people."

"Two's better."

Kiril's snort might almost have been an aborted laugh.

She left, and came back with a man and a woman. "You may return to your room in the men's lodge," she said to Kiril. "The windows are too small to provide an escape route. But I require a commitment from you to cause no trouble. If you refuse your word, you'll spend the night in our jail. Trust me, you're better off at the lodge."

She and Kiril stared each other down. Marla won. "Very well," he said with dignity. But he shot Joss a look that promised a nasty retribution.

They watched Kiril leave with the guards, then she handed him the power cell. "This is what's been causing the disruption? It's heavier than it looks."

He nodded. "It's good that so few Weavers are here. That thing gives me the creeps."

"Do you want someone else to carry it?"

"I'll be okay." He gave her a sad smile.

"Do what you need to do." She put her hands on his arms and squeezed. "And good luck."

"Thanks. I just hope the plan works."

He stopped by a barn and grabbed whatever he could find by way of a container. It turned out to be a leather bucket used for hauling fodder. Then he left Stanstead's lantern light and made his surreptitious way to his stash of tools, where he filled the bucket with dirt and snuggled the cell into it, burying it as well as he could. The relief wasn't complete, but was instantaneous. Then he gathered up the pick, shovel, and water flask, and plunged into the darkness of the countryside.

Another hot morning. Joss had spent most of the night securing the power cell. What was left went to deciding how to approach Kiril. In the end, he decided on up-front honesty as his best, possibly his only, option.

The guard was gone, and Kiril's door was ajar. He knocked and went in. "Good morning, sir."

Kiril scowled. Standing stiffly upright, he commanded the room, despite his bare feet. He'd bathed and changed; his hair was still wet. The place was immaculate, the bed tightly made.

Got more sleep than I did, Joss thought.

Kiril strode to the window in the far wall before turning to face Joss. His voice was icy, but masking an underlying ferocity.

"I don't believe we have anything to say to each other, beyond that when a ship does arrive from Terra, I'll see you hanged."

"Perhaps," Joss conceded. "Let's get breakfast. They usually serve eggs."

"Under guard? No, thanks."

"The guard's gone. You're free to come and go as you please. Sandals still wet?"

"Damned uncomfortable."

Joss agreed; his own sodden footwear had rubbed blisters during his long hikes in the night. "We'll turn them in and pick up new pairs before we eat."

"Isn't your plan to keep me under lock and key?"

"Don't be ridiculous." Between the fight yesterday and serious sleep deprivation, Joss had little tolerance for Kiril's petulance. "I needed to be alone."

"Why? I question your commitment, Sergeant."

He'd hoped to avoid plain talk before breakfast, but what the hell. Taking into account Kiril's mood, he didn't expect the day to improve. "Your first loyalty is to Terra. I see that, it's part of what made you a good commander. But we're not going back, you're not my superior anymore, and I won't let the cell be used as a bargaining chip."

"And that's your opinion of me."

"That you'd use it against them? Pretty much, yeah. You said as much, don't forget. But our loyalties have changed, or at least mine have."

Kiril crossed to the bed and sat on the mattress, his face a mask. Joss thought he slumped a little. He waited out the fragile silence.

"You did the same as me, in a sense." Kiril's voice was subdued, as if forcing himself to reveal a shameful secret. "We both clawed our way up the ranks. This mission's been my sole focus for years. For me it meant status, possibly making general. Proving I had what it takes. Do you know how hard it is to let that go?"

Joss sensed a sea change in the other man and stayed quiet.

"I'm sure there's a good life to be had here, and a lot we don't understand," Kiril continued. "But their Aura... that airy-fairy stuff flies in the face of our technology. I'm not ready to concede it's real."

"But your leg, and the burns. By rights, you should be dead."

"That's blunt."

"But true."

"So the most you're willing to do is play the odds. Terra might or might not send an exploration pod, or a ship full of settlers, but we can't count on rescue."

"More or less, yes. I plan to spend the rest of my life here. Make a contribution."

Kiril stood and returned to the window, which looked over the bustling plaza. "I want that cell, Joss."

"You won't get it. It's more dangerous than you realize. Last night's work was shielding, not just hiding it. Most people can't tell the difference, but for the Weavers it's a form of dying. Like how Willow reacted at the crash site." Although Kiril probably had no recall of that time, it was etched in Joss's memory.

Kiril sighed. "What's next?"

Joss shrugged. "Offhand, I'd say sandals, then breakfast."

He led the other man down a couple of side streets to the textile center, where they dealt with the sandals. Neither of them spoke until they returned to the plaza.

"I'm troubled by how much this energy stuff means to you," Kiril said. "I gave you more credit."

Joss heard his former commander's confusion, but didn't reply immediately. Instead, he watched the activity swirling around them. People at the well, heading toward the dining hall, on their way to work, kids everywhere. He'd debated with himself when to admit his own connection to the energies. Given Kiril's words, the time had come. Besides, too many knew for it to remain a secret. As they crossed the plaza Joss said, "As it turns out, sir, I'm one of them. I can sense the Aura."

They stopped at the door to the hall. "I refuse to believe that."

"That's why the cows. I understand them. I have a minor ability, nowhere near the strength of Willow or Dal, but I know when our cell is active. Not as powerfully, but it affects me, too."

Kiril stared at him as if he'd become subhuman. "We spent two years with that thing. It didn't bother you then."

"True. Either something's changed in me, or there was nothing to compare with. Until you're aware of the Aura, whatever the cell's radiating has no effect. And believe me, the Aura is real."

Kiril huffed a gust of air through his nose, signaling his disbelief.

"So I'm willing to help with a radio, but we need to come up with some other means of powering it. Concentrated solar, maybe. But the bottom line is, if another ship turns up, we'll deal with it then. It's out of our hands." He pulled the door open, gesturing Kiril to precede him.

They queued and carried heaping plates of eggs and bacon to an empty table, then he walked over to where Beatris sat. "How are things this morning?"

She beamed at him. "Same as always. Thank you."

"You're welcome. I'm glad to know it worked."

"If we can stop worrying about that – whatever it was – you'll be a hero."

He grinned at the thought of his supposed heroism. "The cell's secured, but temporary. You'd still be better off to neutralize it somehow."

Her smile dimmed. "Well, nothing's perfect. You've hurt your face. Come by after breakfast and I'll Heal it."

"Thanks, we both will."

At his own table Joss sat across from Kiril and reported. "The woman over there's a Healer. Your jaw must be as sore as mine. She'll fix us up." Although he'd pulled his punch, there had to be a bruise under the beard. He certainly felt it in his fingers.

"I'd rather not."

"Your call. Try the pastries. There's some kind of fruit in them. They're good."

Kiril stalked out of the hall before Joss finished his second cup of caff; the bitter stuff was growing on him, and after his sleep-deprived night, he needed its artificial energy boost.

Until he heard from the Motherhouse, he'd kick back in Stanstead, practice his swimming, hang out in the pastures with the cows and sheep – stupid animals, sheep. Learn all he could about the culture that had become his own. Mollify Kiril.

And try to figure out how to build a radio receiver.

Chapter 16

Willow sat near the back of the dining hall, the only room large enough to hold all the Weavers in residence at the Motherhouse, watching and listening as everyone told everyone else the best way to dispose of the power cell. Without consensus, the level of tension, even acrimony, was unprecedented.

Bryar sat on the far side with others of the water clan. He looked agitated, his usual tranquil face tight across the bones, his eyes narrowed. At least his element was safe from pollution by the cell. Nobody considered water a suitable medium for disposal, other than one flippant suggestion that they sink it in the western ocean. But the tides and currents, the impossibility of recovery should the plan fail, scuttled that idea.

Fire? A nasty, acrid smell had blanketed the crash site, but no smoke. How did it burn, without starting a conflagration? Greasy soot had coated the men and the area around the wreck. Anyway, the non-fire hadn't succeeded in destroying the power cell.

And fire brought on the specter of air. Who could predict what poisons fire might release? The air clan, including five of the six Scribes present, argued eloquently and forcibly against fire or any other strategy that risked polluting the air. Blowing it up, for instance.

And that left earth. More than half of the Healers were earth clan. At the moment, earth offered their only defense. Stones, boulders, and dirt now covered the cell, according to Joss, who had recruited Beatris to convey the message to the Motherhouse. The rubble proved to be an effective barrier so far; the Aura held as strong and stable as in the days before

Joss and Kiril had been so unexpectedly imposed on them. Nevertheless, Willow was uneasy. Using the land this way, leaving even a small patch of it in constant contact with the negating energies... warning bells clanged in her mind.

The others of earth clan agreed.

The debate dragged on, and Willow's thoughts chased themselves in circles. Everyone received an opportunity to express an opinion, but on a midsummer day when herbs came to their full potency in the sun, being trapped indoors proved a severe test to her composure.

The bell rang for an early supper. They'd been at it since mid-morning, with a couple of breaks thrown in, and the debate had become repetitive. Willow crossed her fingers that tomorrow she'd be free to harvest the herbs. Do her job. Even when it didn't disrupt the Aura, the cell disrupted her life.

Over the evening meal the three of them talked, she and Bryar and Quinn, but not with their usual ability to read each other. It was more as if they'd each determined to run roughshod over opinions and feelings. Quinn, especially, but then she'd always been the most abrasive, Bryar the gentlest.

She, the most stubborn, or so they told her.

"If you have any better ideas, let us know." Quinn said, her tone combative and laden with sarcasm. "Maybe take it up north and melt it in a forge? With an absolute guarantee of no repercussions."

"We'll come up with something," Bryar, ever the peacemaker, put in. He laid a calming hand on Quinn's forearm. "Not helpful, love."

She shook him off. "Minding our manners is the last thing we need. We need hard decisions, while you're hiding from the facts, and Wils can't think past dessert —"

Willow reared back, offended. "Not fair, Quinn. My concerns are as legitimate as yours. If I want a treat, maybe that just makes me more human. Lay off."

"Look," Bryar said.

Arwen came in with the Old Man. The two of them made their way through the buffet line and settled at a table a little distance away from the others, carrying on a whispered conversation.

"Now what? Secrets? That does it. I've had enough." Quinn threw down her napkin and stood.

Bryar grabbed her hand before she could storm off. "Let's go for a walk. This isn't like us."

"Losing our lives isn't like us, either," she snapped. But then she relented. "Okay, fine. Finish your dessert. I'll meet you out front."

Arwen called her before she'd taken three steps toward the hatch for dirty dishes. Quinn sent them a shrug, changed direction, and joined the elder two.

"What now?" Bryar was as much on edge as any of them, even if more skilled at holding his tongue.

"Fresh air has to be better. I doubt we'll get Quinn back, though."

Willow and Bryar finished their meals and struck off on a circuit of the Motherhouse valley, a familiar path that encircled many of the cultivated fields and followed the river as it wound around the east side of the complex. The walk helped calm her, as well as giving her a chance to hear Bryar's most recent, half-composed ballad. But it failed to release the nagging worry that their lives were off kilter, rocking unsteadily like a poorly constructed child's top. She doubted she'd escape the low-level dread besetting her until the cell was disposed of, sealed, destroyed... whatever it took to rid themselves of the thing.

The next afternoon, at the tail end of a hot day spent in the meadow, harvesting and processing healing herbs, Willow relaxed on the level place above the green. She was watching Bryar down below teaching their daughter trills on her flute when Quinn emerged from the Centra, her mouth in a tight line. She posted a notice outside the door, then climbed the slope and folded her long legs on the grass.

"Nothing worth going to check," she said. "Just a meeting tonight. Yes, there's a plan." She seemed anything but happy about it. "It's damn risky. Ezra agrees with you, Wils. We can't leave the thing buried. And we can't destroy it. That eliminates every possibility using our known technology. We're casting in the dark, here."

Bryar and Romarin moved on to a duet, while one of the older classes, soon to be divided into guilds, gathered around Beatris, who had spent the morning in the fields with Willow. The agriculturists from the village wheeled barrows of food to the dining hall. The sun had baked them all day, although clouds piled up in the sky now. Everything as it should be. Except the cell.

The cloud cover rolled over the sun, shading the late afternoon. Ominous, she thought, then mentally lectured herself not to construct absurd portents in her head.

"Can you tell me?" she asked.

"Sustainer of breath, convince me this is a good idea," Quinn muttered.

"Quinn?"

"Sorry." Quinn's fingers dug into the grass and uprooted a divot. She looked at it, surprised, and tamped it back into the earth. "I'm in a state. We've *never* risked using the energies this way. We don't even know if we can. And with no inkling of the ramifications."

"And?"

They both watched the activity on the green as they'd done hundreds of times over the years while they shared their joys and concerns, loves and animosities. Willow reached over and gave her friend a little shake. "Whatever it is, it isn't happening this minute."

"This is breaking a confidence, but I'll say it involves linking. Arwen will explain it after evening meal."

"When we're well fed and receptive, right?" Quinn's mood had affected Willow, and her reply held an edge of irony.

Quinn relaxed marginally and returned Willow's gentle shake, her mouth twisted in a semblance of a grin. "You're good for me. We'll deal, we always do. And most likely the three of us won't be involved."

Willow raised her eyebrows.

"They'll be looking for volunteers. Arwen and Ezra are developing a candidate list."

"You don't expect our names on it."

"For different reasons, no. But Willow, listen."

Willow cocked her head, letting her pale hair fall sideways in the still air.

"If one of us does get on that list, it'll be you. If it is, don't volunteer. It could be a suicide mission."

"You are not serious. Look." Irritated, Willow waved a hand at father and daughter with their flutes. "Romarin bids fair to be among the most powerful Healers we've ever seen. I've known it since she started working with me, when she was about three. She hardly needs the instruction, except formulary – and discipline," she added, grinning. "Do you think there's anything I wouldn't do to preserve this life for her? Despite the risk?"

"If it doesn't work, she'd be better off with a flesh-and-blood mama, rather than memories of a martyr."

"It has to work. This is our world at stake."

"Nevertheless, my argument's solid."

"So is mine, but thanks for trying to protect me."

Usually their standoffs resulted from differing premises based on their clan affiliations. This time they both had started from the same place, the honey-haired girl fingering her flute as Bryar coached her through an old dance tune.

There being no way to breach the impasse, Willow held her tongue, wondering when the list would be posted, and whether to expect her name to be on it.

Clouds still covered the sky, casting a weird, dark light over the green without the relief of rain. Bryar disliked mornings like this; he'd take pouring rain over this half-light casting ominous shadows on the day. The small scene across the green from him did nothing to ease his nerves, already exacerbated by the meeting last night.

Using templates to seal the power cell... the idea gave him shivers. Was it even possible to manipulate the Aura that way? To find the right weaves?

Ezra, Arwen, Quinn, and Dorcas, another Scribe, thought so.

He approached the Centra's main door cautiously. Only a fool stepped into the middle of a spat between Willow and Quinn.

Quinn saw him. "Lists are posted," she called, giving him no option but to join them.

"You can't stop me," Willow was saying. Bryar knew that expression on her face. She looked soft, but underneath her usual complaisance lurked a rock-solid resolve – in his less charitable moments, he thought of it as pig-headedness – and once she made up her mind, only irrefutable arguments, marinated in enough time for her to reconsider, ever swayed her.

Not for Quinn the gentle persuasiveness he favored. "Of course we can't," she said as he walked up. "But if you can't see it's stupid to —"

"Hi," he said, stopping Quinn before she launched into a torrent of words Willow wouldn't listen to anyway. He insinuated himself between the two women, these women he loved as a part of himself, and scanned the list of those eligible to volunteer for the seal-the-cell exercise.

Fifteen from the Healers' guild, four from Bards, three from Scribes, chosen from those resident at the Motherhouse. That made sense. Besides being the largest of the guilds, the Healers dug much more deeply into the Aura than the Bards, manipulated templates in more ways, understood more about the weaves. The Scribes, though... only ten members the last he'd heard, but surely they were all qualified. He looked the question to Quinn.

She shrugged. "Two are traveling. They eliminated the newest and the elderly. Then they took another couple of us off for good measure."

"You know why," Willow said. "You'll be head of council one day. They won't risk you."

"Ah." Quinn pounced. "You recognize the risk, at least."

"Even if I didn't, you've been harping on it since we got here." Irritation joined anger in Willow's voice. "As it happens, I spent most of last night working with others in earth clan, trying to isolate the root of our unease. That thing's poisoning the land. We're convinced of it. There's no choice."

"And you're on some kind of crazy self-sacrificing kick today," Quinn said.

Bryar tuned them out and turned his attention to the list. No surprise to find Willow's name, the way her powers grew with each passing year. Quinn's name was missing, although she was by far the most adept of the three of them at manipulating the energies. He agreed with Willow; she'd be protected as the heir apparent to Arwen. Within the next couple of years, by his reckoning.

He hadn't expected to find his name on the list and felt only gratitude that it wasn't there. He was no hero and never strove to boost his energetic connection to the Aura beyond what he needed for his work. A lover, not a fighter, Quinn had commented once.

The women continued bickering. "Volunteering for this is inviting your own death," Quinn said. "I have —"

"A premonition? Or information we lack?" he asked.

"Neither." Quinn shot him a look that told him to shut up. "Just an uneasy feeling. This is untried technology. Things could go wrong in ways we can't conceive of."

"As I understand it, I don't see how," Willow retorted. "But that's irrelevant, because I'm volunteering. We need eight. I won't let this fail because others are afraid. I won't allow the land to die because no one cared enough."

"You're speaking in unwarranted hyperbole," Quinn shot back.

"I am not. I am of earth. You are air, and you haven't got a clue. It will eat away at us until nothing's left. It's a threat to life." This irate, Willow would be deaf to argument or persuasion.

"You never liked burying it in the first place," Bryar said.

"Certainly not. And I was right."

"You can't prove it's spreading," Quinn said.

"It is. We found traces last night. But anyone with the ability to tune in to earth energy senses it."

"Don't do this, Wils. Please." Quinn was begging now, something he'd swear had never happened before.

"I expected your support," Willow threw at them. "But I will do this, with or without it." She yanked open the door to the Centra and stormed inside. Her footfalls echoed on the stone paving until she turned a corner and the walls absorbed the sound. The door slammed closed.

When Bryar faced Quinn, tears stood in her eyes, rare for his hard-headed, logical friend. He pulled her into a hug. Nearly as tall as he and no cuddler, he expected she'd put up with his efforts to comfort her, then politely back away. But this time, the strongest woman he knew shuddered against him, fighting off sobs. He cupped her face with his big hands and wiped her cheeks with his thumbs. Then he kissed her eyelids and whispered, "It's going to be okay. It has to be."

"By all that sustains us, I hope so," she said.

By all that sustains us, so do I.

"Perhaps more than eight will volunteer. She might still be excluded."

"Perhaps."

He could do nothing about the Aura, or Willow.

But he could support Quinn. She exerted such a dominant presence, it was easy to forget she was as vulnerable as any of them. This morning her dark skin shone in the strange overcast, and where he'd missed them the tear tracks stood out on her cheeks. He kept her close as they crossed the green together. He hoped to convince her to join him in one of the shared rooms in the guest lodge, to accept the release of loving. It was little enough, given the crises swirling around them, but that, at least, was his to offer.

Chapter 17

Willow sat in the conference room with the three men and four other women chosen – six Healers, one Bard, one Scribe. Most had reached their middle years, and all were confident workers of Auric weaves. The clans were equally represented, because their work would be done in a circle. Being most purely of earth, Willow was to anchor the northern, the earth position.

Ezra sat at the head of the table and said little, but missed nothing.

Arwen laid out the plan: to link, meld their individual workings, and release the resultant template to wrap and seal the power cell, hopefully forever. The group had spent the morning, as well as the previous afternoon, developing and mastering the weaves.

This was far from any use of a template they'd tried before, although all Weavers learned to link and build weaves during their training. Linking caused a serious drain on the one providing the supplementary energy, but this time there would be no secondary participant; the success of the scheme relied on balance, each direction equal to the others.

Next to her on her left, Dal represented earth and air, both organic and cerebral. On her right, in the northwest, was another Healer, a woman a decade older than Willow, whom she knew only slightly. Dorcas, the only Scribe, was to be in the southeast combining air and fire, logic fueled by passion. Martin, a Healer, held down the south, then came the single Bard in the southwest, a mix of passion and emotion. Not like Bryar, she mused, allowing her mind to wander for a moment. Although water predominated in his makeup, he carried the extra solidity of earth.

Her attention snapped back to the meeting. Arwen was laying out the plans for the afternoon, testing the weave on an object that didn't matter. If it went well, tomorrow they'd begin a trek via a seldom used route to a valley in the hills north of Stanstead, hiding their movements to keep the location of the cell secret, known only to those in the room and Joss.

The meeting broke up at long last. "Opinion?" Dal asked her as they made their way to the dining hall for a late lunch.

"I'm confident. It'll be hard, but it feels like a viable plan."

"Working on a buried object?"

"We'll find out this afternoon."

"I can think of a hundred things that might go wrong, but no reason to believe any of them will."

Willow grimaced. "The forced march to Stanstead worries me more. Trying to get there in three days – that is certain to use up whatever energy we have left."

"They won't let that happen." Dal squeezed her hand. "And it's a chance to see a part of the Midland none of us ever explores."

"True." More an animal track than an actual trail, there were no settlements along the northern route, so it allowed them to get to the power cell's location undetected.

Dal gave her a quick shoulder hug and walked off. With a plate filled with bean cakes and vegetables, she found a place on her own. She needed space, so when Quin entered the dining hall and looked around, Willow met her eyes and shook her head. Quinn joined another group, and Willow thanked all that sustained them that her friends understood her occasional need for solitude.

An hour later, fortified in body and mind, she gathered with the others in a natural field a quarter hour's walk from the Motherhouse. They grouped around an innocuous rock the size of two clenched fists together, partially buried in the soil.

"We'll seal it, then test it," Arwen said. "If it's movable, for instance. Martin's brought his dog along, so we can see how he reacts. But keep him away until we're done," she cautioned.

Martin, a thin, red-headed Healer, nodded. "He's tied up at the trailhead."

The Old Man appeared at the end of the path. He stood on the edge of the meadow with the dog and watched, but didn't approach.

"Let me remind you, if anyone is in distress, sink to your knees, and we stop immediately. Dorcas will monitor the weaves and give the signal to release the completed template onto the stone. Questions?"

There were none. As they formed a circle in their designated places, the stone in the center, Willow read a mix of excitement and trepidation from their faces and postures.

After joining hands, they entered the meditative state they learned as children, the one that best facilitated work with templates. Dorcas counted them in, and they began.

From within her trance, she gradually became aware of the currents flowing through her. She had never experienced this melding of directions before; she doubted any of them had. Free of conscious thought other than their shared intention, she sank into the flows, until it was impossible to distinguish herself from the energy coursing through her. Then she began weaving her part of the template.

Willow was swaying on her feet when she heard Dorcas begin the countdown to release. The words came to her from far away as she rounded up enough consciousness to perform the simple exercise they'd practiced.

When Dorcas shouted, "Now!" the woven energy flew up from their joined hands, then settled and condensed around the stone.

They dropped hands and sank onto the rough grasses and weeds in the field. "Ground," Arwen's voice commanded. "Give yourselves time to come back."

By working in the circle, they prevented any single directional energy from dominating the weave. But no matter the clan affiliation, they all turned to the earth when they exhausted their personal reserves and needed to recharge, or when they ventured so deeply in the Aura that it was hard to restore normal reality. Arwen passed out cakes and water; Willow accepted hers, hoping it would fend off the headache niggling at her temples.

After a while, Dal got to his feet and approached the stone. "I can sense it," he reported, "but it's not noticeable unless you're looking for it."

"Touch it." Quinn stood beside the Old Man. She must have arrived during their trancework.

Dal's fingers didn't quite make contact with the surface of the stone. "It's odd. Like an invisible film. I can't get through it."

Willow remained seated, as did several others. She expected to need every hour of the next three days to rebuild her reserves. Her hands explored the uneven ground and scrubby weeds.

My land. My clan.

"Shall we see what the dog does?" Arwen said.

Martin nodded but didn't rise, so the Old Man brought Martin's dog over. He sniffed around the circle but paid no attention to the rock, even when Ezra encouraged him toward it. Then he flopped down next to Martin and fell asleep.

"Does the protection continue underground?" Arwen asked.

Willow, along with Dal and the Healer to her right, closed her eyes. She felt an awareness of the other two as she allowed her consciousness to sink into the earth. After a brief pause, she nodded.

"Seems to," Dal said. He picked the stone up and moved his hand over the bottom. "Weaker there, though. We'll have to allow for that."

Arwen muttered, "Damn," under her breath, then surveyed them. "When you're ready, go to the Motherhouse and relax. Pack for the trip. I'll see you at evening meal."

She turned away and left with Ezra. Quinn hesitated, then followed them. The eight who made up the circle were in less of a hurry to rush off. Soaking in the earth energy, they'd all settled on the ground. For a time, no one spoke.

"Everyone okay?" Dorcas asked.

"As if I'd been hollowed out," Martin said.

"Same here," the Healer who'd been in the west agreed. "I'm empty."

Willow stood. "And wobbly, but I'll be better off if I walk. Is anyone ready to go?"

A group of Healers joined her, and they made their silent way to their lodge, Willow speculating to herself that the entire journey to the cell might not be adequate to recover from the experience.

Four evenings later, Joss trekked to the valley as he'd done three times before, waiting for them to turn up. Grateful that his training had included stealth, he took care not to be noticed, no mean feat for a man his size. When he arrived just before darkness engulfed the Midland, he found the small group huddled together in the south of the field – as far from the cell as they could get.

No one looked particularly happy.

Arwen spotted him and waved him over. Once he'd exchanged introductions and greetings, she filled him in on their plan.

"How long will this take? Are you doing it tonight?"

Arwen's gaze swept the others. "We'll wait until tomorrow at first light, when everyone's rested. This is a dangerous business, Joss. We require everyone at peak."

He dug into his pack and pulled out a bag of pastries. "I pinched these from the dining hall. Thought you might enjoy them. Over there you'll find a spring." He gestured to the northwest. "I've been using it. As far as I can tell it's pure. Is there anything else you need?" Returning to Stanstead, then coming back in the dark, didn't thrill him, but he'd do it.

The pastries generated muted enthusiasm. The Weavers looked worn out and ready for a night's rest.

Arwen shook her head. "Save the treats, folks. You'll be glad tomorrow, and we can't risk anyone noticing Joss pilfering more."

As he turned to leave, his eyes snagged on Willow. He'd been happy to see her here, surprising himself by the depth of it. He supposed it was relief at seeing a familiar face, since her participation in whatever they planned didn't make him happy in the least. The thinnest in the group, in the failing light she looked ethereal.

But that wasn't his call. They needed him to slip in and out of Stanstead, managing the logistics, nothing more. He understood that, but not the bolt of happiness that shot through him when he saw her again.

The next morning Joss sat with Arwen, Quinn, and Beatris, who had been included in the expedition as a precaution, and watched the circle that surrounded the rocks covering the cell. Those on the northern side stood slightly uphill of the others, and most of them balanced on the scree field. He estimated close to two hours since they had joined hands and linked, although he wasn't clear what that meant, and he read the strain on several of their faces and bodies. His immediate companions contributed to his own stress; he picked up on their worry.

He leaned over to Quinn and asked, "Should it be taking this long?"

"The trial lasted half an hour." She never took her eyes off the circle. "But this is different terrain, and the power cell, not a stone."

"The rocks shielding the cell may affect our ability to reach it," Arwen added. "Or there may be some effect on us we don't sense. Since it's buried, there's nothing to focus on."

"They know to signal problems," Quinn said. "But it worries me that—"

Without warning, the man in the southern position convulsed, a spasm so violent that his hands wrenched away from those on either side of him.

A millisecond later Willow's body jerked and her face emptied. She stood for several long seconds as if unaware of her surroundings before falling to the ground.

The circle broke up. None of the participants remained standing; most wore blank looks. Someone whimpered. Beatris ran to the convulsing man. Dal had been knocked backward by the force of whatever just happened; he pulled himself up and struggled on hands and knees across the rocks toward Willow. She'd gone straight down, then slumped forward and to her left. Her head struck a rock as she fell; she lay with her body twisted, motionless.

The Weavers collapsed, most not moving but looking more stunned than injured, but the woman on Willow's right emitted a thin wail of pain. Joss vaulted over them to get to Willow's side.

He knelt by her to feel for a pulse, and detected a faint thrum under his fingers. "I need help," he said to Dal. "I'm not sure she's breathing. Is anything broken? Can we move her?"

Dal moved his hands over Willow, not quite touching. Strain contorted the man's face, but he neither protested nor commented. After a short time, he nodded. "Try to support her head."

Joss got his arms under her and carried her to flatter ground across the valley, where he laid her on the field and began CPR. Dal, who had staggered after them, started to object, then subsided as he grasped Joss's actions.

Joss moved by instinct, his entire focus on Willow. He couldn't imagine this world without her in it.

After an eternity she gasped and coughed, and her whole body seized up before relaxing. But at least her chest moved, taking in oxygen.

"I'm taking over," Dal said. "Keep everyone away." He trembled and had no color, but he put his hands on her head.

Joss risked looking around. A few Weavers had shifted off the rocks to the grass; a couple were able to sit, but none stood. Arwen and Quinn moved among them, dispensing drops from a small bottle. Another Healer crawled from person to person, speaking quietly, resting her hands on each one in turn. An eerie quiet blanketed the field, punctuated by an occasional moan.

Beatris came over. She watched for a moment, then Dal gestured for her to return to the man who had convulsed, now lying limp on the ground.

She shook her head. "Gone." She touched his shoulder. "Link if you need to," she said.

Dal returned to his trance. Beatris sat next to him, shifted to get comfortable, then was still.

Willow's limbs were intact. Her hands, though...

Joss walked over to the woman who'd been on Willow's right and now stared into the distance in a state of shock. He bent down to turn her left hand toward him. It had sustained burns so severe that there was charring in places. Dal's right hand must be the same, yet he hadn't hesitated to use it in Willow's healing.

And Willow's hands...

"Joss." Quinn's imperious voice shot across the circle. When he looked up, she said, "We need transport to Stanstead."

"I can get a cart, but we'll have to carry them to the trailhead."

"How long will it take?"

He checked the position of the sun. "After lunch. I'll bring food."

"Thanks. It'll help." She dismissed him and turned to the Weavers.

"Pass out the pastries," he said.

Quinn looked startled, as if she'd forgotten the bag of treats, then nodded and crossed the field to the small mound of their packs and supplies.

Joss surveyed the group. By his reckoning, only two of them needed the cart, Willow and the man who... by *gone*, did she mean *dead?* He glanced at the red-headed Healer.

Yes, that's what she meant. Joss knew somehow that he wouldn't be getting up again.

The others might be unsteady, but they'd be able to walk by the time he returned. Willow was in the best hands possible. Nodding to himself, he rose and jogged across the field to the trail.

A minute later he heard feet pounding behind him. Quinn drew up beside him, scowling, and said, "I've been ordered to accompany you."

"Why?"

"To make sure you do what you say you'll do? You're not my favorite person right now."

She strode ahead of him. He read anger in every step.

"I started her breathing," he said. "I gave her breath back."

"And took Martin's away," she shot at him.

They didn't speak for the rest of the walk to Stanstead.

Joss wasn't surprised when Kiril appeared at the barn door. He'd caught sight of his former commander off and on over the last few days, but they hadn't spoken. They both had some adjusting to do.

"Planning a picnic, Sergeant?"

Joss heard the sarcasm in his voice, and cold rage battled against a lifetime's deference to his superiors. "Willow's injured," he snapped, "and a few others."

"What happened?"

"The Aura —"

"Are you about to give me another song and dance about the glories of the Aura, like some beneficent god who's come to heal all wounds? Because if you are —"

Joss glimpsed Quinn's outraged expression. "No. I'm telling you that today the Aura killed a man."

Kiril's eyes locked on his, hard. "Are you serious?"

"I saw it."

Kiril paled under his beard. His demeanor changed instantly. As the commander of their ship, he'd always been pragmatic; now, he moved straight to the immediate concern, rather than asking for particulars. "What do you need?"

Quinn shot him a look approaching pure hatred. "Food. Fast, and enough to feed eleven, plus yourself. We could use another able-bodied man."

"Give me fifteen minutes," Kiril said

"I'm coming with you."

Kiril wheeled and left them, Quinn on his heels.

Joss sighed. The moment the circle fell apart, he'd known that any hope of keeping their plan secret had disappeared. Hell, by tonight the town would host an exhausted group of Weavers dealing with death and injuries.

Then there was Kiril. Joss couldn't think of any way to keep him from figuring out that the gathering had something to do with the power cell. His ex-commander was no fool. He'd realize the scree slope provided the perfect cover.

Kiril and Quinn returned as he finished harnessing the donkey. "Let's get moving," Quinn said, and heaved a pair of baskets into the cart. Kiril followed suit. Joss led the donkey out of the barn. Ten minutes later they cleared the town and struck out on the path leading toward the field.

Quinn strode ahead of them. Joss guessed that she needed to be alone with her thoughts. "Just so you know," he said to Kiril quietly, "any idea that the Aura is a figment of their imagination, or mass hysteria, or anything like that – what I saw tells me that this thing is more powerful than we dreamed."

"Report, Sergeant."

"One Healer is dead, and it damn near killed Willow. Some serious burns. We can't afford to make light of this, Kiril. We don't understand its rules... the implications are scary."

Kiril's face was serious. "I regret Willow was injured. Isn't she supposed to be a master at working with this energy?"

"This was a new technique to them." One day he'd tell Kiril what they'd been trying to do, probably, but he chose not to bring it up now. "I don't know what kind of shape she'll be in when she wakes up, but she won't be doing any healing for a while."

"I'm sorry."

Kiril sounded sincere. To survive in this world, they had to adapt, without the support of their old structure. That couldn't be easy for a man trained from childhood for a senior position in the corporation or the military. Being from the upper management caste, humility didn't come easily to him. But he'd find a place here, sooner or later. His willingness to trek to the meadow was at least in part to hunt for the power cell, Joss had no doubt. But his concern for Willow marked a positive step toward becoming a productive member of this new society.

He trudged along, leading the donkey, his stomach knotted with worry about what they might find when they got back to the site of the disastrous circle.

Chapter 18

Bryar's mood was as black as the midnight skies over the land on a clear night, made worse by this night being not clear but one of light rain colder than it should be, with Summer Solstice only four nine-days past. It soaked through his tunic to chill his back and shoulders. Overhead, shimmery dark gray clouds promised a change from drizzle to downpour.

Nor was his mood improved by the man who stepped out of the shadows as he crossed the plaza on his way to the guest lodge. He'd find Quinn there, since the Scribes didn't maintain their own accommodation in Stanstead.

Joss towered over him like a menace. Bryar recognized his own fanciful mind at work, because Joss had never shown himself to be other than watchful and helpful. Still, his mood soured further.

"What do you want?" he spat as the other man fell into step beside him.

"How is she?"

He forced the words out through clenched teeth. "In a coma, and likely to die."

There was a pause. "No. That can't happen." Joss sounded as if the rain and humidity had flattened the resonance in his voice.

"A nice piece of work. She saves you, then you repay her by killing her."

"I get that you're bitter," Joss said. "But this isn't my fault. Blame it on that damn fool scheme you people devised."

Bryar was silent, unwilling to admit the truth of Joss's words.

"Surely there's something they can do. I've seen the power of your healing methods."

"You don't have the foggiest idea, do you?" Bryar stopped and faced the other man across the darkness. "You have no concept of the Aura, or how it sustains our world. What your box is destroying – it's everything to us. The health of our land, our pattern for how to live." He fought to keep his voice steady; the loss of the Aura would be as devastating, in a different way, as losing Willow. The light touch of her mind, her skin against his... he drew himself back to the present. "The energies fuel our lives. You swagger into our world as if it doesn't matter, with no true awareness of what you've done."

"You think that? That I don't care about what's happened? I felt it. I know... well, not enough. But I know."

"Go away," he said with concentrated rudeness. "Just leave us alone."

"I apologize for intruding. But I had to know."

"Now you do."

As Bryar turned into the arch leading to the lodge, Joss faded into the night as silently as he had appeared.

He had thought she might be in bed, but he found Quinn in the small kitchen tucked in a corner of the common room. She stood at the cookfire, unsmiling. "When did you get here?"

"Not long ago. I brought Romarin."

"You knew?"

He shook his head. "No, but Mari did. She had us on the road by noon."

"You must have traveled day and night."

"She's her mother's daughter," Bryar confirmed. "But at least I have an excuse for being up at this hour. You should be asleep. You can't function if you drive yourself to exhaustion." Quinn's brown skin didn't show dark circles under her eyes, especially in lanternlight, but he detected a sag in her features and wondered when she last had slept.

"So you heard what happened?"

"I talked to Dal. There's this hollow place in my mind where Willow should be, but isn't. Damn, Quinn, this scares me."

"Me, too."

Her voice was small. He crossed the room and pulled her into his arms.

When she regained her composure, she said, "Kicked you out, did they?"

Bryar grimaced. "Dal said my energy wasn't helping."

She nodded. "Too much anger."

"Mari stayed with her, though."

"Is that wise?" Quinn twisted free and returned to the cookfire, where a bubbling stew reawakened Bryar's appetite after three days of dry rations. Of Quinn, Willow, and himself, Quinn wielded the best kitchen skills.

"She's as stubborn as Willow, and she's been a Healer since she was four years old. She may be a long way from finishing her training, but Dal's with her." Bryar moved to the table and sat, propping his chin on his hands as he watched Quinn.

"That's all right, then. He's a sensible man." She busied herself in the kitchen.

"He told me he'd make her a bed in the healing room when she ran out of steam. We passed Arwen and the others on their way home earlier today. I'm sorry about Martin."

"Not half as sorry as I am. I approved the scheme. I believed it would work."

"You tried to talk Willow out of it. You doubted."

"Nothing that stood up against Arwen. I wish I'd tried harder. How is she?"

"Dal says no change. That buffoon crossed the plaza with me. We'll rue the day those two landed here."

"We already do."

"He claims he felt it, when Martin broke the circle."

"He may be telling the truth. With that whisperer thing, Joss might connect more deeply to our life than we choose to admit. And he's forging a home here, although what sort remains to be seen. Not the other man, however." Quinn took up a cloth and wiped her hands, her movements slow and controlled. She picked up a bowl, put it down again.

"I'll invite them to dine," she said.

"You're joking. At *midnight*?"

"Not in the least. This whole mess hinges on that damn cell, and Joss is the one best positioned to explain it. If they know anything that can help us, we can't afford to waste an opportunity to learn from them. It won't help Willow, but it might save our world."

"Then talk to him another time. I refuse to be in his presence tonight. Not with Willow — " He broke off, unable to continue.

"You can be an idiot," she stated coolly. Not for her to show emotion; she fought every lapse into feeling. Bryar read her state of mind from her unconscious actions, her restless motion as she paced, the way she kept wiping her hands against her thighs. In normal circumstances, Quinn was a model of stillness.

But he was too tired to be polite. "And you can forget your constant quest for information. If Joss could help Willow, he would have by now."

"He cares about her, and you don't want to share her." Quinn's pacing took her to the summoning cord by the door. She tugged it, and they waited in silence, hovering too close to an argument to risk words, until a messenger kid appeared. "Find the man Joss," she instructed. "Tell him – no, *invite* him – to join us for a meal. Kiril, too, if they are together."

"Yes, ma'am." The boy ran off into the darkness.

"I don't like it."

"Nor do I. But brooding won't help. Taking positive action might."

As usual, Quinn spoke the truth. Bryar recognized it. Nothing obliged him to be happy about it, though. Since Kiril and Joss had invaded their world, they'd been thrust into a maelstrom of life-changing events alien to his quiet lifestyle.

The two men appeared a quarter hour later. Odd, Bryar thought, that they also would be awake in the night. They seemed no more at ease in each other's presence than he and Quinn were after their cross words.

Quinn waved them to seats around the table as she ladled up the stew. Before she joined them, she leveled her steely look at Joss. "We require information."

"I could do with some myself." He leaned forward, forearms on the table. "There's too much I can't figure out. It concerns the Aura, and the way our power cell disrupts it, but I don't understand why, or where your energy field comes from."

Quinn sat and pointed her spoon at Joss. "That power cell's your doing," she said, her voice hard.

"The Aura is integral to life," Bryar added. "It's not merely the Weavers, it's everything. Years of training only scratches the surface. It simply *is*."

"Although we can't be certain it's always been here," Quinn added, addressing Bryar. "Our history doesn't go back so far. And the legends say nothing, as you yourself know."

"No?" Kiril, who had been eating and listening, rested his spoon in his bowl and swallowed before speaking again. "How far back do you go?"

"Three hundred ninety years," Quinn told him. "We are now in the third season of the three hundred ninety-first year."

"That's it?" Kiril said. "What happened before that? You must have creation myths. You didn't just materialize here."

Quinn shrugged. "Maybe we did."

"That aura of yours doesn't hold the answers?" Kiril's gaze glanced off Quinn's for a moment – animosity bouncing between them like an animate thing – then he looked away and returned his attention to the stew.

Bryar had yet to take a bite. Aromas from the meat and barley had set his juices flowing earlier, but now his stomach resisted food, as if it had shrunk to the size and hardness of a dried pea. The other two men, however, ate with full appreciation of Quinn's efforts.

"This is irrelevant," she said. "What is relevant is the nature of your box, that *cell* you brought to the Midland. Because so far we've been unable to contain it."

"It's contained now." Kiril's eyes locked with Quinn's. "The scuttlebutt around this place is you've got your mystical powers back."

"They believe it's poisoning the earth," Joss put in quietly. "They can't leave it where it is. We have to help them control it."

Kiril and Quinn exchanged glares laden with distrust. "*We* don't have to do a damn thing," he said.

"Life could become awkward for you if you don't," she shot back.

"Look." Kiril settled back, as if preparing to deliver a lecture. "When we started hearing about the Aura, we assumed it was smoke and mirrors. I concede we were wrong, but you can't tell me how it works, can you? After how many years of your culture, you still haven't found any answers. So no, we're not obliged to help you. Our purpose here is to prepare the way for the rest of our people when they turn up. That should be your priority, too, because this Aura thing is unlikely to survive our civilization. Hell, it can't even withstand our power cell."

The man's tone left Bryar ready to punch him, throw him out into the night, arrange a fatal accident... He pulled himself back. However arrogant the bastard might be, Quinn was right. They needed him, or at least needed to keep him close.

In the meantime, Bryar could almost see the shift in Quinn's mind. "Tell me about this civilization of yours." At last she took a bite of the stew, but he suspected a show of nonchalance rather than appetite.

Kiril fell silent. Joss, however, put down his spoon and addressed Kiril in a slow, controlled voice. "I think you're wrong. Whatever energies are at work on this planet, we need to learn to live with them."

Kiril's face was all hard planes. "The best ways to utilize local resources, right? Go for it, Sergeant. You're capable of being logical and objective, your infatuation with the Aura notwithstanding. That's why they selected you for this mission, in spite of —"

"My caste, Commander? You can say it. I'm not likely to forget."

Kiril said nothing. His spoon tapped a tattoo on the edge of his bowl.

Quinn watched the interchange with interest. She'd be filing this tidbit about the thing called *caste* for future inquiry, no doubt.

"We must speak of your box," she said. "Your cell. What it is, what kind of energy it creates, the effect it has. It's possible your knowledge will give us a clue about what happened to Willow. Because you're right, we don't understand the energies we work with daily. And bear in mind, if the land dies, you die with it." She reached across the table and briefly put a hand on Kiril's, stopping the irritating tapping. He looked down, surprised.

Bryar noted a tightening of Joss's features when Quinn mentioned Willow. Interest or guilt? The other one, Kiril, wouldn't know the meaning of guilt.

"Have you got something to draw with?" Joss asked.

Quinn rose without comment and rummaged in the cabinet under the windows. She straightened a minute later with a handful of pens, an ink bottle, and a sheaf of paper seconds that still had one clean side.

Joss frowned at the pen, picked it up and balanced it in his hand. "This is the first I've seen here of paper or pens." He dipped the tip in the inkwell and began to sketch, sinuous curves, adding explanations along the way.

The others leaned over the drawings as they emerged from Joss's hand, even Kiril who presumably was familiar with the workings of the cell. Stew sat forgotten; eventually Bryar, struggling to keep up with the explanation, cleared the bowls from the table. A candle gutted and earned only an annoyed glance. His back began to ache and his head to spin as the hour grew later and Quinn pumped for ever more information.

Finally, Joss laid down the pen. "That's it. The fundamentals of energy waves."

"Thank you," Quinn said.

"Don't tell me you really understood him." Kiril leaned back, tipping his chair onto its back legs, and smirked at her.

Quinn's kept her voice level, refusing to rise to his bait. "Not all of it. I've seen remnants of these concepts in the Aura, but I've never been able to interpret them. Whether it will be of any use now…"

"A bloody uneducated aerospace engineer," Kiril muttered.

Bryar started to speak but thought better of it. Quinn used templates in ways alien to both him and Willow. She kept secrets and took unnecessary risks, going so deeply into the Aura. But she allowed nothing to come between her and her quest for information.

Joss's discourse had consumed the few remaining hours of the night and, as far as Bryar was concerned, accomplished little other than distracting his exhausted mind from Willow. The room fell silent. Quinn rose to make a pot of tisane and arrange a tray of cheese and fruits. The two strangers looked at each other and away again as if neither understood the other, much less the dynamic they found themselves in.

Bryar picked up the tray to carry it to the table, then froze. A subtle shift barely brushed against his consciousness. His gaze flew to Quinn. It had touched her, too, there was no mistaking the sudden hope in her face.

She nodded, a short, terse movement.

"Come on." He shoved the platter at a bewildered Joss, and the two of them bolted, abandoning their guests.

Dal, gray with fatigue in the dim pre-dawn light, blocked their way at the door of the healing room. "You three," he said with a hint of exasperation. "Bonded like littermates. Only one of you can see her for now, whoever's calmest. Her recovery is not yet certain."

"You go," Bryar said. "I'm the furthest possible from calm."

Quinn hugged him. "Do what you do best," she murmured, then vanished through the curtain. Her voice filtered out into the pre-dawn, then, sleepily, Mari's. Dal gave him a nod and followed Quinn. The heavy curtain fell into place.

The rain had stopped. Bryar took his agitation into the Healers' courtyard, where he stood for a moment under the clouds before he whispered words to concentrate the energy around the healing room.

Sustainer of life, send your net of healing to support us as we restore our friend to life. Sustainer of beauty, maintain us in all that is good and joyful.

A rim of light edged the eastern horizon. The Aura swung overhead, full and strong and beautiful, its colors shimmering azure and green against the sky, weaving protection and care. Its unique gift to him, to be able to see its shifting moods and hues.

Sheltered under the eaves, the bench by the door to the healing room was dry. Bryar settled on it and pulled out the pocket flute he carried everywhere. A single bird sounded a note, which he used as the basis for an extemporaneous composition. The notes danced from his lips, borne from the wood of the flute into the air.

His music carried its own freight of healing and love, but did little to assuage his unease. Willow might be awake at last, but she still hadn't filled the place in his consciousness where he expected to find her. It was as if some piece of her was missing.

Chapter 19

Midway through their second day on the road, Bryar caught up with Quinn and Beatris, leaving Dal to lead the donkey cart carrying Willow back to the Motherhouse. "What do you think?" He didn't bother to keep the worry from his voice.

"She's grieving," Beatris said.

Because Willow's connection to the Aura had vanished, as if it had been surgically excised from her mind.

"I agree." Quinn trudged along; she'd never hidden her dislike of traveling from place to place, and looked forward to reaching the Motherhouse, two days hence, with single-minded focus. "She doesn't know how to relate to us. And she doesn't believe we can fix it. Hell, I'm not so sure myself."

Was it fixable? From Willow's few comments, Bryar was skeptical. This differed from her experience at the crash site, she'd told them before they left Stanstead. There, her loss of Aura connection had been like an impenetrable barrier. She'd never doubted its presence, but had been unable to touch it. Now, she experienced what must be the norm for almost everyone in the Midland. He couldn't even imagine that level of emptiness.

Behind them, the donkey cart halted. He turned to see Dal give Willow a hand to step down. Progress of a sort; while she had mostly recovered from her physical wounds, she still wore light bandaging around her hands and hadn't walked at all yesterday. He left the two women and joined them as Mari danced up. Mari was nearly Willow's height, and he wondered how tall she would be when fully grown. His daughter glowed, her skin tanned, her hair catching the sun. She'd made a crown of field daisies and placed it on Willow's head.

"Thank you," Willow said without enthusiasm.

As usual, Mari bubbled over with the joy of discovery. "We passed a patch of baneherb, at least I'm pretty sure that's what it is. It looks so different covered in these pink flowers and—"

"Not now, Romarin."

Bryar heard the impatience in Willow's voice.

So did Mari. Her excitement drained away. "Oh. I'm sorry. I only wanted to..." Her voice trailed off.

He put his arm around their daughter. "Show Dal, why don't you? He might tell you some other uses for it."

With a look at Willow, Dal handed him the donkey's lead rope and walked the downcast girl to the plant – and out of earshot.

"That wasn't necessary," Bryar said. She was never short with Mari. Never. Mari was a loving, cheerful spirit and the light of their lives. "There's no reason to inflict our problems on her."

"My problem. It's nothing to do with you."

"You can't believe that." Bryar sighed and brushed her cornsilk hair from her face. "It's going to work out. You'll see."

Willow turned on him. "Why do you expect me to act as if my whole life isn't forfeit?" As she spoke, her voice rose. He stopped, forcing the donkey to halt as well. Ahead of them, Quinn and Beatris looked back, frowning. "Just imagine my future. I could become a hedge healer or an archivist, like they wanted me to be in the first place. Work in a laundry or a dining hall. The possibilities are endless." She dodged him and circled the cart.

He dropped the donkey's lead and followed her, grabbing her arm. "Stop it," he hissed. "Yes, you should mourn. But damn it, you will *not* hurt our daughter."

She reared back as if he'd slapped her. Then she dissolved in tears.

The rare times Willow cried, she left him with only one option. He gathered her up and held on for dear life, all the while kicking himself. He'd been a fool. She faced a bleak reality and didn't need encouraging, hollow sentiments. Their determined cheer, assuming everything would be fine, might be a total lie.

She pounded on his chest, pushing to get away. Then gave up and sagged against him.

"I'm so sorry," he whispered as her sobs eased.

"I'm afraid." Her voice broke as she forced words out.

"I know. But we stick together. Okay?"

She straightened and revealed the depth of her bleakness. "You and Quinn won't want me around, now that I'm not a Weaver anymore."

"Stop that. We aren't going anywhere. I can't imagine any other possibility, and you shouldn't either." He palmed the tears from her cheeks; his eyes held hers.

With a choked sigh, she broke away and turned from him, walking back toward Mari and Dal. He heard her say to Mari, "It's okay. Tell me about it." By way of apology, she touched their daughter's shoulder.

Relief flooded Mari's face as she picked up her chatter, right where she had left off. Dal gave Willow an assessing look, then joined Bryar. Willow walked with Mari, listening attentively until the unaccustomed exercise tired her, and Dal helped her back into the cart.

Deeper in the hills than Stanstead, the Motherhouse complex stood on rocky land. Few fields bore crops, although sheep and goats were plentiful. Willow and Quinn had lived here for eight formative years while their teachers forged them into competent Weavers. The wild landscape was imprinted in the marrow of their bones, Willow reflected as they made their way from the Motherhouse to the river. The tumultuous water had etched a deep gorge a short walk from the complex, frothing and surging, barreling past their higher position on the path that followed its channel, tearing toward an unknown destination.

Willow wasn't completely sturdy on her feet, but being inside, subject to the inquisition, was more than she could bear any longer. "Does any other river in the Midland carry so much violence?"

"There's one further north that's worse. I suppose Bryar's out in it, but it does nothing for me. For you, water's vital, with its profound connection to earth fertility. Your work relies on water to nurture the plants."

"My former work." She tried, and failed, to keep a tinge of bitterness from her words.

"No glimmer?"

Willow shook her head. "Every once in a while, I think something's there, but it's a phantom memory, or wanting it so badly I imagine it."

"At least you still have the plants." At Willow's hard look she added, "Sorry. Not helpful."

Following the exhausting, confusing trip back to the Motherhouse, she'd endured two days of incessant poking and prodding, an invasion of her mind as Healers and Scribes tried to find a hint of the Aura's continued existence within her. Arwen and Quinn were the most tireless in their explorations. She cringed at the thought of her innermost secrets being exposed to their scrutiny – if they were. Quinn never said. Willow hated that anyone might read her that deeply, even Quinn.

And why bother? Her Healing power, her ability to weave templates from the Aura, had fled, leaving no trace behind. She knew it, and they knew it. A walk to the river put distance between herself and the uncomfortable days just past, dispelling – she hoped – some of the sadness and soreness.

"What do you make of that?" Welcoming any distraction, Willow diverted their attention to the man who stood unmoving on the riverbank. Joss had turned up at the Motherhouse late yesterday. Since quietly arriving and settling in the guest lodge, he had seemed aimless, avoiding the Weavers, spending his day studying the river, the hills, the sheep.

"What about him?"

"An enigma? Why did he come here?"

"Not an enigma, exactly," Quinn said, "although I don't know what drove him to the Motherhouse. Basically, he's earth, grounded in the so-called real world, but he understands animals, and that doesn't mesh with any reality he can grasp. His challenge is dealing with people, unless they're in command, telling him what to do."

"Commanders," Willow muttered. "Is their civilization so horrid that they don't form ordinary friendships?"

"If nothing else, he and Kiril are not friends. This military of theirs dictated their roles – from what they said, it's a hierarchy. If you're not at the top of the pack, you follow the rules. Take orders."

"Terrible." Such a way of living appalled her. It would be like enduring life under her mother's thumb forever.

"And then there's his reaction to women. To him we're exotic and therefore threatening. We make him uneasy."

They both studied the man below them, letting the tumultuous river drown their words.

"Based on our shared history," Willow said, "I should have the stronger connection with him, but he's more comfortable with Bryar. You don't suppose...?"

"No. He doesn't desire men."

Willow didn't ask why Quinn was so sure, but didn't doubt for a moment that she was correct.

Quinn's eyes narrowed as they focused on the solitary man by the river. "Given how they separate the sexes on his world, this is an out-there idea, but I suspect he's virginal."

"Are you kidding?" Willow turned her attention from Joss to her friend.

"Our first sexual experiences mostly happen when we're young. But from how they describe their civilization, women are taboo, and dangerous. If you could bring yourself to have sex with him, you'd do him a favor."

"Bring myself? It would be no hardship, if he were interested."

"He is, I believe. He's never learned how to show it."

"Let's go down river."

They turned away from Joss. Willow pulled an abricoe pastry from her satchel and broke off half for Quinn, handling the treat gingerly. Despite her healed hands, she still experienced residual tenderness. The women ate and walked, following a narrow path that skirted the steep river bank.

"He shows signs of empathy," Quinn said. "He'll want to protect you."

"Just what I need," Willow grumbled.

"I agree, none of us is any good at being taken care of. But as things are now, you might benefit."

Willow chose not to respond to her friend's assessment of her situation. "If what you say is true, our culture must be a shock. He hasn't been here a full season yet."

"He's spent enough time with the agriculturists to know how it is here. He's becoming one of us, and he needs to figure out his place, in this as much as anything."

Quinn sometimes chilled Willow. Even lovemaking became a clinical experience, a subject to be studied. Quinn and Bryar had a physical relationship, but she wondered how it profited either of them. When she reflected on her times with Bryar, how they'd laugh and enjoy each other, play until the moment loving transcended play and turned deeper, the essence of them both... she couldn't imagine that simple joy between Bryar and Quinn.

But that was none of her business. Bryar benefited, as did Quinn. She let it go.

"I'll consider it. But I cannot see it my mission to enhance Joss's experience of life in the Midland. He'll find a partner when he's ready."

"For him, you'd be hard to improve on." Quinn received her shocked look calmly. "I'm convinced he's intrigued by you and probably desires you. Never mind." She reached over and squeezed Willow's free hand. "It was just an idea."

"Which you conjured up to distract me, as well as help Joss?"

"Nothing wrong with solving two problems at once."

And now I'm a problem.

A problem to be solved. At least sadness dominated her reaction, not hostility. Perhaps in time she'd even become resigned to her new status.

Archivist. Hedge healer.

Quinn took the lead as the path narrowed. She followed her friend along the river, going nowhere.

Chapter 20

Slightly out of breath, Bryar caught up with Quinn on the green as she left the dining hall the next morning. "Any idea where Willow is?"

"Haven't seen her since yesterday. We walked the river. What's happening?"

"She missed breakfast, and she's not at the Healers' lodge. It may be nothing, but I've got an uneasy feeling..."

Quinn had a long history of trusting Bryar's instincts. She picked up on his worry and nodded. "We're supposed to meet mid-morning."

"She may not show. She hates those sessions."

"Partly because she doesn't believe we can restore her."

"Can you?" The question sprang from genuine curiosity, not a challenge. If anyone could bring back Willow's connection, it was Quinn.

"To be honest, I'm beginning to doubt it. There's no trace in her mind, no alien weaves. Where we connect to the Aura, there's only... emptiness. Without that, I don't have anything to build on."

"You won't quit trying, though. I know you better than that."

"If she'll let me."

Bryar crossed the green to the Bards' lodge. He wanted to keep Willow tucked in a comfortable corner of his awareness, where she lived whenever their journeys took them within a handful of days of each other. That space had been empty since the accident. He tried to dismiss his worry as resulting from Willow's mental state, her stubborn refusal to accept anything that smacked of sympathy. For all the good it did him. Better he lose himself in his work, a ballad he was composing, a new recitation about the ill-fated circle and the danger of the Aura – which might never be performed, but he'd breathe more easily once he committed his reflections and feelings to poetry.

And recorded the result safely in a template, he thought with a taste of Willow's bitterness. Over the last nine-days his unexamined faith in the land's energies had evaporated like dreamed words to an unremembered melody.

Willow didn't turn up for her session with Quinn and Arwen. "You think she ran." Arwen's flat voice echoed Quinn's lack of surprise.

"Yes, I do. Willow's both intensely private and still healing from the accident. She's overwhelmed."

Arwen smacked the conference room table in frustration. "Even though it's for her own benefit."

"Even though," Quinn confirmed. "She gave no hint, yesterday. It may have been impulsive."

"A poorly chosen impulse. Check her accommodation in the Healers' lodge, please. See if she left any clue to her destination."

"I'll check, but it isn't necessary. She's gone home."

Arwen shot her a puzzled glance, brows raised. "Not to her native hamlet, surely."

On this subject Willow had always maintained a stony silence, beyond acknowledging her mother's adamant opposition to her desire to be a Healer. "No, I meant the cabin she holds south of here, near Hallan Hot Springs. It's where she goes when she needs time to regroup."

"Fool girl." Arwen was already on council when Quinn first entered the Motherhouse, so it came as no surprise that she still viewed the three of them as irrepressible teenagers.

"I'll go after her."

Arwen shook her head as she strode to the door. "No, I want you here until we're sure what's what with the power cell. You've run into Joss?"

"We saw him yesterday, by the river. Why's he here?"

Arwen paused with her hand on the doorframe. "He turned up with the trading caravan late yesterday. Said he'd hoped to talk to Ezra. I wouldn't mind talking to the Old Man myself, come to that."

"Rebecca was pining for home." Few people brought out Quinn's softer side, but the Old Man's elderly wife touched something bordering on the maternal in her. Having spent much of her journey year at their compound, she could imagine the challenge of living with Ezra, with his mysterious skills. That was a side effect of being skilled in template weaving, the need for a contact with reality, in case you slipped out of both stability and perspective.

Arwen was made of sterner, or at least less sympathetic, stuff, however. "Pining or not," she said, "we could use him now. Tell me what you find."

She left, her sandals patting along the corridor.

Quinn petitioned for admission to the Healers' lodge and, with the porter on duty accompanying her, surveyed Willow's room. It was immaculate and appeared, in fact, untouched. Willow had taken a change of clothes and not much else, other than possibly some remedies from the Healers' workroom.

Just before lunch the Aura disintegrated. From her window on the second floor of the Scribe's lodge, she saw the dismay on the faces of those crossing the green. Everyone had slipped into the old stability, as if the fluctuations were things of the past.

Short-sighted, all of us.

Over the mid-day meal, Arwen announced an embargo on travel; nobody was to leave the Motherhouse until further notice. The risk, at that moment, was perceived to be too great, and nobody could predict who might be needed. Across the table from her, Bryar's voice was quiet and intense. "Someone has to go to Willow."

"I agree." She let her eyes shift to her right where Joss hunched over his bowl, oblivious to his surroundings. The barest glance, but Bryar caught it.

"No. Not him. Not when he's caused —"

"We can't honestly blame him for crashing here. And it must be the other one, Kiril, who's unearthed the cell."

She understood Bryar so well. He'd weigh the advantage of finding Willow against the minor betrayal of sending Joss, rather than himself, and tear himself apart worrying about whether to trust their friend to the big man. Quinn herself harbored no doubts. Even if she hadn't spent more than enough time mapping Joss's mind patterns through his Auric connection to know that he'd never hurt Willow, his pensive face, as he sat alone, hunched over a bowl of lentil stew, told her as much. Besides, Joss felt today's disruption and was as distressed by it as any of them.

She'd never tell Bryar any of this, though. The Scribes kept many of the skills they exercised private to the point of secrecy. So she contented herself with putting her hand on his arm and squeezing. "With this unprecedented lockdown, we can't escape. He can. He's not a Weaver."

Bryar scowled. "She's vulnerable."

"So is he. And yes, I am confident he won't hurt her."

He drew his arm away and returned to his stew.

"Meet me mid-afternoon, our place by the river. I'll tell Joss."

However much he disliked her plan, Bryar was tractable. He'd be at the river later, he'd agree to sending Joss after Willow, and after a while he'd forgive her.

And she'd bear the brunt of the inevitable tongue-lashing from Arwen, once Arwen realized Joss had gone.

Quinn and Bryar were sitting on a grassy bluff overlooking the river, enduring the uncomfortable silence that had risen between them, by the time Joss turned up. "You're late," Bryar growled.

The man blushed. "Sorry. Telling time without tools isn't in my skill set." He dropped onto a rock slab that formed a natural bench.

"It gets better," Quinn said. "The longer you spend with the land, the easier it is to work with time accurately."

"I hope you're right," Joss replied, his voice tight. Like her, he must suspect Kiril had moved the cell. "Every agriculturist I've met has a better sense of time than I do."

"I expect you'd benefit from formal training."

He nodded. "Ezra suggested it, too. Overall, whatever's messing in my mind, it's getting stronger. Or maybe I'm just getting used to it. Things were fuzzy at first. Now they're clearer."

"Where is the power cell, Joss?" she asked in an abrupt change of topic. "What's he done with it?"

A flash of anger in the quiet man's eyes. "I wish I knew. He promised he'd leave it, but..." Joss's mouth twisted in frustration. "I swear I could kill him right now."

"Willow's gone," Bryar said.

Alarm, hastily suppressed, flashed across Joss's face.

"But we know where she'll be," Quinn said. "She has a cabin south of here, at Hallan Hot Springs. Whether she admits it or not, she needs our support."

Joss was silent, staring at the tumultuous river. Finally, he said, "The Motherhouse wants you two to stay put."

"Exactly," Bryar said. "Cross-country isn't feasible, and they'll be watching the roads."

"And we'd be missed," Quinn said. "We both have duties here. But you could go."

That hung between them. She watched Joss as he sorted it out.

He shrugged. "Of course I'll help. But what's the point?"

Quinn shifted on the grass, wrapping her arms around her legs. She put her head on her raised knees, gazing out over the river. "It's tough, feeling as if you're alone in the world. It would make it easier for us and her too, knowing she has allies."

Joss measured out his words. "It seems to me that she's a person who needs to be alone occasionally."

She tore her gaze from the manic river to look back at her companions. "True. So we'll leave it for a couple of days. Give her that time to settle."

"Her place is easy to find," Bryar added. "Only a single turn off the track south."

"It's not a good track, nobody uses it except for trade between the hot springs area and the Motherhouse. Most people who visit the springs take a route that passes south of Stanstead."

Joss shifted his gaze from one to the other of them. The way their words bounced off each other must drive home to him their shared sense of urgency. He nodded. "If Willow needs me, I'll go. After all she did for us, I owe her."

"You can say that again," Bryar muttered.

The matter of sending Joss after Willow solved, Quinn stood and dusted her hands. Both men rose with her. "South out of here until you come to the main east-west track, then left. Her cabin's white, to the left of the track, sitting on the side of a hill overlooking a small lake. If you get to the bottom and find a hamlet by a larger lake, you've gone too far. For a Weaver, it's a solid two-day walk. Leave day after tomorrow at first light, before anyone's around."

Nothing remained to be said. She turned from them and started back to the Motherhouse, sensing Bryar behind her. When, after a few steps, she looked over her shoulder, Joss was staring out over the water to the forest on the other side.

The man was a puzzle with a hidden key – although she conceded that Kiril presented the greater conundrum.

Chapter 21

By leaving the Motherhouse before sunrise, he'd made good time. It was early afternoon the next day when, footsore, Joss dropped onto a hillock part way down a long, leisurely slope, across the track from a compact whitewashed cabin. Assuming this was, in fact, Willow's home, she'd picked a fine spot. Forest shaded the surrounding hills, but the cabin nestled in meadowland, punctuated by copses of trees or shrubbery, that continued into the valley below. A couple of goats grazed nearby; he wondered why they didn't venture into the richer feast of the garden upslope of her door. The garden swirled around a bench, its rows filled with all sizes and shapes of plants. Not efficient, but so like her.

Behind the building and downhill, a waterfall tumbled into a small perched lake, rippling the placid surface. Joss reckoned a good swimmer would reach the far side in a quarter of an hour. He'd worked on his swimming while he waited in Stanstead; he'd be able to make it across, just. A well-used footpath led from her door to a pocket of grassy beach bordered by a boulder that jutted out over the water.

The main track carried on to a hamlet, which he assumed was Hallan Hot Springs, set next to a much larger lake in the valley. Cultivated fields, roofs and tiny people going about their business lined the lakeshore. One larger building provided accommodation for those seeking a warm-water vacation, or so he speculated.

An idyllic spot. Impossible to imagine anything negative happening here.

For all that his feet still needed toughening, the walk had been a welcome respite. For the first time in a long time, he felt at home in his body. With limited nourishment and overdoses of stress, his strength had melted away during the last month in the pod. Now, given regular exercise and the best food of his life, he'd regained much of his muscle mass and stamina. The two days on the road had been enough to test, but not to tax him.

The terrain was hillier than Stanstead's, not as untamed as around the Motherhouse. Rounded peaks undulated around folds holding lakes, gentle meadow slopes, copses where the leaves rustled with the slightest movement of the air. He'd heard more birds in the last day than in a lifetime on Terra. Flowers dotted the grass in front of him with red and yellow. The light breeze alleviated the heat from the summer sun.

He studied his hands and arms; an unfamiliar brown, not pasty white. Suntan didn't happen in Northam Corporation, not with the filters blocking the sunlight.

This had to be the place, but Joss was in no hurry to find out for sure. Settling on the hillock, he let tranquility wash over him. In the eight weeks – six nine-days, he corrected himself – since the crash, he'd become familiar with an alien way of life and learned skills that no longer existed on Terra. He'd never seen so many trees, or a lake that actually reflected blue, or cows, or a hundred other things everyone here took for granted. But while he readily explored each discovery, sometimes they overwhelmed his ability to absorb it all. This short respite gave him a chance to catch his breath, without the constant need to learn a new skill or a new perspective on life.

Women, for instance. He wished his unruly mind didn't insist on swiveling back to the mystery of women. They left him unsettled, the way they were always around, involved in the same activities as men, casual and close and everyone mixed up together. On Terra, the things that went on here were punishable by flogging, castration, or death. Thanks to a lifetime of the Corporation's dictates on necessary population control, he couldn't shake the belief that the sexes should stay well away from each other. Given Terran living arrangements, he might go a decade without laying eyes on a woman – and then only from afar. They had their own cities, their own work. But here, men and women *enjoyed* each other.

And then there were the animals, the way they infiltrated his mind. Animal whisperer, the skill was called. He hadn't told anyone that he sensed things about people, too. Strong emotion, the kind that took over a person's mind. The emotion thing troubled him enough that he'd joined a trading caravan to the Motherhouse in search of Ezra, not trusting anyone else with this unsettling awareness. The meeting with Quinn and Bryar had sent his senses spiraling, they both cared so intensely about Willow – and by extension about his agreeing to go on this pilgrimage to her. And neither had bothered to shield their feelings.

Idly rubbing his jaw, he hoped that either Willow or the men's lodge in the hamlet had a razor. A beard worked for Kiril, but two days' stubble in the heat drove him crazy.

Willow stepped out of the cabin. As she pushed aside the curtain covering her door, he caught a glimpse of her face. *Bleak.* She followed the path to the lake and sat on the boulder, unmoving, her bare legs folded under her. If she'd noticed him, she gave no sign.

Joss rose and made his way toward her.

She looked up as he reached the beach. Expressionless, she stood and dove into the water. His breath caught in his throat, waiting for her to surface. He'd picked up her total lack of joy and purpose, and if she never came up from those depths, his own swimming skills were far from sufficient to save her.

Finally he spotted her, farther out in the lake than he expected and stroking toward the far shore. Without considering his actions, he shucked his tunic and sandals and plunged in.

The water, neither warm nor cold, felt soft against his pale torso. Drawing on his courage and his new-learned skills, he set out toward her. To his amazement, it grew warmer the further he went. A hot spring?

"Go away," she shouted.

"No." That cost him a mouthful of lake. He choked, spat, and plowed on.

She disappeared under the surface and reappeared next to him. "If you can't make it, don't expect me to rescue you."

His feet kicked aimlessly while he struggled to keep himself upright and above water. "You couldn't anyway," he gasped. "I'm twice your size."

"Water's a great leveler." She struck out for her beach. He followed. When after an eternity he collapsed on dry land, she stood over him and asked, "Why are you here?"

He ignored the question until he'd caught his breath. "Because you are."

"Go away, Joss."

"Sorry. Can't do it." One last gulp of air and he pulled himself up to stand next to her, keeping his eyes fixed on the distant shore of the lake instead of her wet tunic.

"I want to be alone."

"You've had five days alone."

"Let me guess. Quinn said five days was enough."

He watched her shuttered face and detected no emotion. She hadn't forgotten how to shield herself, a skill he'd noticed in Weavers at the Motherhouse. One minute, emotion poured out, clobbering his senses; the next minute a barrier descended, shutting him out – mercifully, he'd thought at the time, but not now. For Willow, it was her way of keeping herself invulnerable, but he doubted it was the best for her, or what she really wanted.

"They sent me." No need to say who he meant. "They want to know you're all right."

"There's nothing right about it," she snapped. "This is my new reality, and they might as well accept it. From now on, I'm just like everyone else in the land. Life going on as usual, only without..." She made a gesture with her hand that conveyed her sense of the world, and her hopelessness in the face it. "Just like everyone else."

She spun and walked quickly toward the cabin, her tunic clinging. Anger and frustration poured off her in waves, assaulting his fragile awareness. *People whisperer?* She didn't want him here, and she wasn't coping.

But as a member of the Amalgamated Expeditionary Force, the third exploration pod they'd launched, he'd survived unimaginable things. He'd lived in cramped, unnatural circumstances and seen gruesome death and damn near died himself. Every instinct told him to shelter her from the calamity that had fallen on her head.

That blasted tunic triggered a reaction in his body, similar to the needs he'd dealt with at the gymnasium on Terra, or in the bathing rooms here, but different. He hastily looked away.

After she disappeared into the cabin, he waited a while, letting the warm day dry his skin, then rose, donned his tunic, shucked out of the wet trousers – a common style of dress in the summer, even among men, he'd observed – and followed. When he stepped inside, she waved him into a chair pulled up to a rickety wooden table and continued stirring something in a bowl. She'd changed into dry clothing, but her hair hung in limp, wet clumps around her face.

The substantial curtain covering the entrance had been hooked to the side. When he fingered it she said, "Leather." Animal skins, but he didn't sense any residual fear or pain from the hides. A small table and two chairs, cupboards holding a few dishes and foodstuffs, a cookfire, a pump and basin, comprised the room's furnishings. A door to the left of the entry led, he supposed, to a bedroom. The simplicity, the rightness, relaxed him, as if it were part and parcel of the land outside.

"Tell me about the lake. The warmth surprised me." A weak conversational gambit, but given the embargo on any topic that mattered, the best he could do.

"Hot springs throughout the region. People come to soak in mineral pools."

"For health?"

"Mm."

He watched her from the table, letting her movements, the early afternoon peace, lull him...

"I don't need a babysitter."

The abrupt words startled him awake. He must be more tired than he'd realized.

"Bryar and Quinn didn't give me a choice. The Motherhouse isn't allowing anyone out, or they'd be here themselves. You forgot this. Quinn sent it." From within his pack he dropped a linen-wrapped bundle on the table.

Brisk and efficient, she brought over two plates of grain cakes. "Why?"

"The lockdown's not because of you. There's been another Auric disruption. It lasted almost three days." *As she couldn't have known.* "My guess, and Quinn agrees, is that Kiril's moved the power cell. And I may kill him next time I see him. He swore he wouldn't touch it."

"There might be a justification. Perhaps someone else found it." She put bowls of thick syrup and sliced fruit on the table, then ladled some of each over their cakes.

"Bryar's afraid for you. He's told me as much."

"That is Bryar's concern, and unwarranted. What do you want from me, Joss? You're not here to be sure I'm eating properly and getting enough sleep."

"No, I guess not. Open the package."

"I didn't forget it. I've left that life behind."

"Your sash isn't some rag. You earned it."

"I don't need the reminder." She picked the bundle up and carried it into the other room. Whatever she did with her Healer's sash, she returned empty-handed.

They ate in silence. These grain cake things – well, they were better than the tasteless stuff you got served on Terra, but maybe they were an acquired taste. He added more syrup.

When they'd finished eating, he said, "I owe you. You saved Kiril's life, and probably mine."

"And you think to repay the debt by making sure I don't harm myself?"

"That never crossed my mind," he lied. "But there's no need for you to be on your own."

"You're wrong. Go back, tell them I'm fine and to leave me alone." She carried their plates to the basin and pumped water.

"Let me do that."

"No."

"I'm not leaving, so find ways I can help. Kitchen work, whatever."

Again she lapsed into silence, washing and drying the dishes. He went outdoors and draped his wet trousers over a bush to dry, then leaned against the wall. A goat came up and gave him a gentle butt. He reached down to scratch behind her ears and received a positive vibration. Goats definitely had more going on in their heads than sheep. And he gained the consolation of knowing that one living thing around here approved of his presence.

She joined him, rubbed the goat – who shoved against her, almost bowling her over with the strength of her fervor – and said, "I have two cultivation sticks. Start with the vegetables."

"Tell me what to do."

"You'll figure it out." She held out one of the flat-ended sticks they used to weed and cultivate crops.

"Where will you be?"

"Doing the herbs."

She disappeared around the corner. He cringed at the afternoon heat, but set to work. They'd talk later, once she came to terms with the idea he wasn't going away.

He learned her patterns. As she did every day, Willow sat on the boulder, looking out over the water. He had been watching her for three days, waiting for her to speak, helping her when she let him, sleeping on the floor of her cabin at night.

And listening, catching her feelings as she unconsciously released them to float like wisps on the fragrant air whenever she relaxed the hard clamp she kept on her mind. He picked up a vast hollow place she hadn't learned how to fill, tinged with inevitable sadness. Today, however, that sadness trended toward wistfulness.

All this emotion stuff bade fair to drive him nuts. It had been bad enough that day he talked to Quinn and Bryar by the river. Now, he risked overload. In a lot of ways, he was grateful she kept herself so contained. A military man doesn't mess around with feelings... not since he was a boy, anyway, alone in his bed in the dormitory and longing for something he couldn't define. Some of the guys formed attachments or adopted a stray animal for the barracks, but that kind of thing led to vulnerability.

And now he'd somehow become a repository for emotion. If he'd been uncomfortable about understanding the animals, this newer development scared him witless. Physical assault was easy, but this assault of feelings kept him awake nights.

Puts you in a good position to help Willow, jackass.

His fate? But damn, he hated it. He needed to learn to screen himself before he went mad.

He ambled down the hill and settled next to her. "What do you see when you stare like that?"

She'd drifted a long way away, lost in a daydream or a memory. "A path wraps around the lake. Beyond are more meadows, fields, trees. They plant barley in the valley northeast of Hallan. When it waves in the wind, it shifts and changes as if it's many colors, not one."

"Why don't we walk over and see it?"

"Memory's good enough. It has to be, when the colors are muddy."

"Because of the Aura."

"Because there is no Aura."

"For you."

"For me," she agreed.

"Talk to me," he said. "Tell me how it is."

The expected anger didn't surface; instead, she settled into a soft, dreamy state, her body and facial muscles finally relaxed. A warm breeze that trickled across the lake lifted her long, pale hair as she gazed into nowhere. "Empty, as if the life has been drained out of living. As if the colors have faded into grays. And as if I am without purpose."

Exactly what he'd read from her, but the loss in her voice was enough to clog his throat. "At least you've got support. So many people care about you. And Arwen and the others are frantic to find a solution."

The quirk of her mouth carried too heavy a freight of all the negative things about her situation to be called a smile. "The Motherhouse can't fix me. They can't even neutralize the cell. The energies – the way I explain it to myself, the template overloaded and burned itself out. I expect everyone was secretly glad when I left, and I doubt they'd let me in if I went back. Weavers think of it as home, but that's not who I am anymore. I don't know who I am," she concluded on a note that wrung him out, made him long to comfort her. Except he had no idea how.

As for the Motherhouse, he was sure she was wrong, but his arguments had no teeth, so he said nothing.

"I'll be fine, Joss," she said after a while. "I'll become a hedge healer, or a village archivist, as my mother intended. One way or another, I'll be fine."

He doubted it, but he maintained his silence. She had drifted away and wouldn't hear him.

That evening, after a meal of potatoes and beans from the garden, Joss said, "Relive it for me. It's a rotten thing to ask, but they trained me to believe you don't get over a trauma until you release it. It's called debriefing. What's happening now isn't healthy."

She sighed. "I'm tired."

"So am I." He'd once again spent the better part of the afternoon digging weeds in her garden under the sun. The back of his neck felt tight; he rubbed it, hoping the burn wasn't too bad. "The sooner you talk, the sooner we can go to bed."

"I've done this – debriefing. With Arwen and Quinn. Over and over."

"What happened, yes, but did you tell them how it's affected you? Or did you leave them to figure it out for themselves? Bryar and Quinn are your friends, and they're afraid for you."

As usual on these hot, sunny days, she had tied back the curtain; light and a breeze scented with grass and wildflowers filled the little cabin. He experienced her home as a restful place to escape for a while and wished she did as well.

Instead, she gave another deep, heart-wrenching sigh. "No matter how right you are, I hate this. In the cupboard above the pump, there's a bottle."

He brought it over, with two small mugs. "How much?"

She showed him with her fingers. "It's strong. A luxury."

"What's it called?" he asked as he poured.

"Brandy. I trade for it along northern routes. Medicines made from it are more palatable, and it's as potent as what we distill at the Motherhouse."

"At home they serve beer in the bars once a week – that's seven days to you. More at major festivals. If you drink too much, you'll be sorry tomorrow." The words made him flinch. At home? He hoped never to return to the world he'd once called home.

Her answering smile was, at best, tentative. "I learned that lesson a long time ago."

When he sipped, the stuff burned his lip, then burned all the way down, leaving behind a hint of apple on his tongue.

"Weaving my part of the template and maintaining the flow at the same time was a struggle." She held herself straight, facing her memories with courage. "The speed of the energies, and the beauty... it hypnotized me. Everything in me longed to release myself and let it take me. That's one reason we spend years learning to work with templates. Given an eight-way link with eight times the power... if we hadn't trained so deeply, the Aura could have claimed us."

"I've heard you're among the best."

"Was. Not the most powerful by a long measure, but reliable and skilled at manipulating the weaves."

The drink flowed more easily, the more you drank. Joss consciously limited himself. This was for her benefit, easing her into memory, not to be squandered to control his own stress levels.

"So, I remember clenching my neighbors' hands, like a death grip. And being frightened, but exhilarated, too. As if I might whirl right off the land and be lost in the template forever if I let go. And it was uncomfortable. My skin itched, and I started going hot and cold, as if I had a fever. I forgot technique, purpose, everything except building the template. I suppose I came close to collapse."

"You were swaying on your feet. Several of the others, too. Arwen kept me away."

"Just as well. Keeping the flow under control was challenging enough, without allowing anyone not a Weaver near the circle."

"And then the other man collapsed."

She nodded and gripped the mug on the table, but she had gone far away, reliving the events that had cost her her identity, her way of life.

"Martin. A seizure, they said. The shock when he broke the connection – like the static that builds up in the winter. Everything crashed, the energy plowed into me from both directions and ripped me apart. As if it turned me inside out, sucking at me and I couldn't hold onto myself. And it hurt, so terribly…"

"But you didn't fall. Not at first."

"No? I don't remember. The shock and the burning in my hands, then nothing until I woke up in the healing room."

"I held you on the cart. I worried you'd be jostled." He remembered the slight weight of her, her perspiration-stiffened hair falling over his arm.

"After the energy blasted through me, there was a sense of being drawn – that didn't come from the power cell," she said. "The sensation felt different. A pull, not a block."

"The shielding from the rocks held. No one noticed any disruption. Something else caused it."

"The Aura. There's no other possibility." She took a tiny sip of the brandy, then her head jerked up, her eyes locking on his. "Wait… I believe… Joss, I think it pulled from the left. The fuel cell was in front of me, south of me, but I felt a pull from the side. Just for an instant. But that doesn't make sense."

"Toward the east." Forget rationing the brandy. He topped up his own mug, then hers.

Still remembering, she frowned, dropping her gaze back to her mug. "I'm almost certain… Ezra warned me, something about the east. What he told me that day… it was so vague, I didn't take it in."

Joss sipped the brandy. "Your people didn't originate here. They came from Terra, like Kiril and I did, since we speak the same language. Quinn says, three hundred ninety years ago."

He filled the sunlit silence by taking her through his thoughts, step by step. "The Aura might be intrinsic to the planet, sure. But it's threatened now by the power cell on our exploration pod, and that suggests to me that it's not. The earliest ships from Terra probably drew their power in different ways. Perhaps there's a remnant still here on this planet that modifies the usual energy frequencies and gives you, some of you, access to the Aura. For all we know, it created the Aura. If that's true, whatever it is, it's in the east."

The longest speech he'd strung together in months, years, other than technical information. Talking didn't come easily to him, but she needed to hear.

She was in no hurry to respond. His analysis agitated rather than reassured her.

"I believe – I *used to* believe – that the Aura is integral with the land. We honor it with our words and actions. We believe it sustains us, and the Midland. If it's just another box like yours..."

Sensing her distress, Joss leaned forward and put both of his hands on her shoulders. "This is speculation, not hard fact. And even if my theory is true, that doesn't negate your respect. Healing doesn't happen without the Aura."

"It does, but not as smoothly. Hedge healers can make basic remedies and use them."

"Still, what you do is extraordinary. However the Aura came into being, it's deserving of the honor you give it."

She shrugged. "Gave it."

"No." Joss stood, and by gripping her shoulders more tightly managed to pull her up with him. Aware of the way he towered over her, he nonetheless shook her gently. She wouldn't meet his eyes. "Listen to me. Don't abandon your rituals. Don't pretend the Aura blinked out of existence because you can't access it right now. It deserves more, and so do you. We're going to heal this thing, Willow. I don't see how, yet, but we will fix it."

She twisted from his hands and crossed the small room to the washing basin, where she rinsed her brandy mug and turned back to him. The hopelessness she carried with her filled the cabin. "Thank you. But you are wrong. And it hurts more when it's thrown in my face."

Joss didn't know what possessed him; the impulse came out of nowhere. In two strides he was beside her and folding her in his arms. She shuddered and emitted a sad, lonely moan. Then he was holding her against his chest while she sobbed, one big hand cradling her head, her silky hair against his palm –

What the hell was he doing?

Panic hit him, burning in his gut, forcing him to wrench himself free, his heart pounding. He knew better. He'd been a good student, an obedient citizen of Northam Corporation. A rule follower. His hands shook, literally shook, as his visceral response to the danger she represented struck him.

She must think he was mad. But if so, she gave no clue. Instead, she brushed the hair from her face and wiped the tears from her cheeks. "Good night, Joss," she said, and disappeared into her sleeping chamber.

The sky hovered on the edge of darkness, filtering the rosy glow of sunset into the room. He left the cabin, allowing the curtain to close behind him, and walked toward the fields, wondering what he had just done.

Chapter 22

The next morning, Willow stood at the corner of her cabin, where the vegetable garden and herb garden merged, and watched Joss. Polite but distant, he'd barely spoken over breakfast and seemed to prefer his own company. He wore only trousers, and the muscles of his back shifted as he wielded the cultivation stick, clearing weeds, creating a small cairn of early potatoes to be laid out on the grass to cure. The work absorbed him; no daydreaming, the way she always did, drinking in the peacefulness of the place and the task, in no hurry to finish.

For her, the previous night had been cathartic, snapping her out of her self-imposed refusal to accept her new reality and leaving her with a new determination to make life bearable, whatever it took.

Thanks to Joss.

The day had dawned overcast, promising rain before evening. Rain, to wash the land and release its aromas and remind her of Bryar... She stopped that thought in its tracks. Mari was all they shared now. He was a Weaver, and she wasn't. They refused to admit it, but her connection to Quinn and Bryar had been severed. Soon neither of them would notice her absence from their lives.

Mari. A pang went through her. She missed her daughter.

She stood still on the slope, surveying her domain. Her first impression of Joss had been wildly in error. Not a brute at all, but a logical, determined man who worried a problem to death rather than let it get the better of him.

Turning from her scrutiny, she picked up her cultivation stick. The herbs prospered, but there would be no harvesting today. Herbs demanded hot sun to bring out their healing properties, not overcast.

Weeding gave her space to think, though, and Joss provided plenty of food to feed her thoughts. It had never, in her wildest imaginings, occurred to her that the Aura came from something external to the land itself. To her, it was a part of existence, a fundamental component of the fabric of their world. If he was right, a human-made thing caused the Aura to be. That cast their entire belief system into jeopardy, because an artifact could be found, manipulated, even destroyed.

As if you need more worries.

Over their mid-day meal, which they carried to the raised patch of grass across from the cabin, she said, "To confirm your theory would mean going back through the Aura. No one's powerful enough, not even Quinn or Arwen."

"Because?" Joss ate with the appetite of a laborer, which reminded her that living here now meant arranging for food. Weavers didn't need to concern themselves with such things, but an ordinary person bartered, or attached herself to the nearest hamlet, with access to their stores of food and needles, clothing, flints, and shoes, in return for work. But Hallan supported a resident healer already, so she doubted she'd find a position here. Yesterday she had traded vegetables for flour, then filled the cottage with the aroma of baking bread, but her small vegetable garden was insufficient to sustain a regular trade.

One of the goats that roamed the slopes surrounding her home bleated. She liked the goats; perhaps she'd learn to make cheese from their milk, except she'd never seen these goats in foal, so that meant getting a male goat, then she'd need to —

She snapped herself into the present. Joss had asked a question... how long ago? "Templates lose their stability that far back in history. According to Quinn, the furthest it's safe to go is about a hundred years."

He sought facts, not speculation. "So I've heard. It's really that dangerous?"

"Yes. Scribes are far more skilled than the rest of us, but even they can get lost in the weaves. It's not right to ask her, because she's a daredevil where template work is concerned. No benefit is worth the risk."

"The benefit lies in learning more of your history, and by extension whether there's an exterior generator for the Aura."

"But not at the cost of jeopardizing anyone."

"I agree, but it's frustrating, coming up against a dead end like that. And I wanted a reason to lure your friends here. I've decided to go get them."

Startled, she put down her spoon. "Why?"

"Because you need them."

"I don't want them."

"I'm going, Willow. There's no point arguing."

"The lockdown..."

"Getting back out might be a problem," he conceded. "Going back, the worst that can happen is they'll be annoyed with me. I'll leave tomorrow morning at first light."

He obviously considered the matter settled, but she was unsure how she felt about seeing Bryar or Quinn again or about Joss's imminent departure. After they cleaned up from lunch she wandered away, aware that his eyes followed her until she crested a hill and disappeared down the other side.

Joss. He had supported her, forced her to confront the demons that bedeviled her mind, tried out ideas on her. She hadn't felt truly alone since she first handed him the cultivation stick. He had as many demons, as much upheaval in his life, and he handled it with... grace, she decided. Courage, and grace.

And last night, the terror contorting his face when he realized he had embraced her...

She no longer doubted the accuracy of Quinn's speculation, that day on the riverbank. He had little or no experience of women. It was consistent with his stories about his planet, this alien Terra.

On the other hand, after last night there was no denying his reaction to her, either.

She directed her feet to a small meadow hidden in a fold of the hills not too far from her cottage. She settled on the wild grass, kept short by feral goats, and brushed her palm across the blanket of tiny daisies.

In one matter, his words drove her to acceptance of what she'd been denying ever since it happened. Honoring the Aura, calling on the energies for support, formed the backbone of her life, and she would be wrong to give up her practice now.

Sustainer of the land, tell me what to do about this man. Pour your beneficence over us, blessing us and guiding our decisions.

Grant me the strength to walk this new road, devoid of color and life.

As the words filled her she stood, raising her arms in a movement so natural it was instinctive, turning to honor the directions, then facing north. The earth, her home, where her body came into its deepest attunement even without the Aura humming through her.

She sank into meditation and remained there, still, until she was clear in her mind. Then, resolved, she turned and started for her cabin and Joss.

Willow retrieved a ground covering from her cupboard, then located Joss across from the cabin, where he sat stroking one of the wild goats. "Come," she said.

He stood and gave the goat a final head scratch. "Where are we going? Give me a minute to wash my hands."

She could hardly believe this was the same man as the filthy beast who dragged her through the underbrush all those nine-days ago. Fastidious, he washed himself regularly and always wore a fresh tunic, and in his short time with her he had once gone to Hallan, to the men's lodge, for a shave.

After he cleaned up, they set off on the track to the meadow. When they reached the spot she'd chosen, sheltered from the sun and close to a brook that gurgled as it flowed toward the waterfall, she spread the blanket. "Are you happy here?" she asked as they sat.

"Here, in this field, or here, in the Midland?" Joss called himself an engineer, a foreign term. To her it meant he constantly sought clarification as he figured out how everything worked.

"Both, but for the moment, where we are now."

He stretched out on his back without answering, his eyes drooping shut.

"Joss?"

"Everything's still so new. I'm never sure how to react. Things aren't always logical. But something about this..." He gestured at nothing in particular.

"Because you are of earth. Despite training or aptitudes, the land pulls you."

Grinning, he squinted up at her. "No point resisting, eh?"

"None."

Because you connect with the Aura. However faint, however much you do not understand, you possess what I lost.

The unexpected flash of bitterness was out of place today; she shook it off and settled next to him. From somewhere he'd procured a town tunic, with its front opening held closed by ties. Probably the clothiers in Stanstead hadn't had anything else his size in stock. She played with the fasteners, loosening the first knot.

His eyes flew open. "What are you doing?"

"Wait. Close your eyes."

"Not going to happen. Willow..." He lifted a hand to stop her, but she captured it and laid it back on the blanket. She opened the next fastener, and the next, and spread the shirt open.

"Feel it," she whispered. "The air against your skin, the breeze."

She placed her hands on his torso and felt his body spasm, in tension or... fear? Judging from the way his muscles quivered under her palms, he held himself still by force of will.

He'd filled out and put on muscle since the day she'd taken the salve to the ford. She explored the tight curls on his chest, then stroked her hands up over his powerful shoulders, back down along his sides, again and again, the harmonizing movements she'd done a thousand times before. Finally, he released the tension that wrapped around him like armor and relaxed into her touch. Her fingers traced his navel, brushed his nipples. He groaned, softly. A different tension gripped him now; she smiled to herself at the rightness of it, the two of them, the soft air...

When she moved to the ties at his waist, he started to sit up. "Don't, I'm not —"

She caught his arms below the elbow, to the extent her fingers would reach around the muscle and sinew. "Joss. Let me share this with you."

He faltered, his face unreadable, but let her push him back onto the blanket. She freed the ties and opened his trousers. "Feel the sun," she murmured. "Feel the breeze. Feel me." She caressed him, her mouth following the path of her hands.

He groaned more loudly, but he no longer fought.

She straightened and removed her tunic, then took his hands and placed them on her breasts.

Blood suffused his face along with panic as he jerked away. When he tried to rise, she pushed him down and straddled him, leaning her weight on his shoulders. "Feel, Joss. Close your eyes and feel." She reclaimed his hands, this time moving them over her skin, encouraging him to touch, to explore.

In the end, it took very little teaching.

When their shuddering eased, although he still filled her, he rolled them both over so they lay side by side. His corded arms bound her against him, and his breath flowed unevenly.

"You haven't done this before," she said, for his ears alone.

He shook his head and stroked her hair, drawing it out through his fingers.

She lay still, enjoying the feel of his hands, listening to the rustle of the trees overhead and the cheerful burbling of the brook. Outside their patch of shade, the sun warmed the land to fragrance. "Shared pleasure is a beautiful thing, not something to be afraid of."

He rolled away, emptying her. His words were wrenched from him. "Don't you get it? Where I'm from, they'd execute us. It's sinful. A moral transgression against the corporation."

"Do you believe that now?"

He stayed turned away, mute.

"This is your home, Joss. Here, our union is not wrong."

His body shook. She let a little time pass, then used her fingers to wipe his tears, her mouth to kiss his broad back. She settled against him, an arm flung over his chest and her legs nested behind his, prepared to stay there for as long as he needed her to.

Joss jolted awake, instantly on the alert. Something had changed. After a moment he sorted out that he lay on a mat in the late afternoon sun, as naked as the day he was born. Naked to –

To her. To Willow.

For her to see him…

Joss scrambled to his feet, only belatedly realizing that her arm had been locking him to the ground, and snatched up his clothing. He wondered how he'd ever get dressed, given the shaking in his legs.

She stood and claimed his tunic and trousers. Just took them away. The muscles in his fingers refused to resist. She dropped the clothes. "Look at me," she said, leaving no doubt it was a command.

Not that it mattered. Not looking was beyond him.

Willow. A woman.

He had never seen an unclothed woman.

As her eyes lingered on his body, his whisperer senses registered her pleasure. A lightness danced across her face as she smiled and reached out.

He swore under his breath, but he could no more stop her than freeze the rotation of the planet on its axis. No more stop his body's reaction to her than return to the stultifying life on Terra.

She pulled his head down to brush his lips with her tongue and locked her mouth to his.

Sin, a crime against the corporation. But if it were possible to fuse their two bodies, make them inseparable, he would do it. Dangerous or not, sin or not.

How could this be sinful?

Willow gave a little leap and wrapped her legs around him. Logic, right and wrong, all the considerations that made this impossible fled from his mind. He filled her again, drove himself into her, and found his release with a deep cry that echoed in the surrounding hills.

They walked back to her cabin without speaking. Joss was obviously overwhelmed, but Willow had no regrets. Despite Quinn's belief about the benefit to him, an initiation into the ways of the Midland, she accepted that their lovemaking had been as much for her as for him.

She reached out her hand. He accepted it without hesitation, but his eyes focused in the far distance.

Willow was grateful for his silence, because she needed time to think. The afternoon had affected her, too, and in ways new to her. She was sure of three things, though. First, for her their union had been more profound, more shattering, than any previous lovemaking. She had anticipated the playfulness she and Bryar shared, or possibly the simple drive for release that characterized most of her few other assignations, but it hadn't been like that and she couldn't twist it to be so. Something had happened between them, impossible to define and unique in her experience.

But she wanted to understand, because her second sure thing was that she had never felt as sheltered, or as fulfilled, as in Joss's arms.

She consigned those thoughts to the back of her mind and turned to the matter of dinner. New potatoes with butter and mint from the garden. A broth made from her small stock of dried meat. Greens grew rampant this time of year, but she was out of honey so there would be no sweet afterwards.

Planning their evening meal occupied her for the rest of the walk to the cottage. Because the third sure thing was, she was starving.

The thought produced a smile, something else she owed to Joss. She'd honestly begun to wonder if she'd ever smile again.

Chapter 23

Joss wanted to stay with Willow that evening, but he couldn't. Just couldn't.

He walked to Hallan instead, where he spent time in the small men's lodge, getting a shave, listening to the other men joking around, visiting the baths with an older man who quizzed him, reasonably enough, about what he brought to the table – by which the man meant, what he offered in exchange for the facilities he made use of at the lodge.

In Stanstead, after the town got over their skepticism, they accepted him as part of the agricultural team. Besides that, he was strong and growing more so as food, exercise, and sleep transmuted the inevitable muscle atrophy of the journey into the powerful strength he'd displayed on Terra. From building construction to fencing, to scything the grass for winter fodder, he was capable of assisting with most anything they needed.

He was clever with his hands, too. He could and did build things, and since his arrival had produced a few simple figures, dolls and animals, from a knife and a tree branch. The toys delighted Willow – the only time she'd smiled until... he gulped and fought back his physical response to the memory. She had claimed one, which vaguely resembled a goat, for herself. He'd take the rest to Hallan for the kids. Someday soon Kiril would expect him to use that cleverness, plus his store of Terra-based information, to produce a radio. Right now he had no idea where to find the materials and doubted his expertise in the absence of reference files.

As they sat soaking in hot, sulfurous water, he conveyed most of this to the elder. Omitting his alien origin and the animal whisperer thing, though. He still didn't trust the evidence of his own mind far enough.

"Sound as if you'd be useful," the man said. "Planning on settling, then?"

"I don't know yet. It feels good here."

A stronger than usual whiff of the chemicals in the water floated through the steamy room, causing him to wrinkle his nose. One of the other men who drifted in and out of the baths noticed and laughed. "Folks come from far and wide for the waters. Says it heals 'em."

"And maybe it does at that. They leave thinkin' so, anyways."

"You're stayin' up hill with the Healer, Willow, right?" another man put in.

Joss nodded, then allowed himself to go limp and sink under the surface a moment. The heat from the water relaxed his exhausted muscles and being naked in a bunch of men no longer bothered him much.

Progress.

Surfacing, he said, "There's been trouble. I doubt she'd consider herself a Weaver these days. She still works with her herbs and stuff, though."

"We wondered why she wasn't holding clinics. She's been to the village a few times, but just to the market. When she's here, we sort of expect her to take care of us."

"She wants to," Joss said. "Do any other Weavers come through here?" The little-used northern track connected only to the Motherhouse, but a more important road from the west dead-ended at the hamlet. No one lived in the hills to the east, and not for the first time he wondered why.

"Not often. Healers, once or twice a year. We mostly get by."

Mostly. Willow would be heartbroken, if she heard.

"I wish I could say otherwise, but you may not see her for a while. She's not well." His throat clenched for a moment, hurting for her. "She's – she can't Heal anymore."

The faces of the men in the pool showed consternation.

"Damn."

"Poor gal."

"Didn't know that was possible."

"Why not?"

"The Aura – I can't say I understand it," Joss said. "The Motherhouse tried to fix it and it backfired."

"You use strange words. What's that mean, backfired?"

"Didn't work. And bad consequences."

The man nodded. "You talk funny, too. You're not from around here."

"No, quite a way north." He'd decided to use distance as his cover story. No way was he going to try to explain Terra, the crash, the power cell.

Conversation drifted away from him and toward plans for harvest. The hamlet, like most, was largely self-sustaining, as reflected in their unwillingness to part with their hard-to-replace knives and razors, coming as they did from the Northland. If he needed a shave, he went to the men's lodge in Hallan. If he wanted to whittle, he used the knife Quinn had slipped to him before he left the Motherhouse. For safety, she'd said. Most people didn't own their own knives.

His stubble hadn't concerned Willow, although he'd reddened her skin in places. And the water's temperature accounted for the rising heat on his face.

The long summer evening drifted toward nightfall as he parted with the men and made his way up the hill to Willow's cabin. The goats greeted him, and he rubbed their heads. They'd been lying just outside the vegetable garden, making him wonder again why they left her plants alone. Some magic she'd once woven, he supposed.

A good place. Far from anything he'd imagined for himself, but then Terra offered nothing like this. Joss didn't deal routinely with words like *serenity* or *beauty*, but looking out over the lakes and the hills as they turned purple in the fading light, the Hallan valley resonated with him. Something positive. Something worth fighting for.

After he left tomorrow, he doubted he'd be free to settle here in the foreseeable future. He wondered if he should consider crossing the mountains to the east, seeking out the origin of the Aura. The thought worried him for reasons that remained obscure. He needed the Old Man. Joss sensed a wisdom there, a deeper understanding of this new life he'd literally fallen into.

And the prospect of devoting six months or a year to training hadn't been resolved, but so much had opened to him by chance, he had to wonder what more there might be. His mechanical ability and work ethic had brought him here, but it was up to him to make his way forward.

Anyway, Willow wanted him to train. That alone was sufficient argument.

She.

The memory of the pure exultation she'd taught him would always be entangled with fear, not only of what happened, but that he'd hurt her, so slight under him.

Slight but strong. Willow's slender frame hid muscle. Necessary, given the work she did, the distances she covered. The way she'd managed her end of Kiril's litter, despite his expecting her to collapse on him any minute, gave evidence to that.

And then there was Kiril. His former commander didn't figure into his calculations. He was lost and angry, although he'd never admit it, and they were no longer a team. Nothing to be done about that. Kiril would adapt, or he wouldn't.

He occasionally wondered whether his positive feeling for the valley stemmed from Willow's presence in it. No, he concluded, despite her undoubted influence on his perceptions. Even if she left and never returned, he believed he would consider staying. As for her Auric connection, somehow that had no effect on his reaction to her.

The main room of the cabin had been tidied, and she'd lowered the curtain defending her bedroom. He moved quietly as he prepared for bed, surprised by his own fatigue.

Plenty of time to work through his questions tomorrow, trekking back to the Motherhouse to rouse Quinn and Bryar. He sank into sleep with a vague hope that he'd get a chance to kiss Willow again before he headed north.

Sometime in the night Joss sensed a shift, a change of density in the air. Instantly alert, he rose onto an elbow and fixed his eyes on the curtain, defined by a trickle of starlight around the edges. The curtain twitched, swayed, and a hand pushed it aside. Willow soundlessly stepped in.

He spoke without thinking. "I didn't know you'd gone out."

"Go back to sleep." Her voice conveyed bone-deep weariness, beyond what might logically be expected from the time of night. His whisperer senses registered more, distress to the point of despair. She dropped her sandals and a small pack by the door and padded barefoot toward the bedroom.

"Tell me what's wrong." Then, having damn near *demanded* she confide in him, he mentally cursed himself. Shouldn't he have produced a more sympathetic, softer question, given, well, everything? The more deeply enmeshed in the man-woman thing he became, the more it confused him.

She stopped, fisting the curtain that defended her private space. He made out her silhouette, dark against dark. "A boy came for me. For a childbirth. Oh, Joss." She changed direction, collapsed in a chair, and lowered her head to her folded arms on the table.

He considered lighting a candle or the cookfire, but hadn't mastered fire creation with a flint. It would take more time than it was worth. *One day,* he promised himself. But Willow's distress took precedence over his lack of fire-building skill. Instead, he rose and looped the curtain over the hook to let in starlight and a breath of fresh nighttime air. He kicked his bedding against a wall, then knelt by her chair and put a hand on her back. "Tell me."

"I never knew. I never even imagined." Her muffled voice seemed to come from far away, as if a reflection of a memory.

"Imagined what?"

"She'd been in labor for a full night and day. Jana sent the boy to find me, she's the local healer, and…"

He waited.

"We nearly lost them both. Jana saved them. Not me…"

Again she trailed off. Joss half hoped she'd fallen asleep, but her jagged energy told him otherwise.

"Tell me," he said again. Purge her of tonight's events so she could sleep.

Ignoring his hand, she shook off her torpor and crossed to the cookfire, creating a small blaze within a couple of minutes. By its light, her face looked gaunt, her eyes enormous.

She placed a pot of water over the fire and waited for it to boil without giving any sign she was aware of his presence. Then she added an assortment of herbs, covered the pot, and smothered the fire. Whatever was to come would be in darkness.

Her choice.

But the simple act of making a tisane restored her equanimity; sounding calm and determined, she said, "I will never use the phrase 'hedge healer' again. I hadn't realized the extent Weavers denigrate them. In all our years of training, no one ever taught how difficult basic healing is. We access the Aura and work with templates and... and they can't do that. They work with what they're given. An ordinary village healer is closer to the earth than I am."

Because his bulk occupied far too much of the tiny room, he'd long since moved to his usual chair in the corner. "You have the same skills," he pointed out.

"Once." She set two mugs on the table, moving by rote through the darkness. "Now, I know less than they do. Saving the baby... I didn't believe we could. Without the Aura, I didn't know how to bring him to life. I panicked. Jana handled everything."

The plate covering the pot rattled as she carried it to the table. Joss was on his feet in a moment, taking it from her unsteady hands, settling her in a chair. As he poured their tisanes, the air filled with the aromas of mint and bitter, healing herbs.

He sat. "The baby's okay?"

"Yes. He's sickly, but alive. The mother's weak. I'm worried about her milk, but Jana knows what remedies to use. My mind blanked. I'm tired, Joss. I'm just so tired."

"Drink your tisane."

Emptiness consumed her, as if her essence had been lost in the night. If Joss weren't governing himself with an iron grip, he would be totally freaked by her lack of mental substance. *God*, but he wished he didn't read her emotions so clearly. She stared across the cabin at nothing, her eyes blank and unfocused.

Get the tisane into her, he told himself, then get her to bed.

"They work so hard," she said. "With the Aura, it was easy. No one ever taught me how to heal without Entrée."

"Tisane, Willow. Please."

"Yes."

She sipped, wrinkled her nose – which gave him a preview of the taste – then sipped again. He tried his own. Bitter, as he'd expected. The mint helped, but not much.

"I'm a fraud."

"Don't say that."

"I should apprentice to Jana. Learn again how to do this. I'm not part of my own element anymore."

"You did the best you could tonight. No one can ask for more than that."

She finished half of the mug before she shoved it aside. "I can't face this." She was talking to herself, not to him, her mind far away. Even the jagged fragments of feeling had disappeared, masked, perhaps, by the medicines in the drink.

You will not panic. The words might be a mantra.

Joss let silence settle between them while he sorted out his thoughts. Bottom line? The middle of the night was no time to deal with life crises.

He stood, raised Willow up, and led her into the bedroom, holding the curtain aside, encouraging her forward.

She sank onto the straw-filled muslin mattress covering the platform that occupied most of the room, and unexpectedly grasped his sleeve. "I'm afraid to be alone," she said, so quietly he wasn't certain he had heard correctly. Until she tugged, bringing him down next to her.

Joss moved his big body to the far side of the platform and pulled her close. She slept in minutes, as if finding safety in his arms. He, however, lay awake into the night, listening to the serenade of insects outside, holding her against her occasional shudders as she dealt with whatever terrors assaulted her dreams.

Chapter 24

Leaving Willow the next day felt like a rotten idea, and in fact Joss delayed his departure until after lunch; a reasonable precaution given her precarious emotional state. Even though she could hardly wait to be rid of him. Working through this new blow to her self-identity and pride was nothing she intended to share.

Right now, he valued the separation as much as she did, despite his worry. Two days on the road gave him the space to sort through the confused emotions brought on by his last full day and night with her. When he reached the Motherhouse, while he wouldn't go so far as to say he understood all that had happened, some of the mental knots had loosened. He'd settle into his new reality, same as all the other new realities that had assaulted his training, his experience, and his convictions since finding himself in the Midland. He just needed time.

And he'd rather do the settling with Willow, a bald fact he was nowhere near coming to terms with.

The stealth techniques they'd learned in survival courses came in handy. Joss figured he couldn't afford to be seen, especially in the restricted Weavers' lodges, because Arwen and her council were fully capable of preventing him from delivering his messages or leaving again. He'd hoped to catch Bryar or Quinn outdoors, and alone. After several hours he gave up on that idea. Fallback plan, visit them in their rooms, even though the lodges were off limits except to guild members. Willow had mapped the locations for him; he kept his fingers crossed for the accuracy of her memory.

Arwen stalked the grounds of the Motherhouse, watching everything, periodically raising her head as if listening or seeing something invisible. A scary woman, Arwen. Joss would swear she'd detected his presence, although to the best of his knowledge she never saw him.

Because so many of the Scribes were in residence, getting into their small lodge proved tricky. After an hour of watching from the shadows of a rainy evening, he sensed a break in the to-ing and fro-ing and seized it, slipping into her quarters sight unseen. Quinn wasn't there. When she finally came in, well after dark, Joss took the precaution of wrapping one arm around her waist and simultaneously planting his other hand across her mouth. As he expected, she fought like a fury, kicking backwards, digging an elbow into his gut. "It's me," he whispered.

He let her go, and she turned on him, furious. "What the hell do you think you're doing?"

"Trying to keep you from screaming."

Fortunately, Quinn wasn't the type to act in rage. Her anger would be cold and rational. If she sought revenge, it would be calculated, not done in the heat of the moment but a stiletto driven in slowly when you least expected it. He'd rather stay on the good side of Quinn.

"A bit heavy-handed?" Sarcasm dripped from her tongue. "But perhaps manners aren't your strong point. You're more about brute force, right? I want to say get the hell out of my room, but I suppose there's a reason you're here."

He let the insult bounce off him. "Willow needs you."

"Why?" She stowed her satchel and shook the water from the oiled cape she'd worn against the steady rain.

"Exchange of information. But more than that, she needs her friends."

Quinn turned that hard stare on him. "That's all you're sharing?"

"Right now, yes. How's the Aura these days?"

"Stable." She kicked her sandals into a corner and pulled off the rain-soaked trousers she wore beneath her tunic.

"Have you heard from Kiril?" Joss asked.

"Shouldn't I be asking you that question?"

He bit his irritation back. "Not where I've been."

She conceded but with ill grace, standing in front of him with her arms folded across her chest. "No, nothing. I assume he's in Stanstead."

"Can you leave?"

"Not legitimately, but anything is possible. Whether it's advisable..."

"In this case, yes. Will you get in trouble?"

Quinn shrugged the question off. "Her cabin?"

He gave a terse nod. "How soon?"

"Depends. I'll be there. It might take a while."

The Scribes' lodge had fallen quiet. He listened at the door to be sure, then slipped out, moving silently along the corridor.

Bryar was easier. The Bards had congregated in their common room; music and laughter poured into the lobby. Joss tapped on Bryar's door on the second floor and stepped in.

He sat on his bed, tuning a stringed instrument Joss didn't recognize and singing the notes under his breath. He looked up as Joss came in but showed no surprise.

"You expected me?" Joss asked.

"Quinn said you'd be coming. How is she?"

"Willow? She's been better. She needs you." He didn't pursue the question of how Quinn communicated between the lodges.

"I wasn't sure. Before she vanished, she wanted nothing to do with us."

Joss caught a pang of hurt, meant to be private, under Bryar's words. Sometimes – most of the time – he wanted to kick this whisperer thing to the gutter and live a normal life. "Animals do that when they're injured. Go to ground." Another of those odd scraps of information that turned up in his head these days.

"So I hear. She's at her cabin?"

Another nod.

"Did she take her flute with her?"

"If she did, she hasn't used it." There'd been no music. Not even absentminded humming.

"Find it. You are going back?"

"As soon as I can. Did my leaving cause trouble?"

Bryar's mouth twisted, caught between amusement and frustration. "Not much. Quinn and I got a dressing down. I suspect Arwen knows either of us might vanish like you did, but I doubt she'd go out of her way to stop us. She's as worried as we are. Blames herself."

"Why the flute?" Joss asked.

"She plays. It helps her when she's upset." Bryar stood and slipped the stringed instrument into a fitted leather case while Joss fought down a twinge of jealousy at this tiny window into Bryar's life with Willow. "It's one thing I can do for her. About the only thing, really."

"You're her friend. That's as important."

"Just find the flute. It'll be a day or two before I can escape, so you take it to her."

Bryar words struck him as true. A heaviness surrounded Willow these days, rendering her deaf and blind to the wonders of the natural world that had been her mainstay. Music might not assist in restoring her powers, but it would soothe.

"She asked that you tell Romarin where she is and that she's okay."

"Of course I will. Poor kid's worried."

So are you. More than Bryar admitted.

He got the instructions for finding Willow's suite before he snuck out. Her quarters in the Healers' lodge proved to be the hardest yet, because the place buzzed with activity; he waited until deep in the night to sneak in, shielding his lantern. The flute lay on a shelf in her wardrobe. He put it in his satchel and added a change of clothing, a hairbrush, things to make her life more comfortable.

From the dark dining hall he filched some of the dried rations the Weavers carried with them, then he worked his way out of the environs of the Motherhouse. He'd a lot rather have a roof overhead than camp in the rain, but he wasn't willing to risk getting trapped. Two days and he'd be back with Willow. Doing whatever he could, even if it was just tending her garden; and for them both, continuing to reconstruct the elements of a life.

Chapter 25

In the midafternoon heat, Willow's little cabin felt like a party site, with four people filling the main room. Bryar sat across from Joss, picking idle tunes on his chitarre. He had arrived the day before, Quinn a few hours ago. It made sense that she'd have a harder time escaping the Motherhouse, being on the council and at Arwen's beck and call. She busied herself in the small cooking area, while Willow prepared to go to the garden for fresh produce,

Joss sat at the table watching everything – but mostly watching Willow. He was a cipher, quietly observing, keeping his thoughts to himself. Something had changed. However much it intrigued him, Bryar couldn't pinpoint the shift in energy between Willow and Joss.

Willow stopped by the door and put a hand on his shoulder. "Come with me."

"Sure." They shared a smile and a look, the same as always. Almost the same.

He stowed the chitarre in its case and laid it on her bed, the only safe place with so many people filling the cabin. He was glad to get outside, gladder still to spend one-on-one time with Willow.

When he stepped through the door, she was on her knees in the vegetable garden. "You do salad greens," she commanded.

"And you'll do...?"

"Beans. Early beets, if they are ready. There is vinegar from last year's wine, and I traded for a dish of honey."

He grinned as he squatted by her row of new greens. Trust Willow to remember the nasty rash he'd developed on his hands the last time he picked beans. He filled the bowl she'd handed him before he spoke again. "Talk to me, Wils."

She looked up from the bean plants, her brown eyes calm but shuddered. "What do you expect me to say?"

"Uh-uh. Don't do that." He set the bowl on the ground, pulled her to her feet, and walked her out of the garden, onto the grassy hillock across the track from the cabin. There he wrapped his arm around her. "We've always said everything to each other. Now you're mum. I need to hear you."

She turned away from him, staring downhill toward Hallan. "You are my best friend, you and Quinn. But too much has changed..."

"And you're afraid we'll abandon you? Come on. With twenty-five years of friendship between us? Willow, despite what happened—"

"But it did happen, didn't it? I am not the same woman."

He let it hang for the space of a breath. "I'm not the same man. We were children when we started, and we've weathered all manner of change. There's no reason we can't weather this as well."

"I am no longer a Weaver."

The flatness in her voice chilled him. "But you don't know—"

"Stop it." She turned on him and snapped out the words. "Do not hold out hope when there is none. I will find work, ply my craft in Hallan or some other hamlet. I will be fine. But do *not* hold out a false hope."

She was right, and he hated it.

"Did Joss bring your flute?"

"He did."

"Have you played it?"

"I have not been in the mood."

"We'll play duets this evening."

"I doubt I can, without..." She made a gesture with her hand.

"You don't need the Aura. You'll remember the music."

"Do not push me, Bryar. The changes in my life present difficulty enough."

He turned from her to stare out across the valley. "You're fighting me off. You've never done that before."

"I am sorry. But none of your stories and songs tell of a woman in my predicament. Is that not true?"

As deeply attuned as he was to rhythms, he flinched at her use of her childhood dialect. When he first met Willow, she almost never contracted two words into one, giving her sentences an unusual, awkward cadence. Over the years at the Motherhouse, then as a Weaver, she had released her earlier speech patterns. He wondered why they should return now. Her life as a child in the far west had not been particularly happy.

"It's true. No stories to help."

When he pulled her against him, she came willingly enough, but without a sense of surrender or even relaxation. He had hoped to take her out to a meadow, or swim across the lake, and make love with her after their meal. Her self-imposed isolation told him she wouldn't be receptive, for possibly the first time since they became lovers over twenty years ago.

Children. We were children. The woman in his arms now was far more complex. He had nothing to offer beyond his music and his body. When Willow rejected those, she left him empty-handed.

"There is work to do," she said into his shoulder. "The others will want their meal."

"Okay." He kept her hand in his as they walked back to the garden to finish harvesting the vegetables.

After Quinn worked her magic over Willow's cookfire, they carried their dinner to the hillock and sprawled on the grass, eating, enjoying the breeze, not saying much. Despite his size, Joss lounged as comfortably as the rest of them, speaking only to compliment Quinn on her cooking.

Quinn put her spoon in her empty bowl and said, "Why did you call us here?"

Trust Quinn to take the conversation to the heart of their concern.

When Willow didn't answer, Joss spoke. "We've talked a lot about what happened. What she experienced."

"At the Motherhouse as well," Quinn interrupted, impatience in her voice. "Have you got something new?"

Joss glanced at Willow, as if waiting for her to lead the conversation, before he nodded. "Maybe. It concerns the origin of the Aura and your history as a civilization."

"There's the mystery of sharing a language with you, and the simple fact that we're only in year three ninety, with the first two hundred years closed to us and only scanty records from the biblios for the hundred years after that." When Quinn's eyes narrowed that way, she was paying close attention.

"The Aura may not be intrinsic to the land." Joss said bluntly, then fell silent, letting his words sink in.

"We believe it to be a part of us. What holds our civilization together." Quinn sounded defensive, reflecting Bryar's reaction.

Joss nodded. "It is and it does. It doesn't follow that it always did."

A gust of wind shook the leaves of a solitary tree uphill from them. One of the goats studied them from a little distance, her head cocked. After another long silence, Quinn said, "Ezra implied that, when he told some of us it originated in a specific place, somewhere across the hills. But what is it, if not intrinsic? Created?"

Bryar looked at Willow, but she watched her hands, weaving a chain of clover flowers.

"When Willow collapsed," Joss said slowly, as if picking his words with care, "she had a sense – only a sense, this isn't definite – that the energy pulled from her left, to the east."

"Like a magnet," Willow confirmed, looking up, "sucking it from me."

"We don't know what's on the other side," Quinn said. "We can't cross the hills."

"Why not?" Joss asked.

"It's proscribed." Quinn's voice was curt, subtly demanding they not push for more information; she knew more than she was telling. "Nobody goes that direction. Another civilization lives there, not like us. There's no communication."

"But whatever generates the Aura is over the hills," Joss said.

A stunned silence blanketed the peaceful afternoon.

"By not intrinsic, you mean a thing, like your power cell?" Quinn asked, incredulity in every word.

"Exactly."

"Sweet Sustainer," Bryar mumbled.

Nobody spoke. Bryar felt a little sick. His mind shied away from this new concept of the Aura as if it were poison. Across from him, Willow's clover chain lay forgotten in her lap. Quinn looked from Joss to Willow, then off into nowhere. Working through the implications, logically, step by step.

Quinn broke the silence. "Auric energy flowed around the circle, and diffusely across it to form a sphere, working through the eight templates and melding them into one. When the circle fell apart, the energy collided in Willow from two directions. The collision left nowhere for the excess energy to go, so what you're saying is, it was pulled from her. Looked at that way, it probably saved her life. And if you're right and it is a – thing…" The word carried a freight of revulsion, as if Quinn wanted to gag. "If we could find this thing, learn what it is and how it works… what good would it do?"

"That's why you're here," Joss said. "To figure out if it's worth an expedition."

"Could it help us solve the problem of your cell?" Quinn asked.

"I'm skeptical. Even if we did find it, surely other people on their side have tried to control it in the past. It's not lying around waiting for us."

"I expect it's warded," Quinn said absentmindedly; her thoughts were elsewhere.

"All I'd want to do is confirm the hypothesis," Joss said. "I understand how our cell works, but why it affects life here as it does… something about this place transmutes the radiation, and if we're right, that could well be the case with the other source, too."

Quinn nodded. "We'd need a Weaver to locate this mysterious generator, if it does exist."

Joss made a self-deprecating gesture with his hand. "I was able to track our power cell. I could try to home in on it, but I expect you're right."

"Your weak connection might work in our favor, but you lack experience," Quinn said. "And I'd never be allowed to go. There's stuff going on in the Scribes' guild... sorry, can't tell you. And don't forget winter's coming, with no way to cross the hills."

"Hold it," Bryar said. "Even if we found it and could get near it, we couldn't do anything with it. We can't experiment with the Aura."

"You're right," Quinn said after a pause. "Finding the truth wouldn't solve any of our problems. I do know this much," she added. "What they do with the Aura east of the hills is unlike our workings. And it's as if the Aura itself is stronger."

Bryar saw a flash of life cross Willow's face. She sat up straighter, focused on Quinn. "If they're so powerful," she said softly, "Someone over there might know how to help me."

"Insanity," Quinn said. "Too many unknowns."

"I'm not convinced we should risk crossing the hills," Joss said. "Does it make sense to tackle this from another direction? You've said your history only goes back a hundred years or so. Why? If we go through a template, back to the origins..."

"You don't know what you're asking," Quinn snapped. Bryar knew the signs; her nerves were on edge. She didn't like the way the conversation was going.

"It's dangerous," he added. "You can lose yourself and never get out."

"Like getting lost in your mind?" Joss asked. "I read about that, back on Terra. A form of mental illness."

"Don't do it," Willow said to Quinn.

Quinn fiddled with the grass and clover surrounding her, then met their eyes in turn as she scanned the circle. "I can't. I would, but I'd require deeper linking than we've ever tried. Scribes, probably the whole guild. But experiments with templates can go awry much too easily. And Arwen would never authorize it."

"I am not asking you to," Willow repeated, insistent.

"We've come full circle," Quinn said. "I snitched some honey cakes from the dining hall before I left. Back in a sec." She started to stand.

"I'm not interested in any of the rest of it." Willow spoke forcefully, drawing their attention. "The people over there... if they know other ways to work with the Aura, I have to go. I'm an empty shell here, and I have nothing to lose."

"Wils..." Quinn began.

"I mean it. Don't argue with me, Quinn."

Was it being left out of consideration for this journey that led him to speak up? Later Bryar would wonder what mad impulse made him say, "I'll go with you."

Three sets of eyes looked at him, Joss neutral, Willow surprised, Quinn worried.

"You are no explorer," Willow said gently. "This will be risky."

Quinn sat back down and touched his hand. "We have no idea what you'd be facing."

He could withdraw his offer without shame. He was a musician, a man who told the stories, not the one who forged them. He wanted beautiful things, comfortable beds, congenial companions...

"No. I'll do it. I'm ready for a challenge."

"It'll be more than a simple challenge," Joss said. "Those hills of yours, they're closer to mountains. Is there even a trail? We might get lost, the weather could close in before we find our way out the other side. If Willow goes, I do, too. Frankly, I'd rather she stay here, but I understand her reasons."

"This is real?" Quinn asked. "All three of you are ready to put your lives on the line on the chance there's someone trustworthy over there who might – *might* – help Willow?"

"The Motherhouse can't do anything for me," Willow said. "If they're so much stronger, it's worth any risk." The longing in her eyes brought a lump to Bryar's throat.

Quinn sighed. "Wait. Let me mull it over." She rose and went to the cabin. When she returned she carried a plate with the promised honey cakes.

"Not hungry," Bryar said. The queasiness that had arisen with the idea that the Aura was caused by an artifact hadn't left him.

"Eat the things," Quinn grumbled. "I broke a few rules to get them."

Bryar helped himself to a cake, and the scene returned to normal. Except for Joss's presence, it felt comfortably familiar, the three of them, kids then adults, but always together.

And that had probably been Quinn's intention all along.

Willow took a bite, then stretched out on the ground. The few clouds in the sky already reflected the orange and red hues of sunset; the days were getting shorter. Joss bit into his cake, gave it an approving look, and devoured the rest in two bites. Bryar held out an arm to Quinn, and she settled in his embrace as they shared one cake, then another.

The same as always.

When they finished the treat, Quinn said, "You're serious."

"Yes," Joss said. "But we should wait until we're sure we've learned all we can here."

"No," Willow said again. "That means spending the winter here. I want this over with."

Bryar merely nodded, letting their conclusions play out as they would.

"All right." Quinn left no doubt of her discomfort with the decision, but she wasn't stopping them. "At least Willow's given us a valid reason to undertake this foolishness. There's a trail going east."

"Really?" Willow sat up.

"Where?" Bryar asked.

"When you take the track north from the Motherhouse, after half a day you come to a fork. To the left is Ezra's – but don't try to follow it," she added. "He's tweaked the energies around his home, so you won't find him unless he wants you to. The right hand fork may lead into the hills. I've never heard of anyone who's taken it, and I can't find anything in the templates in the last fifty years. Makes me wonder how it stays open, because it's definitely a track, not made by animals, and uninhabited, at least for a day's walk. I'm not sure it goes through, but it's a possibility. I bet Arwen knows. Or Ezra."

"Getting to it means taking the road back through the Motherhouse," Joss said. "Is that going to be a problem?"

Bryar's mouth twitched. "Being hauled up before Arwen is nobody's idea of a picnic in the sun, but Quinn and I are already in trouble."

"If we're lucky, we can get the council's agreement," Joss said. "And stock up on provisions. It's better than starting out unprepared."

"I suggest that Bryar and I leave tomorrow," Quinn said. "This trek needs to happen well before the winter sets in. You two follow in a few days, after Arwen's calmed down and I have a chance to present the plan. She won't be happy about sending you," she said to Bryar. "But you're closest to Willow. I'm not thrilled, either. But other than putting both of Mari's parents at risk, I don't have any arguments to stop you." Quinn surveyed them once again, then she got to her feet. "I'm walking to Hallan and back. Get some exercise before bed. Anybody want to come?"

"Sure," Bryar said, and scrambled up to join her, licking the remains of the sticky cakes from his fingers and hoping the exercise would settle his mind.

Chapter 26

In the end, Willow and her friends decided to walk together – could she consider Joss a friend? The word seemed inadequate. Perhaps the task facing them, and the uncertainty about the Aura's origin, left them all just slightly out of focus, in need of an anchor point. Two days after their strategy dinner on the hill, they'd shared a hearty lunch, using up perishables, and set off for the Motherhouse.

By then her clover chain was dry and brown. Like me, she mused. Nothing but a brittle husk, the life of the seed inside withered and dead.

They should be planning, making lists, discussing options. They should be strategizing for the confrontation with Arwen – because confrontation it certainly would be. Instead, the final day of their walk had passed, so far, with little or no conversation.

She lived with a weary, attenuated hatred for the changes in her life. Hated, for instance, Bryar's choosing to cross the hills with her. He wasn't the stuff of heroes. Supremely talented, strong in body, but hardly inclined to challenge himself. The very fact of his determination to undertake this journey heightened her dread of what was to come.

She had always found comfort in Bryar, not only his lovemaking but also the way he knew her, one of the few she ever let in that deeply, but now something had shifted between them. Why? The afternoon with Joss? She and Bryar both had other lovers, but still turned to each other. That afternoon had changed their dynamic. And yet she kept Joss at bay, too, as if what little was left of her was too small and fragile to risk sharing. Not that he'd tried to approach her.

No wonder she walked in silence.

Bryar stuck by her side, his face expressionless. Up ahead of them, Quinn expounded on something or other, sketching in the air with her hands. Joss followed her speech and her gestures attentively, which Quinn would appreciate. A born teacher, she did not tolerate wasted time.

They stopped for an early lunch under a shade tree, two hours from the Motherhouse. Thin cloud obscured the sun and cooled the morning. From the small rise where they sat, Willow could see the track snaking its way through the rolling landscape to the destination she used to think of as home.

Over dry bread and fruit, Quinn said, "No point sneaking in. There's too much to do, and Arwen's going to have our hides, Bryar's and mine anyway, as soon as she finds out we're back. Might as well get it over with."

Bryar groaned.

"How strict is this obedience thing?" Joss asked. "In the military, to do what you two did, they'd have shot me."

"It's more tradition than rule," Willow said. "To live as a Weaver requires discipline, years of training. Deference to our ways. It's just how it is. No one questions it."

"With some flouting of the rules built into the system," Bryar added. "Our escape routes, for instance. When we were kids, we thought they were so secret, but they were aware of every one. Probably used them themselves."

Willow dredged up a smile, for his sake. "If we had ever gone missing from a crucial lesson, we'd have been in big trouble. We were teenagers."

"Steam needs a release," Quinn said. "Remember when you and Bryar snuck off to make love? First time for both of them," she added in an aside to Joss, who made no acknowledgement. "The whole class was in on it. I suspect council knew not only what was happening, but where, and when to expect you back. Didn't the dining hall save the evening meal for you?" She laughed, and Bryar joined her.

Willow smiled through the heat flooding her face to the roots of her hair, earning a puzzled look from Quinn. She'd never blushed at the memory of that first loving before, both of them so young, life so magical...

Joss ignored the byplay. "This is different, though. This lockdown business..."

"Everybody's scared," Quinn said, returning to seriousness in an instant. "We can't be sure from one day to the next if we'll be able to access our templates. It's crippling. But the reality is, we are independent people. Our ties to the Motherhouse, and especially the guilds, work in our favor, so we keep them strong. But once we've finished training, we're on our own."

"The council doesn't control you?" Joss asked.

"Let's say, not so far," Quinn said cautiously.

Joss nodded but said nothing.

"So, we march straight to Arwen, right?" Bryar asked.

"Expect the tongue-lashing of the year."

"Joss should go to the guest lodge," Willow said. "There's no reason for Arwen to take issue with him."

"No," Joss said. "We're in this together. And I'm the one who came back to get Quinn and Bryar."

"It's masterful, the way Arwen does it," Quinn said around a mouthful of dried fruit. "She's been on council since we were in training. She scared us then, and it's carried forward."

Bryar laughed. "Right. We're grown up, and we're still shaking like babies." He took a final bite from his waybread and stood. "Let's get this over with."

Arwen's office and workroom, a small stone cubicle buried deep in the Motherhouse, felt dark, claustrophobic, and cold after the warm temperatures and open spaces of their trek. The explosion and tongue-lashing weathered, Bryar found himself lined up with the others facing her desk, feeling every bit as guilty as Quinn had predicted. He wanted to squirm when Arwen's gaze drilled into him, but refused to.

Quinn, their unofficial spokesperson, said, "Willow needed us."

Arwen turned to Willow. "There was no reason for you to leave in the first place. This is your home."

Beside him Willow radiated tension, but when she spoke her voice was level. "No, ma'am. Not anymore."

"Reconsider that. You're a part of this community. And you," she said, her gaze spearing Quinn this time. "In a position of trust, I expect you to set an example."

"For instance, exemplifying the bonds of friendship," Quinn replied, no uncertainty in her voice. "Going to the aid of a person who needed me. The lockdown is too restrictive."

"Was. We've lifted it, but only a few Healers have left. The fact remains, you snuck out instead of speaking to me first."

Quinn offered no further justifications.

Arwen sighed, exasperated. "Given the choice, I'd confine you all to your lodges for the next nine-day. Regrettably, you're too old for that."

Bryar turned his grin on the frustrated older woman. "We regret it too, ma'am. But not much."

Arwen slapped her hands on the table and stood. "Dare I hope you will be staying for a while? You and I have work to do," she said to Quinn. "And as for the rest of you…"

"No, ma'am." Quinn spoke quietly, but the words fell like a death knell in the small stone room.

"No?" Arwen sat back down.

Bryar stepped forward, just half a step but enough for him to assume responsibility for what came next. "Quinn's staying. Give us a chance to tell you what we've learned."

"This is going to take a while, isn't it?" Arwen again stood. "I suggest we carry our discussion to the dining hall. You look like a row of recalcitrant children, standing there."

"We feel that way, too," Bryar told her. But he grinned again and managed to eke a returning smile from her.

They followed her across the green to the hall. Around cups of caff – he noticed that Willow clutched hers, as if it were a lifeline – Quinn explained what they had learned of Willow's tragic loss, and what they intended to do.

Arwen fixed her eyes on Quinn. "At least you're right about one thing. It would be suicide to go that far into the templates. We'd never allow it." She gulped her caff, then set the mug down, rotating it on the table, her eyes focused on her hands as she did so. The four of them watched her, waiting.

"I am of two minds," she said. "Bryar, you and Willow are senior Weavers. I don't like putting you at risk. This is a job for a Scribe."

"Crossing the hills is that dangerous?" Joss asked. It was the first time he had spoken since they had filed into Arwen's workroom an hour or more ago.

"Yes, and this applies to you as well," Arwen confirmed. "You're unique, and still a mystery to us, nor are your powers fully developed."

"Why are the hills prohibited, Arwen?" Quinn asked.

Another long pause. "Their culture is much different from ours. They use templates in ways we don't understand. Whether that poses a threat to you, I can't say."

"Does it have a name, this other land?" Willow asked.

"Yes. Borgonne." She shrugged. "I don't have all the answers you want. It should be in the Aura somewhere, but I've never found it. I've never found much trace of their civilization at all. That in itself concerns me, because there should be a record of their usage, at least. Nobody can hide accessing the Aura."

Bryar shivered. He remembered being taught, long ago, that skilled Scribes could track your activities, but it hadn't crossed his mind in years. It felt like a violation.

"I intend to spend the next day or two searching," Quinn said. "With the name, I might have better success. The more information they have, the better. I wish I could go as well —"

"No," Arwen said flatly.

"You don't need to tell me. I'll do what I can from here."

All five mugs sat on the table now. "Anything else?" Arwen asked after a silence that set his nerves on edge. "I won't tolerate any more of this sneaking off. If you're going, go prepared, and with backup. What you did was folly."

"Yes, ma'am," he and Quinn said in tandem. Willow seemed to have retreated into herself, and Joss sat back in his chair, signaling non-participation.

"There is a town a half day's walk from the hills, called Orlan. You will go no farther than that," Arwen continued.

"Spend a day studying and learning, then return. I won't have you venturing into unknown territory with no supplies or backup until we know more. Bryar, be alert for any changes in the Aura, especially anything directional. You, too," she added to Joss. "Don't even think about finding the origin of our energies, not this time."

"Have you been there?" Quinn asked.

"No." Arwen was short. "I met someone from there once, a long time ago. He wasn't forthcoming."

"We need a few days to prepare," Bryar said when nobody else spoke up. "Quinn told us about a track that goes in the right direction."

Arwen looked at Quinn, who said, "The trail east from Ezra's track."

She nodded. "That's the only possibility I know of. I suppose I shouldn't be surprised you found it."

Quinn smiled.

"It's a long walk, without support," Arwen continued. "You'll need supplies for at least a nine-day, maybe more, in one direction. Forage where you can, and be aware that you'll have to restock when you've crossed the hills. I'm not sure what you can barter with. It'll be colder, so be prepared."

No one asked where Arwen got her information. All Scribes held a trove of facts they didn't share, except as needed. And Arwen had been a powerful Scribe for many years.

"You are free to utilize the stores and the kitchen. Check in with me before you leave. Do *not* broadcast word about this jaunt. I'll notify council, but I don't want it to get out to the children. That track isn't common knowledge, and I intend it to stay that way."

Both of Romarin's parents going off into the unknown. Bryar agreed with Arwen; no good could come of her learning of their plan.

The entire community of Weavers avoided the trail north, as if it didn't exist. He'd never wondered why, but even as apprentices they'd never explored to the north.

Or the east.

"One more thing," Arwen said.

They all stared at her; something in her voice said what came next was important, and secret.

"The hills... by now you all must have realized they are spelled. Non-Weavers can't cross them; they get confused and end up where they started after a day or two. You should all be fine, but I don't know if there are other hazards. So, Willow, I want you to stay on the track, even to sleep. Let the others do the foraging. It may be the only safe place, when we simply don't know what might happen to you if you go too far from the route."

Bryar swallowed. This trek suddenly seemed bigger, more intimidating, in ways he couldn't imagine.

Their meeting with Arwen wasn't over yet. Willow spoke up, almost timidly. "And if I make it safely? Will I find someone to help me?"

Arwen froze in the act of standing, then sat again. "There is a man..."

Willow thought with some certainty that she had relied too much on her rolling pack. Arwen had assured her that the trek would be too rough to use it, and she looked with dismay at the pile of supplies on her table. Only a few basic remedies, but heavy clothing, her winter bedroll, water and tools... once she added provisions, the weight would be unmanageable. She had never walked this far before without stops for food and lodging along the way.

Well, no help for it. With Bryar and Joss undertaking this trek for her, she had no right to complain.

A messenger kid appeared to announce a visitor. At the door to the Healers' lodge she found Joss, looking uncomfortable. Since the magical time in the meadow, and that night, they had hardly spoken or been alone. She was glad to see him. His size, but even more his stillness, made her feel safe.

"I'll carry some of your stuff," he said without preamble.

"Thank goodness. I was wondering how I'd manage. Come in." She led him upstairs, where he filled her small lounge. After sorting through her packing, he said, "I'll handle the food." He picked up her sheepskin vest and her bedroll. "These are bulky. Can you handle the rest?"

Hesitant, she nodded, then spoke. "Joss...?"

He was already at the door, her vest and bedroll in his big hands. "Hmm?"

"We haven't talked. Perhaps we should."

No question whether he caught her meaning. A hint of color rose over his unshaven cheeks.

"No." Without another word he turned and disappeared.

No.

He thought he had a lot to deal with. He had no idea how confusing he was.

But at least he'd removed her packing concerns. After a lifetime of independence, she wondered if she could grow accustomed to being taken care of.

She returned to her work, arranging her remaining belongings in her pack, then went downstairs to the Healers' workroom.

She found Dal there, frowning over a remedy. He didn't look up when she came in, but said, "Check this out, Willow."

She recognized the leaves. "Crampweed. For arthritis and menstrual problems. What is wrong with it?"

"The energy's attenuated and... well, out of balance. Not right for its purpose."

He set a small bottle on the workbench and stood to give her a hug. "I hear you're leaving."

"Yes. On a worrisome trek."

They settled on stools at the bench. Dal returned to fiddling with the remedy.

"Why worrisome?" he asked.

"No one goes to the hills. And without a Healer."

"You're a Healer."

"Any village healer surpasses my abilities. As I have proven," she added, thinking back to the childbirth, her reliance on Jana.

"You're wrong about that. Hedge healers work with a minimum of knowledge and a limited palette of remedies. That's why they got the nickname 'hedge'. You have a much larger pharmacopeia at your disposal."

She propped herself on an elbow, resting her head on her hand, and reached across the workbench for the small bottle. Frowning, she held it up to the light. "It's a peculiar color for crampweed."

"It's a student project, but I doubt this particular student made any energetic mistakes in its formulation."

"She's strong?"

"He, and yes. He'll be an excellent Healer. But this..."

"Harvested during one of the dead times?" The expression had come into common use around the Motherhouse for the periods when the Aura failed them.

"That's my guess. I'll ask him to repeat the exercise. It tells us something I'd rather not know about the energy fluctuations."

"Predictable, I suppose."

"Tell me what's really concerning you, Willow." Dal took the bottle from her and filed it, and the leaves, with the other students' remedies.

Her head still on her hand, her hair spilling onto the workbench, she said, "The hills are unknown. What if I fail to recognize any of the plants? What if one of us is injured or falls ill?"

"What if you can't singlehandedly solve all the problems of the Midland? No one expects you to work miracles."

"But we do work miracles. Every day."

"No. We use what's available. And so will you. What did you pack?"

"The basics. No more, because of weight."

"Not good enough. Help me."

The next half hour returned Willow to the wonderland of the herbs, as she and Dal sorted through the supplies and chose or rejected remedies, not in solution but dried, light and easy to carry. When they finished, ten packets lay on the workbench.

"Add this and you're ready to go." He poured alcohol into a small flask, corked it, and handed it to her. "This will see you through, without adding too much weight."

She found a cloth bag and stowed the herbs and flask. "Thank you. My mind must be overloaded."

"You've worked yourself into a state, so you forgot the basics, the non-template tools. Are you sure about this journey?"

"No, but nobody has produced a better option. It's not just my problem. We need to solve the mystery of the power cell, and Joss hopes if we can learn more about the other one—"

Dal's head jerked back. "Surely there can't be another of their devilish devices."

"Keep this to yourself, please." She outlined their theory about the origin of the Aura.

When she finished, he looked at her sadly. "I wish I hadn't heard that."

"It is a theory only. But we must learn more, or we may never be able to control the energy from the cell. Or restore what I lost."

"I want that above all. Be safe, Willow. You're important to me."

"As are you to me." She kissed Dal's cheek. "Shouldn't you be in Stanstead?"

"I'd like to be. The guild needs me here for now. Charlotte understands."

Did anyone understand her? It must be a nice feeling.

She picked up the bag and climbed the stairs to her room to finish packing.

Chapter 27

The rounded, forested peaks appeared before them in layers, every turn in the trail revealing more, higher ones ahead of them. Between these and a high, bright mist that obscured the sun, Willow often had no idea what direction they were walking, leaving her with a sinking feeling that they made no forward progress whatsoever. The track never ascended to the summits, depriving them of perspective, but maintained a reasonably level elevation, following the contour of the slopes in wide sweeps, then descending to cross lush but chilly valleys.

In the valleys they found sparkling rivers, dense riparian forests, and glades of ferns. When they climbed, the air grew cooler, and conifers released a refreshing scent as they trod on the needles littering the path. At lower elevations the big-leaf trees, only a few of which she recognized, provided a dappled shade.

Her earth-based instincts drew her to the largely unfamiliar understory vegetation – but to what end? Only the Aura made it possible to read them, form a picture of their healing powers. Now, they were just plants. That awareness haunted her, for all she did her best to block it from her mind. Conscious of Arwen's stricture, she explored only within a pace of the trail, although she sensed nothing menacing in the surrounding forests.

The total absence of towns or people, however, unnerved her. Having lived her entire life in the Midland, she had never been more than a day or two, at most, from habitation.

One day they walked for hours through a steady downpour, and one night the thunderstorms visible from the

Motherhouse as they accumulated over the hills cracked directly overhead, terrifying her. The tarp they used for a covering proved useless that night. Nobody got much sleep, and they were all grouchy the next morning, trudging forward in wet clothes and boots.

Usually taciturn, Joss became a man of even fewer words, lost in his own thoughts. He shared without complaint in the tasks that kept them going, including trapping animals for their evening meals, although she and Bryar both were more skilled than he. All three of them developed blisters, and he submitted to her ministrations without demur, but shifted away as soon as she finished. He had made no comment about their time of loving in the meadow, and showed no interest in repeating it, so she left him alone.

Bryar also had fallen silent, which troubled her. Did he regret his decision to participate in this expedition? By any criterion, it exemplified folly. When an action had been proscribed for longer than anyone could remember, further back than the accessible records in the Aura, there was a reason.

She tried to talk it over with them one night, seven days out, huddled close to the fire in the middle of the track, in deference to Arwen's warning. Willow knew how to make a fire manually, and she supposed Joss did as well although she had never seen him do so, but tonight, as usual, Bryar had drawn from the Aura to light their small pile of kindling. Nevertheless, she shuddered against the cold as she faced down their deadpan faces.

"I'm prepared to turn back, if you wish it. This journey made some kind of sense, in my cabin. But we were warm and well fed, so it was easy to play with theories and not enough facts. The reality is, we can't hope to accomplish anything. None of us is a Scribe. We are all exhausted, and our supplies are running low, not to mention Arwen's orders." Now that she'd had space to think, Arwen's words chilled her; what she knew about the mysterious Borgonne wasn't positive.

"We agreed," Bryar said. He sounded weary, and his movements told her the cost to him in terms of energy and spirits. She had not even heard his flute, echoing through the forest in the evening, in days. "Leave it alone, Wils."

"I am one person, and not the first to suffer a tragedy. You put yourselves at risk and incur more than your share of discomfort, doing this."

Bryar sprawled on the ground, like her staying close to the fire. "There's no point in discussing it," he said, an edge to his voice. "We're here. That's enough, okay? Anyway, this isn't only about you."

Bryar was rarely so tactless.

"He's right," Joss said, his first words all day not related to the mechanics of their journey.

And his last ones, it seemed. Although it wasn't yet nightfall, he pulled out his bedroll, wrapped himself in it, turned away from them, and settled in for sleep.

"I am grateful. I just wish—"

"Join me," Bryar said, perhaps sensing that his words had wounded her.

She glanced at Joss, then shifted around the fire. They sat for a while, leaning into each other, watching the flames.

"Quinn wanted to be here," he said quietly. "It should be the three of us. Don't fuss. It's an adventure, and it keeps me from growing stale."

"You'll never do that. But adventure is not what you usually seek."

"No. But helping you is."

She fell asleep next to Bryar, his arm heavy over her shoulders, as they had slept so many times before. But that did nothing to ease the niggling worry that dogged her tired footsteps as she trudged along the hillside in the morning.

"Oh, my," Willow breathed.

Every hill they'd climbed she'd believed to be the last, until another appeared ahead. Not this time. The track, which had left the bed of a stony and gullied, steep-sided ravine, rounded a corner and opened abruptly upon a vista such as she had never seen before. The climb out of the ravine had required hands as well as feet; she bent over to catch her breath before standing straight on the rock that formed a lookout and taking it in.

Twelve days on the trail had left her stronger, but also more fatigued; she still found the ascents a challenge. No landscape as dramatic as this existed in the Midland. During her life as a Weaver, she had traversed short-grassed plains and rolling hills. Before her, and well below her, golden grasses grew long and swayed in an irregular breeze, causing ripples to move across a plain that stretched forever, broken by the occasional copse or the trace of a stream. From her height it looked like a piece of finest fabric, the silk she had seen once or twice that came from the Southlands.

The track continued in long switchbacks down the east flank of the hill, toward a settlement in the distance. Bigger than Stanstead, she estimated, although the extent of the plain played tricks with her perspective. Reddish buildings huddled around a square, but she saw no sign of green space. A black tower on the northern outskirts dominated the town.

The Midland had grasslands, but nothing like this. The waving grain ran to the limits of her sight.

Joss arrived next at the lookout. Bryar had stayed back to set up camp, grumbling about a new blister on his foot. They were all tired, dirty, and more than ready to reach the end of the hills.

He winced as he reached her side.

"What is wrong?"

"Nothing. A pain in my head. Not worth worrying about." He breathed deeply and said no more.

She turned her attention from Joss to the landscape before them. "It is exquisite."

"If you say so."

"Have you ever seen anything like this? Does it look like Terra?"

"There are prairies, but I've never been there. Does it matter?"

"Don't be a grouch."

He nodded toward the town. "Is that where we're going? Orlan?"

"I suppose so. I wonder what the tall building is for."

"No idea. Defense, maybe. We might not receive the welcome you expect. Not everyone's as peaceable as your people."

Yours, too. We're your people now.

He frowned and rubbed his temples.

"Still hurts?"

"Yeah. As if my head's been pumped full of gas."

"I have a remedy for that type of headache. Let's go back."

Bryar appeared, scrambling up the ravine, scowling. "More of the same?"

Her excitement returned. "No, wait till you see. Oceans of grass. It's amazing."

Joss sat on the boulder while Bryar hauled himself out of the ravine. "Tell me we made it," he said between pants.

"We did, Bry. We're here."

She held out her hand. He took it and stood in one smooth movement.

His inhuman cry pierced the air. Bryar's hand jerked from hers as he reeled, his eyes rolled up behind his lids. He tripped on the edge of the ravine and crashed backward down the slope.

Joss skidded into the ravine before she recovered her wits. When Willow picked her way to them, stunned, she found Joss kneeling beside Bryar's limp, unconscious body, testing for a pulse. He gave her a curt nod as she knelt across from him. "Weak, but there."

Willow began a mechanical scan of Bryar's bones. He showed little sign of life, his breathing barely detectable.

"Your pack. Where is it?"

She'd left it at their planned campsite, downslope. She gestured and Joss hurried away.

Bryar had landed on his back, one arm wedged under him, the other outflung. She removed stones and smoothed the land before risking turning him to free the trapped arm. His wrist was purple and beginning to swell. She remembered a rivulet they passed half an hour ago. Cold water. They needed cold for the wrist.

She felt Bryar's head, feeling for bumps and watching his empty expression. Concussion, certainly. Without the Aura, she couldn't assess his body or isolate his injuries.

When Joss returned with her pack, she said, "Your headache?"

"Gone. I think we just found out why nobody crosses the hills."

"But what caused this?" As she spoke she stroked Bryar's forehead, brushed his chest and abdomen, watching his face for signs of pain.

"The Aura, as a guess. As soon as we cleared the trees above the ravine. First my head, then Bryar got the full dose, and you..."

"I felt nothing. That confirms it, doesn't it? And this has happened because of me."

"None of that." Joss squatted beside her and put his big hand under her chin, turning her head, forcing her to look at him. "A man's down. Right now he's our only focus. Do you understand me?"

She shook his hand off.

"Listen to me, Willow." He passed her a flask. "Drink, and if there's something for shock in that bag, take it. Now." His hard voice demanded she follow his orders.

She rummaged in the pack, found the vial she needed, and numbly dosed herself.

"Tell me what you've learned."

"Concussion, sprained wrist, nothing broken that I can detect manually."

"We risk moving him, then," Joss said.

"I'd rather not."

"We can't stay here. When it rains, this ravine will be a death trap. Help me."

He'd brought a selection of sticks and some rope from the campsite. Together they fashioned a frame to immobilize Bryar's head, as much as they could.

Her fault.

"There's a place not far downslope," Joss said. "Grassy, flat, and well below the lookout. I'll carry him."

"We should make a litter. Like we did with Kiril."

"No. Kiril was lighter and the land was level. As steep and rough as it is here, you couldn't stay in control. Hell, I'm not sure I can. It's a risk we'll have to take. I won't be able to see my feet, so stay close and let me know before I take a wrong step."

Bryar was compact rather than tall, but heavy boned. She watched, heart in her throat, as Joss lifted him, grimaced under the strain, then staggered as he found his balance. Bryar hung from his arms as if he were –

"Now," Joss commanded. "Watch. Warn me what's ahead." His foot edged forward across the loose stones and dirt of the ravine.

One step at a time, they moved along the steep, uneven, and rutted surface.

"Damn!" His foot slid out from under him. He landed on his back, Bryar on top of him, after skidding his body length down the slope. Gingerly he picked himself up, never releasing his hold on Bryar. "Breathe," he snapped at her, then began the slow descent again.

At the site Joss had chosen, he maneuvered his way up the ravine's wall, then stood still for a moment, catching his breath and his balance, before settling Bryar on the bed he'd created from two of the bedrolls. They left the makeshift neck support in place.

Bryar's face was pasty. Willow straightened his arms and legs and again put her hand on his forehead. "Cold."

"Shock."

She nodded. "I will need your help."

Joss made a small fire, struggling with a fire stone, and boiled water. She moistened Bryar's lips with two drops from the same vial she had used for herself, then they attended to his wrist and the cuts and bruises that peppered his body. When they finished, they wrapped him securely in the remaining bedroll.

"Now?" he asked.

"Now you."

"I'm fine."

"Prove it," she said, her patience no better than her nerves.

As she expected, his back was covered in abrasions from the fall. He sat still with ill grace while she cleaned and doctored them.

"Now we wait." She stowed her supplies as he got to his feet, surveying their new camp.

"Willow...?"

"Hmm?"

"He might be aware of you. It might help if you lie next to him. Hold him. Wherever he is, I think he's frightened."

Their eyes met, she on the ground beside Bryar, he towering over her. She wondered, in a flash, about the way he read the animals, picking up on their... what? Not thoughts, not emotions, whatever animals do. Did he experience the same with humans?

He was right, though. She sensed it, not through the Aura but because she knew Bryar so well. Wordlessly she stretched out on her side, folding her arm to rest her hand on his shoulder.

"I'm going hunting," Joss said. "Shout if you need me."

He disappeared down the trail, leaving her alone to whisper encouragement to her oldest and dearest friend.

Two days into their vigil, and still they waited. Joss leaned against a boulder, ignoring the painful fullness that invaded his head whenever he ventured to the lookout, and stared out at the valley. He no longer doubted. He was aware of everything Bryar felt. That didn't happen with everyone; Willow, for instance, he often found impossible to understand. Perhaps he'd tapped into the other man's mind because Bryar's everyday thoughts had shut down, exposing something raw and primitive. Bryar was beyond frightened, but Joss saw no point in telling Willow that. He was panic-stricken, locked in unconsciousness or coma or whatever.

And Joss knew it. He read Bryar's emotions.

He hated knowing, but it all made sense. His whole life he'd been able to recognize patterns, to fix things, rid them of incongruities to make them work together properly. The connections had once again fallen into place. The proscription on traveling over the hills, the Auric energy, the animal whispering thing…

Not that his understanding provided insight to reviving Bryar. He had to awaken, and soon. Joss wasn't sure how they would deal with the alternative.

Words played constantly in his mind, and he let them, hoping they'd somehow feed through the Aura to their target: *Wake up, Man. Come back to us. Wake up, Bryar.*

He went off by himself daily, giving himself respite from Bryar's agony, coming back with some small animal or other to be skinned and, under Willow's direction, cooked. They needed the meat; their provisions were almost exhausted. She scavenged the area around the campsite for edible vegetables, but found little. Willow continued with the shock remedy and added one for a low fever. Bryar moaned occasionally, and this morning he had clung to her hand. Positive signs, but he had not regained consciousness.

Twice he had spent the night pressed against her, sandwiching her between the two men, because Bryar needed their bedding, and nights were cold. Desire hadn't entered the picture. Protecting her had.

The rain held off. Even with a tarp, rain would be disastrous. But he couldn't ignore the high cloud moving in from the east.

That evening Willow sat next to him as they ate a skimpy supper. "I've reached a decision," she said. "I can think of no other solution."

He waited.

She took a breath. "I will seek help in the town. We cannot wait here any longer."

As he knew as well as she did. Still, he said, "I can't let you do that. In situations like this, it's never good to separate."

"With your size you might be perceived as a threat. Your strength is more valuable here. It is best that I go."

"Willow, that's just crazy. You have no idea what kind of reception you'd get. What if they locked you up or hurt you…" He'd learned by now that the Weavers wandered the Midland with impunity, because of the unwritten agreement that no one would harm them. That might not be the case in this new land.

No trouble reading her at the moment; he recognized the stubborn set of her jaw. "This is not my preference, but I am going. I will reach the town in a long day, probably, so I will leave at dawn tomorrow."

"He'll wake up, Willow. You should be here when he does."

"And when the rain begins, he risks pneumonia. I must do this."

For the first time since they left on this crazy trek, he hauled her into his arms and held onto her.

After a minute she pushed him away. "We are out of alternatives, Joss."

"You will come back?" A stupid thing to say, but it forced its way out.

"Yes. With help for Bryar."

He sighed and tangled his fingers into hers, feeling worse than helpless.

Chapter 28

The town made Willow uneasy. It was bigger than Midland towns, the buildings higher and crowded together, the streets narrower.

She arrived as the sun began its descent behind the hills, after a day of struggling to keep her footing as she descended the last hill, then crossing the endless plain, which held less appeal once she actually traversed it, the never ending grain overtopping her head.

People hastened along the roads at the outskirts of the town, but no one paid any attention to her or responded to her attempts to begin a conversation. She finally stopped a harried-looking man by stepping in his way. Like others she saw, he wore the same linen tunic and pants she did, although of a darker brown. He glowered.

"Excuse me. I am sorry to interrupt you, but I must locate a Healer. Can you tell me where to go?"

"I don't know you." The flat statement was a denial of assistance.

"I am a stranger here. Please, where will I find a Healer?"

"We don't take much to strangers."

The blatant hostility in his voice sent a shiver up her spine. She remained silent, planted in his path.

Thwarted in his obvious desire to escape her, he sighed. "Ask at the marketplace." He gestured to a crossroad. "That way."

"Thank you. I am grateful." She stepped aside.

"Watch out for yourself," he said as he brushed past her.

As she followed the narrow lane that led into the town, she kept her senses alert. The buildings stood close together, two or even three stories tall, of a hard, reddish material. No courtyards fronted them; they opened directly onto the street. The same red squares paved the lane, providing an uncomfortable walking surface after the relative softness of the dirt road from the hills.

The marketplace, the open space at the center of town visible from the lookout, appeared before her unexpectedly when she rounded a building. She watched for a time before venturing farther. Merchants were packing with little bustle, just the weary folding of tables and tents.

She approached a woman on the edge of the market. "Excuse me, I am seeking a Healer. It is urgent."

The apples in a basket beside the table triggered a growl from her stomach, but from the cold look the woman gave her, she didn't dare ask for one. The waybread in her pack would stave off the worst of the hunger pangs.

"I ain't here to give directions to vagrants," the woman snarled before turning her back and resuming her work.

"I have traveled a long way, and I need a Healer. Please..." The rumbling of a hand cart across the red surface, another merchant heading home, half drowned her words.

"Them as don't earn their keep don't find much welcome."

"I am here only because a life is at stake."

"Humph." Her attention focused on Willow's pack. "The healer's a busy man. What do you got to offer?"

"Offer?"

"Pay. Healers don't work for free, any more'n anyone else. You got anything valuable in that pack?" The woman straightened and approached her.

Willow took an involuntary step back. "Only some bread and a bedroll." A bedroll that should be at the campsite with Bryar, but Joss had insisted.

"A common beggar, ain't ya? Less you give somethin' in return, you won't find a welcome, that's the law of it. Take that street." She jerked her head toward one of the wide paths radiating from the marketplace. "You'll see his herbs and stuff hanging in the window."

"I work with herbs myself. I need a person skilled in the energies—"

"What nonsense are you talking? And stop eyeing my apples that way. Sounds like you've got nothing worth trading."

With a flash of guilt, Willow realized she was once again staring at the basket. Her stomach clenched. "The Aura, the power that—"

The woman spat onto the pavement. "Nobody but the Mages mess with the Aura. Ordinary folks keep well away."

"Herbs alone will not help."

"Then you're a damn fool, and that's a fact." The woman returned to her packing. "He's in the tower, the Mage is. But only an idiot goes there uninvited."

Surrounding buildings blocked the view of the tower from the marketplace, but she remembered it was on the northern edge of the town. "I take this road, am I correct?" She pointed to a track opposite the one leading to the hedge healer.

"It's your funeral."

Willow directed her feet north. Whether or not this Mage person proved to be the man Arwen had told her about, he might be able to tell her how to heal Bryar.

She approached the tower through a small flagstone courtyard. Made of black stone and taller than any other building, it loomed over the town and the plain. She saw no windows on the ground floor. A metal device hung centered on the heavy wooden door; she guessed it served as a knocker, so she lifted it and let it fall.

When nothing happened, she held onto it and rapped it against the underlying metal plate three times.

The man who opened the door wore black, slim-cut trousers and shirt, and a belt with a silver buckle. Thin and tall, well into middle age, his hair matched his clothing with hints of gray at the temples, and his eyes—

Commanding, impatient, and black as his clothes.

"What?" he snapped.

Given a choice, she would turn and run. But Bryar lay back in the hills. She schooled herself to calmness. "I need a Healer, one with Entrée."

"I'm no Healer." He started to shut the door. Surprising herself, she inserted first a boot, then the rest of her, into the gap.

The man gaped at her, but recovered his hostile demeanor instantly. His voice was hard. "I recommend you leave. You are not wanted here."

Willow had been on the road since daybreak. She was tired, footsore, hungry, and frightened – and not about to be turned aside now. Swallowing and summoning the dregs of her courage, she said, "Nor do I want to be here. But a friend is injured, and I believe the Aura caused it." She saw a spark of interest awaken in him. "He is unconscious. I need help to know what the problem is, and to restore him."

The man stared at her, studying her for so long that Willow fought the urge to bolt. Then he turned away. "You are courageous, I give you that."

Not knowing what else to do, she followed him, leaving the door ajar. He led her past a flight of stairs, along a hall that cut the tower in half, before turning into a room near the back. Dark and forbidding, it contained an elaborate desk of carved wood, assorted chairs and tables, a shelf of books and manuscripts, and an assortment of unfamiliar objects – tools or ornaments, perhaps.

No windows. She shivered.

"Sit," he commanded, gesturing at a chair placed before the desk. "Tell me what happened. I expect you to be precise and not waste my time with opinions. Then I will decide whether to involve myself. If I choose not to, you will leave here and never return, and not speak of our encounter. Is that clear?"

She nodded and gratefully lowered herself onto the chair as he circled the desk to sit across from her, but before she spoke she fished in her pack and retrieved a piece of the hard waybread, her first food since nibbling a portion of it at midday.

She took a bite, chewed, and forced the dry stuff down. Then she explained where they had come from and what had happened to Bryar, and to a lesser extent, to Joss.

He listened, his gaze fixed on her as if he were trying to work out what species she belonged to.

When she finished, he rose and pulled a rope against the wall. They waited in silence until an elderly man, hunched almost double by age or infirmity, appeared. "We have a guest for supper," the man in black said. "Set another plate."

"Yes, sir." He backed out of the room.

"You will stay here tonight," he informed her, "a privilege I grant to very few. Do not abuse it, and do not speak of it. Now, as we will dine together, I suggest we complete the formalities. Tell me your name."

Spend the night in this forbidding place? Share a roof with this intimidating man? She clung to the thought of Bryar and attempted to swallow her discomfort along with the waybread.

"Willow."

"You may call me Gauvain, and I do not believe you. However, I will allow you your alias for the time being. You will wish to bathe before we dine, as your appearance is appalling. I assume you brought clean clothes?"

Willow allowed herself a private sigh of relief. That was the name Arwen had entrusted to her. However, the assumption was insulting, and she took it as such. "No. I have been on the trail for most of two nine-days. Naturally my clothing is soiled."

Gauvain jerked the cord again. When the older man appeared, looking alarmed, he barked, "A fresh outfit for this woman. Something to render her appearance tolerable. Take her to the large guest bedroom. Provide water for her to bathe."

"Yes, sir." He spoke to the floor.

"Get out of my sight, both of you."

The man scuttled from the room. Willow stowed the remnant of her waybread and picked up her pack before she stood. Gauvain had turned his focus to a document on his desk. He waved her away without looking up.

Cowed, although she refused to admit it, even to herself, she followed the older man, who awaited her at the bottom of the flight of stairs. As she mounted the steps, hoping she was not making the mistake of her lifetime, he said, "Don't worry about him, Miss. He's grouchy of an evening, but he won't do you harm."

"Are you sure?"

He hesitated before he answered. "As sure as can be, Miss. It's a rare privilege to be invited to dine."

"I see."

The man opened a door to a room double the size of her cottage, with a bed large enough to sleep four and tapestries on the stone walls. Underfoot lay a thick rug. The whole thing was done up in in a rich, deep blue; she mentally ticked through her list of known dyes and wondered how he achieved that particular shade and intensity. And for that matter, what dye created the black of his clothing? Black dye was unknown in the Midland.

"You'll wash through here, Miss." He showed her to an attached room equipped with a large tub, big enough for her to sit in. "Turn the handle there for hot water. Leave the tub filled when you finish. Rain has been scarce, so water is reused."

The man pointed out a stack of washing cloths and towels, much thicker and more luxurious than any the Midland offered; explained the other facilities in the bathing room; then bowed himself out. "Fresh clothing will arrive within the half hour. Leave your soiled things by the bed. They will be clean by morning."

"Thank you." Willow felt giddy with the newness and the luxury of it. Even her little cabin had a pump inside, but to turn a handle and produce hot water? And the richness of the bath linen, the bed linen, the rug...

As the man scurried through her door, closing it quietly behind him, she crossed to the window and looked out into the dusk. The hills were not visible, so she faced east. Being out of sight of them made her lonely. Joss and Bryar waited for her in those hills.

She pulled off her dirty clothing, kicking it into a pile, and went to prepare her bath.

Much later she peeked through the anteroom door and breathed a sigh of relief. No sign of the old man, and a tunic and skirt awaited her. She shed the towel, which wrapped completely around her, and donned the outfit. The fabric was silky and unfamiliar, the color a deep reddish purple. Elaborate embroidery decorated the neckline, and the skirt used enough material to create two skirts at home. She ran her fingers through her hair, clean for the first time since they left the Motherhouse, and sat on the bed.

Was this how everyone lived here?

No, she told herself. This was how Gauvain lived.

She stepped into the middle of the room and began her ritual, hoping to draw on it for courage.

Sustainer of life, source of all the powers that be, send your blessing to us. Powers of water, flow kindly through Bryar, and restore him. Powers of earth, flow through Joss and me, show us the way to best care for him. Sustainer of energies, powers of fire, grant that the man Gauvain has no evil intent, but uses his power for healing. Bless this land, bless my land.

She continued with her invocation in silence as darkness gathered in the room. There was no candle, but the dark suited her as she sank to the floor and settled more deeply into meditation, a place where, in times past, she achieved her deepest connection to the Aura.

A sharp rap on the door jolted her from her reverie. Not waiting for her to reply, Gauvain stalked in.

"Whatever are you doing, fool woman?"

She breathed in then out to calm her heart. "Meditating. And I did not know where to find a light source."

That flummoxed him. "I hadn't considered that you might not... naturally, anyone who stays here provides their own light."

"Once I could have done so."

He held out a hand to help her rise, but she ignored it and struggled to her feet, fighting off the voluminous skirt. "By any chance," she asked, "is it time for the evening meal?"

"It is. As I assumed you knew."

"You did not say."

"No, I suppose I didn't. Come." He left her to follow in his wake, down the stairs to a room every bit as elaborate as the first. Two filled plates and two drinking containers waited on opposite sides of the table. She chose the nearest one and sat.

"You are a Weaver," he informed her.

"Was. Was a Weaver."

His eyebrows went up. "Further mysteries. As I remember your Motherhouse, you may not have seen a goblet before. Elegant, is it not? I trust you enjoy wine?"

She picked up the stemmed mug. "It is all right, in small quantity. I prefer beer."

"This one will please you. Eat."

He sat and ignored her as he consumed his dinner, which consisted of a chop seasoned with flavors she could not identify, potatoes, and greens. Basic food made fancy by a sauce and wine. She ate, allowing herself to enjoy her first proper meal in days.

Gauvain leaned back and said, "There is power in a name."

She paused before enjoying her next bite. "Really?"

"Those who know your name hold an energetic bond to you. You are wise to disguise it if you need to preserve your self."

"I repeat, Willow is my name."

"No. Besides whatever is buried deep in your childhood, which you choose to ignore, Willow denotes flow, flexibility. You have neither. You are firm as the earth, and stubborn. You cannot claim relationship to a willow."

"You are mistaken, and I certainly can. A willow shelters, and heals pain and fevers."

"I am never wrong when I read energies. You intend to hide your true name, from me and yourself, but that will wait. Tell me what is going on with the Aura. The fluctuations originate on your side of the hills."

Bothered by his words but not neglecting her meal, she explained about Joss and Kiril, their crash landing, and the cell that had been the start of their troubles.

"There is more to this. Why attempt to cross the hills? Nothing you say provides sufficient justification. The proscription is well known, and any Weaver learns this."

Her part of the story seemed almost incidental after Bryar's calamity. She swallowed.

"I was a Healer once. The cell... there was an accident." She explained the failed circle, the energy draining toward the east, her lost connection.

She had caught his attention; he followed her words closely. "Fascinating, but still insufficient justification for invading my land. There are others in the Midland, Arwen for instance, who would be delighted to explore the challenge you present."

"They tried and failed. Someone residing here might be better able to restore my powers."

He barked out a laugh. "You came all this distance, at considerable risk, in search of healing that may be impossible? I admire your grit."

"Have you ever lost your Auric connection?"

The question sobered him in a flash, but didn't reduce his arrogance. "No, except through this cell of yours. Nor will I. I guard my powers assiduously."

"There is little I would not try. But that was before what happened to Bryar. His fate is now the most important."

His brows raised in disbelief. "There's more to your story? You do lead a life of high drama."

"My friend, a Bard, crested the hill to view your land. Something felled him. He lies in a coma now. He is the reason I am here."

"A trivial situation, in light of your own." In an instant he was on his feet and around the table, raking his fingers into her hair and resting his palms on her head.

She froze. He, however, moved his hands, exploring her skull as she sat rigid, her fork unmoving in her hand.

At last he released her and returned to his seat. "More and more curious. I suspect that your unheralded arrival works to my advantage as well as yours. I wish to see this cell."

"Odd, after I described its effect. But I no longer know where it is or who controls it. It has been moved and is probably buried since I am told the Aura is stable."

And I do not want you to get your hands on it. You are not trustworthy.

"Your thoughts are as plain as your face. You intrigue me, Willow whose name is not Willow. I had every intention of throwing you out in the morning, but I think it would amuse me to help you after all. We depart immediately after breakfast. You will be prepared to leave and will not delay us by the ridiculous things women insist on doing before they appear in public."

The elderly man appeared in the door. "Shall I clear the plates, sir?"

"Yes." Gauvain didn't ask her if she had finished. She watched with some sadness as the last bites of the chop vanished when the man claimed her plate. "And arrange for a horse and cart. I will expect them here before breakfast."

"Yes, sir. Will you drive, sir?"

"Yes. Take that mess away." He waved at the plates.

The wine goblets remained on the table. Gauvain picked his up and drained what was left. Then he dismissed her as abruptly as he had the older man. "Go to your room. Take a candle if you want." He made an idle gesture toward the mantelpiece, and a candle burst into flame. She had been able to do the same, once. "Make sure you are on time tomorrow, and whatever you do, do *not* wear that ghastly outfit you arrived in. I prefer not to pollute my vision."

He rose and left, leaving her feeling confused and weary. The travel had taken its toll, and dining with Gauvain exacerbated her exhaustion.

Grateful that she had limited her own wine consumption to a couple of sips, she retrieved the candle in its holder from the mantle and walked carefully back to her room, kicking the unfamiliar full skirts out of her way as she went.

Willow had heard of horses, although she couldn't say how, other than from Bryar's epic poems. They turned out to be similar to donkeys, but larger and much, much faster. As they raced across the plain, following the track to the hills, she held on for dear life. Clearly enjoying his control of the powerful beast, Gauvain steered the cart at breakneck speed to the base of the hills before he halted. At this rate they could reach Bryar before midday.

"We leave the transport here and proceed on foot," he informed her, as if she weren't intelligent enough to figure it out for herself. He jumped down and went to tether the horse, leaving her to manage on her own. Mercifully, the previous evening she had found a somewhat more tailored blue skirt in a less slippery fabric waiting on her bed, although even in this garb she faced a challenge alighting from the high seat of the vehicle. Gauvain's domineering attitude made her reluctant to kilt the skirt, and the shorter length of the tunic precluded her removing it completely. She scrambled from the high seat, twitching the fabric out of the way, on her own.

Clouds had rolled in overnight, casting the hills into a dim, eerie light after the greater brightness of the plains. Gauvain had been silent during the ride, absorbed in controlling the horse, but as they climbed he demanded every piece of information she could give him about the power cell, her own disability, Bryar's condition.

When they stopped for a rest – mercifully, for although Willow was winded, Gauvain showed no effect from the strenuous climb – he said, "You continue to intrigue me. I believe I might be willing to help you."

"How? Can you restore my connection?"

He ignored the question. "I wonder if Arwen knows what she has in you," he mused.

"I wonder how you know Arwen."

"The boundary between our two lands is more permeable than you think. You've rested long enough. I intend to repair your friend and be home in time for a decent meal."

She drove herself forward, as eager as he to reach their camp.

Joss returned from the rivulet for water just as Willow strode into their camp dressed in something out of costume drama, followed by a man in black. He set the pot on the grass and folded his arms, eyeing the stranger.

A vulture, and dangerous. Allowing Willow to go on her own had been a mistake. At least she seemed unscathed as she settled next to Bryar.

The vulture looked at him and made a hard gesture with his head, downslope. "Leave," he said imperiously. "I tolerate no amateurs."

"Joss, this is Gauvain," Willow said. "How is he?"

"He's trying to come around. You should stay close, he needs you."

She held one of Bryar's hands in both of hers and didn't so much as look at Gauvain, who also folded himself onto the ground, studying Bryar. As if sensing... what?

The man looked up. "You possess some trivial connection," Gauvain said to Joss, "but you'll never amount to anything. Now, get away. Do not disturb me." Having spoken, the vulture ignored him.

Willow was stroking Bryar's arms, his injured wrist. "This might be a good opportunity to hunt," she said.

He caught her unspoken message: let him do his work. And he needed to deal with the flood of relief that had bowled into him when he saw her coming around the turn in the path, as well as his instant antipathy for the man called Gauvain.

Joss ignored the command and knelt beside her, searching her face. The vulture passed his hands over Bryar, his eyes unfocused.

"You're okay?"

"I'm fine, Joss."

"He knows you're here. Don't leave him."

"I won't." She moved a hand from Bryar's to touch his. "Thank you."

Somewhat mollified, he gathered up the equipment he needed for a hunting expedition and took himself off down the path, planning to stay within earshot. However great his relief at seeing Willow again, he didn't trust the vulture an inch.

❖

Willow watched Joss walk away, then focused on Bryar, once again stung by her inability to help him. Gauvain ignored her. His hands moved repetitively over Bryar's head and torso, much as she herself had done so many times, aligning energies. She prayed he would not bring further disaster to them.

Bryar's hand tightened around her fingers. She returned the squeeze, but her eyes stayed on Gauvain.

While she waited she allowed herself the respite of sinking into the day, attuning herself to the earth. With the clouds, it was dark and still in the forest bordering the track. The conifers, which had seemed so rich and right, felt forbidding. No birds sang. The stillness soothed her and made her uneasy in equal measure, portending as it did a storm, and soon.

"Stop fretting," Gauvain snapped. "I'm not conducting this experiment to see my labor wasted by anything as stupid as rain."

He'd been in her mind. And she hadn't known it.

Over and over he passed his hands across Bryar's motionless body. Her friend, her lover, the father of her child, now helpless, and according to Joss, afraid.

"Without the life force animating us, we are shells," Gauvain said. "Those with no Entrée go through life in an attenuated state, unable to tap the full richness of existence." It sounded like a classroom lecture. "Your friend will recover. Be grateful that he fell as he did. With any greater exposure to the energies on my side of the hills, if he lived at all it would be as a shell."

Gauvain dropped his hands and glared at her. "I require focus and privacy to work. There's a feyness about you that creates an unpleasant distraction in my mind. One hour. Afterwards, we will speak of the future."

By now she was used to his attempts to intimidate her, although they still did. But this was Bryar. "Can you explain what happened, and what you will do to repair it?"

"Trivial." He shrugged, then stood and dusted off his black trousers. "This man's Entrée is not above average, but healthy. In all probability he would recover on his own, given time. You Weavers cannot handle the increased Auric strength east of the divide. Experiments have been conducted with introducing the energies gradually, like an inoculation, but with limited success. From what you say, your gigantic friend experienced discomfort, but his powers are too weak for it to disable him. And as for you, I would welcome an opportunity to probe your loss of connection. The Aura is not benign. It demands respect."

"For Bryar, is it a block, or a burn-out?"

"More like a skin overfilled with wine, so that it bursts. There are energetic pathways that need to be repaired if he is to hold and contain energy again. That I can do."

"Not the same as my condition. That is a relief."

"No. Not at all. Go away, woman. Persistence is a quality I normally admire in a student, but at the moment I look forward to a clean house and a good dinner. Your presence slows me down."

"You consider Bryar an experiment."

"A means to expand my knowledge. *Go!*"

"You will call me when you finish." It was not a request.

Gauvain reared back, his blue eyes ice cold. "Be careful how you speak to me."

She stood her ground. "Be careful how you speak to me."

Their eyes met and locked. Gauvain smiled. "Oh, yes, I shall enjoy this," he said, then flapped his hand at her as if he were swatting away a fly, at the same time honeying his voice into a facsimile of manners. "Go. If you please, milady."

Willow bent and kissed Bryar's forehead. "I'll be close," she whispered to him. Then she stood and dropped into the ravine, planning to sit on the boulder overlooking the plains, studying once again the alien landscape.

Gauvain missed his elegant lunch, she thought. It was approaching midafternoon before he climbed from the ravine to the lookout. The lines either side of his mouth seemed deeper, as if he had been under immense strain, and his skin, already pale, now was chalky.

Joss sat close by, silent and still as always, sheltered from the plain by a boulder.

"You," Gauvain said to Joss. "Leave us. Your friend is awake, although not yet moving, and understandably nervous about being alone."

"I'll go," Willow said. She rose and took a step toward the ravine.

"No, you will not. I wish to speak with you before you return to your pitiful campsite."

Again a meeting of wills. In the end she said to Joss, "It's all right. We can't leave him on his own."

Joss glared at Gauvain in a way that threatened painful retribution should anything happen to her, then dropped into the ravine and disappeared around the bend.

"Very pleasant," Gauvain said, sitting and gesturing for her to join him. "This aspect renews one's perspective. I may bring my apprentices here."

"You have something more to tell me?" She wanted to be with Bryar, not make polite chat about the view.

"Yes. I've decided to restore your powers to you. In return, you will agree to apprentice with me for half a year. Thereafter, I will decide if you are worthy to stay longer."

"You can do that?" A buzz of anticipation began in her head at the word 'restore', so she scarcely heard past the promise of regaining her connection.

"Yes, I believe so, although your case is unique in my experience. I expect a season of gradual restoration to guard against the sort of shock your companion experienced. During that time, you will study in my apprentice class. I suspect you will advance rapidly once we complete your repair."

"Repair," she repeated. "I'm another experiment, am I not?"

"Of course." He seemed surprised that she should ask. "But it is a situation from which we both stand to benefit."

"When?"

"Ever practical, aren't you? I accede to your soft-hearted notion that you are needed here, but I expect you within a nine-day. You will come alone, and I recommend you not keep me waiting. My apprentices know not to anger me."

Willow looked not at Gauvain but at the gently swaying grass. She bore an intense antipathy to this man, and she would be sure that Bryar's condition was as promised before she committed herself. But the lure of the Aura, of seeing the land in all its depth and richness, of Healing again, being a part of the world of the plants…

"Go back to your friends," he said. "Send them home, and if you have courage enough, come to me. If you don't, I suggest you work in the Motherhouse kitchens. Live out your pathetic life being minimally useful."

Without another word, he stood and started down the track.

She shouted after him. "You guarantee it will not rain?"

She saw him clench his fists. "No. It will not rain." From his tone, she suspected she should say no more. He still scared her.

Willow watched him go for a minute, then clambered down the steep bank of the ravine and returned to Bryar and Joss.

Chapter 29

Joss watched as Willow shoved her meager belongings into her pack, folding the town outfit carefully; it was incongruous out here in the wilds, but she insisted on taking it, planning to change into it when she got to the foot of the hills. All that satin or whatever, even more ridiculous with her hiking boots. Another way this morning was off balance.

He scanned the remains of their campsite, their home for the last seven days, seeking something, anything that might delay what came next. Bryar crossed the clearing to wrap his arms around Willow; Joss wished he dared do the same.

No matter how many arguments he and Bryar had presented, no matter how heartfelt their fear for her might be, she was determined to do this foolhardy thing, and to do it alone, while they returned to the Midland without her.

Still, none of them rushed to separate.

Willow broke away. "Dawn is long past. We must go."

Steel in her voice. Bryar and he were the softies here, not her.

She approached him and took his hands. "You will safeguard Bryar? And yourself?"

"I will." He liked the man. And he'd do it for Willow.

She rose on tiptoe and kissed his cheek. "May the land sustain you."

"And you." The meaning wasn't clear to him, in practical terms, but as part of this new world, he honored its meaning to her.

She next went to Bryar. "You will see Romarin?"

"Of course. I'll tell her what's going on."

"And Arwen, and Quinn?"

"Yes, love. You're fussing."

"No." She gave them a rueful grin, her first of the morning. "I am delaying. And for no good reason."

She placed her hands on his arms, he on hers.

"Flow of water sustain you," she said.

"Stability of earth sustain you."

After a few more seconds, Bryar backed away and slung his pack onto his shoulders – they had redistributed the weight until such time as he recovered fully from his ordeal. He looked at Joss and nodded.

"Just go," Willow said behind them.

Joss shouldered his own pack, and they both turned toward her, then away. Single file and without speaking, he and Bryar left her there at the deserted campsite.

Willow watched them leave. When they were out of sight and hearing, she picked up her own pack, refusing to waste any more time, and climbed the ravine to the boulder that marked the effective end of the Midland, the beginning of the land on the other side of the hills.

The beginning of her new life.

Part of her wanted to linger at the lookout and cry, or sit silently as the wind blew silken patterns across the grain. She would do neither. She had a journey to complete, and having done it before, she knew she needed the full day to get to Gauvain's tower before sunset.

She did look back, though, along the ravine to the point where it turned toward the campsite, longing to be walking home with Bryar and Joss. Then, having wasted enough time in fruitless sentimentality, she started the trek to the tower and Gauvain.

To My Readers

Hello, and thanks for choosing *The Healer*. The story continues with Book 2, *The Bard*.

If you enjoyed this book, well, I don't need to tell you how much reviews mean to writers.

To keep up with my writing, whether fantasy or romance, visit my website, http://lizanncarson.com.

Happy reading,

LizAnn

About LizAnn Carson

It's interesting, trying to condense who you are into a paragraph or two. For openers, I live with one husband and two cats, on the west coast of British Columbia, in a city that's large enough to have all modern conveniences, but not so large as to have hours-long traffic jams or heavy duty pollution. I can follow a trail to my local supermarket, or I can be downtown in twenty minutes.

Yes, I spend most of my time writing (and editing, formatting, critiquing for other writers, battling computer problems, and occasionally tearing my hair out). But beyond that, I enjoy a variety of crafts. I love the new craze of coloring books for adults. Recently I have been learning to play early music (Baroque and earlier) on my baritone ukulele – it works! I walk a lot and enjoy weight training. Once, a long time ago, I owned a yarn shop, and for a while I taught English as a Second Language. My career, on the other hand, was in the world of computer systems development.

You'd be very welcome to drop in at my website: http://lizanncarson.com.